A Book Of

CAPITAL MARKET AND FINANCIAL SERVICES

For
M.Com. Part II : Semester IV
As Per New Syllabus, June 2014

Dr. Mahesh Kulkarni
M.Com., M.Phil., L.L.B., D.T.L., Ph.D.
Research Guide, University of Pune and YCMOU, Nashik

Dr. Suhas Mahajan
B.A., M.Com., Ph.D.
Research Guide, University of Pune and YCMOU Nashik.

NIRALI PRAKASHAN
ADVANCEMENT OF KNOWLEDGE

N0256

CAPITAL MARKET AND FINANCIAL SERVICES (M.Com.)   **ISBN 978-93-5164-451-4**

First Edition   :   **December 2014**

©   :   **Authors**

Published By :
NIRALI PRAKASHAN
Abhyudaya Pragati, 1312, Shivaji Nagar,
Off J.M. Road, PUNE – 411005
Tel - (020) 25512336/37/39, Fax - (020) 25511379
Email : niralipune@pragationline.com

DISTRIBUTION CENTRES

PUNE

Nirali Prakashan
119, Budhwar Peth, Jogeshwari Mandir Lane
Pune 411002, Maharashtra
Tel : (020) 2445 2044, 66022708, Fax : (020) 2445 1538
Email : niralilocal@pragationline.com

Nirali Prakashan
S. No. 28/25, Dhyari,
Near Pari Company, Pune 411041
Tel : (020) 24690204Fax : (020) 24690316
Email : bookorder@pragationline.com

MUMBAI
Nirali Prakashan
385, S.V.P. Road, Rasdhara Co-op. Hsg. Society Ltd.,
Girgaum, Mumbai 400004, Maharashtra
Tel : (022) 2385 6339 / 2386 9976, Fax : (022) 2386 9976
Email : niralimumbai@pragationline.com

DISTRIBUTION BRANCHES

NAGPUR
Pratibha Book Distributors
Above Maratha Mandir, Shop No. 3, First Floor,
Rani Jhanshi Square, Sitabuldi, Nagpur 440012,
Maharashtra, Tel : (0712) 254 7129

JALGAON
Nirali Prakashan
34, V. V. Golani Market, Navi Peth, Jalgaon 425001,
Maharashtra, Tel : (0257) 222 0395
Mob : 94234 91860

BENGALURU
Pragati Book House
House No. 1, Sanjeevappa Lane, Avenue Road Cross,
Opp. Rice Church, Bengaluru – 560002.
Tel : (080) 64513344, 64513355,
Mob : 9880582331, 9845021552
Email:bharatsavla@yahoo.com

KOLHAPUR
Nirali Prakashan
New Mahadvar Road,
Kedar Plaza, 1st Floor Opp. IDBI Bank
Kolhapur 416 012, Maharashtra. Mob : 9850046155

CHENNAI
Pragati Books
9/1, Montieth Road, Behind Taas Mahal, Egmore,
Chennai 600008 Tamil Nadu, Tel : (044) 6518 3535,
Mob : 94440 01782 / 98450 21552 / 98805 82331, Email : bharatsavla@yahoo.com

RETAIL OUTLETS
PUNE

Pragati Book Centre
157, Budhwar Peth, Opp. Ratan Talkies,
Pune 411002, Maharashtra
Tel : (020) 2445 8887 / 6602 2707, Fax : (020) 2445 8887

Pragati Book Centre
676/B, Budhwar Peth, Opp. Jogeshwari Mandir,
Pune 411002, Maharashtra
Tel : (020) 6601 7784 / 6602 0855

Pragati Book Centre
Amber Chamber, 28/A, Budhwar Peth,
Appa Balwant Chowk, Pune : 411002, Maharashtra,
Tel : (020) 20240335 / 66281669
Email : pbcpune@pragationline.com

PBC Book Sellers & Stationers
152, Budhwar Peth, Pune 411002, Maharashtra
Tel : (020) 2445 2254 / 6609 2463

MUMBAI
Pragati Book Corner
Indira Niwas, 111 - A, Bhavani Shankar Road, Dadar (W), Mumbai 400028, Maharashtra
Tel : (022) 2422 3526 / 6662 5254, Email : pbcmumbai@pragationline.com

www.pragationline.com   info@pragationline.com

Preface ...

Capital Market and Financial Services has emerged as an interesting and exciting area, as it has experienced phenomenal changes in respect of theoretical contents and their practical implementation in the actual practice. The basic purpose of the book is to acquaint professionals and students of business studies with the contents and radical changes in capital market and financial services.

There are a number of references available on the subject of Corporate Financial Management. A few of them are fairly comprehensive and elaborative in nature. The present text book is expected to serve better the interest of the post-graduate students of colleges, management institutes and departments of commerce and management of recognised universities. This book is specifically written as per the revised syllabus prescribed for M.Com. students of University of Pune w.e.f. 2014. We do hope that this text book will definitely help to meet the growing requirements of the students of business finance from the varied faculties of Commerce and Management. This book adopts a modern and novel approach to enable students acquire sound knowledge, basic concepts and structure of capital market and financial services.

All the topics included in the syllabus are explained in simple but apt language, with a sizable number of examples in order to suit the needs of such readers. Equal emphasis has also been given on graphical presentations to simplify the financial theories and practices. The book has been designed to serve as a self-sufficient text for M.Com. students. It will definitely add to our satisfaction if this book would be more useful as a reference for practicing consultants, professional managers, dynamic entrepreneurs and enthusiastic teachers of the subject concern.

We sincerely thank the senior faculty members from various colleges, management schools and financial organisations for guiding and constantly encouraging us in our enterprise and the students community who inspired us to write this unique book.

We are very thankful to **Shri. Dineshbhai Furia, Shri. Jigneshbhai Furia, Mrs. Nirja Sharma, Mr. Malik Shaikh, Mr. Prasad Chintakindi, Mr. Sachin Shinde** and the entire staff of Nirali Prakashan, Pune for their earnest help in bringing out this book with vigour and accuracy. We have taken maximum efforts to make the text error free. Nevertheless, we do not rule out the possibility of certain shortcomings or misprints still remaining, we will be grateful to the reader if such errors are being pointed out from time to time.

We must concede that this book would never have been written without the support, encouragement and inspiration of our family members, many, many thanks to them.

Any criticism or valuable suggestion for further improvement of this book will be gratefully acknowledged and highly appreciated.

<table>
<tr><td>9ᵗʰ **December, 2014**</td><td>**Dr. Mahesh Kulkarni**</td></tr>
<tr><td>**Angarki Chaturthi**</td><td>**Dr. Suhas Mahajan**</td></tr>
<tr><td>**Pune.**</td><td></td></tr>
</table>

Syllabus ...

1. **Capital Market :**

   Meaning, Functions, Structure, Characteristics, Participants of Capital Market - Capital Market Instruments, Equity Share, Preferences Shares, Debenture, Bonds - Innovative Debt Instruments - Forward Contracts, Futures Contract - Options Contract, Trends in Capital Market.

2. **Stock Market :**

   Stock Exchange : Organization-membership-governing body - Bombay Stock Exchange, National Stock Exchange and Over the Counter Exchange of India (OTECEI).

   1. **Primary Market :** Functions of Primary Market - Issue Mechanism, Participants

   2. **Secondary Market :** Objectives, Functions of Secondary Markets, Stock Broking, e-broking, Depository System-Functions and Benefits-Stock-Market trading-Derivatives Trading.

3. **Financial Services :**

   - Merchant Banking-meaning-functions and services rendered. Mutual Funds :

     Meaning, functions-Types-Open and Closed Ended Funds - Income Funds, Balanced Fund, Growth Fund-Index Fund. Portfolio Management - Meaning and Services, Credit Rating - Meaning and Need, Various Credit Rating Agencies. Foreign Direct Investment.

4. **Securities and Exchange Board of India (SEBI) :**

   - Background, Establishment, Functions, Powers, Achievements and Regulatory Aspects, Recent Changes and Emerging Trends.

***

Contents ...

***

List of Figures ...

***

1...

Capital Market

Contents ...

New Issues Market and Stock Exchange are the most important components of the **Capital Market** where the share, debentures, bonds and other securities of various companies and Government are traded. New Issues Market is the Primary Market where the issuers can sell the securities but cannot buy. Stock Exchange or Secondary Market is an association of the member brokers who assist, facilitate and regulate trading in securities where one can buy and sell the securities. Thus, **Capital Market** comprises two components viz.: New Issue Market or Primary Market where companies issue the securities directly to the public and Stock Market or Secondary Market where the existing securities are bought and sold.

Financial System

The economic growth of a country mainly depends upon the mobilisation of scarce resources through conversion of public savings into productive investments. Public savings can be converted into useful investments through various intermediaries and instruments. Intermediaries help the people to invest their savings whereas the instruments help them to earn a sizable and secured rate of return on their investments. Hence, the **'Financial System'** of a country incorporates different intermediaries, instruments and markets which help the people to channelise their savings into resourceful investments.

The major function of the financial system is the provision of money and monetary assets for the quality production of goods and services. The "**financial system**" is a broader term which brings under its fold the financial markets and the financial institutions which support the system. The major assets traded in the financial system are money and monetary assets. The basic responsibility of the financial system is to mobilise the savings in the form of money and monetary assets and invest them into productive ventures.

Financial Market

Financial Markets can be referred to as those centres and arrangements which facilitate buying and selling of financial assets, claims and services. Sometimes, we do find the existence of a specific place or location for a financial market as in the case of stock exchange.

Generally speaking, there is no specific place or location to indicate a financial market. Wherever a financial transaction takes place, it is deemed to have taken place in the financial market. Hence, financial markets are pervasive in nature since financial transactions are themselves very pervasive throughout the economic system, e.g. purchase of shares, debentures, granting of loan by financial institutions, issue of equity shares, deposit of money into a bank, repayment of loan installment and so on.

Classification of Financial Markets

The **Classification of Financial Markets** is shown in Figure 1.1 as follows :

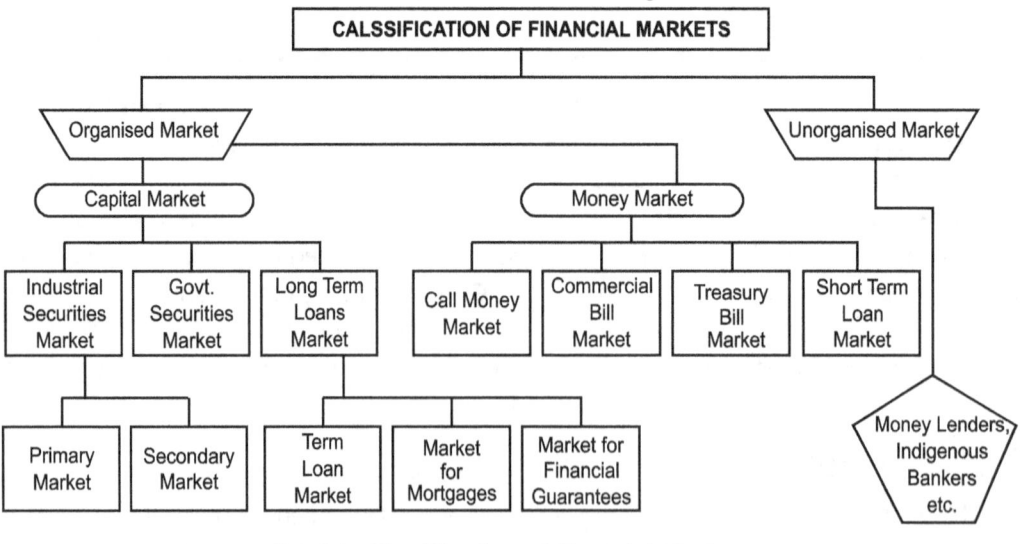

Fig. 1.1 : Classification of Financial Markets

1.2

Unorganised Markets

Unorganised Markets are the markets in which the regulations concerning their financial dealings are inadequate and their financial instruments are not standardised.

These markets inclusive of money lenders, indigenous bankers, traders etc., who lend money to the public. Indigenous bankers also collect deposits from the public. There are also private finance companies, chit funds etc., whose activities are not controlled by the RBI. Recently, the RBI has taken steps to bring private finance companies and chit funds under its strict control by issuing non-banking financial companies (Reserve Bank) Directions, 1998.

These investment and finance companies, housing finance, chit funds etc., also mobilise and channel savings into investment. They are only partly controlled by the Reserve Bank in respect of resource mobilisation through deposits. For the rest of their activities they are controlled and regulated like any other company by the Registrar of Companies, under the Companies Act. Similarly, moneylenders and indigenous bankers are licensed under the State laws and regulated by the State agencies. But there is hardly any system of regulation on them worth the name.

Organised Markets

In the **Organised Markets**, there are standardised rules and regulations governing their financial dealings. There is also a high degree of institutionalisation and instrumentalisation. These markets are subject to strict supervision and control by the RBI or other regulatory bodies. These organised markets can be further classified into two viz.: Money Market and Capital Market.

Money Market :

Money market is a market for dealing with financial assets and securities which have a maturity period of upto one year. In other words, it is a market for purely short term funds. The money market may be subdivided into four viz.: i) Call Money Market, ii) Commercial Bills Market, iii) Treasury Bills Market and iv) Short-term Loan Market.

a)   Call Money Market :

The **Call Money Market** is a market for extremely short period loans say one day to fourteen days. So, it is highly liquid. The loans are repayable on demand at the option of either the lender or the borrower. In India, call money markets are associated with the presence of stock exchanges and hence, they are located in major industrial towns like Mumbai, Kolkata, Chennai, Delhi, Ahmedabad etc.

b)   Commercial Bills Market :

It is a market for Bills of Exchange arising out of genuine trade transactions. In case of credit sale, the seller may draw a bill of exchange on the buyer. The buyer accepts such a bill promising to pay at a later date specified in the bill. The seller need not wait until the due date of the bill. Instead, he can get immediate payment by discounting the bill.

c) Treasury Bills Market

It is a market for treasury bills which have 'short-term' maturity. A treasury bill is a promissory note or a finance bill issued by the Government. It is highly liquid because its repayment is guaranteed by the Government. It is an important instrument for short term borrowing of the Government.

d) Short-term Loan Market

It is a market where short-term loans are given to corporate customers for meeting their working capital requirements. Commercial banks play a significant role in this market. Commercial banks provide short term loans in the form of cash credit and overdraft. Overdraft facility is mainly given to business people whereas cash credit is given to industrialists. Overdraft is purely a temporary accommodation and it is given in the current account itself. But cash credit is for a period of one year and it is sanctioned in a separate account.

1.1 CAPITAL MARKET

The word "**Capital Market**" is used in a wide sense including new issues market, stock market, money market, government securities market etc. The information about these markets and their operations would hopefully sharpen the tools of management as they are down to earth, practical and operational.

1.1.1 MEANING

The **Capital Market** is a market for financial assets which have a long or indefinite maturity. Generally, it deals with long term securities which have a maturity period of above one year. Capital Market may be further divided viz.: Industrial Securities Market, Government Securities Market and Long Term Loans Market.

a) Industrial Securities Market

As the very name implies, it is a market for industrial securities namely : i) Equity shares or ordinary shares, ii) Preference shares, and iii) Debentures or bonds. It is a market where industrial concerns raise their capital or debt by issuing appropriate instruments. It can be further subdivided into :

a) Primary Market or New Issue Market and b) Secondary Market or Stock Exchange.

i)   **Primary Market :**

Primary market is a market for new issues or new financial claims. Hence, it is also called New Issue market. The primary market deals with those securities which are issued to the public for the first time.

ii) **Secondary Market :**

Secondary market is a market for secondary sale of securities. In other words, securities which have already passed through the new issue market are traded in this market. Generally, such securities are quoted in the Stock Exchange and it provides a continuous and regular market for buying and selling of securities.

b) Government Securities Market

It is otherwise called Gilt-Edged securities market. It is a market where Government securities are traded. In India there are many kinds of Government Securities - short term and long term. Long term securities are traded in this market while short term securities are traded in the money market. Securities issued by the Central Government, State Governments, Semi-Government authorities like City Corporations, Port Trusts etc.

c) Long Term Loans Market

Development banks and commercial banks play a significant role in this market by supplying long term loans to corporate customers. Long term loans market may further be classified viz.: Term Loans Market, Mortgages Market and Financial Guarantees Market.

i) Term Loan Market

In India, many industrial financing institutions have been created by the Government both at the national and regional levels to supply long term and medium term loans to corporate customers directly as well as indirectly. These development banks dominate the industrial finance in India. Institutions like IDBI, IFCI, ICICI, and other state financial corporations come under this category. These institutions meet the growing and varied long-term financial requirements of industries by supplying long-term loans.

ii) Mortgage Market

The mortgage market refers to those centres which supply mortgage loan mainly to individual customers. A mortgage loan is a loan against the security of immovable property like real estate. The transfer of interest in a specific immovable property to secure a loan is called mortgage.

iii) Financial Guarantee Market

A Guarantee market is a centre where finance is provided against the guarantee of a reputed person in the financial circle. Guarantee is a contract to discharge the liability of a third party in case of his default. Guarantee acts as a security from the creditor's point of view. In case the borrower fails to repay the loan, the liability falls on the shoulders of the guarantor. Hence the guarantor must be known to both the borrower and the lender and he must have the means to discharge his liability.

Distinction between Capital Market and Money Market

The distinction between Capital Market and Money Market is briefly shown as follows :

Capital Market	Money Market
i) Capital market refers to the market for raising of financial resources by the business enterprises, firms, government, semi-government, bodies and other organisations. The market comprises some who demand and other who supply these resources.	i) The money market is the collective name given to the various firms and instruments that deal in the various grades of near money.

Capital Market		Money Market	
ii)	It is a market for long-term funds exceeding a period of one year.	ii)	It is a market for short-term loanable funds for a period of not exceeding one year
iii)	This market supplies funds for financing the fixed capital requirements of trade and commerce as well as the long-term requirements of the Government.	iii)	This market supplies funds for financing current business operations, working capital requirements of industries and short period requirements of the Government
iv)	This market deals in instruments like shares, debentures, Government bonds etc.	iv)	The instruments that are dealt in a money market are bills of exchange, treasury bills, commercial papers, certificate of deposit etc.
v)	Each single capital market instrument is of a small amount. Each share value is ₹ 1, 2, 5 or 10. Each debenture value is ₹ 100.	v)	Each single money market instrument is of large amount. A TB is for a minimum of ₹ 1,00,000. Each CD or CP is for a minimum of ₹ 25,00,000.
vi)	Development banks and Insurance companies play a dominant role in the capital market.	vi)	The Central bank and Commercial banks are the major institutions in the money market.
vii)	Capital market instruments generally have secondary markets.	vii)	Money market instruments generally do not have secondary markets.
viii)	Transactions take place at a formal place viz., stock exchange.	viii)	Transactions mostly take place over-the-phone and there is no formal place.
ix)	Transactions have to be conducted only through authorised dealers.	ix)	Transactions have to be conducted without the help of brokers.
x)	The unorganised capital markets are not in existence.	x)	The unorganised money markets are in existence. The indigeneous bankers and money lenders are still the major source of short-term loans for the small borrowers.

Nature of Capital Market

Capital market management has both **macro and micro aspects**. In **macro aspect**, the capital market is window of the economy in the capitalist market oriented countries. Raising of resources through issue of securities, borrowing and lending in the organised sector of the economy are functions and activities in the capital market. The financial resources raised through the capital market if used for investment and for productive activities would generate further outputs and incomes of the people and promote growth.

Capital market management involves various disciplines, much more than in banking. E.g. various laws, requires legal expertise, funding business requires banking knowledge, hire purchase and leasing requires a different expertise. Mutual funds, brokerage firms, portfolio managers and a host of other agencies require knowledge and expertise in personal management, marketing management, funds management, investment management etc.

In short, capital market management is different and more specialised than banking. It requires a different cadre of specialists to man the increasing work of financial institutions. It is more practical and operational and the expertise needed is different

Capital Market Intermediaries

The term **Capital Market Intermediary** includes all kinds of organisations which intermediate and facilitate financial transactions of both individuals and corporate customers. Thus, it refers to all kinds of financial institutions and investing institutions which facilitate financial transactions in capital markets.

These intermediaries mainly provide long-term funds to individuals and corporate customers. They consist of term lending institutions like financial corporations and investing institutions like Life Insurance Corporation, General Insurance Corporation etc.

The **Capital Market Intermediaries** are shown in Figure 1.2 as follows :

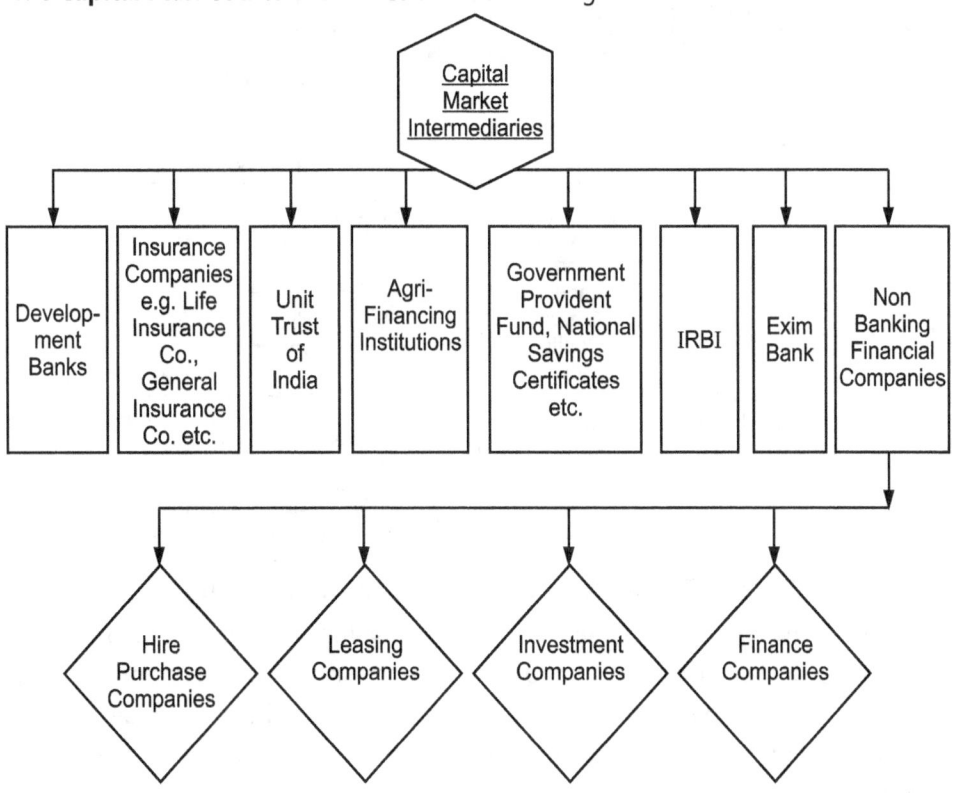

Fig. 1.2 : Capital Market Intermediaries

The capital market is a wider term encompassing all long term borrowings and lendings, issue of long term securities, and all unsecuritised debt of long term nature, the new issue market in particular relates to the new issues of marketable securities by existing or new companies. Thus, economic growth and activities in the capital market are closely related.

The major borrowers in the capital market are the corporate sector and the government sector, who spend more than their income and invest more than they save. The lenders are the household sector and the foreign sector in the case of India as they have positive savings and net surpluses to lend. These four sectors are related to each other. These sectors constitute the economy and the financial system is generated out of such borrowings and claims on money.

The **Relation between Economy and Capital Market** is shown in Figure 1.3 as follows :

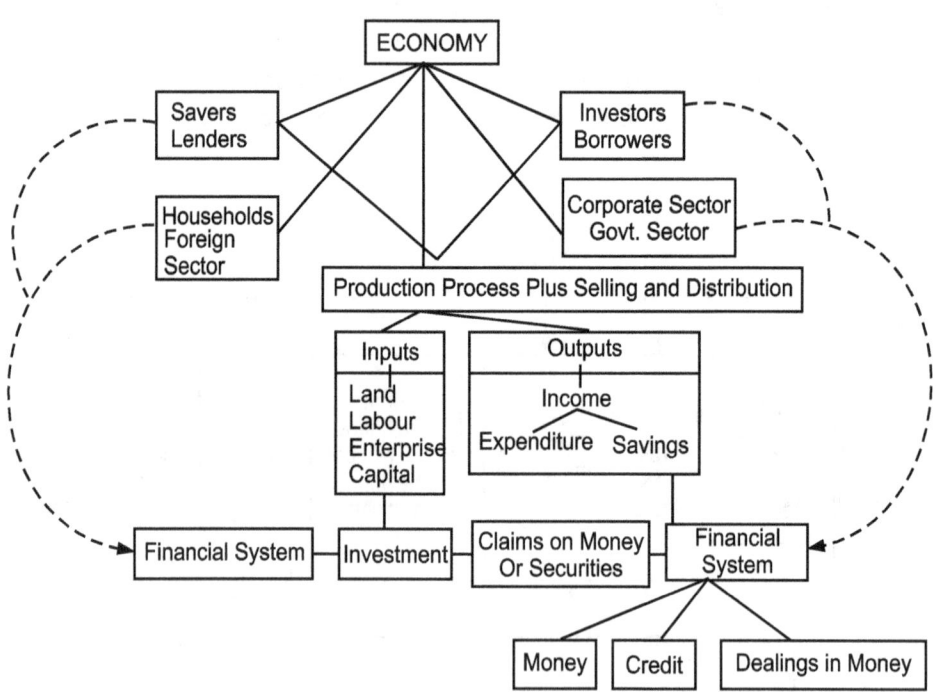

Fig. 1.3 : Relation between Economy and Capital Market

As shown in the above figure, the economy is understood to refer to productive activity including selling and distribution of goods and services. In the process of production, the inputs are the factors of production namely land, labour, enterprise and capital. Out of four factors of production, the capital is generated out of savings, lending to investment which is a part of the financial system. The claims of money are generated through money/savings, lent for investment and expenditure.

Capital Market Management

The study of **Capital Market Management** should thus encompass the totality of the financial sector services excluding the banking sector, but inclusive of money market and other financial markets. With the liberalisation of industrial and financial policies in India the integration of various segments of financial markets was accelerated and the role of private sector in the capital and money markets has increased. The **Study of Capital Market Management** is shown in Figure 1.4 as follows :

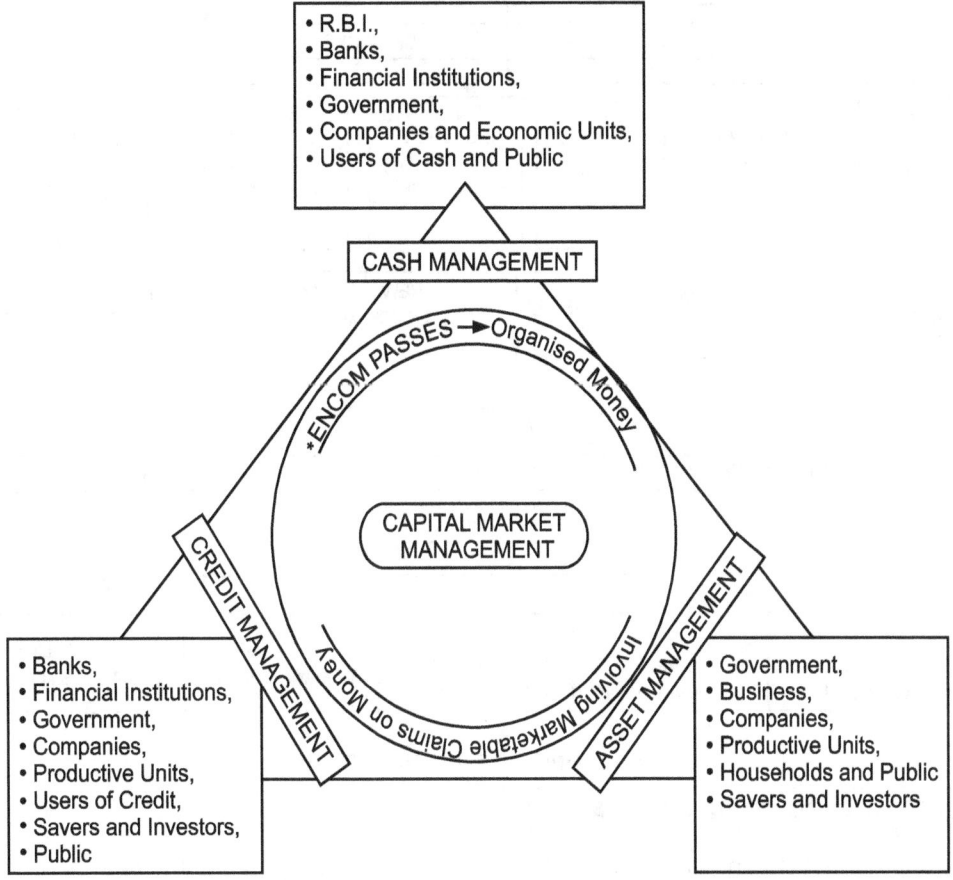

Fig. 1.4 : Study of Capital Market Management

Conceptually, money flows into various markets, namely product markets, factor markets, financial markets etc. These money flows into financial markets reflect the investment and disinvestment process, conversion of money into future claims of money and vice-versa. The need for cash and economising of cash are the basic principles of corporate finance. This leads to the use of near money like credit, master cards, bills, drafts and other instruments of credit. These result in claims on money both of short- term and long-term nature. If these instruments are of short term nature, these relate to money market and if they are of long term nature they belong to capital market. But in view of growing integration of markets, capital market management includes a study of both these markets.

The following chart on **"Capital Market Management"** (CMM) shown in Figure 1.5 depicts the various services rendered in the 'Capital Market' and their management as a science of study. The chart is self-explanatory which brings out various services rendered and the intermediaries rendering these services and the emerging markets therefrom.

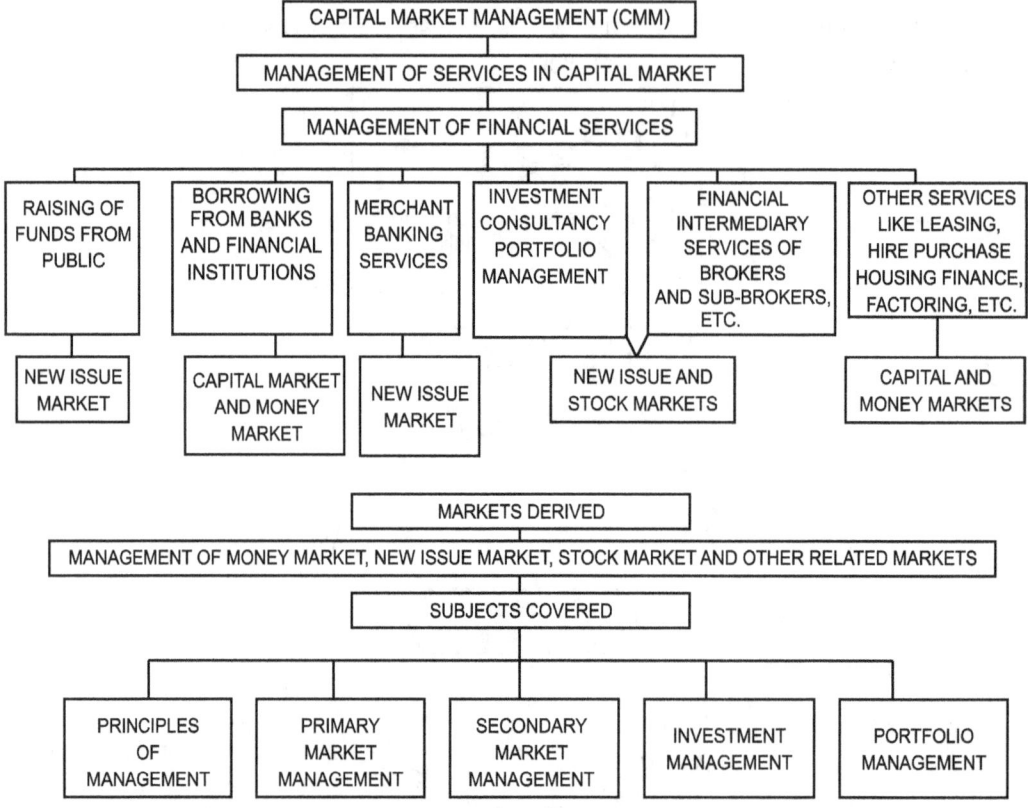

Fig. 1.5 : Capital Market Management

1.1.2 FUNCTIONS OF CAPITAL MARKET

Capital market operations consist of primary market operations and secondary operations. While in primary market investors exchange their savings for securities by corporate with a view to receiving expected returns, investors exchange their holdings with other investors in the secondary market. Mutual funds is another indirect method of capital market investment for individual investors. There are various types of functions of capital market, however, **some important functions** of this market are as follows :

i)   A capital market serves as an important link between those who save and those who aspire to invest these savings. The capital market is a medium through which savings of the community are made available for industrial and commercial enterprises.

ii) The operations of different institutions in the capital market induce economic growth. They give quantitative and qualitative directions to the flow of funds and bring about rational allocation of scarce resources.

iii) A healthy capital market consisting of expert intermediaries promotes stability in values of securities representing capital funds.

iv) Capital serves as an important source for technological upgradation in the industrial sector by utilising the funds invested by the public.

v) The capital market serves as an important source for the productive use of the economy's savings. It mobilises the savings of the people for further investment and thus avoids their wastage in unproductive uses.

vi) It provides incentives to saving and facilitates capital formation by offering suitable rates of interest as the price of capital.

vii) It provides an avenue for investors, particularly the household sector to invest in financial assets which are more productive than physical assets.

viii) It facilitates increase in production and productivity in the economy and thus enhances the economic welfare of the society. Thus, it facilitates "the movement of stream of command over capital to the point of highest yield" towards those who can apply them productively and profitably to enhance the national income in the aggregate.

ix) A well organised capital market provides the essential attributes of liquidity, marketability and safety of investments to the investors.

x) Non-government public companies used to approach the capital market for major part of their financial requirements. The major instruments issued include equity shares, preference shares, debentures, bonds etc.

The functional basis of market is thus seen in the mobilisation of savings for investment, increase in both savings and investment in the economy and to improve productivity of capital by activating the idle balances and increasing the velocity of circulation of money and credit and their use for productive purposes. These trends will lead to increased output of goods and services in the economy and larger industrial growth.

1.1.3 CAPITAL MARKET STRUCTURE

As per the chart shown below capital market includes issues of two major categories marketable and non-marketable, whether marketable or not, these are issued by government and government departments, companies, P.S.Us., mutual funds, UTI, etc. The non-marketable securities or claims are issued by post offices, as savings certificates, deposit receipts etc., non-securitised loans and advances of banks and financial institutions, deposits with banks and companies and securities of private limited companies and finance company deposits/loans, etc. The marketable securities are issued through new issues market and are traded through the stock market. The players through whom these issues are managed are mainly merchant bankers, registrars, brokers, underwriters, mailing agents etc.

The main players in the stock market are brokers, investment consultants, portfolio managers, investment managers etc. The **Capital Market Structure** is shown in Figure 1.6 as follows :

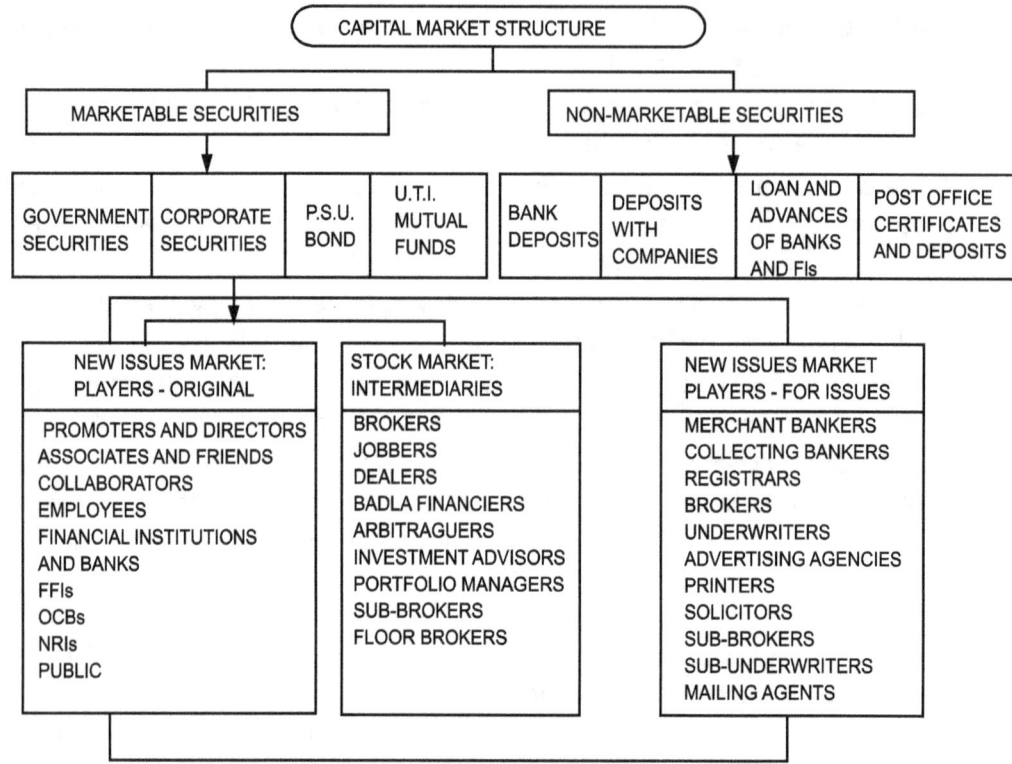

Fig. 1.6 : Capital Market Structure

1.1.4 CHARACTERISTICS OF CAPITAL MARKET

Some of the important **Characteristics of Capital Market** are as follows :

i)   Capital market refers to the market for raising of financial resources by the business enterprises, firms, government, semi-government bodies, P.S.Us and other organisations. Definitionally, the market comprises some who demand and others who supply these resources. The methods of raising these resources are: (a) from the public, b) from the banks and financial institutions, and c) from foreign sources.

ii) The term capital market is a wide term encompassing all long-term claims of money-lendings and borrowings. It thus includes all term lendings by banks and financial institutions and long-term borrowings from foreign markets and new issues by companies and raising of all resources from public through issue of new securities, deposits, loans etc.

iii) The capital market study should really encompass both the marketable and non-marketable segments. In view of the fact that demand and supply forces and trading activity is confined only to the segment of marketable securities.

iv) Capital market management involves various disciplines, much more than in banking. For example, various laws, requires legal expertise, funding business requires banking knowledge, hire purchase and leasing requires a different expertise. Mutual funds, brokerage firms, portfolio managers and a host of other agencies require knowledge and expertise in personal management, marketing management, funds management, investment management etc.

v) Capital market management is different and more specialised than banking. It requires a different cadre of specialists to man the increasing work of financial institutions. It is more practical and operational and the expertise needed is different.

Money Management :

Money Management refers to use of money in such a way that the investments generate an appreciation much higher than the fall in the value of money and investor's net worth will continue to grow faster than the average rate of inflation.

Any saver will have some specific objectives or motives behind his saving. He may be providing for a future, or for a larger accumulation of wealth. His objectives may be set out as follows which is called **"Panchasutri of Investment.**

i) Income at regular intervals.

ii) Capital appreciation or gain in wealth.

iii) Safety of funds.

iv) Marketability and liquidity of assets.

v) Hedge against inflation or fall in value of money.

All of the above objectives are fulfilled by investments in stock and capital markets. The most important objective, namely to protect the value of his money requires planning for proper money management by the investors.

Avenues of Investment

Savers channel their investment into various categories of avenues, depending on the characteristics of these avenues and their own asset preferences.

These avenues may be classified into two broad categories : (a) Non-Financial (Physical) Avenues and (b) Financial Avenues.

(a) Non-Financial Investment Avenues		
i. Gold	i. Consumer Durables	i. Curios
ii. Silver	ii. Commodities.	ii. Vintage Cars.
iii. Diamonds	iii. Land, Buildings, etc.	iii. Antiques

(b) Financial Investment Avenues	
Non-stock Market Avenues	**Stock Market Avenues**
i. Postal Savings ii. Bank Deposits iii. Company Fixed Deposits iv. Insurance Policies, Life, Accident, etc.	i. Gilt Edged Securities - State/Central Governments ii. Semi-Government Securities and P.S.U. Bonds

v. Annuities	iii. Corporate Securities
vi. U.T.I. Units/Schemes	a) Shares-Equity-Bonus-Rights
vii. Mutual Fund Schemes	b) Debentures, Convertible and Non-convertible
	c) Preference shares

Cash and credit are parts of money management which are provided by the Government, RBI and Banks and are used for purchase/sale of securities, borrowing/lending. Savings are income minus expenditure of individuals, households, companies and any other bodies, corporate or non-corporate and these funds are used for purchase of securities or lending for any purpose to borrowers or companies or any other issuer of securities.

When credit is extended or in case of cash flowing in business, management of money becomes the basic objective of both issuer of security and the purchaser of security. The following Figure 1.7 shows the Institutional Role in Money Management viz.: Reserve Bank of India, Commercial Banks and Financial Institutions.

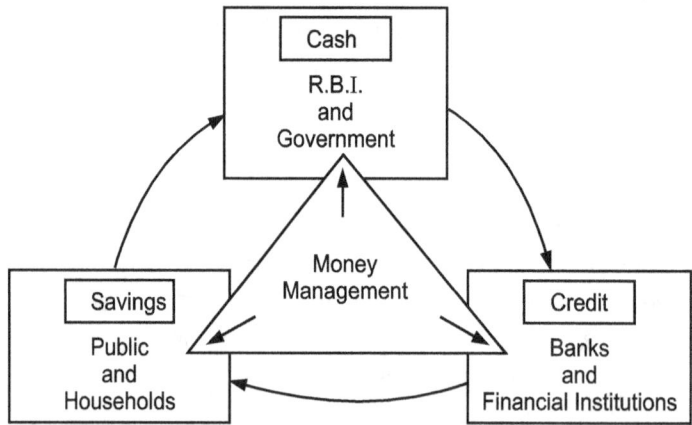

Fig. 1.7 : Institutional Role in Money Management

Basic Components of Capital Market

Two basic components of Capital Market are: i) the new issue and ii) the stock market.

In the former, the existing companies or the new companies raise funds from the public through issue of securities for their project financing, expansion, modernisation etc. In the latter, namely, the Stock Market, the existing securities are bought and sold for helping investors to disinvest and fresh investors to enter into the market. The public can only buy in the new issues market but cannot sell. But in the stock market, they can sell as well as buy the securities. The new issues market and stock market are complementary and investors should be familiar with operations in both.

Issuers of Securities :

The players in the market are the companies issuing securities, intermediaries and brokers who match buying and selling orders and finally the public at large who are the investors in the stocks. The players in the market vary from one segment of the market to another. There are a number of segments in the securities market, depending upon the issues of securities :

i)   Corporate securities,   ii)   Government securities,

iii) Securities/Instruments of P.S.U.   iv)   UTI and mutual fund schemes.

Once we identify the marketable securities, we have a recognised market for them, controlled and regulated by the SEBI and the government.

The market structure of such regulated market segments is as follows.

SECONDARY MARKET STRUCTURE

New Issues Market	Regular Stock Exchanges (21)	Over the Counter Exchange of India (1)	National Stock Exchange (1)
New issues of new companies and further issues of existing companies	For big companies with paid up capital above ₹ 5 crores and ₹ 10 crores as the case may be Trading and physical operations includes Principal exchanges like Mumbai, Kolkata, Delhi and regional exchanges like Cochin, Indore, etc. The B.S.E. and D.S.E., are on electronic trading and others are to follow suit.	Computerised trading for smaller companies with paid up capital of ₹ 30 lakhs and ₹ 25 crores. No trading started operations in Oct. '92.	Recognised in April '93 and started operations later, only in Govt. securities and national market instruments. Equity Trading started in Nov. 1994 - Computerised trading, with countrywide trading network.

Capital raised in the capital market is of various maturities, depending upon the objectives of a borrower. Thus, funds may be required for working capital or short-term accommodation or for project finance, expansion, modernisation and diversification etc. The funds flowing into the market may therefore be in the form of cash, credit and savings and meet the requirements of cash, liquid funds or medium and long term capital assets.

Reforms in Capital Market

The organised financial system is vitally related and influenced by the economic and financial policies of the government. The latest economic policy encompassed reforms in industrial, trade and commerce and financial spheres. Industrial policy liberalisation, freeing of trade and commerce and financial deregulation were the major pillars of these reforms.

The recent economic reforms also encompassed a series of measures to promote investor protection and encourage the growth of capital market. The government controls on new capital issues and entry into the capital market were relaxed. Thus, the Capital Issues Control Act was abolished and the post of Capital Issues Controller was also abolished. Free entry into capital market for new issues by companies and free pricing of shares for new issues has been ensured. The control of SEBI on all players in the capital market and stock market, including merchant bankers, mutual funds, registrars, brokers, sub-brokers, portfolio managers, consultants etc. was strengthened and made effective. The objectives of such regulation by SEBI were to promote investor protection, ensure fair practices by intermediaries and brokers and encourage the growth of a healthy capital market in India.

1.1.5 PARTICIPANTS OF CAPITAL MARKET

There are 23 Stock Exchanges in India, increase in turnover took place mostly in the large exchanges at the expense of smaller ones. Presently, 6 top exchanges account for 99 percent of turnover with BSE and NSE taking the leading role of stock market participation in the country.

Securities Market Participants :

The securities market essentially has three categories of participants, namely, the issuers of securities, investors in securities and the intermediaries, such as merchant bankers, brokers etc. While the corporate and government raise resources from the securities market to meet their obligations, it is households that invest their savings in the securities market.

It is advisable to conduct transactions through a SEBI registered intermediary, as they are accountable for their activities. The list of registered intermediaries is available with exchanges, industry associations etc.

Segments of Securities Market :

The securities market has two interdependent segments: the primary (new issues) market and the secondary market. The primary market provides the channel for sale of new securities while the secondary market deals in securities previously issued.

1.1.6 CAPITAL MARKET INSTRUMENTS

The instruments and non-security forms of investments that are used in the capital market are as follows :

A) Security Forms of Investment

1) Corporate Bonds /Debentures
    i)   Zero Coupon Bonds (ZCBs)
    ii)   ZCBs with the option to convert interest earned to equity on maturity
    iii)   Bonds with detachable warrants.
            a)   Convertible
            b)   Non-convertible
2) Public Sector Bonds
    a)   Taxable
    b)   Tax free
3) Preference Shares
4) Equity Shares
    a)   New Issue
    b)   Rights Issue
    c)   Bonus Issue

B) Non-Security Form of Investment (non-marketable)

1) National Savings Schemes
2) National Savings Certificates
3) Provident Funds
   a) Statutory Provident Fund
   b) Recognised Provident Fund
   c) Unrecognised Provident Fund
   d) Public Provident Fund
4) Corporate Fixed Deposits
   a) Public Sector
   b) Private Sector
5) Life Insurance Policies
   a) Whole Life Policies
   b) Limited-payment Life Policy
   c) Convertible Whole Life Assurance Policy
   d) Endowment Assurance Policy
   e) Jeevan Mitra
   f) The Special Endowment Plan with Profits
   g) Jeevan Saathi
   h) The New Money Back Plan
   i) Marriage Endowment/Educational Annuity Plan with Profits
   j) Bima Sandesh Premium Back Term Insurance Plan
   k) New Children's Deferred Assurance Plan
   l) Jeevan Dhara
   m) New Jana Raksha Plan with Profits
   n) Jeevan Akshay Plan
   o) Jeevan Balya Plan
   p) Jeevan Kishor
   q) Jeevan Griha
   r) Jeevan Sarita
6) Unit Schemes of Unit Trust of India (Some are marketable among these)
   a) Unit Retirement Benefit Plan
   b) Re-investment Plan
   c) Unit Linked Insurance Plan
   d) Capital Gains Unit Scheme
   e) Children's Gift Growth Funds
   f) Parents' Gift Growth Funds

g)   Monthly Income Unit Scheme with extra bonus plus growth

h)   Mastershares

i)   Mastergrains

j)   Equity Linked Savings Scheme

k)   Growing Monthly Income Unit Scheme

l)   Mastershare Plus.

There are many other UTI schemes on similar lines and a number of commercial banks and financial institutions have set up Mutual Funds. Various schemes including the Personal Equity Plan and Tax Saving Schemes, have been launched by many public sector and private sector Mutual Funds.

7) Post Office

a)   Recurring Deposits

b)   Time Deposits

c)   Monthly Income Scheme

d)   Social Security Certificates

e)   National Saving Certificates

8) Others

a)   Rahat Patras or Relief Bonds

b)   Kisan Vikas Patra

c)   Deposits in Banks

i)   Recurring Deposits

ii) Time Deposits.

Ownership Securities

There are different ways by which the required amount of capital can be raised. A small scale business organisation requires small amount of capital. It can be raised privately by few individuals through the savings, from friends and relatives, loans from the banks and financial institutions, etc.

A Joint Stock Company is a large scale business organisation. In order to finance its activities, a company needs large amount of capital, which is not contributed by a few individuals but it is contributed by the public at large. A Joint Stock Company can raise the capital by issuing the shares and debentures to the public and loans from the banks and financial institutions. The other source of financing is the re-investment of a portion of profits known as "Retained Profits". Accepting deposits from the public is another method of obtaining funds by the company. Figure 1.8 shows the **Medium of Raising Capital** as follows :

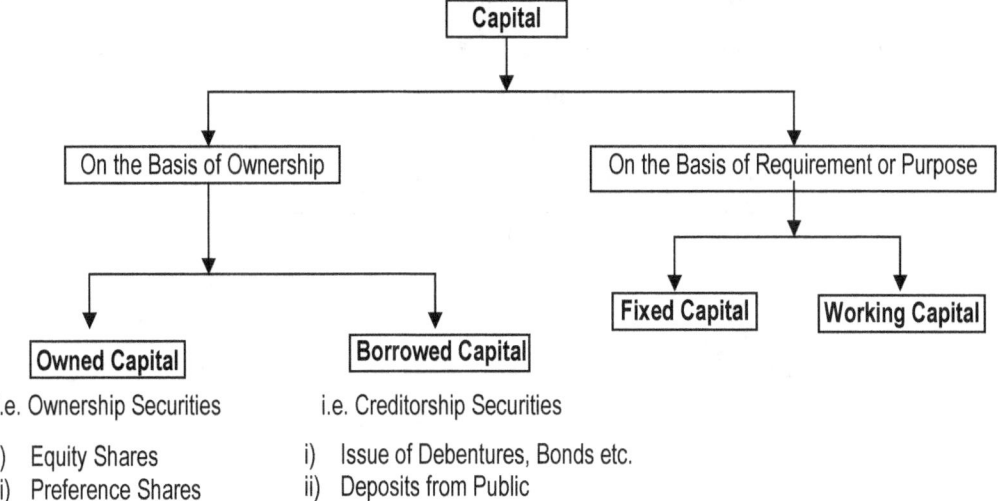

Fig. 1.8 : Medium of Raising Capital

Owned Capital

The capital raised by issue of shares to the members of a Company is known as **'Owned Capital'** or 'Permanent Capital'. This capital is not required to be returned by the company to the investors throughout the life time of the company, except the 'Redeemable Preference Shares' where the amount invested is returned after the expiry period. The owned capital can also be raised by retaining profits or by capitalisation of reserves.

Share Capital

Meaning :

Joint Stock Company needs funds to meet its various types of requirements. Some funds are required for a long period to meet long term needs. E.g. to purchase fixed assets like Buildings, Plant and Machinery etc. Some funds are required to meet short-term needs. Long-term needs of a company are met by issue of shares, particularly the fixed capital requirements. The capital raised by issue of shares is known as **Share Capital**. The finance needed by the business organisation is termed as capital. The share capital cannot be returned to the shareholders during the life time of the company.

Definition :

Definition of Share Capital as given in **Finance Dictionary** is "the portion of a corporation equity obtained from issuing shares in return for cash or other consideration".

In other words, the share capital of a Company is the money subscribed by the shareholders for the purpose of the company.

The Share Capital of a Company is known by different stages of its development. Figure 1.9 shows **Classification of Share Capital** as follows :

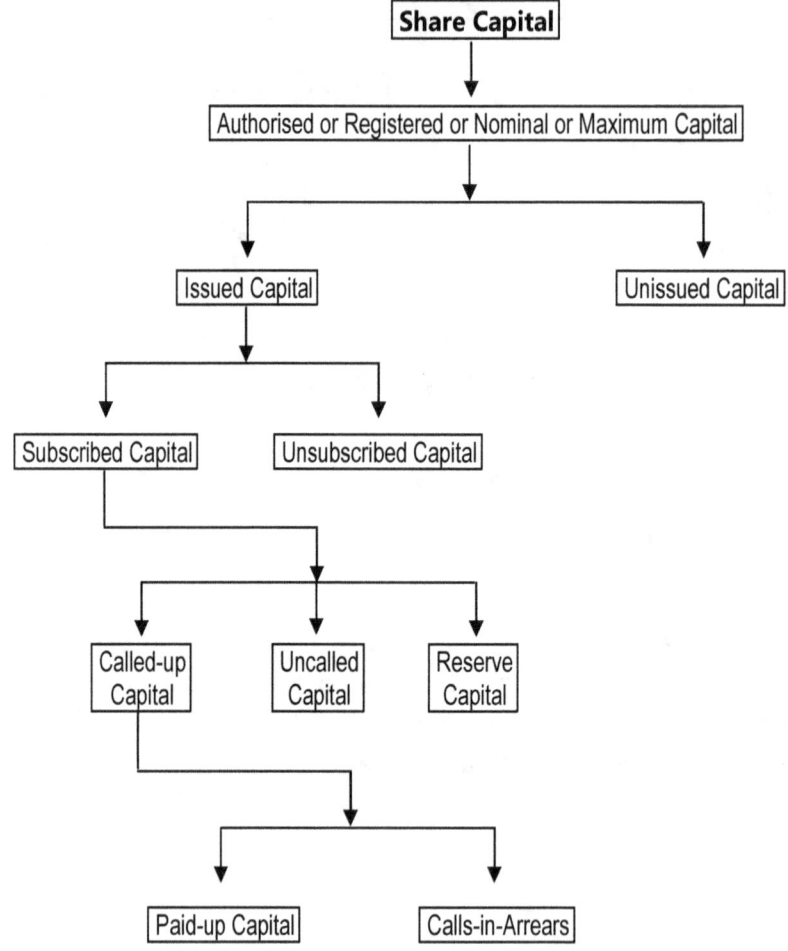

Fig. 1.9 : Classification of Share Capital

The share capital is also classified for the clear understanding and it has a statutory cover.

i) **Authorised Capital :**

This is the maximum capital that the Company can raise which is authorised by the Memorandum of Association. The company does not issue all this to the public. It will be released gradually according to the capital needs of the corporate enterprise. This is also called Registered Capital or Nominal Capital.

ii) **Issued Capital :**

It is that part of the authorised capital released to the investors for subscription.

iii) Subscribed Capital :

This is the capital subscribed by the investors for the offer given by the corporate enterprise. Sometimes, there will be over-subscription and the company will make allotment as per the decisions of the Board of Directors in consultation with the local stock exchange. Some subscribers will be allotted in full (i.e. Firm Allotment). Some are allotted pro-rata and some applications are rejected.

iv) Called-up Capital :

It is that part of subscribed capital called by the Company to make contribution towards the share capital. The company may call full or partial money.

v) Paid-up Capital :

It is that part of called-up capital received by the Company and finally appears in the Balance Sheet. This is the actual capital contribution made by the investors.

The major **Classifications of Share Capital** are illustrated as follows:

Balance Sheet of Activa Co. Ltd., Ahmedabad as on 31st March, 2014

Liabilities	₹	₹
Share Capital :		
i) Authorised Capital :		15,00,000
1,50,000 shares of ₹ 10 each		
ii) Issued Capital :		
1,00,000 shares of ₹ 10 each at		
₹ 5 per share issued	5,00,000	
iii) Subscribed Capital :		
1,00,000 shares of ₹ 10 each		
at ₹ 5 per share subscribed	5,00,000	
iv) Called-up Capital :		
1,00,000 shares of ₹ 10 each	5,00,000	
at ₹ 5 per share called-up		
v) Paid-up Capital :		
1,00,000 shares of ₹ 10 each at		5,00,000
₹ 5 per share paid-up		

Shares

Meaning :

Share Capital of a Company is split up into a large number of equal parts or units, each of such part is called a **Share**. e.g. the total capital of a Company may consist of ₹ 1,00,00,000 divided into 10,00,000 shares or parts of ₹ 10 each. A share in a Company is one of the units into which the total capital of the Company is divided. A person who holds the shares of a

Company is called as a **Shareholder** and becomes one of the owners of the Company. Therefore, the capital so raised is known as **'Owned Capital'** and the shares are called 'Ownership Securities'.

A share is a fractional part of the capital of the Company which forms the basis of ownership of certain rights and interests of a subscriber in the Company. A share is the interest of a shareholder in a definite portion of the capital. It expresses proprietary relationship between the Company and the shareholder.

Definition :

According to Section 2 (46) of the Companies Act, 1956,

"**Share** means a share in the share capital of a Company and includes stock except where a distinction between stock and share is expressed or implied".

Characteristics :

The important characteristics of a share are as follows :

i) A share is a conclusive evidence of the share capital of a Company, without which there will be no capital.

ii) A share is the fractional part of the total share capital of a Company.

iii) A share is categorised as goods which can be purchased, sold or mortgaged.

iv) Every share has a definite nominal or face value, for e.g. ₹ 10, ₹ 1, etc.

v) As per Section 83 of the Companies Act, each share in a company having a share capital must bear a distinctive number for identification.

vi) As per Section 82, the share is a movable asset of the shareholder and hence, it is transferable in the manner provided by the Articles of the Company.

vii) A share certificate is issued for each or of a certain number of shares held by any shareholder.

viii) A share is the interest of a shareholder which confers certain rights on its holder.

ix) A share certificate is not a negotiable instrument, although it can be transferred.

x) A shareholder gets income on his shares which is called dividend.

xi) Every shareholder is liable to the Company within the provisions of the Articles, Memorandum and the Companies Act.

Stock

Meaning :

The term '**Stock**' is used in the definition of a share given in Section 2 (46) of the Companies Act, 1956. Every Public Company with share capital can convert its fully paid-up shares into stock or vice-versa (Section 194). The conversion of shares into stock is possible only when the Articles of the Company permit for the same. The conversion requires passing of an ordinary resolution by the members at a general meeting. A notice of such conversion must be given to the Registrar (Section 94) within 30 days.

Stock in a Company means, "a bundle of fully paid shares put together for convenience, so that it may be divided into any amount and transferred into any fractions and sub-divisions without regard to the original face value of the shares".

However, a Company cannot issue stock originally, i.e. at the time of its incorporation, while the shares can be issued originally direct to the shareholders. When the shares are converted into stock, the share certificates issued to the shareholders are called back by the Company and 'Stock Certificates' are issued in place thereof. A stockholder enjoys the same rights and privileges as that of a shareholder.

Distinction between Shares and Stock

The important points of distinction between Shares and Stock are as follows :

Shares	Stock
i) **Meaning :**	
A share is a share in the Share Capital of the Company.	Stock is simply a set of fully paid shares put together in a bundle.
ii) **Paid-up Value :**	
The shares may be fully paid-up or partly paid-up.	Stock is always made up of fully paid-up shares.
iii) **Distinctive Number :**	
A share has a definite number by which it is distinguished from other shares.	Stock has no such distinctive number.
iv) **Nominal Value :**	
A share has a nominal value.	Stock has no such nominal value.
v) **Transferability :**	
Shares can only be transferred in round numbers, not by any part of it.	Stock can be transferred in any fractions.
vi) **Direct Issue :**	
A public company can issue share directly to shareholders.	A company cannot issue stock directly. It may issue shares first, and when they are fully paid-up, can be converted into stock.
vii) **Registration :**	
Registration of a share capital with the Registrar is compulsory before issuing shares.	Stock can be issued only after passing an ordinary resolution if Articles permit. A notice of such conversion is given to Registrar.
viii) **Which Company can issue ?**	
Private as well as Public Company can issue shares.	Only Public Company having a share capital can issue stock.
ix) **Right to Issue :**	
Right to issue shares is received from Memorandum of Association.	Right to convert shares into stock is received from the Articles of the Company.

Types of Shares

There are different kinds of shares in any company with varying rights as to dividends, voting etc. Figure 1.10 shows the **Classification of Shares** as follows :

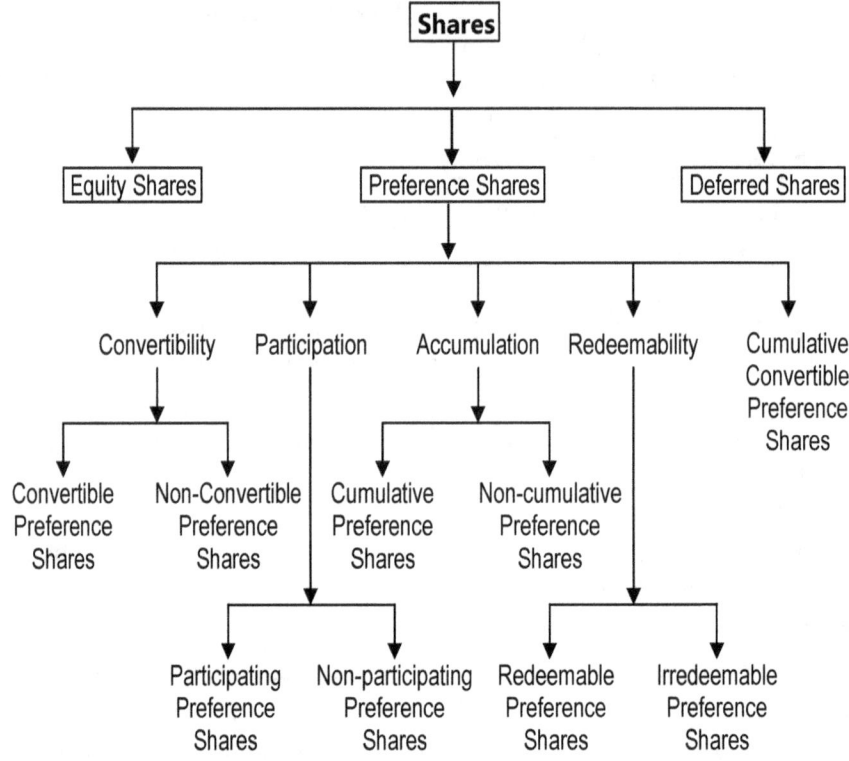

Fig. 1.10 : Classification of Shares

1.1.6.1 EQUITY SHARES

Meaning and Definition

This is the most popular type of shares nowadays. According to Section 85 (2) of the Companies Act 1956, "**Shares** which are not preference shares are known as **equity shares or ordinary shares**".

A major portion of the authorised capital of companies is always in the form of ordinary shares. Equity shareholders have the residual rights of the Company. The dividend on these shares is paid after the dividend on preference shares have been paid. The rate of a dividend on such shares depends upon the amount of profits available and the intention of the directors. A large part of the net profits of a Company, after paying the fixed dividend on preference shares (if any), is paid as dividend to the equity shares. If no profits are left after paying fixed preference dividends, the holders of equity shares get no dividends. In case the Company goes into liquidation, (i.e. winding up) the amount of equity share capital will be repayable only after every other claim, including that of preference shareholders, has been settled. The equity shareholders have normal voting rights on every resolution placed before the company at any general meeting. Equity shares are always irredeemable. Equity share capital is not repayable during the life-time of the Company, hence it represents, permanent capital of the Company.

The fortune of equity shareholders is tied up with the ups and downs of the company. These shareholders have the chance of earning good dividends and also run the risk of receiving nothing. Therefore, equity shares are bought only by those who are prepared to take the risk. Because of the risk attached to these shares, the equity share capital is also called as 'Risk Capital' or 'Venture Capital' of the company.

These shares are entitled to receive the entire surplus profits after preference shares are paid fixed dividend. If no profits are left after payment of fixed dividend to preference share holders, these shares get no dividend. The same applies to the return of capital on winding up of the company. Hence, capital raised through such shares is called as 'Risk Capital'. The fortune of equity shareholders is tied up with ups and downs of the Company. If the company fails, the risk falls mainly on them. If the company is successful, they enjoy great financial rewards. These share holders enjoy normal voting rights on every resolution placed before the Company at the general meeting [Section 87 (1) (a)]. These shares are always irredeemable. (Except in case of buy back of shares).

Characteristics

Some of the important **characteristics of Equity Shares** are as follows :

i) The equity share capital is the **permanent capital** of the company. It is not repayable during the life-time of the Company.

ii) The equity shareholders enjoy normal **voting rights**. They are entitled to vote in the general meetings of the Company.

iii) The **rate of dividend** on equity shares is not fixed. It depends upon the profits earned by the company and the recommendation of Board of Directors.

iv) Equity shareholders receive the dividend on their shares only after the preference dividend has been paid. Further, the equity shares rank behind the preference shares for repayment of capital on winding up of the Company. That is why the share capital raised through such shares is called as **'Risk Capital'**.

v) Equity shares are issued without any **charge (security)** on the assets of the company. If the Company wishes to raise further finance through mortgage of property and other assets, it can do so freely.

vi) Equity shares of a public company are **freely transferable**. The Articles of Association lay down the procedure of transfer of equity shares.

vii) The benefit of **Bonus shares** is available only to the equity shareholders. Out of the accumulated past profits, a Company may issue bonus shares to the existing equity shareholders.

viii) When a company needs more finance for the expansion purpose, a company may raise additional funds by issuing further shares. At such times, the company has to offer the shares first to the equity shareholders called as **Right Issue**.

Different Values to Equity Share :

'Equity Capital' is a term which denotes the capital contributed by the owners of the Company, Different values are attached to equity shares which are : a) Par Value, b) Book Value c) Market Value and d) Issue Price.

a) Par Value :

This is also called the face value of the share. This value is specifically stated in the Memorandum of Association and is also written on the certificate. This value may be ₹ 1, ₹ 2, ₹ 3, ₹ 10 or ₹ 100. Of these values ₹ 10 is the most accepted denomination. Next comes ₹ 100 denomination. To arrive at the face value, the entire capital authorised to issue will be divided by a number and this number is called 'par value'. e.g. A company is authorised to issue ₹ 10 crores divided into 1 crore units of ₹ 10 each, ₹ 10 is the face value and each unit is called the share.

b) Book Value :

Book value takes into account the equity capital and the owners funds. This value is arrived at by adding reserves and surplus to paid-up capital and dividing the same by the number of equity shares. e.g. A company has a paid-up share capital of ₹ 10 each and a surplus of ₹ 1 crores. The book value will be,

$$\text{Book Value} = \frac{\text{Share Capital (+) Free Reserves}}{\text{Number of Equity Shares}}$$

$$= \frac{₹ 1,00,00,000 \text{ (+) } ₹ 1,00,00,000}{10,00,000 \text{ Shares}}$$

$$= \frac{₹ 2,00,00,000}{10,00,000 \text{ Shares}}$$

$$= ₹ 20 \text{ per share}$$

As and when the reserve or surplus increases or decreases, the book value varies accordingly.

c) Market Value :

Normally, this refers to the realisable value of the share in the market. If the shares are listed on the stock market and traded on trading days the price can be easily ascertained as the price is regularly quoted by the exchange. But some companies, though they list their shares in the stock exchanges, do not have the regular trading on the exchange. In such cases, their will be irregular quotation and the market value cannot be easily ascertained as the quoted price differs from the current rate. In case of unlisted shares, only guess work will be done, taking into account the earning capacity of the company, dividend policy, risk involved, the management thinking and the size of the company.

d) Issue price :

This refers to the price at which the shares are issued to the public after obtaining the permission to issue at that price from the appropriate authority (Controller of Capital Issue). The companies which have gained the image in the market may issue the shares at the price over and above the face value and this additional price is called 'Premium'. The newly floated companies normally issue the share capital at the face value. However, the Indian Company's Law does not permit to issue at a price lower than face value.

Rights of Equity Shareholders :

Some of the important Rights to Equity Shareholders are as follows :

i) Right to Income :

The equity investors have a residual claim to the income of the firm. The income left after satisfying the claim of all other investors belongs to the equity shareholders. This income is simply equal to profit after tax minus preferred dividend.

The income of equity shareholders may be retained by the firm or paid out as dividends. Equity earnings which are ploughed back in the firm tend to increase the market value of equity shares and equity earnings distributed as dividend provide current income to equity shareholders. For example, if a firm earns ₹ 15 lakh during the year and pays a dividend of ₹ 8 lakh, the value of equity shares may rise by about ₹ 7 lakh, the amount retained by the firm. The equity shareholders thus receive benefits in two ways : dividend income of ₹ 8 lakh and capital appreciation of ₹ 7 lakh.

It may be noted here that equity shareholders are entitled to receive dividend that is declared by the board of directors. The dividend decision is the prerogative of the board of directors and equity shareholders cannot challenge this decision in a court of law. In this respect, the position of equity shareholders differs markedly from that of supplier of debt capital. Debenture holders, for example, can take legal action against the company for its failure to meet contractual interest payment and capital repayment, irrespective of the financial circumstances of the company. Equity shareholders, on the other hand, cannot challenge the dividend decision of the board of directors in a court of law, however impressive the financial performance of the company may be.

ii) Right to Control :

Equity shareholders, as owners of the firm, elect the board of directors and have the right to vote on every resolution placed before the company. The board of directors, in turn, selects the management which controls the operations of the firm. Hence, equity shareholders, in theory, exercise an indirect control over the operations of the firm. How effective is such indirect control ? Often, such indirect control is weak and ineffective because of the apathy and indifference of most of the shareholders who rarely bother to cast their votes, by post or through a proxy, let alone attend the annual meetings. Scattered and ill-organised, equity shareholders fail to exercise their collective power effectively. Usually, the management of the firm, with the support of a well organised but not a very substantial group of shareholders, is able to hold the reins of control. The proxy system helps the management further. If the shareholders are satisfied, they may sign the proxy in the favour of management, authorising management to vote on their behalf. This system may confer a distinct advantage to the management in the voting process.

iii) Pre-emptive Right :

The pre-emptive right enables existing equity shareholders to maintain their proportional ownership by purchasing the additional equity issued by the firm. The law requires companies to give existing equity shareholders the first opportunity to purchase, on pro-rata basis, additional issue of equity shares capital. For example, if the company had 10,00,000 outstanding shares of equity stock and proposes to issue 2,00,000 additional equity shares, an equity shareholder owing 100 shares has the right to purchase 20 of the 2,00,000 new shares before those are offered to anyone else. The equity shareholders may, however, forfeit this right, partially or totally, as per management's request if this right creates a problem or a hindrance in issuing additional shares.

iv) Right in Liquidation :

As in case of income, equity shareholders have a residual claim over the assets of the firm in the event of liquidation. Claims of all others-debenture holders, secured lenders, unsecured lenders, other creditors and preferred shareholders are prior to the claim of equity shareholders. More often than not equity shareholders do not get anything in the event of liquidation because the liquidated value of assets is not adequate to meet fully the claims of others.

| Advantages and Disadvantages of Equity Share Capital |

A) To the Company :

The most important source of long term funds, Equity Share Capital offers following **Advantages** to the Company :

   i)   It represents permanent capital. Hence, there is no liability for repayment.

   ii)   It does not involve any fixed obligation for payment of dividends.

   iii) It enhances the credit worthiness of the company. In general, other things being equal, the larger the equity base, the higher is ability of the company to obtain credit.

The **Disadvantages** of raising funds by way of Equity Share Capital are as follows :

   i)   The cost of equity capital is high, usually the highest. The rate of return required by equity shareholders is generally higher than the rate of return required by other investors.

   ii)   Equity dividends are payable from post-tax earnings. They are not tax-deductible payments.

   iii) The cost of issuing equity stock is generally higher than the cost of issuing other types of securities. Underwriting commission, brokerage costs, and other issue expenses are high for equity capital.

   iv) Sale of equity stock to outsiders may result in the dilution of the control of existing shareholders though the existing equity shareholders may have the right to maintain proportional ownership when additional equity capital is issued, they may not be able to exercise this right for various reasons. Further, in certain cases pre-emptive rights may be curtailed or forgone.

B) To the Equity Shareholders :

The **Advantages** of Equity Share investment from the **Shareholders** point of view are as under.

i)   They enjoy the right to share the profits.

ii)   They enjoy the right of control.

iii)   They have pre-emptive right.

iv)   They have the advantage of capital appreciation by getting bonus shares.

v)   Equity dividends enjoy tax-exemptions upto a limit of ₹ 10,000 (including earnings of other investments).

vi)   They enjoy more voting right as the rule is 'one share – one vote'.

There are certain **Disadvantages** from the **Shareholders** point of view which are as follows :

i)   There is no definite return on investment. During slack years dividends may be curtailed.

ii)   The right of controls is a myth. In practice, they do not have any control over the affairs of the company as they are scattered, unorganised and can voice their feelings only in the annual general meeting. They do not have power to participate in the day-to-day affairs.

iii)   Equity holders are residual claimants regards earnings and capital repayment and hence it is disadvantageous.

iv)   As the price of equity shares fluctuate widely in the stock market, they are not covered for this risk of fluctuation.

1.1.6.2 PREFERENCE SHARES

Meaning and Definition

According to Section 85 (1) of the Companies Act, 1956, "Preference shares are the shares which carry the following two preferential rights :

i)   **A right to receive dividend at a fixed rate** or a fixed amount before any dividend is paid on equity shares, and

ii)   **A right to receive repayment of capital** on winding up of the company, before the capital of equity shareholders is returned.

Under the Companies Act 1956, both the rights must be attached to the preference shares. If any shares carry only one of these two preferential rights, they will be treated as equity shares. The holder of preference shares enjoy only a preferential right over the equity shareholders. Preference shareholders get dividend at a fixed rate, for example, if a dividend is declared at the rate of 15%, it should be noted that, "his right is not to dividend but to preferential treatment if and when a dividend is declared and distributed". The preference shareholders do not enjoy normal voting rights like equity shareholders. However, these shareholders are entitled to vote in the following cases :

i)   When any resolution directly affecting their rights is to be passed.

ii)   When the dividend due on their preference shares or part thereof has remained unpaid.

Characteristics of Preference Shares

Some of the **important characteristics of Preference Shares** are as follows :

i)   Preference shareholders enjoy a **preferential right** on the **payment of dividend** at a fixed rate out of the profits of the company.

ii)   At the time of winding up of the company, preference shareholders have a preferential right regarding the **repayment of capital** (investment).

iii)   Preference shareholders get a **fixed rate** of dividend every year.

iv)   Preference shareholders do not enjoy normal **voting rights** like the equity shareholders. However, they are entitled to vote when their interest is affected.

v)   As preference shareholders get a fixed rate of dividend, they are not allowed to **participate in prosperity** like equity shareholders except in case of participating preference shares. They will not get more dividend when company earns surplus profits.

vi)   Preference shareholders are not entitled to claim for **bonus shares** or new issues.

vii)   Those investors who **do not** want to take any **risk** regarding the rate of dividend and return of their fund invested, prefer to purchase preference shares.

viii) Preference share do not impose heavy **burden on the finances** because dividend on these shares will be paid only if profits are available.

Kinds of Preference Shares

Different **kinds of Preference Shares** which are issued in the capital market which are as follows :

i) Convertible and Non-convertible Preference Shares :

Convertible preference shares are the shares which can be converted into equity shares within a certain period or upto a specified date. The holder of these shares is given the right of conversion of his shares into equity shares.

In case of non-convertible preference shares, the holders of these shares are not given the right to convert their shares into equity shares. All preference shares are deemed to be non-convertible unless the Articles or terms of issue state otherwise.

ii) Participating and Non-participating Preference Shares :

Participating preference shares are those shares which are entitled, in addition to preference dividend at a fixed rate, to participate in the balance of profits with the equity shareholders, after they get a fixed rate of dividend on their shares. This means they get their regular fixed rate of dividend and additional dividend out of the surplus profits. The participating preference shares may also have the right to share in the surplus assets of the company on its winding up. Such a right must be expressly provided in the Memorandum or Articles of the company.

Non-participating preference shares get only a fixed rate of dividend out of the profits and they do not get any additional dividend with equity shareholders. All the preference shares are deemed to be non-participating, unless stated otherwise in the articles in the terms of issue.

iii) Cumulative and Non-cumulative Preference Shares :

On the basis of payment of the dividend, preference shares may be cumulative or non-cumulative. In the case of cumulative preference shares, if the profits of the company in any year are not sufficient to pay the fixed dividend, the dividend amount accumulates and when the company makes profits in subsequent years, the arrears of dividend must be paid alongwith the current year dividend, before the dividend is paid to equity shareholders.

In case of non-cumulative preference shares, the dividend is only payable out of the net profits of each year. If the company does not earn profit in a particular year, the arrears of dividend cannot be claimed in the subsequent years in which company earns profit. All the preference shares are treated as cumulative preference shares unless contrary is stated in the Articles or the terms of issue.

iv) Redeemable and Irredeemable Preference Shares :

According to Section 80 of the companies (Amendment) Act, 1980, a company limited by shares, if so authorised by its Articles, may issue redeemable preference shares. Such shares may be redeemed (repaid) either after a fixed period or earlier at the option of the company. The paying back of capital is called the redemption.

The Redeemable Preference Shares can be redeemed, only subject to the following conditions :

a)   There must be a provision in the Articles giving powers to a company to issue such shares.

b)   Such shares must be fully paid.

c)   Such shares shall be redeemed out of distributable profits of the company, or out of the proceeds of a fresh issue of shares made for the purpose of redemption.

d)   The premium, if any, payable on redemption of such shares must be paid out of the profits of the company, or out of the company's share premium account.

e)   If such shares are redeemed out of profits of company, the company should create a reserve fund known as 'Capital Redemption Reserve Account', out of its divisible profits for the purpose, which should be equal to the nominal amount of the shares so redeemed.

f)   Notice of redemption must be sent to the Registrar within 30 days after doing so, from the date of redemption.

In case of irredeemable preference shares, the capital is to be returned on the winding up of the company. But the companies Amendment Act, 1988, strictly prohibits the company to issue irredeemable preference shares or redeemable preference shares which are redeemable after the expiry of a period of 20 years from the date of its issue. [Newly inserted by the Companies (Amendment) Act 1996].

v) Cumulative Convertible Preference Shares (CCPS) :

The Government has issued guidelines on 19th August, 1985 permitting issue of another class of shares by public limited companies called "Cumulative Convertible Preference Shares". These guidelines are issued for the guidance of companies proposing to issue cumulative convertible preference shares. The main guidelines in this respect are given below :

i)   The cumulative convertible preference shares can be issued for the following purposes :

   a)   Setting up new projects;
   b)   Expansion or diversification of existing projects;
   c)   Normal capital expenditure for modernisation; and
   d)   Working capital requirements.

ii)   The amount of issue of CCPS will be the extent the company would be offering equity shares to the public for subscriptions. In case of projects assisted by financial institutions, the quantum of issue would be approved by the financial institutions/ banks.

iii) The entire issue of CCPS would be convertible into equity shares between the end of 3 years and 5 years as may be decided by the company and approved by SEBI.

iv)   The rate of preference dividend payable on CCPS would be 10%.

v)   The conversion of aforesaid preference shares into equity shares would be compulsory at the end of 5 years and the aforesaid preference shares would not be redeemable at any stage.

vi)   On conversion of the preference shares into equity shares, the right to receive arrears of dividend, if any, on the preference shares upto the date of conversion shall devolve on the holder of the equity shares on such conversion. The holder of the equity shares shall be entitled to receive the arrears of dividend as and when the company makes profit and is able to declare such dividends.

Advantages and Disadvantages of Preference Share Capital

A) To the Company :

Preference Share Capital offers the following **Advantages** to the company.

i)   The company enjoys a comfortable position as the dividend on preference share may be skipped and it cannot be legally questioned in the court of law.

ii)   Except the redeemable preference shares, which is a negligible portion of the total capital, the company does not face the redemption problem. Even in case of redeemable preference shares, the repayment can be postponed and it will not pose any problems except that it has to pay negligible penalty.

iii) This capital does not carry the voting right except regarding the matter concerned with them. This helps company in control matters.

iv)   While issuing the preference capital, no property of the company needs to be pledged or mortgaged. This helps the company in conserving the assets.

v)   Preference capital is considered to be the part of network and it increases the creditworthiness of the company.

The disadvantages of raising funds by way of preference capital are as follows :

i)   Issuing preference capital is an expensive one as the dividend payable is not a tax-deductible expense.

ii)   Skipping of dividends may pose the control problem.

B) To the Preference Shareholders :

The **Advantages of Preference Share** investment from the **shareholders** point of view are as under :

i)   It earns a stable dividend rate.

ii)   For a corporate investor's preference, dividend income is tax-exempt to the extent of the dividend paid out.

There are certain **Disadvantages from the shareholders** point of view which are as follows :

i)   Legal protection is not given to the preference holders regarding dividend and capital repayment. The company can skip the dividend and also can postpone the capital repayment. The preference holders are highly exposed.

ii)   The rate of preference dividend is not attractive.

iii) The market price of preference share highly fluctuates when compared to debentures.

Distinction between Equity Shares and Preference Shares

The important points of distinction between Equity Shares and Preference Shares are as follows :

Equity Shares	Preference Shares
i) Meaning : According to Section 85 (2), shares which are not preference shares are known as equity shares.	According Section 85 (1), preference shares are the shares, which enjoy preferential right as regards the payment of dividend and the repayment of capital.
ii) Rate of Dividend : The rate of dividend may fluctuate from year to year depending upon the net profit of the company.	The rate of dividend on these shares is fixed.
iii) Preferential right as to the payment of dividend : Payment of equity share dividend is made after the payment of preference share dividend.	Dividend on preference shares is paid before the payment of equity share dividend.

Equity Shares	Preference Shares
iv) Repayment of Capital :	
Equity share capital ranks behind the preference shares for repayment of capital on winding up of the company.	Repayment of preference share capital is made before the payment of equity share capital.
v) Voting Rights :	
Equity shareholders enjoy normal voting rights on all matters affecting the company.	The voting rights of preference shareholders are usually restricted. However, they are entitled to vote when their interest is affected.
vi) Face Value :	
The face value of equity share is relatively low. e.g. ₹ 10 or ₹ 1.	Face value of preference share is relatively high. e.g. ₹ 200 or more.
vii) Redeemability :	
Equity shares are not redeemable during the life-time of the company unless the company decides to buy-back its shares.	Redeemable preference shares are redeemable during the life-time of the company.
viii) Types :	
There are no types of equity shares. All equity shares are of one category.	There are different types of preference shares like cumulative and non-cumulative, convertible etc.
ix) Bonus Shares :	
A company may issue bonus shares to the company's existing equity shareholders.	Preference shareholders are not eligible for bonus shares if issued by the company.
x) Capital Appreciation :	
Equity shares may enjoy capital appreciation with rising dividends.	Preference shares have no capital appreciation. These shares do not participate in prosperity of the company.
xi) Risk Involved :	
Equity shares are subject to higher risk. It is regarded as the risk capital.	Preference shares are less risky and gets dividend at the fixed rate.

Creditorship Securities

Meaning :

A company cannot live on its funds all the time. It has to depend on borrowings from outside. Every trading company, unless prohibited by its Memorandum or Articles, has implied power to borrow money for the purpose of its business. It has also the power to give security for the loan by creating a mortgage or charge on its property. A non-trading company has no implied power to borrow money unless expressly authorised to borrow by their memorandum and articles. A private company is entitled to exercise borrowing powers immediately after its incorporation. But a public company cannot exercise its borrowing powers until it obtains, 'Certificate of Commencement of Business'.

Borrowed Capital means the capital which is required to be returned after the expiry of a certain period. It consists of the amount raised by way of loans or credit. Borrowed capital is also known as creditorship capital or Borrowed funds. Borrowed capital (i.e. funds) can be raised by issue of debentures, by accepting public deposits, loan from banks and financial institutions, etc. A fixed rate of interest is payable on borrowed capital. Borrowed capital is not a permanent capital because it is available for a specific period and is repayable at the end of specified period according to terms and conditions of loan agreement. Borrowed Capital does not affect the owners control over management. Figure 1.11 shows **Medium of Raising Borrowed Capital**.

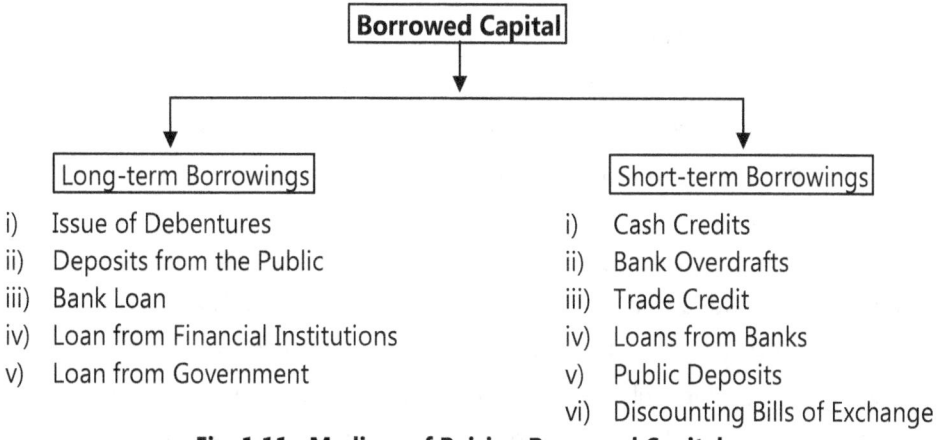

Borrowed Capital

Long-term Borrowings	**Short-term Borrowings**
i) Issue of Debentures	i) Cash Credits
ii) Deposits from the Public	ii) Bank Overdrafts
iii) Bank Loan	iii) Trade Credit
iv) Loan from Financial Institutions	iv) Loans from Banks
v) Loan from Government	v) Public Deposits
	vi) Discounting Bills of Exchange

Fig. 1.11 : Medium of Raising Borrowed Capital

1.1.6.3 DEBENTURES

Meaning and Definition

In addition to the share capital, a company can supplement its resources by borrowings. According to the Companies Act, 1956, the Board of Directors of a company is empowered to borrow funds. Besides issuing shares, a company can raise funds in the form of a debt, such as loans from debt financial institutions, inviting public deposits and issuing debt instruments such as bonds and debentures. It helps a company to have a balanced capital structure. Issue of debentures as a method of raising funds in the form of a debt is widely used in practice.

The word 'debenture' is derived from the Latin word 'debere' which means 'to owe'. Thus, debenture means 'an instrument in writing issued by a company under its common seal, acknowledging its indebtedness for a certain sum of money and undertaking to repay it on or after a fixed future date'.

According to Section 2 (12) of the Companies Act 1956, "debenture includes debenture stock, bonds and any other securities of a company whether constituting a charge on the assets of the company or not". Debenture being a form of loan, interest is payable on the same at certain rate per annum at stated intervals. The holders of a debenture is not a member of the company but merely a creditor.

A debenture is a written acknowledgment of debt by a company under its common seal. It is an instrument used by companies to raise loan capital. Interest is paid to debenture holders at a fixed rate at regular intervals. When capital is required, but not of a permanent nature, it may be obtained through long-term loans. For obtaining long-term loans, issue of debentures is the most common method adopted by companies. The term 'debenture' means acknowledgment of a debt in writing. In the words of **J. Lewis Brown and L. R. Howard**, "A Debenture is a document given by a company in acknowledgment of a debt, undertaking to repay the stated sum on or before a certain date".

A debenture is a tool or device used to raise funds in the form of debt. It is a description of an instrument. The Companies Act allows conversion of debenture into debenture stock which contains description of a debt which is composite in nature and can be divided and transferred in parts.

A debenture is a document issued by a company as an evidence of a debt due from the company with or without a charge on the assets of the company. It is a certificate issued by a company under its seal acknowledging a debt due by it to its holders.

According to the Companies Act 1956, the term debenture includes "debentures stock, bonds and any other securities of a company whether constituting a charge of the assets of the company or not".

The term "debenture stock" is similar to "share stock". It is the aggregate and consolidated amount of borrowings on account of debentures by a company. Fully paid debentures can only be converted into debenture stock. Such stock can be divided and transferred in any convenient parts.

Characteristics of Debentures

Some of the **important characteristics of Debentures** are as follows :

i) It is issued by a company and is usually in the form of a certificate, which is an acknowledgment of indebtedness.

ii) A debentureholder is a creditor of the company. It is creditorship security.

iii) It is issued under the Company's seal. However, it is not necessary.

iv) It is one of a series issued to a number of lenders. But a single debenture may be issued by the company.

v) The rate of interest payable on debentures is fixed, whether or not the company has made a profit.

vi) A debentureholder does not have any right to vote in the company meetings.

vii) It generally creates a charge on the assets of the company. But there may be debentures without any such charge.

viii) Debentures may be issued at par, at a premium or at a discount either privately or through a prospectus.

Classification of Debentures

The **Types of Debentures** are classified as under :

A) On the basis of Security,
   i) Secured Debentures
   ii) Unsecured Debentures

B) On the basis of Permanence,
   i) Redeemable Debentures
   ii) Irredeemable Debentures

C) On the basis of Negotiability,
   i) Registered Debentures and
   ii) Bearer Debentures

D) On the basis of Convertibility,
   i) Convertible Debentures
   ii) Non-Convertible Debentures

E) On the basis of Priority,
   i) First Mortgage Debentures and
   ii) Second Mortgage Debentures

Figure 1.12 shows the **Types of Debentures** issued by a Company as follows :

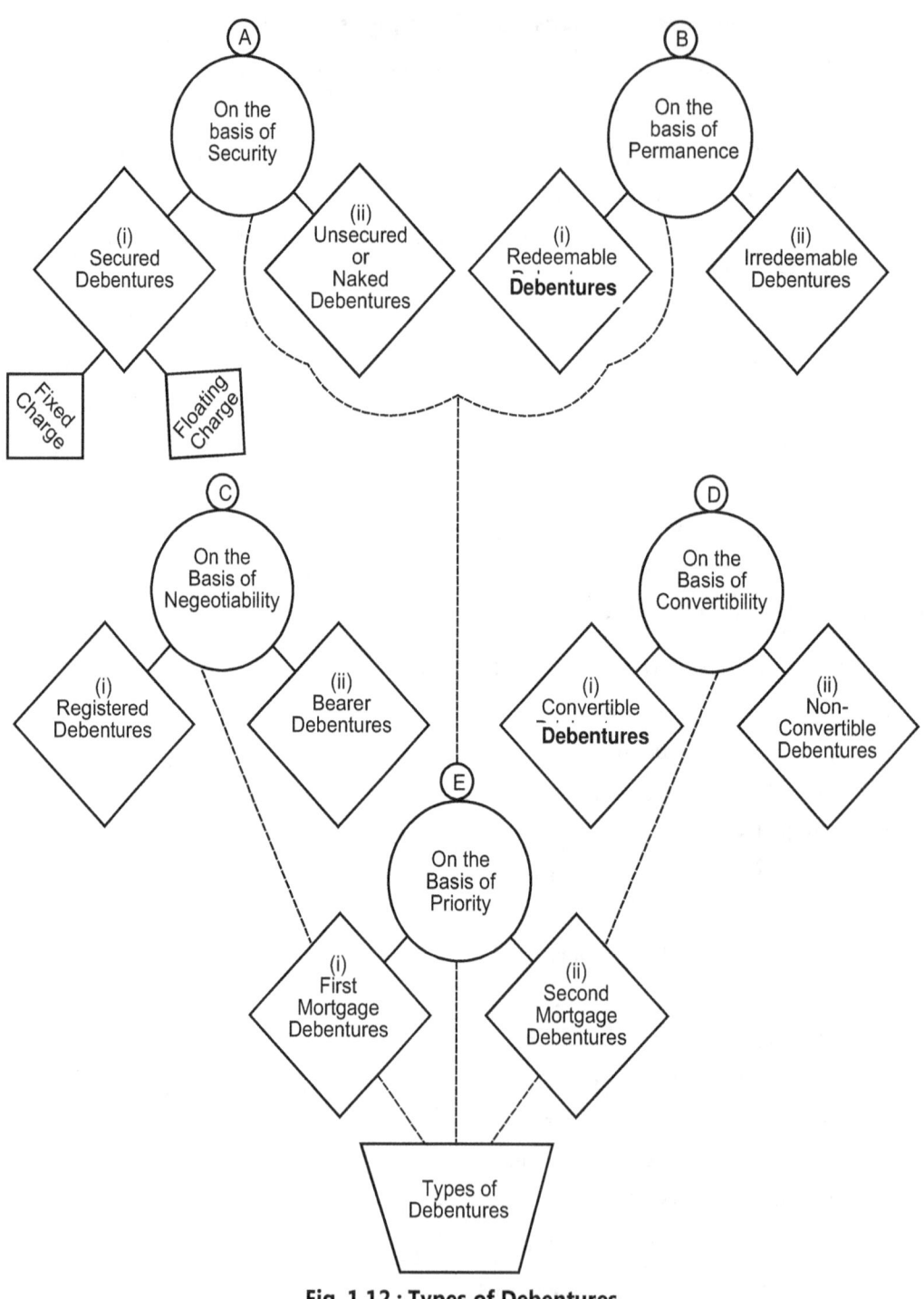

Fig. 1.12 : Types of Debentures

The following are the types of debentures issued by a Company which can be classified on the basis of : A) Security, B) Permanence, C) Negotiability, D) Convertibility and E) Priority.

A) Security :

i) Secured Debentures

These debentures are secured by a charge upon some or all assets of the company. There are two types of charges : i) Fixed charge; and ii) Floating charge. A fixed charge is a mortgage on specific assets. These assets cannot be sold without the consent of the debentureholders. The sale proceeds of these are utilised first for repaying debentureholders. A floating charge generally covers all the assets of the company including the future one.

ii) Unsecured or "naked" Debentures

These debentures are not secured by any charge upon any assets. A company merely promises to pay interest on due dates and to repay the amount due on maturity date. These types of debentures are very risky from the view point of investors.

B) Permanence :

i) Redeemable Debentures

The debentures which are repayable on the expiry of a certain period are called redeemable debentures. In time, the debentures may be redeemed by the company on demand by the holders or at the discretion of the company.

ii) Irredeemable Debentures

A debenture will be treated as irredeemable when there is no period fixed for repayment of the principal amount. These debentures are retained as a part of the permanent capital structure of the company. These debentures are called perpetual debentures. These debentures are repaid at the time of liquidation of the company. The company can redeem such debentures by giving due notice to the holders.

C) Negotiability :

i) Registered Debentures

These debentures which are payable to the holders, whose names have been registered with the company are called registered debentures. The transfer of such debentures requires registration with the company. The payment of interest and repayment of principal is made to those whose names have been registered with the company and duly recorded in the Register of Debentureholders.

ii) Bearer Debentures

The debentures which are payable to the bearer are called bearer debentures. They are treated as negotiable instruments and transferable by mere delivery. Registration of such transfer with the company is not necessary.

D) Convertibility :

i) Convertible Debentures

These are debentures which will be converted into equity shares (either at par or premium or discount) after a certain period of time from the date of its issue. These debentures may be fully or partly convertible. In future, these debentureholders get a chance to become the shareholders of the company.

ii) **Non-Convertible Debentures :**

These are debentures which cannot be converted into shares in future. As per the terms of issue, these debentures are repaid.

E) **Priority :**

i) **First Mortgage Debentures :**

These debentures are payable first out of the property charged.

ii) **Second Mortgage Debentures :**

These debentures are payable after satisfying the first mortgage debentures.

1.1.6.4 BONDS

Bonds and debentures are creditorship securities which help an enterprise to procure funds from lenders. Debenture is merely a written instrument signed by the company under its holders. Through this instrument; the company promises to pay a specific amount of money as stated therein at a fixed date in future together with periodic payment of interest to compensate the holders for the use of funds. The Companies Act, 1956, does not define debenture. It simply states that a debenture includes debentures stock, bonds and any other securities of a company whether constituting a charge on the assets of the company or not. Thus, the Act only states that it is a kind of security which constitutes a charge by way of security on issuing debentures.

Debentures and Bonds :

At the very outset, it is imperative to have clear understanding of two terms, debentures and bonds, used very frequently to denote a security for raising loan capital. In the U.S.A., term bond refers to security instrument that is in lieu of specific assets of the enterprise and the word 'mortgage bond' is very often used as an alternative to the word bond. Debenture, on the other hand, refers to unsecured bond which is not secured by in lieu of any specific assets. Of course, it is secured by all the assets of the company not otherwise mortgaged. In the event of liquidation, debentureholders become general creditors. In our country no such distinction is made between the two terms. For debentures which are secured by pledging certain assets, the term 'secured debenture' or bond is used and unsecured debentures refer to those having no lieu on specific assets. In financial usage also no clear line is drawn between a bond and a debenture

Debentures and Debenture Stock :

The difference between 'debentures' and 'debenture stock' is the same as the difference between 'shares' and 'stock'. A debenture is a document given by the company as an evidence of debt to the holder. On the other hand, debenture stock is the description of the borrowed capital consolidated into one mass for the sake of convenience. Like share, the 'debenture' is always of fixed denominations, indivisible and transferable in its entirety, and like a stock the 'debenture stock' is not of any fixed amount, divisible to any extent and may be transferred even in small fractional amount. In this case, the company issues to each lender a certificate, known as debenture stock certificate, showing the fraction of the debt which the company owes to him.

There is one more important difference between 'stock' and 'debenture stock'. Where the 'stock' cannot be issued originally, that is at the time of its incorporation; 'debenture stock' can be so issued. Unlike a shareholder, a debenture stock holder is not a member of the company. He has no right to attend and vote at general meetings. A debenture stockholder is a creditor of the company. Debenture stock is generally created by a trust deed which varies in its provision from the deed securing debentures.

Debenture Trust Deed :

Where secured debentures are issued by a company, it is usual to execute a trust deed conveying property to the trustees in trust for debentureholders.

Debentureholders of a company, who are usually in large number, may not have the time to look after their interest in the property mortgaged or they may, in order to protect and safeguard their interest, appoint some person amongst them as trustees. A trust deed is in such a case executed, conveying the property of the company to trustees. Under the terms of the trust deed the company undertakes to pay the debentureholders their principal sum and interest and normally charges its property to the trustees as security.

The trust deed contains the terms and conditions endorsed on the debentures and defines the rights of debentureholders and the company. It usually empowers the trustees to appoint a receiver to protect their interest. It also contains other provisions concerning meetings of the debentureholders, supervision of the assets charged, and keeping of a register of debentureholders. Whenever there is a default by the company, action may be taken by the trustees on behalf of all the debentureholders. According to Section 117-A of the Companies (Amendment) Act 2000, a trust deed shall be in a specified form and shall be executed within the prescribed period. A copy of the trust deed shall be open to inspection to any member of debentureholder of the company and he shall also be entitled to obtain copies of such trust deed on the payment of prescribed amount.

Procedure of Issuing Debentures and Bonds :

The Memorandum of Association must contain the provision for borrowing by the company. According to Section 292 (1), the Board of Directors of a company has the power to issue debentures on behalf of the company. After the Board of Directors has decided upon the details of debenture issues the debenture certificates are printed and deed of trust is drawn. The trust deed contains the full details of the property to be mortgaged. The trustees are appointed to safeguard the interest of the debentureholders.

It is convenient to the Company to make trustees parties to the deed instead of all the debentureholders. On the other hand, the debentureholders who are ignorant of law, can protect their rights and can bring an action against the Company through trustees.

Debentures are issued, like shares, by the Company issuing a prospectus whereby the public is invited to apply for its debentures. The debentures may be issued at par or at a premium or at a discount. There is no restriction as regards the maximum amount of discount that can be allowed while issuing the debentures. The holders of debentures are called debentureholders and they are entitled to get a fixed rate of interest either annually or half-yearly. Interest is payable on the face value of the debentures and the interest is a charge against profit. Debentureholders may be asked to pay the whole amount along with the application or to pay the sum in instalments.

Before issue of debentures, a prospectus is issued containing certain information as per the provision of the Companies Act 1956. If the Company has not issued any prospectus, a statement in lieu of prospectus must be filed with the Registrar of Companies at least three days before the first allotment of debentures.

The intending buyer of debentures must apply in prescribed printed form which is generally attached with the prospectus.

Subject to the restrictions imposed by Section 293 of the Companies Act, 1956, a company can issue debentures. The procedure for Issuing debentures by a Company is very much similar to that of an issue of shares. Applications for debentures are invited from the public through the prospectus and the applicants are asked to pay the application money along with the applications. The Company may ask for payment of the whole of the amount alongwith the application or by instalments.

Like shares, debentures may also be issued either, i) at par, or ii) at a premium or iii) at a discount without any legal restriction as shown in Figure 1.13 as follows :

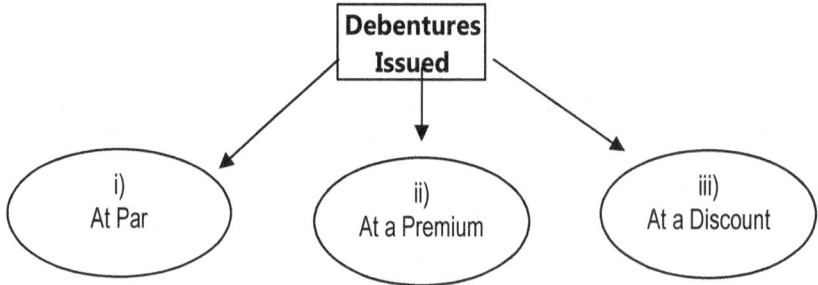

Fig. 1.13 : Issue of Debentures

i)   Issue of Debentures at Par :

Debentures are said to be issued at par when the debentureholder is required to pay an amount equal to the nominal or face value of the debentures, e.g. the issue of ₹ 100 debenture for ₹ 100.

ii)   Issue of Debentures at Premium :

If the debentures are issued at a price higher than the nominal value of the debentures, the debentures are said to be issued at a premium. The excess of Issue price over the nominal value is regarded as the premium amount.

The Companies Act, 1956, does not contain any specific provision as to the manner in which the premium received on the issue of debentures is to be utilised. But from the point of view of sound financial policy, such premium not being trading profit should be transferred to Capital Reserve at the end of the period and the same can be utilised in writing off capital losses like discount on issue of shares or debentures, premium on redemption of debentures, underwriting commission, preliminary expenses, etc.

iii) Issue of Debentures at Discount :

If the debentures are issued at a price lower than the nominal value of the debentures, the debentures are said to be issued at a discount. The difference between the nominal value and the issue price is regarded as the discount.

The Companies Act, 1956, does not prescribe any restriction on issue of debentures at a discount. But the Companies Act, 1956, requires that the discount on issue of debentures, being a capital loss must be shown specifically on the assets side of the Balance sheet till written off under the heading "Miscellaneous Expenditure". Such discount on issue of debentures may either be written off against capital profits of the company or be treated as deferred revenue expenditure and written off against revenue over the period the debentures are likely to be carried.

As well, Debentures may be issued for cash, or for consideration other than cash or as a collateral security also.

iv) Debentures Issued for Cash :

When debentures are issued for cash, the amount to be collected on them may be payable in lump sum or in instalments. Where payable in instalments, debenture application account is opened on receipt of applications. Debenture allotment account and debenture calls account are credited as against debenture account.

v) Debentures Issued for Consideration other than Cash :

It may so happen that the company acquires some assets from the vendor and instead of paying the vendor in cash, the company may allot debentures in payment of purchase consideration. The issue of debentures to vendors is known as issue of debentures for consideration other than cash.

vi) Debentures issued as Collateral Security :

The term 'Collateral Security' implies additional security given for a loan. Where a company obtains a loan from a bank or insurance company, it may issue its own debenture so the lender as collateral security against the loan in addition to any other security that may be offered. In such a case, the lender has the absolute right over the debentures until and unless the loan is repaid. On repayment of the loan, however, the lender is legally bound to release the debenture forthwith. But in case the loan is not repaid by the company on the due date or in the event of any other breach of agreement, the lender has the right to retain these debentures and to realise them. The holder of such debentures is entitled to interest only on the amount of loan, but not on the debentures. Such an issue of debentures is known as "Debentures issued as Collateral Security".

Procedure for Issuing Debentures :

The following is the **procedure for issuing debentures** :

i) **Passing of Resolution :**

In order to issue debentures, the Board of Directors, through its committee, in conformity with powers given by articles, prepare a prospectus, trust deed and other details and then passes a resolution at a duly convened and constituted meeting.

ii) **Consent of the Controller of Capital Issues :**

The consent of the Controller of Capital Issues is to be taken if the issue exceeds ₹ 50 lakhs in a period of 12 months. However, the Board of Directors cannot issue debentures if the company exceeds the paid-up capital and its free reserve. For this purpose, the sanction of the shareholders at a general meeting is required.

iii) **Permission of the Reserve Bank of India for bearer debentures :**

If a company issues bearer debentures, then permission of the Reserve Bank of India should be obtained.

iv) **Consent of Trustees :**

If a company issues debentures under trust deed, then consent of trustees should be obtained. A draft of trust deed, prospectus and debenture bond is also prepared.

v) **Filing of Prospectus or Statement in Lieu of Prospectus :**

The company may issue debentures to the public with or without issuing a prospectus. In case the company issues a prospectus to the public, the company must file a copy of the prospectus signed and dated by the directors of the company, with the Registrar of Companies before the prospectus is issued.

vi) **Restrictions on company regarding issue of debentures :**

The company must receive at least 5% of the issue price of debentures in cash and the company should not make the allotment of debentures within 5 days from the date of issue of prospectus to the public.

vii) **Filing a copy of charges with the Registrar :**

If any assets of the company are mortgaged against debentures, a trust deed should be prepared which should be registered in due course. The particulars of the charges created on the issue are to be filed with the Registrar of Companies within 30 days of its creation.

viii) **Script Certificates :**

Debentures are always fully paid. When the debenture amount is received in instalments, the script certificates are given for payment in instalments and the final certificate is given on payment of the last instalment and in exchange of the script certificates. The company must issue debenture certificates within 3 months from the date of issue of the prospectus.

ix) Record in the Register of debentureholders :

After the allotment, particulars of each debenture are entered in the Register of Debenture holders and debenture certificates properly stamped, sealed and signed by the directors, will be prepared and will be issued to the allottees in due course.

SEBI Guidelines – 2000 for Issue of Debt Instrument :

I.   Creation of Debenture Redemption Reserve (DRR) :

A company has to create DRR in case of issue of debenture with maturity of more than 18 months.

The issuer shall create DRR in accordance with the provisions given below :

1.   If debentures are issued for project finance, DRR can be created upon the date of commercial production.

2.   The DRR in respect of debentures issued for project finance may be created either in equal instalments or higher amounts if profits so permit.

3.   In the case of partly convertible debentures, DRR shall be created in respect of non-convertible portion of debenture issue on the same lines as applicable for fully non-convertible debenture issue.

4.   In respect of convertible issues by new companies, the creation of DRR shall commence from the year the company earns profits for the remaining life of debentures.

5.   DRR shall be treated as a part of General Reserve for consideration of bonus issue proposals and for price fixation related to post tax return.

6.   Company shall create DRR equivalent to 50% of the amount of debenture issue before debenture redemption commences.

7.   Drawal from DRR is permissible only after 10% of the debenture liability has actually been redeemed by the company.

8.   The requirement of creation of a DRR shall not be applicable in case of issue of debt instruments by infrastructure companies.

II. Requirement of Credit Rating :

1.   No public or rights issue of debt instruments (including convertible instruments) in respect of their maturity or conversion period shall be made unless credit rating from a credit rating agency has been obtained and disclosed in the offer document.

2.   For a public/rights issue of debt security, of issue greater than or equal to ₹ 100 crores, two ratings from two different credit rating agencies shall be obtained.

3.   Where credit rating is obtained from more than one credit rating agencies all the credit rating(s), including the unaccepted credit ratings, shall be disclosed.

4.   All the credit ratings obtained during the three (3) years preceding the public or rights issue of debt instruments (including convertible instruments) for any listed security of the issuer company shall be disclosed in the offer document.

III. Requirement in respect of Debenture Trustee :
1. In case of issue of debenture with maturity of more than 18 months, the issuer shall appoint a debenture trustee.
2. The names of the debenture trustees must be stated in offer document.
3. A trust deed shall be executed by the issuer company in favour of the debenture trustees within six months of the closure of the issue.

IV. Distribution of Dividends :
1. In case of few companies, distribution of dividend shall require approval of the trustees to the issue and the lead institution, if any.
2. In the case of existing companies prior permission of the lead institution for declaring dividend exceeding 20% or as per the loan convenants is necessary if the company does not comply with institutional condition regarding interest and debt service coverage ratio.
3. (i) Dividends may be distributed out of profit of particular years only after transfer of requisite amount in DRR.
   (ii) If residual profits after transfer to DRR are inadequate to distribute reasonable dividends, the company may distribute dividend out of general reserve.

V. Other Requirements :
1. No company shall issue of Fully Convertible Debentures having a conversion period of more than 36 months, unless conversion is made optional with 'put' and 'call' option.
2. If the conversion takes place at or after 18 months from the date of allotment, but before 36 months, any conversion in part or whole of the debenture shall be optional at the hands of the debentureholder.
3. (a) No issue of debentures by an issuer company shall be made for acquisition of shares or providing loan to any company belonging to the same group.

   Sub-clause (a) shall not apply to the issue of fully convertible debentures providing conversion within a period of eighteen months.
4. Premium amount and time of conversion shall be determined by the issuer company and disclosed.
5. The interest rate for debentures can be freely determined by the issuer company.

Conversion of Debentures :

Meaning :
According to the terms of issue of the debentures, debentureholders may be given the right to exercise the option to convert their debentures into equity shares or preference shares at a stipulated rate within a specified period. If the debentureholders find the offer is beneficial to them, they will exercise their right and opt for shares, otherwise they may not exercise their right.

Convertible debentures are the debentures, whose holders have the option to get them converted wholly or partly into shares. Convertible debentures are usually converted into equity shares. However, they will be converted into preference shares also if the terms of conversion so provide. It may be noted that debentures or bonds converted into shares cannot be converted back into debentures or bonds later.

Although the Companies Act, 1956, does not prohibit such conversion of debentures into shares, it has to be carefully noted that the provisions of Section 79 are not violated in the process of conversion. In such a case, the actual proceeds of the issue of debentures should be considered in determining the number of shares to be issued in exchange of the debentures to be converted. That is to say, even the debentures originally issued at a discount can be converted in determining the number of shares to be issued. Thus, the issue price of the shares must be equal to the amount actually received from the debentureholders at the time of issue of those debentures. Otherwise, the provisions of Section 79 would be violated, because shares cannot be issued at a discount, except as provided in Section 79.

Terms of Conversion :

The **Terms of Conversion** are stipulated at the time of issue of debentures which are shown in Figure 1.14 as follows.

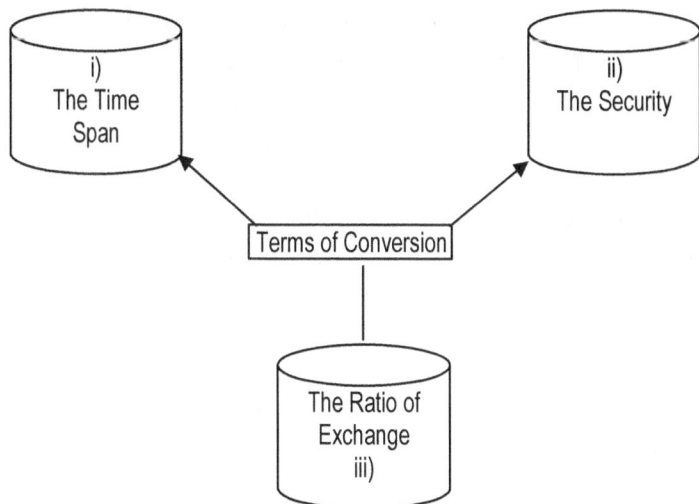

Fig. 1.14 : Terms of Conversion

i)   **The time span**, over which the debentures can be converted;

ii)   **The security** (i.e. equity or preference shares) to be received by the debenture-holders, if they exercise their option of conversion.

iii)   **The ratio of exchange between debentures and shares :** The ratio may be stated in terms of either a conversion price or a conversion ratio. e.g. if the debentures having a face value of ₹ 100, are issued by Atlas Nipco Ltd., Ajmer for a conversion price of ₹ 25 per share, it means that each debenture will be converted into four equity shares. In other words, the conversion ratio can be obtained by dividing the face value of the security by the conversion price.

Moreover, the conversion price may not necessarily remain constant over the time. Many convertible issues provide for increases or "step-up" in the conversion price at periodic intervals. e.g. a debenture having face value of ₹100 may have a conversion price of ₹ 25 per share for the first five years; ₹ 30 a share for the second five years and ₹ 50 a share for the third five years, and so on. This means with the passage of time each debenture will be converted for a fewer number of equity shares.

Legal Provisions regarding Conversion of Debenture :

The issue of convertible debentures is permitted under the Companies Act. However, it must be borne in mind that conversion of debentures into shares must not be such as to amount an unauthorised issue of shares at a discount. It is prohibited by Section 79 of the Companies Act. For example, if convertible debentures are issued at a discount and they are later on to be converted into or exchanged for shares of the same normal amount, the issue of the shares in exchange or conversion will be illegal unless the conditions under Sec. 79 are complied with and the sanction of the Company Law Board is obtained for the issue.

The provision of Sec. 81 of the Companies Act regarding shareholder's pre-emption right (i.e., the right of the existing shareholders to have the new shares first offered to them whenever the company increases its share capital) are not applicable to increase of the subscribed capital of a public company caused by an option attached to debentures to convert them into shares. This is subject to the following two conditions :

i)   The terms of issue of such debentures should have been approved by the Central Government before the issue of debentures or being in conformity with the rules, if any, made by the Central Government in this behalf.

ii)   Such terms should also be approved by the special resolution passed by a company in general meeting before the issue of debentures. Of course, this condition is not applicable in case of debentures issued to Central Government or any institution, specified by the Central Government in this behalf.

Convertibility or Conversion of Debentures

Convertible Debentures can be fully or partly convertible. Figure 1.15 shows the **Types of Convertible Debentures** as follows :

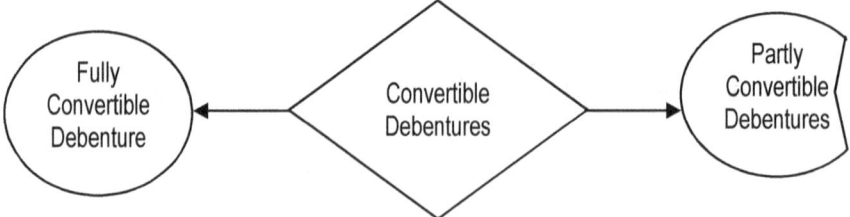

Fig. 1.15 : Types of Convertible Debentures

i)   **Fully Convertible Debentures :** Fully convertible debentures are the debentures which are fully converted into equity shares. They are classified as an equity in future.

ii)   Partly Convertible Debentures : Partly convertible debenture are the debentures which are not fully converted into equity. The convertible portion is known as equity and non-convertible portion is known as debtor loan.

Advantages of Convertible Debentures :

Convertible Debentures are advantageous, both to the company and to the investor.

A) Advantages to the Company

The company stands to gain by raising funds through convertible debentures as follows :

i)   The cost of raising fund is lowered : The company is usually able to sell a convertible debenture at a lower interest rate as compared to the interest rate it would have been required to offer on a straight (i.e., non-convertible) debenture issue. This is because the investor is prepared to accept the lower return now in consideration of the higher gain that he expects to make by sale of shares obtained in future on conversion of the debentures.

ii)   The cost of capital over a period is less : Interest on debentures is allowed as an expense for tax purposes and hence the cost of capital over a period is less to the company as compared to the money raised through direct issue of shares.

iii) It is a good alternative : Raising of funds through convertible debentures is a good alternative particularly when the equity market is bad.

iv)   No immediate dilution of EPS : There is no immediate dilution of Earning Per Share (EPS) when funds are raised through convertible debentures as compared to the situation when the additional funds are raised through equity shares.

B) Advantages to the Investor :

Following are the advantages to debentureholders i.e. investors.

i)   The investor continues to get a regular return on his investment with the possibility of making capital gain through sale of shares obtained on conversion of debentures.

ii)   The Investor gets immediate return on his Investment and therefore purchase of convertible debentures is particularly beneficial to him in case of projects having long gestation period.

Distinction between Debentures and Shares

The important points of distinction between Debentures and Shares are as follows :

Points of Difference	Debentures	Shares
i) Status in company	Debentureholders are the creditors of the Company.	Shareholders are the owners of the Company.
ii) Voting Rights	Debentureholders have no voting right and consequently do not pose any threat to the existing control of the company.	Shareholders have voting rights and consequently can control the total affairs of the company.

Points of Difference	Debentures	Shares
iii) Rate of Return	Debenture interest is paid at pre-determined fixed rate. It is payable, whether there is any profit or not. Debentures rank ahead of all types of shares for payment of the interest due on them.	Dividend on equity shares is paid at a variable rate which is vastly affected by the profits of the company (however, dividend on preference shares is paid at a fixed rate).
iv) Determination of Taxable Profit	Interests on debentures are the charges against profits and they are deductible as an expense in determining taxable profit of the company.	Dividends are appropriation of profits and these are not deductible in determining taxable profit of the company.
v) Classification	There are different kinds of debentures, such as Secured / Unsecured; Redeemable / Irredeemable; Registered / Bearer; Convertible/Non-convertible etc.	There are only two kinds of shares – Equity Shares and Preference shares. (There are different types of preference shares).
vi) Position in the Balance Sheet	In the Company Balance Sheet, Debentures are shown under "Secured Loans".	In the Company Balance Sheet, shares are shown under "Share Capital".
vii) Convertibility	Debentures can be converted into shares as per the terms of issue of debentures.	Shares cannot be converted into debentures in any circumstances.
viii) Forfeitable	As per the provision of Section 122, the debentures cannot be forfeited for non-payment of calls money.	Shares can be forfeited for non-payment of allotment and calls money.
ix) Redemption	At maturity, debentureholders get back their money as per the terms and conditions of redemption.	Equity shareholders cannot get back their money before the liquidation of the company (however, preference shareholders can get back their money before liquidation)
x) Priority in case of Liquidation	At the time of liquidation, debenture-holders are paid-off before the shareholders.	At the time of liquidation shareholders are paid last, after paying debentureholders, creditors etc.

Merits of Debenture Issue

The following are the **merits of raising funds** through **issue of debentures** :

i)   Debentures provide funds to the company for a specific period hence, the company can appropriately adjust its financial plan to suit its requirements.

ii) Debentures provide funds to the company for a long period without diluting its control.

iii) Debentures enable the company to take advantage of trading on equity and thus pay to the equity shareholders, dividend at a rate higher than overall return on investment.

iv)   Debentures are more suitable for investors who are cautious and conservative and who particularly prefer a stable rate of return with little or no risk.

Demerits of Debenture Issue :

The **raising of funds through debentures** is subject to the following **limitations** :

i)   Raising of funds through debentures is risky, since in the event of failure of the company to pay interest or the principal instalment in time, the debentureholder may resort to the extreme remedy of filing a petition for winding up of the company.

ii)   Debentures are particularly not suitable for Companies whose earnings fluctuate considerably. In case of such company raising funds through debentures, may lead to considerable fluctuations in the rate of dividend payable to the equity shareholders.

iii) Every additional issue of debentures becomes more risky and costly on account of higher expectation of debentureholders. They may demand higher rate of interest, besides power to have some say in the management of the company. As such, at times, the management may find it inadvisable to accept their condition and decide not to use debentures as a source for meeting their financial requirements.

1.1.6.5 INNOVATIVE DEBT INSTRUMENTS

Debt Instruments :

Debt-instrument represents a contract whereby one party lends money to another on pre-determined terms with regards to rate and periodicity of interest, repayment of principal amount by the borrower to the lender.

In Indian Securities Market, the term 'Bond' is used for debt instruments issued by the Central and State governments and public sector organisations and the term 'Debenture' is used for instruments issued by private corporate sector.

Debt v/s Equity :

The key differences between equity and debt are as follows :

i)   Debt investors are entitles to a contractual set of cash flows (interest and principal) whereas equity investors have a claim on the residual cash flows of the firm after it has satisfied all other claims and liabilities.

ii)   Interest paid to debt investors represent a tax-deductible expense whereas dividend paid to equity investor has to come out of profit after tax.

iii) Debt has a fixed maturity whereas equity ordinarily has an infinite life.

iv)   Equity investors enjoy the right to control the affairs of the firm whereas debt investors play a passive role - of course; they often impose certain restrictions on the way the firm is run to protect their interests.

Features of Debt Instruments are shown in Figure 1.16 as follows.

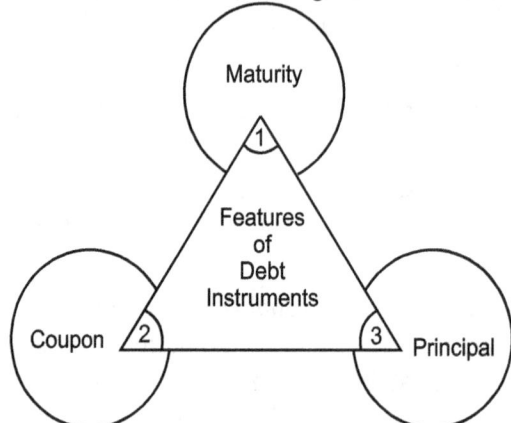

Fig. 1.16 : Features of Debt Instruments

Each debt instrument has three features : Maturity, coupon and principal.

1) Maturity :

Maturity of a bond refers to the date, on which the bond matures, which is the date on which the borrower has agreed to repay the principal. Term-to-Maturity refers to the number of years remaining for the bond to mature. The Term-to-Maturity changes everyday, from date of issue of the bond until its maturity. The term to maturity of a bond can be calculated on any date, as the distance between such a date and the date of maturity. It is also called the term or the tenure of the bond.

2) Coupon :

Coupon refers to the periodic interest payments that are made by the borrower (who is also the issuer of the bond) to the lender (the subscriber of the bond). Coupon rate is the rate at which interest is paid, and is usually represented as a percentage of the par value of a bond.

3) Principal :

Principal is the amount that has been borrowed and is also called the par value or face value of the bond. The coupon is the product of the principal and the coupon rate.

Segments in the Debt Market

There are three main segments in the debt markets in India, viz., i) Government Securities, ii) Public Sector Unit, (PSU) bonds, and iii) Corporate securities.

Participants of Debt Market

Given the large size of the trades, Debt market is predominantly a wholesale market, with dominant institutional investor participation. The investors in the debt markets are mainly banks, financial institutions, mutual funds, provident funds, insurance companies and corporates.

Acquiring Securities in Debt Market

An Investor may subscribe to the issues made by government or corporates in the primary market. Alternatively, he may purchase the same from the secondary market through the stock exchanges.

Salient Features of Innovative Debt Instruments introduced in Capital Market

Various innovative instruments which are introduced in Indian Capital Market are as follows :

i) **Non-voting Shares :**

These are like other equity shares but without voting rights, these Shareholders' rights as to bonus, rights will be on par with voting shares. For surrounding the voting rights a higher percentage of dividends say 2 percent more than other equity dividends may be paid. SEBI has further recommended an overall retraction of these shares to 20 percent of the share capital. This could be issued to residents, non-residents and institutions who are interested more in return than in central. In case the company fails to pay dividends voting rights may be revived to them.

ii) **Detachable Equity Coupons/Warrants :**

There are coupons/warrants attached with the original instruments such as shares and debentures as sweeteners. They are issued free of cost. These give a right to acquire the shares of the issuing company at a concessional rate on a future period. Companies such as TISCO, Reliance Gujarat Ambuja Cement and Essar Gujarat have issued them. If the market price of the shares falls below the concessional rate offered, these become useless. Warrants prices would be maximum when the share prices are close to their exercise price.

iii) **Participating Preference Shares :**

These are those preference shares which have a right to participate in the extra profits available after distributing equity dividends. They may also give rights to participate in the extra profit when the equity share dividends exceed a specified limit agreed upon earlier.

iv) **Participating Debentures :**

As like participating preferences shares, these debentureholders would have a right to participate in the extra profits available after meeting out the demand of equity dividends. They may have agreements with the company to hike up interest rate as and when equity dividend exceed a specified limit.

v) **Convertible Debentures with Options :**

At present debentures are converted into equities compulsorily; but this instrument would be converted into equities only when preferred by the investors. So the option to convert is voluntary and lies with the investor. Recently, Reliance Poly Propelene and Reliance Polyethylene and Nagarjuna Fertilisers have issued them.

vi) **Third Party Convertible Debentures :**

In this, the debenture would be converted into the equities of not the issuing company but into the equities of a third party company probably controlled by the issuing company. Suppose company A issues such debentures, these would be converted into the equities of company C, this requires the consent of both the company shareholders.

vii) Mortgage Backed Securities :

These types of securities are the result of securitisation of the debts of certain companies. The debts available in the balance sheet would be converted into securities and sold off to different investors. But the responsibility to collect the debt and servicing the mortgaged backed securities lie with the company which has sold-off the debt.

viii) Convertible Debentures redeemable at a premium :

In this type of instrument the option to convert them into equities or to redeem them at a premium lie with the investors. If they want they can convert them into equity otherwise they can redeem them with the company at a premium which is agreed upon earlier.

ix) Debt for Equity Swap :

Now there is no possibility of converting equity into debt. But this instrument precisely advocates this whereby equities which were not serviced properly can have the option to convert them into debts, a fixed rate of return over the period after conversion.

x) Zero Coupon Convertible Bonds :

These bonds do not bear any interest during the life period but would be converted into equities at a concessional rate than other convertible bonds bearing interest. So companies which suffer out of cash flow problems during the initial periods may opt for this type of bond. Mahindra and Mahindra and SPIC have issued these bonds already.

xi) Global Depository Receipts :

These are popularly called as GDRS Companies going for Euro bond issues them. These are infact convertible debentures issued in foreign currencies. These securities represent certain underlying equities of the issuing company. After the lock of period, these securities would be converted into issuing companies equities. Some 30 companies have approached the Government for permission. Reliance has already successfully issued them.

xii) Preferred Stock Instruments :

a)   **Convertible Cumulative Preference Shares :** In this, preference shares would have the option to convert them into other forms of securities and areas of dividends could also be accumulated till the conversion. Usually, the dividend rate conversion period and time would be argued upon earlier.

b)   **Adjusted Rate Preferred Stock :** These are those which tie up dividend rates to the market rates of interest.

Add on Products

Add on products are those which are supplied either as sweetener or as prices will be the original instruments. They can be classified under the following heads.

a)   **Warrants :** These are instruments attached with the original instruments as a sweetener. The issuer promises to give equity at a concessional rate in a future priced with no compulsion to accept on the part of the shareholder. These are of different kinds such as Detachable attached, Harmless and naked warrants.

b)   **Loyalty Coupon :** It is an incentive provided to the shareholders in the form of money for not selling the shares within a specified time limit. At the expiry of the time limit money promised would be paid for remaining loyal to the investment.

c)   **Safety Net :** It is our offer to buy the shares back either by a mutual fund. Merchant banker or a trust at a specified or issue Price.

xiii) Short term Debentures :

Companies which want short-term loans from the market can approach through this route and get their funds requirements. These will have all the characteristics of debentures otherwise.

xiv) Debentures issued at a premium and Redeemed at Par :

These are instruments issued to get higher money during earlier periods and pay higher interest charges so as to cover up the premium received during the issue but would be redeemed at par.

xv) Deep discount Bonds/Happy Return Bonds :

There are long-term bonds issued at a discount and redeemed at par value after specified number of years. Recently, IDBI, SIDBI have issued these bonds.

xvi) Double Option Bonds/Regular Return Bonds :

Double option bond is a cumulative bond consisting of two parts. Part A representing principal sum and Part B representing the cumulative interest sum and redemption premium. Regular Return Bond is a non-cumulative bond where interest on the principal sum is payable half yearly, further a redemption premium would also be paid. Recently, IDBI has issued them.

xvii) Negotiable Debentures :

These debentures as like negotiable instrument are transferable from one person to another person through endorsement and delivery.

xviii) Floating Rate Bonds :

Interest rate of Debentures are usually fixed and because during changing price levels these instruments suffer heavily. To overcome this, the interest of the debentures would be allowed to float, according to the rates of inflation. The real return is not affected because of price changes. Recently, SBI had issued their bonds.

xix) Junk Bonds :

These are bonds issued with very high interest rates issued to mobilise resources for takeovers and mergers. These bonds may at times even provide as high 40 percent per annum.

xx) Exchangeable Bonds :

These are instruments which could be exchanged into other types of financial or other at a specified or maturity period.

xxi) Stock Options :

Options are speculative type of instruments. There are two types, they are call option and put option. Call option is a right to buy securities at a specified rate at a specified future time. Put option are securities which are sold at a specified future time. These call and put options would again be quoted in the market. At present in India option trading is banned.

xxii) Serial Bonds :

These are appropriate for issues that wish to divide their bond issues into a series, each part of the series maturing at a different time.

xxiii) Collateral Trust Bonds :

When the security deposited with the trustee of a bond issue consists of the stakes and bonds of other companies, bonds are called as Collateral Trust Bonds.

xxiv) Subordinated Bonds :

These are debentures that are specifically made subordinate to all other general creditors holding claims on assets.

xxv) Direct Lieu Bonds :

These are special bonds secured by one piece of property such as terminal, a dock or a bridge.

xxvi) Prior Lieu Bonds :

These are bonds that have been placed ahead of the first mortgage usually during the re-organisations.

xxvii) Variable Rate Bonds : These are debt instruments with coupon rate of interest which is not fixed but which varies in accordance with some predetermined formula.

xxviii) Index Linked Bonds :

Here, the return out of a bond is linked to certain index say, suppose it is linked to consumer price index the interest payments and principal payment will be increased in the ratio of the consumer price index.

xxix) Junior Mortgage Bonds :

These bonds have a secondary claim to assets and earnings behind senior mortgage bonds.

xxx) Put Bonds :

These are those bonds which allow the bond investor to put the bond back to the issuer before the bonds maturity date at a price called the strike price.

Mutual Funds Related Instruments :

Innovative Instruments in Mutual Funds : In time with the liberalised efforts, mutual funds have been coming out with many new forms of fund mobilisation. Depending on the purpose and characteristics, these securities could be classified under the following heads from Sr. Nos. xxxi) to xxxviii)

xxxi) Close Ended Mutual Fund :

Once the subscription for this fund reaches the predetermined level, the fund is closed hence this name. The corpus and number of unit holders are determined in advance. Most of the mutual funds are of this type. Master shares, master share plus are examples of this type.

xxxii) **Open Ended Mutual Fund :**

The size of tile fund is not determined, the entry to the fund is always open to the investor who can subscribe at any time. These are not publicly traded but are repurchased at anytime at repurchase rate. Can Star Cancigo, Dhanashayoa Dana Vidya are some examples of this type.

xxxiii) **Income Mutual Funds :**

These funds offer a higher return than bank deposits but with lesser capital appreciation. The income out of the funds are periodically distributed magnum triple, Ind Joythi, GK Safe PNB-RIPS, Dhanshri 99 are examples of this type.

xxxiv) **Growth Mutual Funds :**

These do not offer regular income but offer substantial capital appreciation in the long-run. Mastergain, Magnum Express Festival Bonanza, Ind Joythi are examples of this type.

xxxv) **Balanced Mutual Funds :**

Those offer a blend of immediate average return and reasonable capital appreciation. They are known as middle of the road funds. Dhanavarsha can stock are examples of this.

xxxvi) **Tax Saving Mutual Funds :**

Under section 80 C of the Income tax act, a tax deduction is provided on the investments subject to a maximum investment of ₹ 10,000 p.a. SBI Magnum GIFTS, Ind Shelter, Reliance Tax Saves are examples. These are closed ended mutual funds.

xxxvii) **Specialised Mutual Funds :**

These funds are invested in particular sector or industry. There is no diversification and hence the changes to gains and losses are high.

xxxviii) **Off Share Country Funds :**

These are those which are issued in a foreign country in foreign currency but the proceeds are invested in the origin country. India Fund, India growth funds are examples.

Money Market Related Instruments :

xxxix) **Money Market Funds :**

Recently SEBI has brought out the guidelines for money market mutual funds. The proceeds out of these funds would be invested in short-term money markets and the profits would be distributed to unit holders.

xxxx) **Commercial Paper :**

It is a short-term fund raising machine. It is a usance promissory note negotiable by endorsement and delivery. These may be either floating or collateral floating rate notes.

xxxxi) **Certificates of Deposits :**

These are short-term deposits sold at a discount and redeemed at par value on maturity. The difference between the issue price and par table is the return out of those deposits. These deposits can again be negotiable by endorsement and delivery.

xxxxii) **Bankers' Acceptance :**

These are written promissory notes issued by banks to repay borrowed funds from the investors.

Others :

xxxxiii) Counter Receipts : This is a document created by OTCEI. As no physical securities are issued in OTC trading, these are receipts issued as a proof of holding certain underlying securities mentioned there in these have to be transferred like other shares. These are voted only for OTC trading, should the investor want to possess the underlying securities can surrender them and get the proper equities of such companies.

xxxxiv) Stock Invest : It is an instrument conceived and introduced by SEBI whereby investor's can hold the share application money in their own account and earn interest till allotment. Further, this instrument is valid for 4 months and can be obtained in any denominations.

1.1.7 FORWARD CONTRACTS

Meaning

A forward contract is a bilateral contract in which the buyer and the seller agree upon the delivery of a specified quality and quantity of asset at a specified future date at a pre-determined price.

Scope

Forward contracts are typical OTC derivatives. As the name itself suggests, forwards are transactions involving delivery of an asset or a financial instrument at a future date. One of the first modern 'to arrive' contracts-as forward contracts were known-was agreed at Chicago Board of Trade in March 1851 for maize corn to be delivered in June of that year.

From then on, the market has developed tremendously, taking into account the needs of the market players. Consequently, we have today, forward contracts on a variety of commodities and underlying assets including : Metals, Energy products, Interest Rates, Exchange Rates. The **Scope of Forward Contracts** is shown in Figure 1.17 as follows :

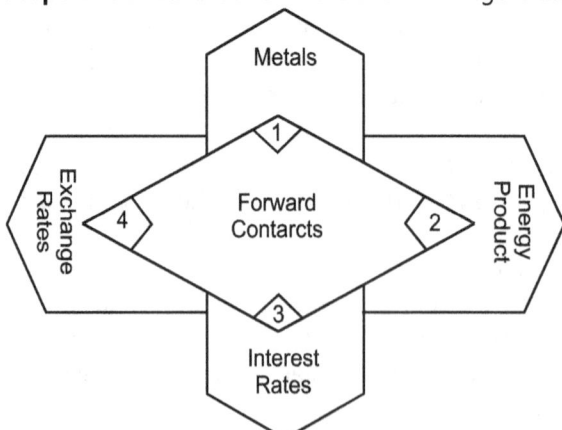

Fig. 1.17 : Scope of Forward Contracts

Characteristics of Forward Contracts

The main **characteristics of 'Forward Contracts'** are as follows :

i)   Forward Contracts are OTC (Over the Counter Exchange Contracts).

ii)   **Not available to the common man :** The presence of credit risk in forward contracts makes parties wary of each other. Consequently, forward contracts are entered into between parties who have good credit standing. Hence, forward contracts are not available to the common man.

iii) **Buyer and seller committed to the contract :** Both the buyer and seller are committed to the contract. In other words, they have to take delivery and deliver respectively, the underlying asset on which the forward contract was entered into. As such, they do not have the discretion as regards completion of the contract.

iv) **Forwards are price-fixing in nature :** Forwards are price-fixing in nature. Both the buyer and seller of a forward contract are fixed to the price decided upfront. For instance, if we propose to sell one US dollar to a bank, one month forward at say ₹ 48.75, we have to sell at the same rate to the bank on the delivery date, irrespective of the fact where the market rate is. Thus, if on the delivery date the market price is ₹ 48.50, we stand to lose ₹ 0.25. On the other hand, if the market price is ₹ 49.00, we stand to gain ₹ 0.25. In both the instances, the customer and the bank are duty-bound to deliver and take delivery of the US dollar respectively, independent and irrespective of whether they stand to gain or lose. In other words, the parties to a forward contract are committed to fulfil their respective obligations.

v)   **Pay-off profiles are linear to the price of the fundamental :** Due to forward contracts are OT contracts and the presence of credit risk in forward contracts makes parties vary of each other, the pay-off profiles of the borrower and seller, in a 'forward contract' are linear to the price of the underlying.

Determining Forward Prices :

In principle, the forward price for an asset would be equal to the spot or the cash price at the time of the transaction and the cost-of-carry. The cost-of-carry includes all the costs to be incurred for carrying the asset forward in time. Depending upon the type of asset or commodity; the cost-of-carry takes into account the payments and receipts for storage, transport costs, interest payments, dividend receipts, capital appreciation etc. In short, Forward Price is inclusive of spot or the cash price plus carrying cost.

$$\text{Forward Price} = \text{Spot or Cash Price} \; (+) \; \text{Carrying Cost}$$

1.1.8 FUTURES CONTRACT

Meaning

A futures contract can simplistically be defined as an agreement to buy or sell *an asset at a certain time in the future at a certain price.* A more comprehensive definition would be as follows. Futures are firm financial agreements to deliver (sell) or take delivery (buy) of a standardised quantity of an underlying commodity/instrument, at a pre-established price agreed on a regulated exchange at a specified future date.

A futures contract is a firm legal commitment between a buyer and seller in which they agree to exchange something say pepper for a specified money at the end of a designated time period, say three months hence. Delivery is necessary and the price is known in advance. The risk is borne by both buyer and seller. Only the risk of uncertainty is not there for the buyer, as the seller bears it, for a reward. The possible risk attached to the upward and downward changes in the actual price at the future stipulated time is there for both buyer and seller. If prices fall below the stipulated price, the buyer suffer loss and if they rise above the stipulated price, the seller suffer loss due to the contracted stipulated price. The loss of one is the gain of the other and it is a zero sum game. Herein lies the speculative element in futures.

Future trading in stock and shares was prohibited in India, for a long time, until March 1995, when they were permitted again alongwith options.

In options, the delivery is optional for buyer but obligatory for seller of the option. The buyer pays the seller a premium in the beginning itself while there is no premium paid on the Future contract. Future contracts can be performed only at the settlement date but not before that. The buyer of tile options has a right to exercise the option either at the expiration date or prior to that. Deliveries and execution of contracts are enforced by the organising authorities.

Futures have evolved out of forwards and are exchange traded versions of forward contracts. They are one of the most popular and widely used derivative instruments.

Types of Future Contracts

The various **Types of Futures Contracts** are shown in Figure 1.18 as follows :

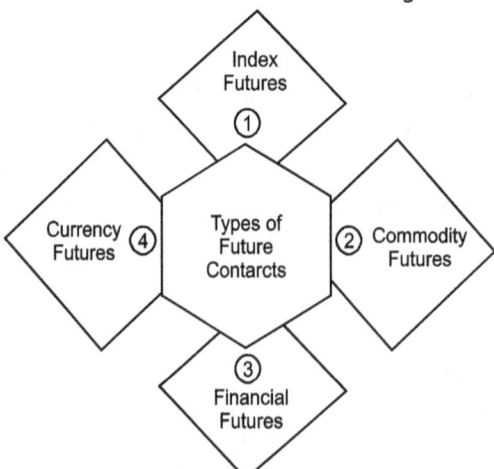

Fig. 1.18 : Types of Futures Contract

1) Index Futures

Index futures are the underlying assets in an index. Most, but not all of these contracts are for stock indices. The more famous of the indices on which futures are traded are Standard and Poor's 500, the New York Stock Exchange index and Tokyo's Nikkei index and such others.

For example, suppose the future contracts are based on NSE Index. The NSE 100, is quoting early in July 2000 at 1200. Each point in the index is valued at ₹ 100, one futures contract on NSE Index will cost ₹ 1,20,000; if at the end of one month, the index rose to 1220, then on the settlement day a cash payment of ₹ 100 × 20 = ₹ 2,000 is to be paid by the seller to tile buyer.

It is assumed that, all the traders in the futures are to be members and each trader is expected to put in "good faith" margin deposit depending upon the value of the total contracts. These margin moneys are marked to the market value or a daily basis. The margins to be kept on futures are less than for normal deliveries, as index futures do not involve full value payments. Thus, an index futures contract is an obligation to deliver at settlement an amount of cost, equal to a number of times (say 100 or 500) of the difference between the stock index value at the close of the last trading day (1220) of the contract and the price at which the future contract was originality struck (1200), The terms of the contract, underlying the futures trading will determine the number of times the difference is to be multiplied. Margin money his to be kept and other conditions are to be observed for any contingent event of failure to make the additional deposit marked to the market value of the contract and the possible failure to honour the contract by either party.

Valuation of Index Futures

If an investor invests in B.S.E. 30 index he will collect dividends on the scrips he holds and his principal value may go up or down depending on the index. In the case of the futures index, the investor will get the same outcome as if he invests all his money in riskless. Treasury bills and enters into a futures contract for future delivery of the index. The futures then must sell at a price equal to today's price of the index plus a premium equal to risk free return plus dividend on the index shares.

Symbolically, it can be shown as under :

F_E be the price of the futures.

F_B is today's price of futures.

I_B is current price of the Index.

D is divided on the index shares.

I_E is the index price at the expiration date.

$$\text{Return to Index} = \text{Index price at Expiration} - \text{Current Index Price} + \text{Dividend}$$

$$= I_E - I_B + D \qquad \text{... (1)}$$

$$\text{Return to Futures} = \text{Futures Price at Expiration} - \text{Current Futures Price} + \text{Interest on Risk Free Asset}$$

$$= F_E - F_B + R_F \qquad \text{... (2)}$$

As I_E will equal F_E at expiration, using the above equations, we can derive, FB as

$$F_B = I_R + (R_F - D)$$

With the help of above equation, it is clear that, the present price of futures, will equal present price of Index plus the "cost of carry", which equals $(R_F - D)$, namely, [lie interest obtainable on risk-free asset (R_f) minus dividend on Index Shares (D). The cost of purchasing the Index Shares is substantially higher than the cost of buying the futures contract for the same index. The money used to buy the futures will involve interest cost and by not buying the shares, dividends are lost. Assume that the money used to purchase the index shares is invested in Treasury bills to give risk free return (R_F). If R_F is less than the dividends lost, the futures price will be below the Index price (that is $F_B < I_B$) and $(R_F < D)$.

2) Commodity Futures :

Commodity futures are those in which the underlying asset is a commodity. It can be an agricultural commodity like wheat, corn, soyabeans or a perishable commodity like pork bellies; or even precious assets like gold, silver, copper etc.

In an organised commodity futures market, contracts are standardised with standard qualities. Of course, this standard varies from commodity to commodity. They also have fixed delivery dates in each month or a few months in a year. In India, commodity futures in agricultural products are popular.

Some of the well known commodity exchanges are as follows :

1) New York Cotton Exchange (CTN) to deal in cotton.
2) Commodity Exchange, New York (COMEX) to deal in agricultural products.
3) London Metal Exchange (LME) to deal in gold.
4) Chicago Board of Trade (CBT) to deal in soyabean oil.
5) International Petroleum Exchange of London (IPE) to deal in crude oil.

3) Financial Futures :

Financial futures are those where the underlying assets are financial instruments like money market paper, T. bills, notes, bonds etc.

4) Currency Futures :

Currency futures are those in which the underlying assets are major convertible currencies like the U.S. dollar, the Pound Sterling, the Euro, the Yen etc.

Financial and currency futures are widely used by financial institutions like banks, hedge/pension funds worldwide to hedge their price risks. Markets in financial futures contracts are a relatively new phenomenon. The first contracts were currency futures in which trading began in 1972 on the International Monetary Market (IMM), which is a part of the Chicago Mercantile Exchange (CME). Since 1972, the growth of these markets both geographically and in terms of instruments have been rapid.

The basic difference between commodity features and financial futures contracts are that in financial future contract cash settlement at delivery date instead of physical delivery is allowed. Very few financial futures are settled in that matter.

Characteristics of Future Contracts

The main characteristics of Future Contacts are as follows :

1) Exchange-Traded, Pricing Fixing Contracts :

Futures are essentially exchange-traded versions of forward contracts. Financial analysts' desire to replicate a cash market strategy without the concomitant credit risk resulted in the development of futures. The futures exchanges are highly regulated world-wide and come under the supervisory purview of governments in various countries.

a) **Price-Fixing Contract :** The important features of an exchange traded product are as follows :

An exchange-traded contract is a price fixing contract in as much as the buyer/seller is obligated to take/give delivery or close-out the positions at the pre-agreed price for the purpose of settlement. As such, the **pay-off profiles** of the buyer and seller are symmetric (like that of forward contracts) as shown in Figure 1.19 as follows :

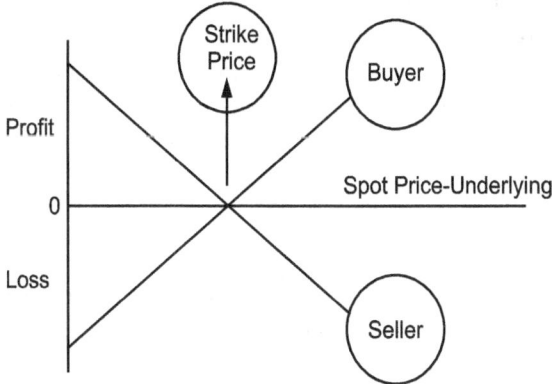

Fig. 1.19 : Futures Pay-off Profiles

b) **The clearing house becomes a seller for every buyer and a buyer for every seller :** The credit risk is sought to be eliminated through the system of margin requirements by the clearing houses established by all the futures exchanges. The clearing house may be a subsidiary of the exchange itself or an independent corporation. The clearing house stands as a counter party for each and every transaction undertaken on the futures market. In other words, the clearing house becomes a seller for every buyer and a buyer for every seller. Once a trade is confirmed, the clearing house guarantees fulfilment of each contract. To support this guarantee, the clearing house sets membership standards, operates a margining system, monitors daily positions, and maintains a guarantee fund that can be called upon in the event of default by one/more members. Under the margining system, the individual buyers and sellers are required to post the daily margins, for the purpose of market-to-market the futures contracts on a daily basis.

c) **Single Period Contracts :** Futures can be used for fixing the price for a single contract period only and are not useful for multiple periods. It therefore follows that futures can be used to hedge a single period price risk of any underlying exposure. In Figure 1.20 the exposure is only from the 6th to the 12th month for which futures can be effectively used as follows :

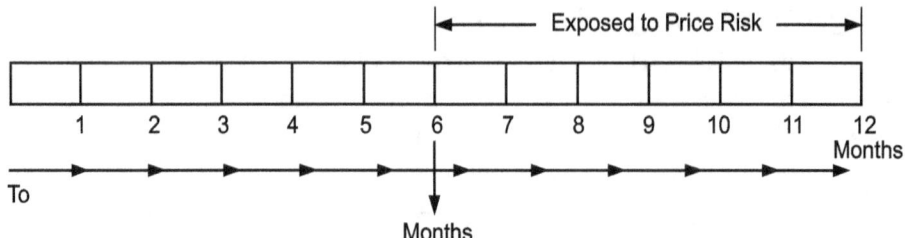

Fig. 1.20 : Single Period Interest Rate Risk

    d)   Standardisation in terms of various factors : Through standardisation, contracts become fully transferable and fungible. As futures are highly standardised products in terms of the quantity and quality of the underlying, settlement dates and market conventions etc., they are traded in one of the most highly liquid markets in the world.

2) No practice to make Down Payment :

    In future contracts, the contracting parties need not pay only down payment at the time of agreement. However, they deposit a certain percentage of the contract price with the exchange with the exchange and it is called initial margin.

3) Hedging of Price Risks :

    Future contracts are used either as hedging or as trading instruments. 'Hedging' is a strategy whereby specific exposures to a particular market, say, currency commodity, etc. are sought to be covered with a view to stabilize cash flows. The decisions in hedging operations are driven due to fear of market movements. Hedging represents a defensive strategy in financial matters aimed at neutralising adverse market movements.

    For example, company pension funds investing in different stock markets can use the stock index contracts to hedge exposure to a particular stock market. Corporate treasurers can use the interest rate contracts to manage interest rate risk. Banks, financial institutions and individuals may use futures contracts as trading instruments.

    The important feature of the futures contract is to hedge against price fluctuations. The buyers of a futures contract hope to protect themselves from future spot price increases and the sellers from future spot price decreases. Parties enter into futures agreement on the basis of the expectations of the future price in the spot market for the asset in the questions.

4) Possesses the Property of Linearity :

    Futures contract possesses the property of linearity. Parties to the futures contract get symmetrical profits or losses due to price fluctuation of the underlying asset on either direction.

5) No Delivery of the Asset :

    In case of futures contract, the delivery of the asset in question is not essential on the date of maturity of the contract. Actually, parties simply exchange the difference between the future and spot prices on the date of maturity.

6) Forward Contract becomes a Future Contract :

For all practical purposes, when a forward contract is standardised and dealt in an organised exchange, it becomes a future contract.

Differences between Forward Contracts and Futures Contracts

The difference between **Forward Contracts and Futures Contracts** are summarised as follows :

Sr. No.	Point for Difference	Forward Contracts	Futures Contracts
1.	Nature	A forward contract is not at all a standardised one. It is tailor made contract in the sense that the terms of the contract like quality, price, period date, delivery conditions etc. can be negotiated between the parties according to their convenience. Basically forward contracts are OTC contracts.	A future contract is a highly standardised one where all the terms and conditions of the contract are standardised and they cannot be altered to the requirements of the parties to the contract. Basically, future contracts are exchange traded contracts.
2.	Process	Forward contracts are private and negotiated bilaterally between the parties with no exchange guarantees.	Future contracts uses a clearing house which provides protection for both the parties.
3.	Existence of Secondary Market	It is a customised contract which is not a standard one, it cannot be traded on a organised market, there is no secondary market for a forward contract.	Future contracts can be traded on organised market/exchanges. Hence, it has a secondary market.
4.	Prices	Prices are not transparent as there is no reporting requirement.	Prices are transparent. Future contracts are reported by the exchanges.
5.	Settlement	A forward contract is always settled only on the date of the maturity. By actual delivery or offset with cash settlement.	A future contract is always settled daily, irrespective of the maturity date, in the sense that, it is "market to market" on a daily basis. Usually, by closing out and cash settlement.
6.	'Modus Operandi'	Generally, parties enter into a forward agreement with the help of some financial intermediary like a bank.	It is not so in case of a future contract. It is mainly facilitated through organised exchanges and the question of a third party does not arise.
7.	Down Payment	The contracting parties need not pay any down payment at the time of agreement. Involves no margin payments.	The contracting parties have to deposit a certain percentage of the contract price as "Margin Money" with the exchange. It acts as a collateral to support the contract.
8.	Delivery of the Asset	The delivery of the asset in question is essential on the date of maturity of the contract.	A future contract does not end with the delivery of the asset. The parties merely exchange the difference between the future and spot prices on the date of maturity.

Sr. No.	Point for Difference	Forward Contracts	Futures Contracts
9.	'Credit Risk'	Credit risk of forward contracts can be substantial, usually requires lines of credit.	Credit risk is largely eliminated by use of margin money and daily cash settlement of profit and losses through the clearing house.
10.	'Used for hedging'	Forward contract used for hedging and physical delivery.	Future contract used for hedging and speculating.

1.1.9 OPTIONS CONTRACT

Meaning

'Options' is the most popular class of derivative instruments. 'Derivative' is a common name given to a class of instruments whose value is derived from another asset called the underlying asset.

"Option" is a derivative security used for the purpose of risk management in the investment market, based on some security. Futures, forwards, swaps, options, etc. are all examples of hedge against risk. Investors are risk averse and want to reduce the risk. Individuals and corporations have a strong urge to reduce or manage risk and this is secured by trading in derivative markets.

Instrument like "options" give the buyer the right but not the obligation to buy or sell an asset. The volatility in share prices require to be hedged. Thus, the larger the volatility the larger is the hedging demand. This is secured through the options. Thus, the volume of options trading and volatility may be corrected but this does not mean that options can cause higher or lower volatility in underlying issues. Actually, 'options' is an instrument or a tool for risk management and no correlation is exclusively found for options to increase or decrease volatility of share prices.

In short, in the volatile environment, risk of heavy fluctuation in the prices of assets is very heavy. 'Option' is yet another instrument to manage such a risk. An 'option contract' gives the buyer an option to buy or sell an underlying asset such as stock, bond, currency, commodity etc. at a predetermined price on or before a specified date in future. This predetermined price is called the "strike price" or "exercise price".

The term "writer" : In an option contract; the seller is usually referred to as a "writer" since he is said to write the contract. It is similar to the seller who is said to be in "short position" in a forward contract. In an option contract, the buyer has to pay a certain amount at the time of writing the contract for enjoying the right to buy or sell.

Types of Options

The two major types of stock options are called calls and puts. There is also a third type of such options which is called double option. The **Types of Options** are shown in Figure 1.21 as follows :

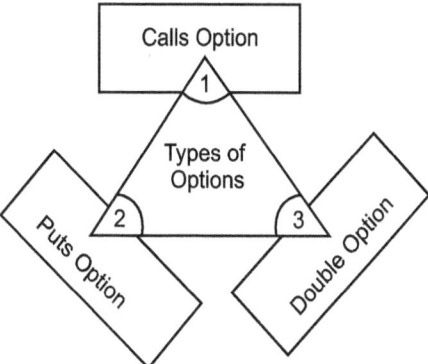

Fig. 1.21 : Types of Options

1) **Calls Option :**

Call give the buyer the right but not the obligation to buy a given quantity of the underlying asset, at a given price on or before a given future date.

2) **Puts Option :**

Puts give the buyer the right, but not the obligation to sell a given quantity of the underlying asset at a given price on or before a given date.

3) **Double Option :**

A double option is one which gives the option holder both the rights – either to buy or to sell an underlying asset at a predetermined price on or before a specified date in future.

Example of Calls and Puts Options :

A call gives the investor the right to purchase 100 shares of a particular stock at a fixed price until a specific date. An investor who purchases a call option locks in a price on 100 shares of stock for a predetermined time. A put option gives an investor the right to sell 100 shares of a particular stock at a fixed price until a specific date. A put locks in a price at which to sell stock rather than a price at which to buy stock. Both puts and calls provide the investor with the right, but not the obligation, to use the option. Stock options are created, or "written", by other investors who wish to earn income from selling the options. The writers then become obligated to sell (if a call has been sold) or purchase (if a put has been sold) the stock if and when the owner of the option decides to exercise the put or call.

In case of call option, the writer of a call option is under an obligation to sell the asset at the specified price, in case the buyer exercises his option to buy. Therefore, the obligation to sell arises only when the option is exercised. On the other hand, the writer of a put option is under an obligation to buy the asset at the exercise price provided the option holder exercises his option to sell.

Values of Call and Put Options :

Puts and calls derive their values from the values of the stock that they can be used to sell or purchase. Stock options pay no dividends or interest and expire without any value if not used by the expiration date. The value of a call option is directly related to the value of the underlying stock (i.e., the option value increases when the stock value increases) and the value of a put is inversely related to the value of the underlying stock (i.e., the option value increases when the stock value decreases). Option values are also affected by the time remaining until expiration, the price volatility of the underlying common stock and the market rate of interest.

Terms used in Options Contract :

a)   **Option Premium :** Option contract, like any other contract must be supported by consideration. The consideration for option contract is a sum of money called "premium". In other words, the premium is nothing but the price which is required to be paid for the purchase of 'right to buy or sell'. In the case of a double option, this premium money is also double.

b)   **Option Market :** Once an option contract is written, it can be bought or sold on the option market. Options market are the markets where option contracts are bought or sold. The first option market namely the 'Chicago Board of Option Exchange' was established in 1973. Thereafter, several options markets have been set up. The option markets may have three different types of structures :

     i)   Auction market with jobbers or market makers (as the present one).

     ii)   Order matching electronic trading.

     iii)   Dealer markets as in Government security.

c)   **Strike Price :** The price at which the right to buy or sell the underlying is exercisable – again agreed upfront. It is also known as the exercise/agreed.

d)   **American Option and European Option**

     i)   **American Option and European Option :** In an option contract, if option can be exercised at any time between the writing of the contract and its expiration it is called as an American option. In this type of option, the right (buy/sell) can be exercised by the buyer at any time during the life of the option contract.

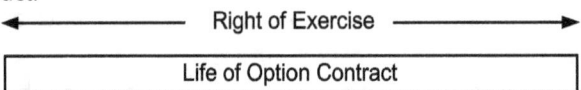

     ii)   **European Option :** If right can be exercised only at the time of maturity, it is called as European option. In this type of option, the right an be exercised by the buyer at the end of the life of the option contract.

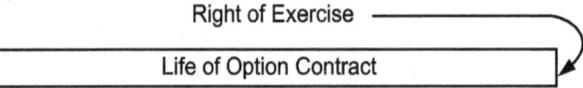

e)   **Intrinsic Value :** The intrinsic value of an option is the difference between the strike price and the spot rate of the underlying. In other words, intrinsic value represents the gain to the holder on immediate exercise of an option.

For a call option, if **spot rate** is greater than **strike or exercise price,** it is said to have positive intrinsic value. In the case of a put option positive intrinsic value accrues, if strike or exercise price is greater than the spot rate. For European options, the concept of intrinsic value is only notional since they cannot be prematurely exercised. On the contrary, if spot rate is lower than the strike price for a call option and if strike price is higher than the spot rate for a put option, their intrinsic value is zero and not negative due to the throw away feature.

f)   **Time Value :** The difference between the total value of an option and its intrinsic value is the time value of the option. Time value represents the additional amount of premium that the option buyer is willing to pay over the intrinsic value for the unexpired life of the option.

g)   **Volatility :** In risk management, risk is measured using standard deviation. Such standard deviation expressed in percentage terms is known as volatility. In options, the value/price of the option is determined to a great extent by the volatility in the value/price of the underlying.

h)   **Investors and Dealers :** Investors are individuals, mutual funds, pension funds, trusts, endowments, portfolio managers, companies etc.

The dealers in these markets are security firms, banks, financial institutions, market makers etc.

i)   **Option Price :** The option price is in the form of premium paid on a contract. The rupee amount of the premium is the price paid (debit) for an option when purchased or received (credit) for the option when sold. The actual amount paid for a contract is quoted price times the number of underlying shares, normally 100 shares, for each contract.

Suppose, the exercise price of A Co. is ₹ 1,500 for a call option and the actual market price is ₹ 1,400, then the call is said to be *out-of-the money*. If on the other hand, the market price of A Co. is ₹ 1,600, which is above the exercise price (₹ 1,500) then the option will have an intrinsic value or real worth and the call is said to be *in-the-money*. The reverse is true in the case of put options.

The premium for an option is almost always greater than the intrinsic, value. This excess value, namely premium minus intrinsic value is called the time value which is the speculative value of the premium paid on the option contract. This is what the buyer is willing to pay above the real worth for the expectation of future profits based on the underlying share. It is this time value which reflects the speculative element in options trading.

As mentioned above, the intrinsic value depends on the share price of the underlying security and the exercise price of the option. Thus, Intrinsic value = Actual share price – Exercise price (call option).

The excess of the option premium over the intrinsic value is called the time value of option. The time value depends on length of the time to maturity or expiration date and optimistic expectations of a rise in price of the intrinsic security. The time value of option thus depends on the speculative element and expectations of future. The more risky the underlying share like Reliance, the more attractive is the option on it. Such options will have a larger time value and the option price will rise with the risk on it, and the volatility of the price of underlying security.

j)   **Settlement :** The uncovered options are called naked options To cover calls – Buy the underlying security or go long in a put of equal or higher premium or maturity. To cover puts - go short in the underlying security or go long in a put.

Normally, option contracts are settled on the next day. If you exercise an option, settlement takes place in T + 5 days. The OCC makes arrangements for the settlement of these contracts in the U.S.A. The collection of margins and regulation of writing of contracts in options and in their trading and related matters, including settlement and clearance are the responsibility of the regulatory authority namely the Options Clearing Corporation, as in the U.S.A.

Characteristics of Options Contract

Options Contract have many distinctive **characteristics** out of which following are the important characteristics of option contract :

i)   **There is no Obligation to Buy or Sell :** In option contracts, the option holder has a right to buy or sell an underlying asset. He can exercise such type of right at any time during the currency of the contract. But in no case, he is under obligation to buy or sell. If he does not buy or sell, the contract will be simply lapsed.

ii) **Highly Flexible Instrument :** Option instruments cannot be made flexible according to the requirements of writer as well as the user. Such option contracts are highly standardised and so they can be traded only in options exchangers. On the other hand, there are also privately arranged options which can be traded "over the counter". Therefore, this instrument can be used according to the requirements of the writer as well as the user. This instrument is a combination of futures and forward contracts.

iii) **Options does not possess the Property of Linearity :** Profits and losses are not symmetrical under an option contract. It means that the option holder's profit, when the value of the underlying asset moves in one direction is not equal to his loss when its value moves in the opposite direction by the same amount. In an option contract, **the gain is not equal to the loss**.

iv) **Settlement :** In option contract, settlement is made only when the option holder exercises his option. If the option is not exercised by the option holder, till maturity, then the agreement automatically lapses and no settlement is required. Generally, this option contract terminates either at the time of exercising the options by the option holder or maturity whichever is earlier.

v)   **Down Payment :** In options contract, the option holder has to pay a certain amount called "premium" for holding the right of exercising the option. If the option holder does not exercise his option, he has to forego this premium amount. Otherwise, this premium amount will be deducted from the total payoff in calculating the net payoff due to the option holder.

1.1.10 TRENDS IN CAPITAL MARKET

A new era in capital market in India was ushered in July, 1991, with starting of a process of financial and economic deregulation. Beginning with devaluation of rupee by about 20% in July 1991, industrial policy was total reshaped to dispense with licensing of all industries except the 18 scheduled industrial groups. Further, removal of MRTP limit on assets of companies, dilution of FERA and foreign trade liberalisation etc. were some of the other reforms.

After a period of sustained growth, the India capital market suffered a slowdown due to the global financial crises. However, since early 2009, the markets have recovered. Indices have gained over 80% and market capital has more than doubled making India one of the top performing markets.

As per the report of Arin Roy and Sreekrishna Sankar (Indian capital markets: Trends and Prospects) which studies trends in retail and institutional segments, with a focus on the issues responsible for the current **lull** in there retail investment space.

Main findings of the study include:

1) Though the Indian equity market is highly attractive with high returns and a high level of investment from both domestic and foreign investors, the market lacks depth and breadth with limited reach and high concentration in trading among a few companies. Geographic breadth is another problem for Indian markets.

2) Indian debt market is underdeveloped, the corporate debt segment is not significant.

3) Indian derivatives market is growing, but needs to develop further in terms of products and investor base.

4) Domestic brokerages are standing up to the challenge of the foreign brokers, leading to a high growth, competitive space where technology adoption is playing a key role.

5) Financial Information Exchange (FIX) and Direct Market Access (DMA) are key growth areas in the institutional segment, with both setting the stage for **algorithms** trading.

6) FIX adoption is already rapidly rising and DMA adoption among the top layers is nearly complete.

"There is significant focus on the adoption of FIX and DMA in the markets. This is mainly driven by the fact that Foreign Institutional Investment (FII) flows are increasing, and in order to gain a share in the business, it is essential to provide compatibility with their systems and requirements" says Sreekrishna Sankar Analyst with Celent's Indian Financial Services Group and coauthor of the report". But there are a lot of rules and regulations in the usage of algorithms: specifically relating to a approval from the exchanges which are turning many traders away from using algorithms. Until some of these rules are modified the uptake of algorithmic trading will not be great.

This report discusses the adoption technology that is driving the next phase of growth in the Indian market, alongwith the regulatory changes needed for further evolution.

Reformation in Capital Market

The recent years witnessed significant reforms in the capital market. It is well known that trading platform has become automatic, electronic, anonymous, order-driven, nation-wide and screenbased. Shouting and gesticulations have yield place to punching and clicking. Speed and efficiency are the hallmark of the current system. Across the system, multitude of market participants trade with one another anonymously and simultaneously. On any trading day, more than 10,000 terminals come alive in 400 towns and cities, information is flashed on real time basis. Transparency is ensured in respect of dissemination of information, price and quantum of the order, but member's identity is sought to be hidden to prevent any bias in response. Today, trading member need not went his way to the Jeejeebhoy Tower in Dalal Street, Mumbai or to any stock exchange building elsewhere, he can comfortably sit at his computer terminal and execute the order.

Another material development, which proved to be of immense relief to the investors, was dematerialisation of the scrips. Now 99% of the scrips in the market are dematerialised. Almost 10% of the trades are in DMAT form.

At the stock exchanges, robust risk management system has been put in place, value-at-risk margining and exposure limits, on-line monitoring of margins and positions, clearing corporation and settlement guarantee fund mechanism for trade settlement - all these have made Indian market now aguably world class, in terms of transparency, efficiency and safety.

Antiquated and abused badla system or ALBM stands abolished. In its place for hedging and trading purposes, a number of derivatives in the form of features and options, both index-based and stocks-specific have been introduced.

Corporate bonds and Government securities used to be traded via telephone exchange.

During last few years, Indian capital market has been regaining its buoyancy. Globally recognised economic fundamentals of the country and widely the confidence of the investors, global and local, in the Indian market, to a substantial degree. The Indian capital market has outperformed many in the world. Note importantly the primary market too has perked up. The depth and liquidity of the market and its absorbing capacity has been indisputably proven.

QUESTIONS FOR SELF-STUDY

I. Theory Questions :

1. What is a 'Financial Market' ? State the classification of Financial Markets.

2. What is 'Capital Market' ? State the divisions of Capital Market.

3. Explain the term 'Capital Market'. What are the functions of Capital Market ?

4. Explain the structure of Capital Market.

5. Define the term 'Capital Market'. Explain the characteristics of Capital Market.

6. What is 'Capital Market' ? State the functions and characteristics of Capital Market.

7. What is 'Share' ? State the important characteristics of Shares.

8. What are 'Equity Shares' ? State the important characteristics of Equity Shares.

9. Explain the important rights to Equity Shareholders.

10. Define the term 'Equity Shares'. State the advantages and disadvantages of Equity Shareholders.

11. What are 'Preference Shares' ? State the important characteristics of Preference Shares.

12. Define the term 'Preference Shares'. State the advantages and disadvantages of Preference Share Capital.

13. Explain the important rights to Preference Shareholders.

14. What is 'Debentures' ? State the important characteristics of Debentures.

15. What are 'Bonds' ? State the important characteristics of Bonds.

16. Explain the procedure of issuing debentures and bonds.

17. State the legal provisions regarding conversion of debentures.

18. What is 'Convertible Debentures' ? State the advantages of convertible debentures.

19. State the merits and demerits of raising capital through issue of debentures.

20. Explain the important features of innovative debt instruments introduced in capital market.

21. What is 'Forward Contracts' ? State the important features of forward contracts.

22. What is 'Futures Contract' ? Explain the various types of Futures Contract.

23. What is Futures Contract ? State the important characteristics of Futures Contract.

24. What is 'Option Contract' ? Explain the types of option contracts.

25. State the important characteristics of options contract.

26. Explain in brief the recent trends in capital market.

27. Distinguish clearly between :

    a)   Primary Market and Secondary Market

    b)   Capital Market and Money Market

    c)   Shares and Stock

    d)   Equity Shares and Preference Shares

    e)   Debentures and Bonds

    f)   Debentures and Shares

    g)   Equity and Debt

    h)   Forward Contracts and Futures Contracts

28. Write short notes on :

    i) Financial System, ii) Unorganised Markets, iii) Money Market, iv) Secondary Market, v) Long-term Loan Market, vi) Capital Market Intermediaries, vii) Economy and Capital Market, viii) Capital Market Management, ix) Functions of Capital Market, x) Capital Market Structure, xi) Characteristics of Capital Market, xii) Money Management, xiii) Reforms in Capital Market, xiv) Capital Market Instruments, xv) Ownership Securities, xvi) Classification of Shares, xvii) Different Values to Equity Share, xviii) Kinds of Preference Shares, xix) Creditorship Securities, xx) Cumulative Convertible Preference Shares (CCPS), xxi) Classification of Debentures, xxiv) Closed Ended Mutual Funds, xxv) Stock Invest, xxvi) Index Futures, xxvii) Commodity Futures, xxviii) Reformation in Capital Market.

2...

Stock Market

Contents ...

Stock Market refers to secondary market where shares and bonds of existing business enterprises of Government or Semi-Government bodies are bought and sold. In simple language, it produces a market for the purchase and sale of corporate securities.

The securities market has two interdependent and inseparable segments, viz. the primary market and the secondary market. The primary market is the channel for creation of new securities through financial instruments by public limited companies as well as government agencies, whereas secondary market deals in securities already issued. The resources in the primary market are mobilised either through the public issues or through private placement. It is a public issue if anybody and everybody can subscribe for it, whereas if the issue is made available to a selected group of persons it is termed as private placement.

2.1 STOCK EXCHANGE

Stock Exchanges are intricately interwoven in the fabric of the nation's economic life. "Without the stock exchange, the savings of the community-the sinews of economic progress and productive efficiency would be used much less completely, and much more wastefully, than they are now." Stock Exchange is an essential concomitant of the capitalistic system of economy. It is indispensable for the proper functioning of corporate enterprise. It brings together large amounts of capital necessary for the economic progress of a country.

It is a two-way market in which investors and speculators' agents, i.e., stock brokers are just as likely to be sellers as well as buyers. Besides, the stock market bridges the gap between governments and municipalities which need to borrow money for long periods or to raise permanent capital and investors who only wish to put up money for comparatively short-time.

Definition

Securities Contracts (Regulation) Act, 1956, defines, Stock Exchange as "an association, organisation, or body of individuals, whether incorporated or not, established for the purposes of assisting, regulating and controlling business in buying, selling and dealing in securities.

Thus, stock market may be defined as the place where second-hand securities are dealt in. Securities which are traded in stock market include the shares and securities of corporate enterprises, Government Securities, debentures and bonds of local self-governments and port trusts. Persons desirous to deal in shares and securities assemble in this market.

It is the citadel of capital and the pivot of money market. It provides necessary mobility to capital and directs the flow of capital into profitable and successful enterprises. It is the barometer of general economic progress in a country and exerts a powerful and significant influence as a depressant or stimulant of business activity.

Secondary market is a place where already issued securities (Share, Bonds) of the Companies listed on recognised exchanges in the market are traded. Secondary markets therefore are another name of the stock markets which comprises four players - Stock Exchanges, Companies, Investors and Brokers.

Indian Stock Markets have a history which dates back to nearly 200 years.

Characteristics of Stock Market

The main characteristics of Stock Market are as follows :

i)   Stock market is the place or market where securities of joint stock companies and of government or semi-government bodies are dealt in.

ii) Stock market refers to secondary market where shares and bonds of existing business enterprises of government or semi-government bodies are bought and sold. Thus, it provides a market for the purchase and sale of corporate securities.

iii) Stock market is an organised market where securities of government and semi-government bodies and corporate enterprises are bought and sold.

iv) Stock market may be registered or unregistered body. It is not always necessary for a stock exchange to incorporate it under the Companies Act. It can operate as a private institution. In our country, stock markets of Mumbai, Ahmedabad and Indore have been organised as private clubs.

v) Transactions in the stock market must accord to the rules and bye-laws framed by the stock exchange to regulate its day-to-day operations.

vi) Unlike the new issue market, stock market deals in second hand or existing securities.

vii) Only individuals can buy and sell securities. The stock market does not provide this facility to corporations and partnership firms. Now Rules have been changed and enrolment of corporate bodies as members of stock exchanges are allowed.

viii) In the stock market only those securities which are listed in the stock market are transacted. Unlisted securities are not permitted to be dealt in the market.

Recognised Stock Exchanges

The stock market in India is regulated under the Securities Contracts (Regulation) Act, 1956. At present, there are twenty-three Stock Exchanges recognised by Government under the Act. They are at Ahmedabad, Bangalore, Baroda, Bhubaneshwar, Mumbai, Kolkata, Cochin, Coimbatore, Delhi, Gawahati, Hyderabad, Indore, Jaipur, Kanpur, Ludhiana, Chennai, Mangalore, Patna, Pune, Rajkot, Over the Counter Exchange of India (OTCEI) and the National Stock Exchange of India Limited (NSE). The Bombay Exchange was granted permanent recognition at the first instance. The other exchanges were given, in the first instance, official recognition for a period of five years and at the end of each term the recognition was renewed for a like period. The exchanges at Kolkata, Delhi, Chennai, Ahmedabad, Hyderabad, Indore and Bengaluru have now been granted permanent recognition.

History and Growth of Stock Markets in India

- It was at the close of the eighteenth century when East India Company was a dominant institution that business in loan securities of the company used to be transacted.

- By 1830's business on corporate stocks and shares in Bank and Cotton Presses took place in Mumbai.

- The organised stock exchanges in India are of comparatively recent origin. There were three stock exchanges in India in 1933, one each at Mumbai, Kolkata and Ahmedabad. However, the history of the unorganised stock business and simultaneously of stock exchanges in India is roughly a history of over a century. Mumbai and Kolkata were said to have some trade in securities mostly in Government securities, and a few bank shares as early as 1836.

- The main impetus to the stock business came only in 1850's when the Companies Act introduced the doctrine of limited liability and when there was massive development in the means of transport and communication. Number of stock-brokers in Mumbai increased to 60 in 1860 with the legendary 'Prem Chand Roy Chand' as their leader.

- In 1874 after the American Civil War, the brokers who thrived out of the Civil war in 1874, found a place in a street (now called Dalal Street) where they would conveniently assemble and transact business.

- In 1875, they formally established in Mumbai, the "**Native Share and Stock Brokers Association**" and the Stock Exchange acquired a premises in the same street and was inaugurated in 1877 named as Bombay Stock Exchange or BSE.

- After this in 1908, Kolkata Stock Exchange was formed. The Madras Stock Exchange came into existence in 1920.

- After the Second World War, Stock Exchanges were floated in all parts of the country namely, Uttar Pradesh Stock Exchange Limited (1940), Nagpur Stock Exchange Limited (1940) and Hyderabad Stock Exchange Limited (1944).

- Under the provisions of the Securities Contracts (Regulation) Act, 1956 the Central Government recognised five exchange in the year 1957, two exchanges in 1958 and one exchange in 1963, namely (a) the Bombay Stock Exchange from 31st August, 1957 (renamed from the Native Share and Stock Brokers Association), (b) The Ahmedabad Share and Stock Brokers Association Ltd. from 10th October, 1957, (c) The Kokkata Stock Exchange from 10th October, 1957, (d) The Chennai Stock Exchange from 15th October, 1957, (e) The Delhi Stock Exchanges Association Ltd. from 9th December, 1957, (f) The Hyderabad Stock Exchange Ltd. from 29th September, 1958, (g) The Indore Share Brokers Association from 24th December, 1958, (h) The Bengaluru Stock Exchange from 16th February, 1963.

- Three more stock exchanges were set up in Cochin (1978), Kanpur (1982) and Pune (1982). Subsequently, another three stock exchanges were opened in Ludhiyana, Guwahati and Mangalore.

- The two new exchanges – The Over the Counter Exchange of India (OTCEI) set up in 1990 and the National Stock Exchange (NSE) set up in 1993 - have quickly gained prominence.

- OTCEI - The first screen-based automatic trading system in India trades primarily in securities issued by companies with relatively small equity base.

NSE aims to provide comprehensive nation-wide trading and automatic post-trade clearing and settlement facilities.

2.1.1 ORGANISATION OF STOCK EXCHANGE

The **Organisation of a typical Stock Exchange** is shown below in Fig. 2.1.

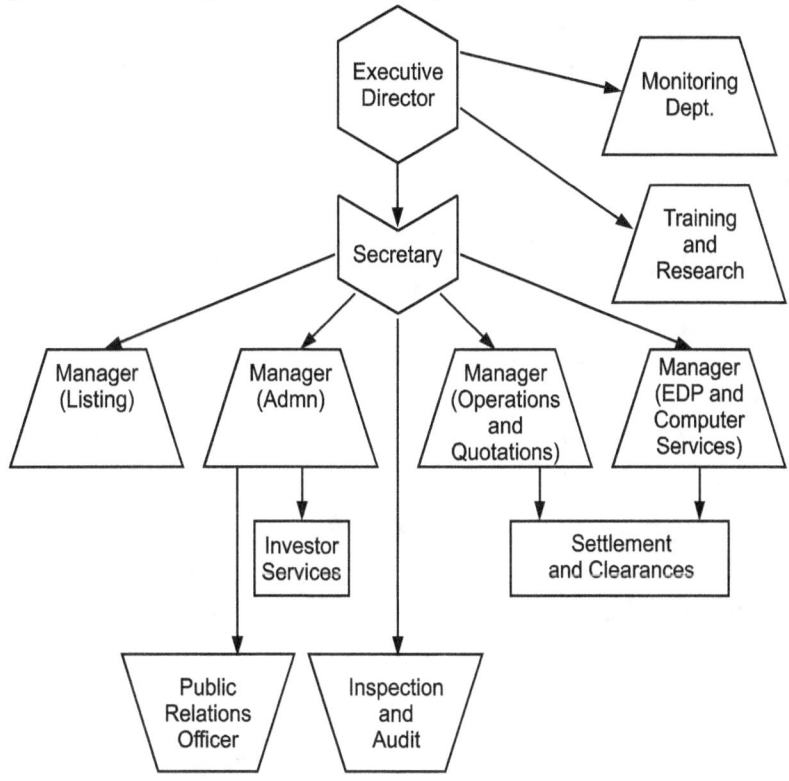

Fig. 2.1 : Organisation of Stock Exchange

In organisational set of a stock exchange, there are following departmentations, under the control of executive director.

i) Secretary for listing, ii) Manager (operations) for trading operations and manager (administration) for general administration of the Exchange, iii) EDP for reporting and recording of data and information for development of the management information system, iv) Training and research. Some exchanges have other departments also like monitoring department, quotations department, public relations department, etc.

Administration of major exchanges is through the committees. These committees of members are appointed by the board of directors for carrying on the functions of administration and management of the exchange. The number of committees may vary from exchange to exchange. All the major items of work are entrusted to the committees for their deliberations and decisions.

The recognised stock exchanges at Mumbai, Indore are voluntary non-profit making associations, now Mumbai Stock Exchange is converted into joint stock company.

While the Kolkata, Delhi, Bengaluru, Cochin, Uttar Pradesh, Ludhiana, Gawahati and Kanara Stock Exchanges are joint stock companies limited shares and the Chennai,

Hyderabad and Pune Stock Exchanges are companies limited by guarantee. Since the Rules or Articles of Association defining the constitution of the recognised Stock Exchanges are approved by the Central Government, there is a broad uniformity in their organisation. In fact, the Chennai Stock Exchange was re-constituted and the Kolkata Stock Exchange had to undergo a major re-organisation as a condition precedent to their recognition by the Government of India.

Administrative Policy :

The administration and implementation of policy is left to the executive director and secretary, who also attend board meetings. They are assisted by a staff of officers, assistants, sub-staff etc., for day to day working of the exchange. The executive director is the chief in charge of stock exchange administration and is responsible to the governing board and the government and keeps a rapport with all concerned agencies. The president as the chairman of the governing board is responsible for policy aspects and is helped by the executive director in implementation of policies. Both the president and executive director have to work in close coordination, so that the government guidelines and board's policy decisions are implemented with the least friction and utmost precision.

2.1.2 MEMBERSHIP OF STOCK EXCHANGES

The regulations governing the admission of members of the recognised Stock Exchanges are uniform in terms of the provisions of the Securities Contracts (Regulation) Rules, 1957. These Statutory Rules provide that no person shall be eligible to be elected as a member if he is less than twenty one years of age; or is not a citizen of India; or has been adjudged bankrupt or proved to be insolvent or has compounded with his creditors; or has been convicted of an offence involving fraud or dishonesty; or is engaged as principal or employee in any business other than that of securities; or is a member of any other association in India where dealings in securities are carried on; or is director, partner or employee of any company whose principal business is that of dealing in securities.

Firms and companies were hitherto not eligible for membership of a recognised Stock Exchange. Steps are now being taken to enlist financial institutions and corporate bodies as members of a recognised Stock Exchange. The enrolment of financial institutions and corporate bodies as members of recognised Stock Exchanges ensuring professionalisation of stock broking and better services to the investors. Individuals are ordinarily not deemed to be qualified unless they have had atleast two years' market experience as an apprentice or as a partner or authorised assistant or authorised clerk or remisier of a member.

Recommendations by High-Powered Committee on Stock Exchange regarding Organisation, Management and Membership

In May 1984, the Government appointed a High-Powered Committee under the chairmanship of Mr. G. S. Patel to make a comprehensive review of the functioning of the stock exchanges in India with a view to ensuring their smooth functioning and for the expansion of their activities, and to make recommendations to the Government in the matter. The Committee had been set up following the suggestion of the Rangrajan Study Group which examined resources availability for private sector in the Sixth Plan period. The final set of recommendations of the High Powered Committee on Stock Exchange Reforms, popularly known as **G. S. Patel Committee**, were made public in May 1986.

Recommendations in connection with organisation, management and membership of stock exchanges are as under :

Organisation and Management :

The Committee recommends that all stock exchanges should have a uniform model and have a legal, status of a company limited by guarantee without shares under the Companies Act. The existing post of President should be abolished and all stock exchanges should be headed by a non-executive Chairman and a Managing Director. The Government should have the final say in appointing the Chairman.

In addition to the Defaults Committee, Arbitration Committee, etc., the stock exchanges must have at least two other committees, one for planning and development of securities business and the other for the purpose of audit.

The Committee does not favour setting up of a Commission on the lines of Securities and Exchange Commission as in U. S. A. It, however, recommends that an apex body called the Council for Securities Industry be established. The composition of the governing body of the Council for Securities Industry should consist of 10 members out of which 4 should be the Chairmen of Stock Exchanges and another 4 should be independent, members from Government officials, experts from the field of corporate finance, commerce, accountancy, management, etc., and 2 from investment and development finance institutions. The Council for Security Industry should be a statutory body with adequate powers to function effectively. The strength of stock exchange division of the Ministry of Finance should be considerably increased and upgraded.

Membership of Stock Exchanges

The Committee recommends that the minimum educational qualifications for new members should be Standard XII. After five years or so, the question of raising the minimum education standard to graduation could be examined. A separate Institute designated a National Institute of Investment and Financial Analysis should be established on an all-India level to offer diploma course for seeking membership of the stock exchange as also for the existing members. With a view to professionalising the existing members, all stock exchanges must conduct from time to time refresher courses. Members of the stock exchanges and others associated with the working of the stock exchanges should have reasonable background in economics, corporate finance, taxation, etc.

The Committee has recommended fixation of security deposits by the members of stock exchange. It feels that there should be a linkage between the volume of business and owned funds of a member in his business. Membership should be always open to any person who is qualified, having adequate experience and has also qualified for a professional diploma. At present, the entry into stock broking business is very easy for members and their close relatives. It has recommended that the norms of eligibility for membership in regard to the educational qualifications, experience and practical training should also apply to those acquiring membership on a hereditary basis or through nomination.

The Committee has recommended that a minimum amount of business be done by each member to remain in business. These norms may be laid down by the Council for Securities Industry. Dormant membership should be terminated. The companies may also be allowed membership of stock exchanges, provided all the directors assume unlimited liability and a majority of directors are members of the stock exchanges. Multiple membership should be allowed to facilitate the arbitrage transactions and interflow of information. The Government should have the power to direct the stock exchanges to increase the membership. There should be specialist members for different types of activities.

Eligibility of Membership

To become a member of a recognised stock exchange, a person must possess the following qualifications :

i)   He should be a citizen of India,

ii)   He should not be less than 21 years of age,

iii)   He should not have been adjudged bankrupt or insolvent,

iv)   He should not have been convicted for an offence involving fraud or dishonesty,

v)   He should not be engaged in any other business except dealing in securities,

vi)   He should not have been expelled by any other stock exchange or declared a defaulter by any other stock exchange.

Apart from individuals, a company is also eligible to become a member provided it satisfies the conditions imposed by the stock exchange concerned.

2.1.3 GOVERNING BODY OF STOCK EXCHANGE

The **Governing Body of a recognised Stock Exchange** has wide governmental and administrative powers. It has the power, subject to Government approval, to make amends and suspend the operation of the Rules, By-laws and Regulations of the exchange. It also has complete jurisdiction over all members and in practice its powers of management and control are almost absolute.

Under the constitution, the governing body has the power to admit and expel members; to warn, censure, fine and suspend members and their partners, attorneys, remisiers, authorised clerks and employees; to approve the formation and dissolution of partnerships and appointment of attorneys, remisiers and authorised clerks; to enforce attendance and information, adjudicate disputes and impose penalties; to determine the mode and conditions of stock exchange business and regulate stock exchange trading in all its aspects; and generally to supervise, direct and control all matters and activities affecting the Stock Exchange.

The board of directors consists of elected members, and they regulate the affairs of the exchange. Traditionally, the committees of members managed the affairs of the exchange, as self-regulatory organisations. Only broker members are represented on the board for a long time. Later government representative and a representative each of RBI and of the public were also kept on the board to represent other interests in the exchange. The recent guidelines of the SEBI in this regard are to give a representation of 50% for non-brokers including those of the government and the public, so that the management board becomes broad based and the interests of all concerned are looked after. The other 50% goes to elected broker members of the exchange.

Powers of Governing Boards of Stock Exchanges

The recognised stock exchanges are managed by "**Governing Boards**". The governing boards consist of elected member directors from stock broker members, public representatives and government nominees nominated by the SEBI. The government also has powers to nominate Presidents and Vice-President of stock exchanges and to approve the appointment of the Chief Executive and public representatives. The major stock exchanges are managed by the Chief Executive Director and the smaller stock exchanges are under the control of a Secretary.

The Governing boards have wide powers such as :

i) Election of office bearers and setting up of committees like Listing Committee, Arbitration Committee, Defaulter's Committee, etc.,

ii) Admission and expulsion of members,

iii) Management of the properties and finances of the exchange,

iv) Framing and interpretation of rules, bye-laws etc. for the regulation of stock exchange,

v) Adjudication of disputes among members or outsiders,

vi) Management of the affairs of the exchange in the best interest of the investors and public interest.

Services rendered by the Stock Market

There are various types of services rendered by the stock market. These services can be examined by three heads i.e. **to the investor**, **to the corporation** and to the **community or society**. **Services Rendered by the Stock Market** are shown below in Figure 2.2.

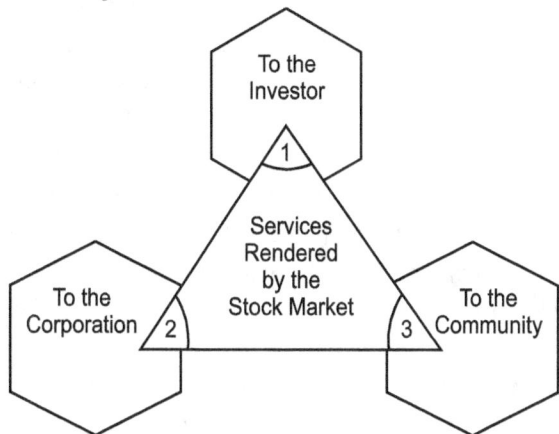

Fig. 2.2 : Services Rendered by the Stock Market

1) **Services to the Investors :**

Stock Exchange provides the following services to the investors.

a) The daily or periodical quotations of the listed securities enable the investor to assess the value of the investment.

b) The publicity resulting from exchange transactions has an educative and advertising effect. People, who may not become interested in the purchase of stocks and bonds, learn something about them from daily stock quotations and their interest frequently develops into action by watching the prices shoot up.

c) The investor assumes less risk by purchasing listed securities as it is minimised by the presence of continuous market negotiability, correct evaluation and facility of liquidating the investment.

d) Liquidity of investment is ensured by a stock market as the investor who wants to withdraw himself from a particular venture can easily do so.

e) Negotiability of the listed security purchased on the stock exchange helps an investor to pledge it as a collateral security for a loan.

f) An investor usually has a feeling of fair dealing when he purchases or sells the security on a well-regulated stock exchange. The brokers who deal in listed securities are thought to be more honest and dependable than the general run of security salesmen.

g) Almost all stock exchanges have set up investor service cells for the purpose of attending to the complaints against broker members and their authorised clerks and the listed companies. The follow up action with members and companies is taken by this cell. There is also a customer protection fund with all stock exchanges to reimburse the clients of any losses incurred due to defaults of members. The cell sends these complaints to the companies, if there are listed companies and request for early compliance.

h) In case of complaints against members, the latter are called to explain their version of the deal which led to the complaint. Sometimes, the matter goes for arbitration by the arbitrators' committee of the exchange, if a large amount of money is involved. Investors are also served by the directory of corporate information and educative and informative handbooks and with daily volume/price data.

i) The stock exchange facilitates an investor to shift from one type of investment to another according to his investment priorities without any significant depreciation in its real value. Accordingly, an investor does not get tied for the better or for the worse to the particular concern whose shares he buys. It is this assurance that he does not have to sink or swim with it, that makes him willing to venture into investments. Moreover, by widening the opportunities for investment, a stock exchange also enables investors to spread their risk by acquiring securities of different industries in varying proportions which is an essential concomitant to modern investment.

2) Services to the Corporation :

Stock Exchanges offer certain services to the corporation as well :

a)   The stock market plays a cardinal role in promoting the level of capital formation by assisting in the effective mobilisation (and also augmentation) of savings and their canalisation into appropriate avenue of investment. This it does by providing an organised market in diverse type of securities to suit the varying notions and whims of a vast mass of savers about liquidity, profitability and risk element in their investments.

b)   The stock exchange, in addition to providing a market already in existing securities, assists in the provision of new capital for industrial and other borrowers. Enterprises whether new or old, when assured of the regular flow of funds through sale of shares and securities at a small capital cost, can confidently embark upon programmes of industrial expansion resulting in increased production, reduced cost and also larger profits to shareholders which in their turn infuse confidence in them.

c)   The opportunity of constant evaluation of returns on one's investment compared to others, the liquidity that is imparted to investment in fixed capital and price continuity that is being ensured, instil confidence in the minds of savers. On the other hand, by creating conditions which reasonably ensure availability of financial resources for creating real capital, whether in private sector or in public sector they give impetus to development.

d)   The stock exchange gains the confidence of investors in securities by safeguarding their interests through tight listing requirements and through regulation and control of the activities of its members. Listing of securities at the stock exchange gives a status to them and thereby it benefits both the sellers and buyers and also encourages investments. The fact that shares are being quoted at a stock exchange augments the seller's ability to dispose them off and the buyer in his turn feels secured of getting accommodation, if need be, by pledging such securities with bankers.

e)   The credit of a corporation is enhanced as soon as its securities are listed on the stock exchange. It gives an impression of being a sound concern. Market for the listed securities is widened. It is an arithmetical truth that a well diversified market in the securities of a corporation is highly beneficial for its management because there is a lesser possibility of group opposition.

f)   The market price of the listed securities tends to be somewhat higher in relation to earnings, dividend and property values because of their improved marketability and attractiveness. The high value assessed for the company's securities may act as a valuable bargaining factor in merger plans.

g)   A corporation gets a good response from investing class when either it has got its securities listed or has expressed the intention of getting them listed in the near future. The well-organised stock exchange is interested in minimised fluctuation in the security price and a company having its securities listed on such a market maintains the confidence of its investors and others who deal with it.

3) Services to the Society :

The economic services, which a well constituted and efficiently run stock market can render to a country with a large private sector operating under the normal incentives and impulses of private enterprise, are considerable. The services rendered to the community, society and ultimately to the Government are as under :

a) Stock exchange serves the nation in several ways through its diversified economic services which include imparting liquidity to investments and providing marketability, enabling evaluation and ensuring price continuity of securities.

b) Alongside extending help to the private sector industrial enterprises, a stock exchange also proves to be a boon for governments who need to borrow large funds for financing developmental programmes which it has taken upon itself for betterment of the economic lot of the people. This it does through providing an organised market for government bonds.

c) A stock exchange creates a cluster of shares and stock brokers, underwriters and other well-versed in financial matters who educate public opinion about the soundness of the new issues and offer expert advice to the prospective investors regarding the appropriate securities and the opportune time for transactions in them.

d) The stock market is an important institution to finance the economic development in a country. The various private and state enterprises have to seek the assistance of stock exchanges for contacting the investors. "It is no exaggeration to say that the sharp increase in industrial activity in the past two decades and more would not have been possible but for the important part played by the stock exchanges in India.

e) In underdeveloped economies not only is the volume of savings low but a large part of it is dissipated in conspicuous consumption and in hoards because of lack of knowledge of investment opportunities, high liquidity preference and other factors mainly of a non-economic character. The stock market promotes conditions which take care of some of these inhibiting factors. It offers a ready market for conversion of securities into cash and thus encourages investment and discourages hoardings.

Stock Market Indices

Stock Index is representative of the price and value of various companies listed on the Stock Exchange. It is a single figure, which sums up the overall performance of the market on a daily basis. A Stock Index is the pulse rate of an economy and reflects the expectations of investors. It measures the general movement of the market. **Types of Stock Indices** are shown in Figure 2.3 as follows.

Fig. 2.3 : Types of Stock Indices

1) **Broad Market Index :** It consists of all the large, liquid stocks of the country and becomes the benchmark for the capital market in the whole country e.g. S & P CNX 500, Sensex.

2) **Specialised Index :** These are industry or sector specific indexes, which act as a benchmark for that particular industry, e.g. CNX Mid Cap, which is composed of companies with market capitalisation between 500-1500 crores, NASDA, which comprises IT shares, CNX 1T sector index, CNX Bank Index, CNX FMCG Indexes.

Determinants of a Stock Index :

Following are the five important **determinants of a stock index** which is called **'Panchasutri of Stock Index'** as shown below in Figure 2.4.

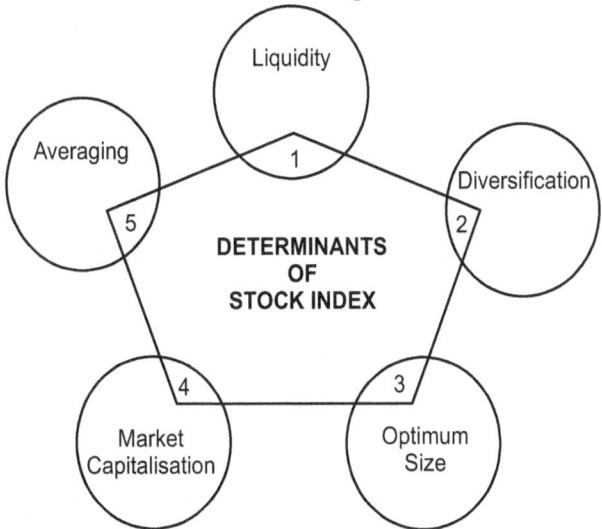

Fig. 2.4 : Determinants of a Stock Index

1) **Liquidity :**

The Index should have stocks with high liquidity. This is measured by the 'impact cost' criterion. Impact cost is measured as –

$$\frac{\text{Purchase Price of Stock} - \text{Market Price}}{\text{Market Price}} \times 100$$

Purchase price of the stock involves transaction costs. Higher the difference between purchase price and market price of the stock, higher will be the impact cost.

2) **Diversification :**

Index should be well diversified i.e. reflect the economy by having a balanced representation of all sectors.

3) **Optimum Size :**

The Index should not be too small as it will not represent the market properly, on the other hand it should not he too big otherwise it may include illiquid stocks in it.

4) **Market Capitalisation :**

The Index should include the stocks of companies that have significant market capitalisation with respect to the index such that any change in the price of the stock is reflected in the Index.

5) **Averaging :**

Index movement occurs due to news about the company and about the economy. The Index must be averaged so as to reduce the impact of company news and is affected only due to changes in economy.

Methods of Index Construction :

There are different types of methods used for constructing index. The following three methods are normally used for the same.

1) Price Weighted Index Method, 2) Equal Weighted Index Index and 3) Value Weighted Index or Market Capitalisation Weight Index Method. Methods of Index Construction are shown below in Figure 2.5.

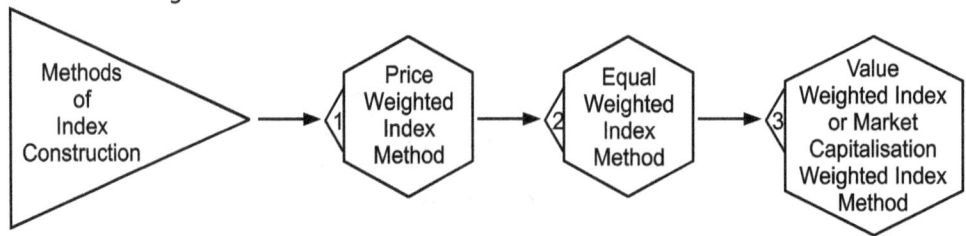

Fig. 2.5 : Methods of Index Construction

1) **Price Weighted Index Method :**

It is the ratio of sum of prices of a certain year (or month or week or day) with reference to base year. e.g. an index comprises 5 stocks which is as follows :

Stocks	Price in Base Year ₹	Price in Current Year ₹
A	80	120
B	55	78
C	72	100
D	30	55
E	65	80
Total	**302**	**433**

$$\text{Price Index} = \frac{₹\,433 \times 100}{₹\,302}$$

$$= ₹\,142.36$$

It is based on the assumption that investors buy one share of each stock included in the Index.

2) **Equal Weighted Index Method :**

It is the ratio of the sum of relative prices of shares in the current year with reference to the base year. e.g. considering the above example :

Stocks	Calculations		Relative Price in Current Year ₹
A	120 × 100/800	=	150.00
B	78 × 100/55	=	141.81
C	100 × 100/72	=	138.88
D	55 × 100/30	=	183.33
E	80 × 100/65	=	123.07
Total			737.09

$$\text{Equal Weighted Index} = \frac{₹\,739.09 \times 100}{500}$$

$$= ₹\,147.41$$

It is assumed that investors assign equal weights to all the stocks included in the Index.

3) **Value Weighted Index/Market Capitalisation Weighted Index Method :**

It is the ratio of aggregate market capitalisation in current year to the aggregate market capitalisation in the base year. For example considering the above example.

Price in Base Year ₹	Price in Current Year ₹	Number of Ordinary Shares Outstanding ₹ mm	Market Capital in Current Year ₹ mn	Market Capital in Base Year ₹ mn
(1)	(2)	(3)	(2 × 3)	(1 × 3)
80	120	15	1,800	1,200
55	78	10	780	550
72	100	25	2,500	1,800
30	55	12	660	360
65	80	20	1,600	1,300
			7,340	5,210

$$\text{Value Weighted Index} = \frac{₹\,7,340}{₹\,5,210} \times 100$$

$$= ₹\,140.89$$

Other Popular Indian Indices

i)   **NSE's S & P CNX Nifty :** It is a value weighted index which comprises of 50 stocks with base period as the closing price of 3rd November, 1995 and base value of Index as 1,000.

ii) **BSE Sensex-Bombay Stock Exchange Sensitive Index :** It comprises 30 shares and is a value weighted index with base period as 1978-79 w.e.f. 1st September, 2003, the free float, government and promoter holdings as well as locked-in-shares are excluded for calculating market capitalisation of the companies and this is called Free Float Cap Weighing.

iii) **The Times Index of Ordinary Share Prices :** It is an Equal Weighted Index comprising 72 shares with a base year of 1984-85.

iv) **The Financial Express Equity Index :** It comprises 100 actively traded shares with base year as 1979. It is a value weighted index.

Stock Market Indices of U.S.

Major U.S. Indices are as under :

i)   **Dow Jones Indices**

   a) Dow Jones Industrial Average Index comprising 30 stocks, current Divisor value is 0.12560864. (It is just an example).

   b) Dow Jones Transportation Index with 20 stocks. Its current divisor value is 0.23720855. (It is just an example).

   c) Dow Jones Utility Index with 15 stocks. Its Current divisor value is 1.5940823. (It is just for example).

       All of these are price weighted indices.

ii) **NYSE Composite Index :** It comprises 2,100 stocks and are calculated as Price Weighted Index with a base value of 5000.

iii) **NASDAQ (National Association of Stock Dealers Automated Quotations) :** It is a market value weighted index. It is a floorless exchange. NASDAQ Indices are calculated as :

Calculation of NASDAQ Indices

$$\text{NASDAQ Index Level} = \frac{\text{Current MarketValue}}{\text{Adjusted Based Period Market Value}} \times \text{Base Value}$$

$$\text{Where, Adjusted Base Period Market Value} = \frac{\text{CMVAA}}{\text{CMVBP}} = \text{PBPMV}$$

CMVAA = Current Market Value after Adjustments

CMVBA = Current Market Value before Adjustment

PBPMV = Provision Base Period Market Value

Major NASDAQ indices are as follows :

a) NASDAQ-100 Index which includes 100 largest domestic and non-financial companies with a base value equal to A 125.

b) NASDAQ-100 Equal Weighted Index, Base value equal to 1000 and same securities as NASDAQ 100 but weight of 1% of the Index.

c)   NASDAQ Financial 100 Index containing 100 domestic and international financial companies having a base value equal to 250.

d)   NASDAQ Biotechnology Index, comprising pharmaceutical and biotech firms and having base value equal to 200.

e)   NASDAQ Composite Index consisting of all domestic and international based common type stocks of 3000 companies and a base value of 100.

f)   NASDAQ National Market Composite Index value which is a subset of NASDAQ Composite Index and has a base of 100.

Other NASDAQ indices are as follows :

- NASDAQ Computer Index
- NASDAQ Health Care Index
- NASDAQ Industrial Index
- NASDAQ National Market Industrial Index
- NASDAQ Insurance Index
- NASDAQ Other Finance Index
- NASDAQ Telecommunication Index
- NASDAO Transportation Index

iv) **Standard's and Poor's**

Major S & P indices are as follows :

- S & P 500 Index.
- S & P 100 Index.
- S & P 400 Mid Cap Index.
- S & P 600 Small Cap Index.
- S & P 1500 Super Composite Index.

Note : All these index are calculated by Free Float Methodology and Equal Weighted Methodology.

2.1.4 BOMBAY STOCK EXCHANGE (BSE)

Bombay Stock Exchange (BSE) was established in 1875. It was started as "The Native Share and Stock Brokers Association" and over the years it has become the premier stock exchange of the country. It is the first stock exchange to have obtained permanent recognition in 1956 from the Government of India under the Securities Contracts (Regulation) Act 1956.

Features of Bombay Stock Exchange (BSE)

The main features of Bombay Stock Exchange (BSE) are as follows :

i)   The Stock Exchange, Mumbai (BSE) was established in 1875 as 'The Native Stock Broker's Association'. Over the past 120 years, BSE has emerged as one of the premier Stock Exchange of the country. It is the oldest Stock Exchange in Asia. BSE is a non-profit distributing, self-regulatory organisation owned by 658 broker members.

ii)   Approximately, 7500 scrips in the form of equity and debt instruments are listed at BSE amounting to over 75% of market capitalisation and 70% of listed capital in India.

iii)   BSE is considered as a pillar of Indian economy. In the past 125 years, BSE has made significant contributions to promote country's economic growth by providing avenues to raise capital through the primary market. It is one of the major sources for generation of foreign exchange.

iv)   BSE has introduced path breaking technologies in recent times. BSE provides trading through BOLT - BSE Online Trading System. BSE has promoted CDSIL - Central Depository Services (India) Ltd. which is equipped with latest technology and provides services at very economical rates. BOSS - BSE Online Surveillance System has various online alerts to monitor the market. BSE introduced trading through Internet. Trading in Derivatives segment has commenced from 9th June, 2000.

v)   BSE Indices are quoted world over as barometer of Indian economy. Various BSE Indices are Sensex (BSE 30). National Index (BSE 100), BSE 200, BSE 500 and Dollex.

vi)   BSE is uniquely positioned as it has separate full fledged Investors Services Cell, Bad Delivery Cell, Research Statistics and Publication department and Trading Institute. Investor protection is further strengthened by specialised funds like Trade Guarantee Fund and Customer Protection Fund so that any default on the part of BSE member does not affect the stability of the market.

vi)   BADLA is a unique feature of SSE. Facility of trading in basket of scrips is also available with the Exchange.

Organisation Structure of BSE

The exchange comprises a governing board having 20 directors which regulates the exchange affairs and decides its policies. Among these 20 members, there are 9 elected directors in the board, of which one third retire every year by rotation, there are 3 nominees of SEBI, 6 public representatives, an Executive Director, Chief Operating Officer, and Chief Executive Officer.

The Executive Director as the Chief Executive Officer is responsible for the day-to-day administration of the Exchange he is assisted by the Chief Operating Officer and other Heads of Departments.

The average daily turnover of the exchange during the financial year 2003-04 and 2004-05 (April-March) was - ₹ 1978.81 crores and ₹ 2050.26 crores respectively.

The Organisation Structure of Bombay Stock Exchange is shown in Figure 2.6.

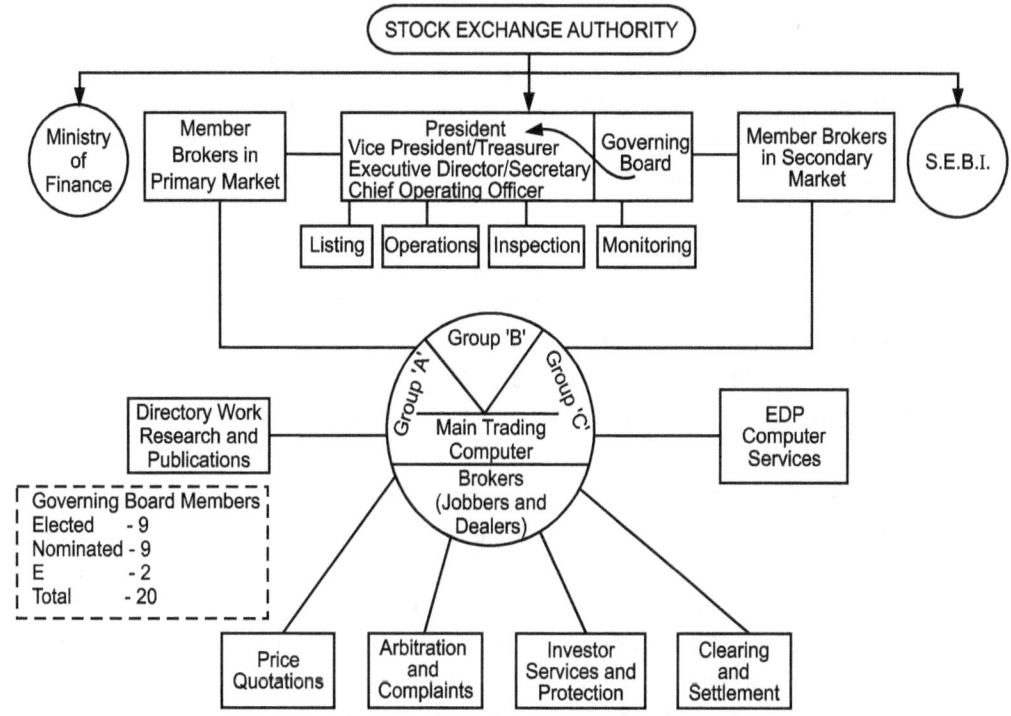

Fig. 2.6 : Organisation Structure of Bombay Stock Exchange

The above mentioned chart shows the organisational setup for management and administration of BSE.

The decisions made by the governing board are implemented by the executive director and secretary through various departments which perform the functions of listing, regulation of trading, provision of settlement and clearance etc. The decisions are sometimes taken by the committees appointed by the governing board for specific purposes. The various departments are seen in the chart.

These departments are function based, keeping the services to be rendered to the members and the public in mind. These departments are all interlinked and coordination on a daily basis is the responsibility of the secretary.

The main departments and their functions are as follows :

i)   **Listing Department :**

To study the project of the company and its draft prospectus and to ensure that the company observes the law and guidelines of the government before being listed and a listing agreement is entered into. To observe that the listed companies follow the clauses of the listing agreement and to see that the company makes fair and equitable allotment of shares and to take any follow-up action with the companies.

ii)   **Operations Department :**

To observe that daily trading takes place in an orderly manner, collect quotations and make them available to members/ public by every evening.

iii) **Computer Department :**

To collect and compile the corporate data, quotations of scrips and turnover of trade, memberwise and scripwise. To build up a management information system useful to the exchange to take action against members and useful to the public and members for better investment decision-making.

iv) **EDP Work :**

The EDP work of building up the corporate database of the exchange is an important item of work of the management. The financial results of the companies and their balance sheet data are available on the computer of the exchange their net profits, dividends, bonus, etc., are all recorded on the computer. The EDP builds up the information base on companies for members and investors to make their investment decisions.

With the help of above mentioned departments the functions of BSE are therefore performing more scientifically by vigorous enforcement of rules without any bias or partiality and giving transparency to its operations. For this purpose, BSE strengthened its manpower expertise, through an appointment of executive director and other experts, 'personnel and implementing proper computerisation and automation. A new management information system is built up for better enforcement of rules against listed companies and against members, brokers in their activity and in their exporting system.

Objectives of the Stock Exchange, Mumbai

Following are the main objectives of BSE.

i) To safeguard the interests of the investing public having dealings on the exchange and the members.

ii) To establish and promote honourable and just practices in securities transactions.

iii) To promote, develop and maintain a well regulated market for dealing in securities.

iv) To promote, industrial development and efficient resource mobilisation by way of investment in corporate securities.

Role of Bombay Stock Exchange

The Stock Exchange is an intergral part of the 'Capital Market', which enables the business enterprises whether in private sector or in public sector to raise the necessary financial resource by providing a market place that brings together the enterprises which need money and investors with investible funds. In doing so, the stock market also imparts liquidity to such investments or an ability to convert their investments into ready cash at short notice, thereby encouraging the flow of savings into productive ventures.

The Stock Exchange Mumbai, which was established in 1875 as "The Native Share and Stock brokers' Association"- a voluntary non-profit making association - has evolved over the years into its present status as a self regulating organisation and the premier Stock Exchange in the country.

It is the most popular stock exchange in the country.

The Exchange while providing an efficient market also upholds the interests of the investors and ensures redressal of their grievances, whether against the companies or the brokers It also strives to educate and enlighten investors by making available necessary informative inputs through the Training Institute.

The Governing Board is the apex body which regulates the Exchange and decides its policies. It comprises 9 elected directors, an Executive Director, three SEBI nominees, a Reserve Bank of India nominee and five public representatives who are persons of public eminence in the life of the city of Mumbai not directly connected with the securities business.

The President, the Vice-President and the Honorary Treasurer are annually elected from among the elected Directors, by the Governing Board following the election of Directors. The Executive Directors as the Chief Executive is responsible for the day-to-day administration of the Exchange.

Listing on Bombay Stock Exchange

A company which wishes to have its securities listed on the exchange has to comply with the listing requirements prescribed by the exchange. These are :

I. **Minimum listing requirements for new companies**

a) **Minimum Capital**

New companies can be listed on the exchange if their issued and subscribed capital after the public issue is ₹ 10 crores and the company should have a post-issue net worth of ₹ 20 crores.

In case of new companies in technology sector –

- Total income from the main activity should not be less than 75% of the total income during the two immediately preceding years.
- Minimum post-issue paid-up equity capital should be ₹ 5 crores.
- Minimum market capitalisation should be ₹ 50 crores.
- Post-issued net worth should be ₹ 20 crores.

b) **Minimum Public Offer**

i) Minimum 20 lakhs securities must be offered to the public and the minimum size of offer to public is ₹ 50 crores.

ii) **Minimum Listing Requirements for companies listed on other stock exchanges.**

- Company should have minimum issued and paid-up capital of ₹ 3 crores and a profit making track record for the last 3 years.
- Minimum net worth of company should be ₹ 20 crores.
- Market capitalisation should be at least two times of the paid-up capital.
- The company should have a dividend paying track record for the last 3 consecutive years and minimum dividend should be at least 10%.

- • At least 25% of the capital issued must be with Non-Promoter Shareholders.
- • The company should have at least two years listing record with any Regional Stock Exchange and sign an agreement with CDSL and NSDL for DEMAT trading.

iii) In case of companies de-listed by BSE and seeking re-listing a fresh public offer must be made as per prevailing guidelines of SEBI and BSE.

iv) The companies who desire to list their securities offered through public issue are required to obtain prior permission to use the name of the exchange in their prospectus which is obtained from a duly formed "Listing Committee" who evaluates the promoters, company, project and several other factors before taking any decision in this regard.

v) **Submission of Letter of Application** – As per Section 73 of the Companies Act, 1956, a company seeking listing of its securities on the Exchange is required to submit a letter of application to all the stock exchanges where it proposes to have its securities listed before filling the prospectus with the Registrar of Companies.

vi) **Allotment of Securities** – As per Listing Agreement a company is required to complete allotment of securities offered to the public within 30 days of the date of closure of the subscription list and approach the regional stock exchange i.e. stock exchange nearest to its registered office for approval of the basis of allotment. In case of book building issue, allotment shall be made not later than 15 days failing which 15% interest will have to be paid to the investor.

vii) **Trading Permission** – The issuer company should complete the formalities of trading at all stock exchanges where securities are to be listed within 7 working days of finalising the basis of allotment for obtaining trading permission.

viii) **Requirement of 1% Security** – The company has to deposit a refundable amount of 1% of the amount of issue with the regional stock exchange before the opening of issue as a security against any default by the company.

Trading System :

Trading is done by members and their authorized assistants for their Trader Work Stations (TWS) in their offices, through the BSE On-Line Trading (BOLT) system. BOLT system has replaced the open outcry system of trading, that used to take place in the trading ring. BOLT system accepts two way quotations from jobbers, market and limit orders filler from client - brokers and matches them according to the matching logic specified in the Business Requirement Specifications (BRS) document for this system. The matching logic for the Carry - Forward System as in the case of the regular trading system is quote - driven with the order book functioning as an "auxiliary jobber."

Earlier BSE had an open outlay system of trading but now it has shifted to a fully computerised mode of trading known as BOLT (BSE OnLine Trading) system w.e.f. 14th March, 1995. In this system member-brokers enter orders for purchase or sale of securities, from Trader Work Stations (TWS) installed in their offices, instead of assembling in the trading ring. So the entire trading is anonymous i.e. buyers and sellers do not know the names of each other. Trading is done from Monday to Friday between 9 : 55 a.m. and 3 : 30 p.m. (now the time has been changed) and the scrips traded have been classified into A, B1, B2 and Z groups which represent certain qualitative and quantitative parameters which include number of trades, value traded etc., for the guidance and benefit of investors. 'F' group represents the fixed income securities. The exchange has also commenced trading in Government Securities for retail investors under "G" group w.e.f. 16th January, 2003.

Settlement System :

Securities traded on BSE are classified into three groups, namely, specified shares or 'A' group and non-specified securities which are sub-divided into 'B1' and 'B2' groups. Presently, equity shares of 150 companies are classified as specified shares. These companies typically have a large capital base with widespread shareholding, steady dividend, good growth record and large volume of business in the secondary market. Contracts in this group are allowed to be carried over to subsequent settlements upto a maximum permissible period of 75 days.

1087 relatively liquid securities are placed in a category called 'B1' group. The remaining securities about 5000 as on 31st August, 1998 are placed in the 'B2' group. All newly listed securities are placed in the 'B2' group. Settlement of transactions is done on an 'Account Period' basis. The period is a calendar week in the case of 'A' and 'B1' and 'B2' groups from Monday to Friday.

During an account period, buy or sell positions in a particular security can be either squared up by entering into contra-transactions or can be further accumulated by entering into more buy or sell transactions.

Clearing System :

The Clearing House of the Exchange handles the share and the money parts of the settlement process in the case of 'A', 'B1' and 'B2' groups.

Transfer of Ownership

Transfer of ownership of securities is effected through a date stamped transfer- deed which is signed by the buyer and the seller. The duly executed transfer - deed alongwith the share certificate has to be lodged with the company for change in the ownership. A nominal duty becomes payable in the form of stamps to be affixed on the transfer - deeds. Transfer - deed remains valid for twelve months or the next book - closure following the stamped date whichever occurs later.

Brokerage and Other Transaction Costs :

i)   **Brokerage :** Negotiable, subject to a ceiling of 2.5 percent of the contract value or 25 paise per share whichever is higher.

ii)   **Stamp Duty :** The Stamp Duty is to be paid by the buyer while registering the share in his name. The rate is 50 paise for every ₹ 100/- or part thereof on the basis of amount of consideration.

Surveillance :

The Surveillance Department monitors the members on daily basis and scrutinises the prices and volumes of the scrips on a daily basis. It monitors the movement of scrips, detects market manipulations like price rigging etc., monitors abnormal prices and volumes not consistent with the normal trading pattern along with the inspection of member-brokers' position to reduce the possibility of default.

As per SEBI guidelines, the following steps are being taken to reduce defaults –

i)   **Circuit Filters :** The exchange applies a daily circuit filter of 20% on all the scrips whose price moves beyond the limit on any particular day.

ii)   In case of large variations in volumes of scrips, they are scrutinised and appropriate action is taken.

iii) The exchange also imposes special margins on scrips where it is suspected that there is an attempt to ramp up the prices by creating artificial volumes. The exchange also transfers the scrips for trading and settlement on a trade-to-trade basis resulting into giving/taking delivery of shares on a gross level.

iv)   The exchange has developed an OnLine Real Time (OLRT) Surveillance System w.e.f. 15th July, 1999 which generates online alerts whenever there is any abnormal variation in price, volume, position taken by members.

v)   Besides this there exists a database with the exchange regarding the lost, stolen or misplaced securities.

vi)   The Risk Management Department of the exchange has developed a client caution database to provide information to member brokers regarding the false/forged certificates issued by clients or sub-brokers. The member brokers have the database available with them and can issue it for further verification.

vii) The exchange has an inspection department to check the records of the member brokers regarding compliance of the risk management procedures.

Opportunities available for Foreign Investors :

i)   Direct investment

Foreign Companies are now permitted to have a majority stake in their Indian affiliates except in a few restricted industries. In certain specific industries, foreigners can even have holding upto 100 percent.

ii) Investment through Stock Exchange

Foreign Institutional Investors (FII) upon registration with the Securities and Exchange Board of India (SEBI) and the Reserve Bank of India (RBI) are allowed to operate in Indian Stock Exchanges subject to the guidelines issued for the purpose by SEBI. Important requirements under the guidelines are as under :

Portfolio investment in primary or secondary markets will be subject to a ceiling of 30 percent of issued share capital for the total holding of all registered FIIs in any one company. The holding of a signal FII in any one company is subject to a ceiling of 10 percent of the total issued capital. However, in applying the ceiling of 30 percent the following are excluded :

a) Foreign investment under a financial collaboration (DFI) which is permitted upto 51 percent in all priority areas.

b) Investment by FIIs through following alternative routes; Offshore Single/ Regional funds GDRs and Euro convertibles.

Disinvestment will be allowed only through a broker of a stock Exchange.

A registered FII is required to buy or sell only for delivery. It should not offset a deal. It is also not allowed to sell short.

iii) Investment in Euro Issues / Mutual Funds Floated Overseas

Foreign investors can invest in Euro issues of Indian companies and in India – specific funds floated abroad.

iv) Broking Business

Foreign brokers upon registration with the SEBI are now allowed to route the business of registered FIIs. Guidelines for this purpose have been issued by SEBI. However, foreign brokers at present are not allowed membership of Indian Stock Exchanges.

v) Asset Management Companies/Merchant Banking

Foreign Participation in Asset Management Companies and Merchant Banking Companies is permitted.

Basket Trading System :

The need of trading in a basket of scrips (forming part of a popular index like BSE Sensex) was felt by the investors who wish to link risk exposure of their portfolio only to the extent of the Sensex movements.

With a view to provide investors with this facility of creating Sensex linked portfolio and also to create a linkage of market prices of the underlying securities of Sensex in the Cash Segment and futures on Sensex, the Exchange has launched Basket Trading on BSE OnLine Trading (BOLT) System w.e.f. Monday, the 14th August, 2000.

In Basket Trading System, the investors would be able to buy/sell all 30 scrips of Sensex in the proportion of current weights in the Sensex, in one go. The investors need not calculate the quantity of Sensex scrips to be bought or sold for creating Sensex linked portfolios and this function would be performed by the system.

Profiling Baskets allow the investors to create their own baskets by deleting certain scrips from the total Sensex basket of 30 scrips but the weight of the scrips would be adjusted in such a manner that the *inter-se* relationship in terms of weights of the remaining scrips is maintained as it was in Sensex Basket.

Moreover, through Basket Trading system, the arbitrageurs would be able to take advantage of price differences in the underlying securities of Sensex and futures on the Sensex by simultaneous buying and selling of baskets, covering the Sensex scrips and Sensex Futures.

BSE 30 Sensitive Index Futures :

Underlying Stock Index	:	BSE 30 Sensex
Contract Size	:	50 times the Sensex
Ticket Symbol	:	BSX
Contract Months	:	3 nearest serial months, 3 series will be open for trading simultaneously
Trading Hours	:	Same as cash market
Last Trading Day	:	The last Thursday of the contract month, unless it is a holiday. If it is a holiday, the last trading day shall be the immediately preceding business day.
Trading Hours on Last Trading Day :		The expiring contract will close before normal trading hours on last trading day.
Minimum Price Fluctuation	:	0.1 Point of the BSE Sensex (equivalent to ₹ 5/-)
Final Settlement Basis	:	Cash settlement, on the last trading day the futures closing price will be calculated based on a set of 60 price points of cash Sensex values taken during the closure trading. The highest and lowest 10 price points will be ignored and the closing price will be computed as an average of the remaining 40 price points will be the closing price. This will be published on the BOLT screen and transmitted through two independent vendors.

Sensex Constituents

BSE - 30 Sensex, is the Benchmark Index of Indian Capital Market, and it comprises 30 scrips.

This is the first Index constructed by the Bombay Stock Exchange. Sensex measures the floating capitalisation of its constituents. SENSEX is calculated using the "Free-float Market Capitalisation" Methodology.

Constituents of Sensex as on 10th December, 2007

Code	Company Name
500410	ACC Ltd.
500425	Ambuja Cements Ltd.
500490	Bajaj Auto Ltd.
500103	Bharat Heavy Electricals Ltd.
532454	Bharti Airtel Ltd.
500087	Cipla Ltd.
532868	DLF Ltd.

Code	Company Name
500300	Grasim Industries Ltd.
500010	HDFC
500180	HDFC Bank Ltd.
500440	Hindalco Industries Ltd.
500696	Hindustan Unilever Ltd.
532174	ICICI Bank Ltd.
500209	Infosys Technologies Ltd.
500875	ITC Ltd.
500510	Larsen & Toubro Limited
500520	Mahindra & Mahindra Ltd.
532500	Maruti Suzuki India Ltd.
532555	NTPC Ltd.
500312	ONGC Ltd.
500359	Ranbaxy Laboratories Ltd.
532712	Reliance Communications Limited
500390	Reliance Energy Ltd.
500325	Reliance Industries Ltd.
500376	Satyam Computer Services Ltd.
500112	State Bank of India
532540	Tata Consultancy Services Limited
500570	Tata Motors Ltd.
500470	Tata Steel Ltd.
507685	Wipro Ltd.

2.1.5 NATIONAL STOCK EXCHANGE (NSE)

NSE is India's leading stock exchange covering more than 160 cities and towns across the country. It provides a modern fully computerised trading system designed to offer investors across the length and breadth of the country, a safe and easy way to invest or liquidate investment in securities. The need for setting up the National Stock Exchange arose from concerns of investors with the state of existing trading and settlement facilities. Investors in many areas of the country did not have the same access and opportunity to trade as their counterparts in Mumbai or the main metros. The NSE network has been designed to provide equal access to investors from anywhere in India and to be responsive to their needs. This translates into a single dynamic market across the country with greatly enhanced liquidity, unparalleled transparency and safety. Investors located in remote corners of the country are now able to transact with investors across the country with ease and efficiency.

National Stock Exchange of India (NSE) was set up in November 1992 under the recommendation of a high powered study group on establishment of new stock exchanges – The Pherwani Committee which recommended the setting up of NSE for removing the defects of the Indian Stock Market and provides equal access to investors across the country. NSE was promoted by leading financial institutions on behalf of the government of India and functioned as a tax paying company just like other existing stock exchanges.

It was recognised as a stock exchange in April 1993 under the Securities Contracts (Regulation) Act, 1956. In June 1994 a Wholesale Debt Market (WDM) segment was started and in November 1994 the Capital Market (Equities) segment commenced its operation. Tile operations of the Derivatives segment commenced from June 2000.

Ownership and Management :

NSE has set up facilities which serve as a model for the securities industry in terms of trading systems, practices and procedures. It has been set up as a public limited company, owned by leading institutional investors in the country. The ownership and management of the Exchange is distinct and separate from the right given to members to trade on the Exchange.

The affairs of the company are managed by its Board of Directors. Decisions relating to market operations are delegated by the Board to an Executive Committee which includes representatives from trading members. The Exchange has instituted several committees to advise it on various aspects of operations. These committees include industry professionals, trading members and Exchange staff. The day-to-day management of the Exchange is delegated to the Managing Director supported by a team of professional staff.

Emergence of National Stock Exchange of India is a landmark development during post liberalisation period. Consequent upon tectonic reforms in new economic policy leading to abolition of the office of the Controller of capital issues, greater autonomy to the Securities and Exchange Board of India (SEBI) for pricing of securities and greater concern for investor protection, need was felt for a country wide screen based online trading house. Accordingly, National Stock Exchanges of India was set up in Mumbai 1992 by all India Financial Institutions (IDBI, ICICI, LIC, GIC and its subsidiaries, commercial banks including State Bank of India with an equity capital of ₹ 25 crores) Key policy decisions are taken by the Board of Directors whereas operational decisions are taken by an Executive Committee under the overall supervision of the Board. NSE is an attempt to overcome the fragmentation of regional markets by providing a screen system which transcends geographical barriers.

Membership of National Stock Exchange (NSE)

Membership on the Exchange focuses upon professional capability of members to provide desired level of services to investors. The Board has laid down minimum eligibility criteria for membership of NSE. Realising the need to upgrade professional standards of market intermediaries, admission standards lay stress on factors such as track record, education, experience, capital adequacy, corporate structure, etc. Admission is a two stage process and applicants are required to clear a written examination followed by an interview.

The capital adequacy requirements are substantially in excess of the minimum statutory requirements as also in comparison to those stipulated by other exchanges. **Eligibility Criteria for Trading Membership of NSE** is shown below in Figure 2.7.

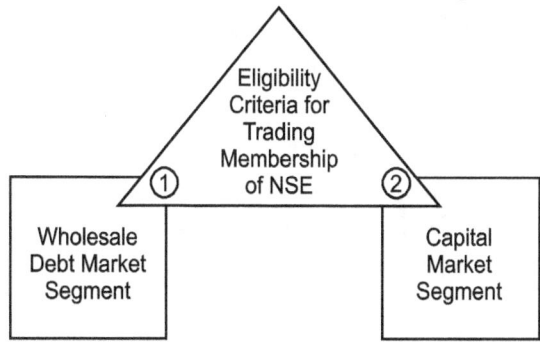

Fig. 2.7 : Eligibility Criteria for Trading Membership of NSE

The NSE admits members separately to the Wholesale Debt Market segment and the Capital Market segment. Only corporate members are admitted on the debt market segment whereas individuals and firms are also eligible on capital market segment.

1) **Trading Membership on Wholesale Debt Market Segment :**

The eligibility criteria for Trading Membership on the Wholesale Debt Market segment of the NSE are i) The persons eligible to become trading members are bodies corporate, subsidiaries of banks and institutions. ii) The whole-time directors or the dealers should possess at least two years' experience in any activity related to banking or financial services. iii) The applicant must possess a minimum networth of ₹ 2 crores.

2) **Membership on Capital Market Segment :**

The eligibility criteria for Capital Market segment are : i) Individuals, registered firms, corporate bodies and institutions are eligible to become trading members. ii) The minimum networth requirements prescribed are as follows – individuals and registered firms, ₹ 75 lakhs; corporate bodies, ₹ 100 lakhs. iii) The minimum prescribed qualification is graduation and two years experience of dealing in capital market must be fulfilled by : minimum two directors in case the applicant is corporate; minimum two partners in case of partnership firms; and the individual in case of individual or sole proprietary concerns.

The eligibility criteria common to both the segments are : i) The applicant must be engaged solely, in the business of securities and must not be engaged in any fund based activities. ii) The minimum paid up capital for corporate body should be ₹ 30 lakhs.

Functioning of Wholesale Debt Market (WDM) :

Wholesale Debt Market or the money market as it is commonly referred to, is a market where pure debt instruments such as Government securities, Treasury bills, Public sector bonds, Corporate debentures, Commercial paper, Institutional bonds and a variety of other debt securities are traded.

Individuals, corporate bodies, institutions, banks, Provident Funds are entitled to invest in the securities available for trading in the WDM segment. Besides, each security has its own feature and persons eligible to invest and the minimum amount may vary accordingly.

There are two types of entities in the system i.e. the Trading members and Participants. Trading Members who meet the admission criteria for membership to the WDM segment, can place orders and execute trades on the system on their own or on behalf of their clients. Participants take direct settlement responsibility for the trades executed on the Exchange on their behalf by an NSE trading member. Participants are large investors such as banks and institutions who are not members of the NSE and cannot therefore directly transact, but effect transactions through the NSE WDM members.

Investor – Grievances :

Common investor grievances observed in NSE are as follows :

i)   Non-receipt of shares sent for transfer.

ii)   Non-receipt of corporate benefits.

iii)   Non-rectification of bad delivery by the broker.

iv)   Non-receipt of funds/securities on sale/purchase.

v)   Introduction of fake, forged and stolen securities.

vi)   Non-rectification of company objections.

vii)   Contract notes not issued by the broker.

a) Investor complaints against Companies :

After initially forwarding the complaints to the company, a consistent follow-up is done. Companies which have a long history of pending investor complaints are instructed to maintain special personnel to tackle the pending complaints on a priority basis. In certain extreme cases, actions like suspension of trading of the securities is also taken.

b) Investor complaints against Brokers :

In the case of brokers, after they are intimated about the complaints, a reply is expected within 21 days of intimation. If necessary, further clarifications are asked for and the issue is settled to the satisfaction of the parties involved. On certain occasions, a personal hearing is granted to the parties involved to try and solve the matter amicably. If all efforts to solve the matter amicably fail then the matter will be referred for arbitration.

c) Role of investor in resolving grievances

According to the NSE, it is mandatory to sign a 'broker-client agreement' by the investor. The broker-client agreement document include the following terms and conditions which relate to order or trade confirmation; brokerage charged by the broker and delivery of security and funds. A clearly spelt out agreement reduces the scope for disputes. A format of the broker client agreement is available with all NSE brokers.

Objectives of National Stock Exchange (NSE)

The main objectives of NSE are as follows :

i) To play the role of a catalyst in Indian security market

The primary objectives for constituting NSE are to establish a nation-wide trading facility for equities, debt instruments and hybrids, to ensure equal access to investors all over the country through an appropriate communication network, to provide a fair, efficient and transparent securities market to investors using electronic trading systems, to enable shorter settlement cycles and book entry settlement system and to meet the existing inter-national standards of securities markets.

ii) To introduce state-or-art technology for providing transparent mechanism

The NSE market is the fully automated screen-based trading system. It uses the electronic trading system and computerised settlement system which is capable of being extended to every corner of the country through the media of electronic network. There is no trading floor as is prevalent in the traditional stock exchanger, nor do dealers use the telephone to arrange money market deals. Instead, the market operates with all market participants stationed at their offices and making use of computer terminals, to enter orders, to receive the current market status, the trades executed and other market related information.

iii) To provide enormous flexibility to trading members

The trading system provides enormous flexibility to trading members. When recording an order, a trading member can place various conditions on the order in terms of price, time or size. Orders are matched automatically by the Exchange Computer System.

National Stock Exchange and its Subsidiaries

NSE has the following subsidiaries :

i) **National Securities Clearing Corporation (NSCC) :** In its effort to further improve the settlement system and minimise risks associated therein, NSE has set up a subsidiary- National Securities Clearing Corporation (NSCC). On par with clearing corporations world over, NSCC will guarantee settlement of trades executed and settled through it.

NSCC was established in August 1995 as a wholly owned subsidiary of NSE. The objective of NSCC was to bring and sustain confidence in clearing and settlement of securities, to promote and maintain, short consistent settlement cycles; to provide counter-party risk guarantee and to operate a tight risk containment system. In April 1996, NSCC started clearing operations. Presently, it carried out the clearing and settlement of trades executed in the equities and derivatives segments and operates Subsidiary General Ledger (SGL) for settlement of trades in government securities. It assumes the counter-party risk of each member and guarantees financial settlement. It also undertakes settlement of transactions on other stock exchanges like OTCEI. The clearing and settlement mechanism of NSCC is in line with international markets.

For deals which are cleared and settled through, NSCC on behalf of its clearing members, the Corporation will become counter-party to the positions for settlement. In the event of a member becoming a defaulter, it will be the responsibility of the Corporation to complete the settlement. This will virtually eliminate counter-party risk of trading on the NSE. In order to do this it will be necessary for the NSCC to implement a combination of risk management measures including margining, tight monitoring and setting up of Settlement Fund so that its integrity is maintained all the time and risks are minimised.

The Settlement Fund is an important element of the guarantee process. The Fund operates like a self insurance mechanism. It is made up of contributions by members and in the event of member's default or failure to meet settlement obligations, the Fund is used to complete settlement. All trading members of NSE are automatically eligible to and are required to become clearing members of NSCC and the Settlement Fund has been set up by transferring 20% of the cash deposit of members to this Fund.

ii)   India Index Services and Products Ltd. (IISL) :

IISL is a joint venture between NSE and CRISIL Limited. It was setup in May 1998, to provide a variety of indices and index related services and products for the Indian capital markets. It has a consulting and licensing agreement with Standard and Poor's   (S & P) for cobranding equity indices. IISL provides a broad range of services, products and professional index services. It maintains over 80 equity indices comprising broad-based benchmark indices, sectoral indices and customised indices. Based on IISL indices, a number of investment and risk management products have been developed within India and abroad. They include index based derivatives traded on NSE and Singapore Exchange (SIMEX) and a number of index funds.

iii) National Stock Exchange of India and (NSEIT) :

NSEIT a 100% subsidiary of National Stock Exchange of India Limited is the information technology arm of the largest stock exchange of the country. NSEIT has state-of-the art infrastructure and skills.

It runs the trading and clearing infrastructure of NSE. NSEIT has the major focus on providing top-of-the line products, services and solutions in the area of trading, broker front-end and back office, clearing and settlement, web-based trading, risk management, treasury management, asset-liability management, banking, insurance etc. It has also been providing consultancy and implementation services in the areas of data warehousing, business continuity plans, status mainframe, facility management, site maintenance, real market analysis and financial news over NSE-Net etc. NSEIT has the plans to release products-for broker back-office operations and enhance neat XS/neat IXS to support straight through processing on the net.

iv)   National Securities Depository Limited (NSDL) :

NSF along with Industrial Development Bank of India (IDBI) and Unit Trust of India (UTI) setup the National Securities Depository Limited (NSDL), the first depository in India so as to solve the problems related to trading in physical securities.

NSDL commenced its operations in November 1996 and since then it has established national infrastructure of international standard to handle trading and settlement in dematerialised form. This has helped to eliminate the risks associated with false, bad or stolen paper.

v) Dot Ex International Limited (Dot Ex) :

Dot Ex was established as a joint venture between L-flex Solutions Ltd. & NSEIT Ltd. Dot Ex was introduced to provide a world-class internet trading platform which allows members of NSE to offer online trading facilities to their customers. With the help of this members of NSE can service a larger clientele by using automated risk management features and thus it increases volume of trading. It also enables the investors to get comprehensive and updated information necessary to trade along with single click convenience to fulfil their obligations. It provide a Dot Ex Plaza where multiple market participants such as members of NSE, depository participants and banks can offer web based services to their customers.

Electronic Trading System of NSE

NSE introduced for the first time in India fully automated screen based trading, thereby eliminating the need for physical trading floors. The brokers can now trade from their offices wherever they are located. They are connected to the Exchange from their workstations to the central computer located at the Exchange via. satellite using VSATs (Very Small Aperture Terminals). Buy and sell orders from the brokers reach the central computer located at NSE and are matched by the computer.

NSE has moved to electronic trading system which helps in providing wider reach and ease in trading. NSE's IT set-up uses satellite communication technology to connect around 400 cities around the country. The trading hardware of NSE can presently handle around 1 million trades per day. NSE's Internet Based Information System (NIBIS) helps in providing trading information over the internet. The exchange applications are being handled by the use of latest software platforms like RDBMS, ORACLE 7, ORACLE FORMS 4-5 etc. It manages its data center operations, system and database administration, development of in-house systems and design and implementation of telecommunication solutions. NSE has more than 4000 VSATs. It has also developed a corporate network connecting all the offices at Mumbai, Delhi, Kolkata and Chennai which enables speedy inter-office communications and data and voice connectivity between offices. NSE has gone online on the internet where live stock quotes can be seen on the website.

The following type of instruments are traded at NSE : i) Equity shares, ii) Preference shares, iii) Debentures, Deep Discount Bonds etc., iv) Warrants, v) Units of mutual funds.

As of now, more than 1400 companies are available for trading on the NSE. NSE is a national market and hence our endeavour is to provide for trading shares that have a regionally well dispersed interest. The companies are selected based on their paid-up capital, market capitalisation, dividend payment and a good track record. The criteria is meant to ensure that only companies that meet certain standards are listed. This list is reviewed at periodic intervals.

National Stock Exchange Indices

An index provides information about price movements of products in the financial, commodities and other markets. Price movements of stocks, bonds, T-Bills etc. are measured through financial indices. Stock Market indices are created by selecting a group of stocks that are representative of whole market or a specified sector or segment of the market. It reflects the overall behaviour of the equity markets.

With the objective of providing a variety of indices and Index related services, NSE has set-up India Index Service and Products Limited (IISL). IISL is a joint venture between National Stock Exchange of India Limited (NSE) and Credit Rating Information Services of India Limited (CRISIL). It has a consulting and licensing agreement with Standard and Poor's (S&P), the world's leading provider of investible equity indices, for co-branding IISL's equity indices.

Major Indices of NSE are as under :

1)	S & P CNX NIFTY	2)	CNX NIFTY Junior
3)	S & P CNX 500	4)	CNX Mid cap
5)	S & P CNX Defty	6)	CNX Mid cap 200

1) S & P CNX Nifty :

NSE 50 Index : The NSE-50 Index is a market capitalisation weighted index comprising 50 scientifically selected stocks having the highest liquidity and largest market capitalisation. Each stock has been given a weightage in the index equivalent to its market capitalisation. The capitalisation of 50 stocks as on 3rd November 1995 is taken as the base capitalisation and this value is set at 1000. Daily price change in index securities is captured in the market capitalisation figure and reflected in terms of index movement. The index value compares the day's market capitalisation vis-à-vis base capitalisation and indicates low-prices in general have moved over a period of time.

Nifty Constituents

S & P CNX Nifty is the first Index constructed by National Stock Exchange. Its construction is slightly different from the SENSEX. As we have seen before SENSEX measures the floating capitalisation of its constituents. However, Nifty takes the Full Capitalisation of its 50 constituents.

Constituents of Nifty as on 10th December, 2007

Symbol	Company Name
ABB	ABB Ltd.
ACC	ACC Ltd.
AMBUJACEM	Ambuja Cements Ltd.
BAJAJAUTO	Bajaj Auto Ltd.
BHEL	Bharat Heavy Electricals Ltd.
BPCL	Bharat Petroleum Corporation Ltd.
BHARTIARTL	Bharti Airtel Ltd.
CIPLA	Cipla Ltd.
DRREDDY	Dr. Reddy's Laboratories Ltd.

Symbol	Company Name
GAIL	GAIL (India) Ltd.
GLAXO	Glaxosmithkline Pharmaceuticals Ltd.
GRASIM	Grasim Industries Ltd.
HCLTECH	HCL Technologies Ltd.
HDFCBANK	HDFC Bank Ltd.
HEROHONDA	Hero Honda Motors Ltd.
HINDALCO	Hindalco Industries Ltd.
HINDPETRO	Hindustan Petroleum Corporation Ltd.
HINDUNILVR	Hindustan Unilever Ltd.
HDFC	Housing Development Finance Corporation Ltd.
ITC	ITC Ltd.
ICICIBANK	ICICI Bank Ltd.
INFOSYSTCH	Infosys Technologies Ltd.
LT	Larsen & Toubro Ltd.
MTNL	Mahanagar Telephone Nigam Ltd.
M & M	Mahindra & Mahindra Ltd.
MARUTI	Suzuki India Ltd.
NTPC	NTPC Ltd.
NATIONALUM	National Aluminium Co. Ltd.
ONGC	Oil & Natural Gas Corporation Ltd.
PNB	Punjab National Bank
RANBAXY	Ranbaxy Laboratories Ltd.
RCOM	Reliance Communications Ltd.
REL	Reliance Energy Ltd.
RELIANCE	Reliance Industries Ltd.
RPL	Reliance Petroleum Ltd.
SATYAMCOMP	Satyam Computer Services Ltd.
SIEMENS	Siemens Ltd.
SBIN	State Bank of India
SAIL	Steel Authority of India Ltd.
STER	Sterlite Industries (India) Ltd.
SUNPHARMA	Sun Pharmaceutical Industries Ltd.
SUZLON	Suzlon Energy Ltd.
TCS	Tata Consultancy Services Ltd.
TATAMOTORS	Tata Motors Ltd.
TATAPOWER	Tata Power Co. Ltd.
TATASTEEL	Tata Steel Ltd.
UNITECH	Unitech Ltd.
VSNL	Videsh Sanchar Nigam Ltd.
WIPRO	Wipro Ltd.
ZEEL	Zee Entertainment Enterprises Ltd.

S & P CNX NIFTY includes of 50 stocks and represents 23 sectors of the economy.

NIFTY is computed using weighted average market capitalisation method. (Ratio of weighted average market capitalisation of all stocks to the weighted average market capitalisation in the base period). The base period is 3rd November, 1995 and its value is 1000.

Criteria for Stock Selection in S & P CNX NIFTY :

- **Liquidity :** Liquidity of a stock is also called impact cost. Impact cost is the ratio of difference between actual Buy/Sell price to the Ideal Price calculated as (Best Buy + Best Sell) /2 i.e. it is the percentage mark-up suffered during buying/selling the desired quantity of Security as compared to its ideal price.
- For being included in the S & P CNX NIFTY the liquidity in terms of impact cost of 0.75% or less.
- The companies should have an average market capitalisation of ₹ 500 crores or more during the last six months.
- The companies should have at least 12%, stock not held by promoters and associated entities (i.e. floating stock).

  S & P CNX NIFTY Stocks represent 60% of the total market capitalisation.

2) CNX Nifty Junior :

CNX NIFTY Junior comprises 100 most liquid stocks in India. It is computed using weighted average market capitalisation method. Stocks in CNX NIFTY Junior are stocks with highest liquidity excluded from S & P CNX NIFTY. The base date for CNX NIFTY Junior is 3rd November, 1996 and base value is 1000.

Criteria for Selecting Stocks in CNX NIFTY Junior

- Liquidity (Impact cost) - The stocks with impact cost of 1.5% or less are included in the CNX NIFTY Junior Index.
- Market Capitalisation of Stocks for inclusion in this index should be ₹ 200 crores or more.
- At least 12% of the stocks should not be held by promoters and associated entities.

  CNX NIFTY JUNIOR represents 10% of the total market capitalisation.

3) S & P CNX 500 :

It is an Index which compares portfolios returns with market returns. The S & P CNX 500 companies are separated into 72 industry indices. The weightage of stocks in the Index is in accordance with the weightage of stocks in the market. For example, A company having 10% weightage in universe of stocks traded on NSE; then pharma stocks in the Index (S & P CNX 500) will also have around 10% representation in the Index. The Index is calculated using weighted average method. 1994 is the base year for the Index and base value is 1000.

Criteria for selection of Stocks for inclusion of S & P CNX 500

- Market Capitalisation.
- It should have industry representation i.e. Industry weightage in the Index must be representative of industry weightage in the market.

- The companies should have high turnover and high trading frequency along with a minimum listing period of 6 months.

- Companies should have positive net worth record of minimum 3 years.

4) CNX MIDCAP :

It represents the stocks of mid cap sector. It is computed on the basis of weighted average market capitalisation with base period as 1st January, 2003 and base value of 1000.

Criteria for Selection of Stocks for CNX Midcap –

- Market Capitalisation – First a list of all stocks in descending order of capitalisation is formed out of which those having more than 5% market capitalisation are excluded. The weightage and the cumulative weightage of remaining stocks is determined. These companies form upto 75% (i.e. 75% and less) of the cumulative percentage of 75%.

- Listing record of minimum 6 months.

- Positive net worth track record of 3 years.

5) S & P CNX DEFTY :

It is S & P CNX NIFTY measured in Dollars. It enables foreign institutional investors and off-shore funds to measure their performance. Its calculation is done as –

$$\text{S \& P CNX Defty} = \frac{\text{S \& P CNX NIFTY at time t} \times \text{Exchange rate as on base date}}{\text{Exchange rate at time t}}$$

Base date is 3rd November, 1995

Base value is 1000.

Exchange rate as on base date = 45.5 and Adjustment factor as on base date = 1.

6) CNX MIDCAP 200 :

It includes medium capitalisation companies and represents 72% of market capitalisation of Mid cap sector. Base date for Index is year 1994 and value is 1000.

Criteria for selection of stocks for CNX Mldcap 200

- Market Capitalisation – Midcap of the company's stock for being included in the index should be between 750-7500 crores.

- The weightage of industries in CNX Midcap is 200. Index represents weightage of industries in Midcap segment of the market.

- Listing record should be a minimum of 6 months.

- Company should have had a track record of positive net worth for at least 3 years.

Other Indices of NSE are –

1.	CNX IT Sector Index	2.	CNX Bank Index
3.	CNX FMCG Index	4.	CNX PSE Index
5.	CNX MNC Index	6.	CNX Service Sector Index
7.	S & P CNX Industry Indices	8.	Customised Indices.

2.1.6 OVER THE COUNTER EXCHANGE OF INDIA (OTCEI)

The OTCEI was set up in 1992 expressly to provide investors with a convenient, efficient and transparent platform for dealing in shares and stocks, and to help enterprising promoters set up new projects or expand their activities by providing them with an opportunity to raise capital in a cost effective manner.

The OTC Exchange is the ideal avenue for small and medium sized companies (with an issued capital ranging from ₹ 30 lakhs to ₹ 25 crores) to raise resources from the market through listing on it. OTC was the first stock exchange in the country to introduce state-of-the-art, screen-based, automated trading systems. Through its network of members, dealers and representative offices spanning the length and breadth of India, the OTCEI has turned the idea of nationwide trading into concrete reality.

Need for OTCEI

The term "over the counter" (OTC) was coined at a time when securities were traded over the counter of different dealers from their inventories. It is a way of trading securities other than on an organised stock exchange. Now, OTC markets are envisaged as floorless security trading systems equipped with computer network through which nationally and internationally scattered buyers and sellers can conduct business more efficiently.

The traditional stock exchanges have failed to provide facilities such as adequate liquidity to small scrips and access to small investors. Investors are losing the confidence in market because of lack of transparency of operations. To overcome these problems, the need for over-the-counter market arises so as to facilitate small investors, which can help in solving the problems of liquidity and inaccessibility. Members and dealers are important constituents of OTC Exchange of India (OTCEI) market. It will not have brokers like traditional stock exchange.

There were many companies which were innovative and had been undergoing technological revolution. These companies needed a platform to raise timely, cost effective and long-term capital so as to carry out their operations and enhance growth. They were unable to fulfill the listing requirement and the minimum capital limit for getting listed on large exchanges. So OTCEI was set-up for providing transparent and efficient mode of trading for smaller companies.

Public financial institutions, scheduled banks, mutual funds, banking subsidiaries, merchant banks and funds approved by SEBI and other non-banking financial companies having a minimum net worth of ₹ 2.5 crores - would be members of OTCEI. The important factors behind the growth of floorless electronic trading system is that it eliminates defects of present trading system which are designated more to maximise brokerage and less to minimise investors transaction cost. OTCEI thus ensures transparency and strengthens investors' confidence in the market.

Legal Status of OTCEI

OTC Exchange of India is a company incorporated under Section 25 of the Companies Act, 1956, with the objective of setting up a national, ringless, screen-based, automated stock exchange. OTC Exchange, recognised as a stock exchange under Section 4 of the securities Contract Regulation Act 1957, is promoted by the all-India financial institutions, insurance companies and merchant banking subsidiaries of banks. The top executives of the promoters are on its Board of Directors.

Promoter of OTCEI

Its promoters are : Unit Trust of India; Industrial Credit & Investment Corporation of India; Industrial Development Bank of India; SBI Capital Markets Ltd; Industrial Finance Corporation of India; Life Insurance Corporation of India; General Insurance Corporation of India and its subsidiaries; and Canbank Financial Services Ltd. Players in the market will be members, dealers, companies and 'investors, supported by registrars/custodian, settlor, bank. OTC operations will be supervised by SEBI and Government of India.

The number of shares held and shareholding pattern of the promoters is shown below in a Table.

Table 2.1: Share of Promoters in OTCEI

Institution	Number of Shares held	Share holding pattern (%)
UTI	20,00,000	20
ICICI	20,00,000	20
IFCI	8,00,000	8
LIC	8,00,000	8
IDBI	17,00,000	17
GIC	1,60,000	1.6
SBI Capitals Ltd.	11,00,000	11
Can bank Financial Service	8,00,000	8
New India Insurance	1,60,000	1.6
Oriental Insurance	1,60,000	1.6
United India Insurance	1,60,000	1.6
National Insurance	1,60,000	1.6
Total	**1,00,00,000**	**100.00**

The top executives of the promoters are on the Board of Directors of the OTCEI, OTC operations are supervised by SEBI and Government of India.

Participants in OTC Market

The various participants in the OTCEI are :

i) **Members and Dealers appointed by OTCEI**

These members and dealers may act as brokers and serve as market makers.

Market making is a process of making two way quotes i.e. buy as well as sell quotes for the same scrip by the sponsor. The maximum permissible spread between the buy and sell is 10%. Compulsory market making has to be undertaken by the sponsor of the scrips for a minimum period of 18 months from the date of public trading. At the end of 18 months, the sponsor may withdraw for market making functions, provided an alternate compulsory market maker has been assigned for the scrip. The sponsor will arrange one or more members/dealers to make market in the scrip sponsored by it, known as Additional Market Maker.

The compulsory and additional market maker must hold atleast 5% of public offering between themselves for the purpose of market making.

The members, in addition, carry out the vital function of sponsorship. The criteria of sponsorship involves :

a) appraising a company at its project.

b) certifying to OTCEI the investment worthiness of the company and its project.

c) valuing the shares of the company.

d) obtaining governmental clearances for the issue of shares.

e) managing the public issue of securities.

f) servicing as a market maker in the issued scrip for atleast 3 years from the date of trading commences.

The member of OTCEI may be an institution, a banking subsidiary, a merchant bank or a finance company approved by SEBI.

ii) Companies, who securities are listed on OTCEI

Every company desirous of listing would have to get sponsored by a member of the OTCEI.

iii) Investors who trade in the OTCEI

iv) Registrar

a) Keeps custody of share certificates.

b) Maintains Register of Members.

v) Settlement Bank

It clears the payment between counters.

vi) SEBI and Government which exercises an overall supervision on OTCEI

| **Features of OTCEI** |

The main features of OTCEI are as mentioned below :

i) The trading will not be in the traditional 'ring' but it will be 'screen-based'. Investors can walk into any of the counters of members and dealers, see the quote-display on the screen, decide to deal and conclude the transaction. All the counters of members and dealers will be connected by a telecom network to the OTC Central computer.

ii) OTC trading also provides for transfer of shares by registrars, upto a certain percentage per portfolio. This results in faster transfers. The concept of immediate settlement, instead of longer settlement periods, makes it better for the investor. Investor will trade, not with share certificates but with a different tradeable document called CR (Counter Receipt). However, he can always exercise his right of having a share certificate by surrendering the CR and again exchanging the share certificate for CR when he wants to trade. There will be a custodian who will provide this facility, along with a settlor who will do the signature verification and CR validation.

iii) The scrips listed on the OTC Exchange will be 'sponsored' by its members. Members, when they sponsor, research the scrip and recommend investment-worthiness of the scrip. As sponsors, members will be compulsorily making market in that scrip, which ensures liquidity. This compulsory market-making provides for availability of both buy and sell quotes for the scrip, from the sponsor of the scrip.

iv) Trading on the OTCEI takes place through a network of computers of OTC dealers located at different places within the same city and even across the cities. These computers allow dealers to quote, query and transact through a central OTC computer using the telecommunication links.

v)   Small and medium sized companies with a paid up capital between ₹ 30 lakhs and ₹ 10 crores maybe enlisted on the OTCEI. The maximum limit has now been raised to ₹ 25 crores.

vi) OTCEI deals in equity shares, preference shares, bonds, debentures and warrants.

vii) A company which is listed on any other recognised stock exchange in India is not permitted simultaneously for listing on OTCEI.

viii) The minimum offer should be 40% of the issued capital or ₹ 20 lakh worth of shares in face value, whichever is higher.

Global Scene of OTC Exchange

An OTC Exchange is totally different from the existing systems of trading shares in the stock exchanges. The objective behind establishing OTCEI was to have stock exchange in the country having automated computerised trading. Unlike the conventional stock exchanges, there is no trading hall or exchange of share certificates. Instead, the trading is done through computers by the dealers operating right from their offices.

In 1971, a ringless electronic security trading system represented by US-NASDAQ (United States, National Association of Security Dealers Automated Quotation System) became operative. It has served as a role model for other countries to emulate and grow-JASDAQ (Japanese Association of Security Dealers Automated Quotation System) in Japan, SEAQ (Stock Exchange Automated Quotation System) in London.

In U.S. more than 90% corporate bonds are traded on the OTC market and most of them are listed on the New York Stock Exchange. Virtually, all the securities traded at NYSE are also being traded over the OTC market through a third market. The 'third market' is subset of secondary market of NYSE and part of the OTC market where primarily, those securities listed on the NYSE are traded. The market consists of security dealer-broker, who make the market in different securities and stand ready to buy or sell securities of any depth (quantity). These market-makers are in direct competition with the specialists of the NYSE.

OTC Exchange of India has picked the Model from the NASDAQ system (National Association of Securities Dealers – Automated Quotations) prevalent in the United States of America. Modifications suiting to Indian conditions have been adopted.

OTC in America was an off shot of the Government efforts to regulate the United Securities Market. Today, NASDAQ market is the fourth largest in the world next only, in turnover, to New York, Tokyo and Korean Stock Exchanges. Its turnover is supposed to be in the range of US $ 670 billion in 1991 which is equivalent to almost 70% of the turnover on the New York Stock Exchange. Some of the biggest turnover names like, apple computer, which started as small venture companies and now grown into multinational giants, still continue to be quoted on the NASDAQ system of USA.

The Indian version of NASDAQ (National Association of Securities Dealers) is what is called as OTC Exchange of India (OTCEI, in brief). It is the country's only electronic screen-based exchange.

Eligibility for Listing on OTC

a)   A company with a paid-up capital of more than ₹ 30 lakhs and less than ₹ 2500 lakhs can list its shares on the OTC Exchange.

b)   Companies engaged in leasing, hire-purchase, finance, investment, amusement park etc. are not eligible for listing on it.

c)   Companies listed on any other recognised stock exchange in the country cannot simultaneously list their shares on it.

d)   Companies covered under MRTP/FERA may be listed on it, if they satisfy the listing guidelines on other recognised stock exchanges.

Conditions :

a)   The guidelines on pricing, underwriting, public offer percentage, promoters' contributions, lock-in period, reservation in issues, instruments etc., as issued by and modified by SEBI from time to time, need to be followed by the company;

b)   The company needs to have one of the members of OTC Exchange of India as a sponsor;

c)   The company should pay one-time listing fee of ₹ 6,000 and annual listing fees of 0.05% of the issued capital of the company;

d)   The company must follow all listing requirements of OTECI and comply with its regulations and provisions of the listing agreement;

e)   The company needs have a minimum of 4 collection centres for application forms, one each from the Northern, Southern, Eastern and Western regions of the country;

f)   All member and dealer counters shall be provided with issue stationery, at least 21 days prior to the issue;

g)   Listing on the OTC Exchange will be permitted only after the Company has obtained necessary statutory approvals such as under MRTP and FERA, etc. and necessary Government clearances such as the License/ Registration, Capital Goods Clearance, Foreign Collaboration Clearance, etc. as are applicable;

h)   Publicity to an issue of securities to the public will be subject to the approval of OTCEI and guidelines issued by SEBI and the Government;

i)   OTCEI will prescribe such time limit not exceeding current statutory provisions on the company and its sponsors to complete the process of allotment of securities, compilation of the list of allottees and refundees and mailing of CRs and refund cheques;

j)   It will prescribe the interest to be paid to investors in case of delay in delivery of CR/refund cheque. It may also levy penalties as decided by it on the company or its sponsor for such delay within the prescribed statutory provisions;

k)   The company will authorise OTCEI empanelled registrar to transfer the shares not exceeding 0.5% of the issued capital per folio. The transfers exceeding this limit will be processed by the company within 18 days from the date of lodgement;

l)   The offer for sale of Document or Prospectus or any other issue document will be subject to clearance by SEBI and/or OTCEI.

m)   Its decision on granting/not granting listing will be final. In addition, the conditions under which a company can be delisted will be specified in the listing agreement; and

n)   OTCEI reserves the right to revise, delete any of the above conditions or add new conditions.

Listing Requirements :

For getting listed on OTCEI :

i)   A company should have a minimum paid-up capital of ₹ 30 lakhs and the minimum offer to the public should be 25% of the issue capital or ₹ 20 lakhs worth of shares in face value whichever is higher. All the issues should be as per SEBI guidelines on Disclosure and Investor Protection.

ii)   Every company that intends to get listed must be sponsored by a merchant banker of the exchange. The sponsor of the issue must arrange for Market Makers to give Buy and Sell quotes in the securities for an initial period of 18 months.

In addition, companies which fulfil the following conditions are eligible to apply :

i)   3 year dividend paying record in the last 5 years.

ii)   Sponsored by a Member/Sponsor of OTCEI.

iii)   Have at least 2 market makers for continuous liquidity to their shares.

In case of companies not fulfilling 3 year 0ividend record/financial institution appraisal or funding criteria may go for Bought-Out-Deals.

Along with the above mentioned norms all Public Limited Companies have to fulfill the following criteria to get themselves listed on OTC.

i) **Company Valuation :**

Net Tangible Assets (or)	₹ 1 crore (or)
Market Capitalisation (or)	₹ 5 crore (or)
Net Income (in latest fiscal year or 2 of last 3 fiscal years)	₹ 0.25 crores

ii) **Shareholding :**

Minimum Total Float (shares)	11,00,000
Minimum Public Float (shares)	5,00,000
Market value of Public Float	₹ 2.50 crores
Minimum offer to the public (as % of total paid-up capital)	25%
Minimum number of shareholders	1000

iii) **Market Making :**

Number of Market Makers	Minimum 2
Duration of Market Making	18 months
Obligation	Mandatory
Market making inventory (at the time of public issue)	Graded

iv) **Company Fact File**

Operating History (or)	1 year (or)
Minimum Market Capitalisation	₹ 5 crore
Corporate Governance	Yes
Compliance Standards	No defaults

Additional Requirements for Finance Companies

Registration with RBI	Compulsory
As NBFC	
Investment Grade Rating	In case of FDs or debenture issues
Continuous Profitability	Past 3 years
Market Making Inventory	
Principal and Additional Market Maker	10% minimum together
Debt Equity Ratio	As per RBI guidelines

Continuous Listing Requirements

The trading in equity shares of the company commences 3 days after the company is listed. Post listing, the company is required to provide a bank guarantee of 1% of the issue amount in favour of OTCEI for complying with continuous requirements. Apart from this, the following are the continuous listing essentials.

i) Company Valuation

Net Tangible Assets	0.75 crores or
Or Market Capitalisation	3.75 crores or
Or Net Income (in latest fiscal year or last 3 fiscal years)	0.15 crores

ii) Shareholding

Minimum Total Float (shares)	8,25,000
Minimum Public Float (shares)	3,75,000
Market value of Public Float	₹ 1.90 crores
Minimum offer to the public (as % of total paid-up capital)	25%
Minimum number of shareholders	1000

iii) Company Fact File

Operating History (or)	N/A (or)
Minimum Market Capitalisation	₹ 3.75 crore
Corporate Governance	Yes
Compliance Standards	No Defaults

Procedure for Listing

- The company first appoints a sponsor. A sponsor does not participate in secondary market activities and only sponsors the issue.
- A sponsor appoints a market maker, who is actually involved in trading and underwriting activities for the issue.
- After this, the registration application (with relevant documents) is submitted to get approval which is valid for 6 months.
- A draft prospectus is then submitted with OTCEI for approval.
- After this Notice of Issue is submitted.
- The basis of allotment of securities is finalised.
- Listing application is filed.

The initial listing fee is ₹ 7,500.

The annual listing fee is as follows :

Paid-up Capital	Amount of Annual Fees
Up to ₹ 3 crores	₹ 7,500
₹ 3-10 crores	₹ 15,000
₹ 10-20 crores	₹ 25,000
₹ 20-50 crores	₹ 40,000
₹ 50-100 crores	₹ 85,000
₹ Above ₹ 100 crores	₹ 1,000 for every ₹ 10 crores or part thereof of the capital

Trading in OTC Exchange

Every investor is required to register with OTC prior to trading. The investor registration is required to be done only once and is valid for trading on any OTC counter in the country and in any scrip. The registration is, at present, done free of cost. The purpose of investor registration is to facilitate computerised trading.

For buying and selling shares on OTC, an investor needs the INVEST OTC CARD which can be obtained from any OTC counter free of any charge just on filling the application form.

Investor Registration : This is a new concept to be introduced by the OTC Exchange of India. Every investor who trades on the OTC Exchange has to be registered with the exchange. He can either apply for registration along with the application for the issue, or he has to get himself registered by giving the investor registration form, duly filled in to any one of the OTC counters. Investor registration is required to be done once and is valid for trading on any OTC counter in the country and is free of cost, for the time being.

The purpose of the investor registration is to facilitate computerised trading. It also provides greater safety of operation to the investors. Each investor will be given a unique investor number and investor registration card, mentioning the registration details. Any modifications to be made, should be similarly applied for and registered. The investor has to reproduce the details, original or modified, exactly as mentioned in his registration card.

Trading Documents : Following are its trading documents : TCR – Temporary Counter Receipt; PCR – Permanent Counter Receipt; SCS – Sale Confirmation Slip;   TD – Transfer Deed; Services Application Form; AAS – Application Acknowledgement Slip; Deal Form.

Trading Procedure : An investor can buy any listed scrip at any OTC Counter; likewise, he can sell any listed scrip at any OTC Counter. The investor can also make an application for services like : transfer of shares, splitting and consolidation of shares, nomination and revocation of nomination, registering power of Attorney, transmission of shares and change of holders names.

Parties involved in OTC Trading are shown below in Figure 2.8.

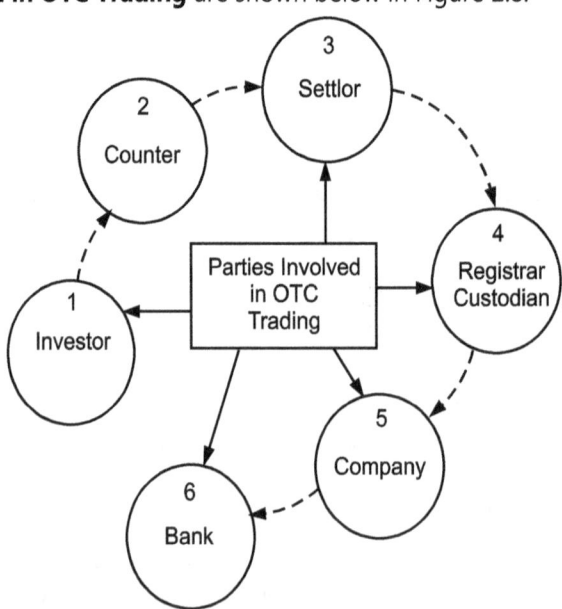

Fig. 2.8 : Parties involved in OTC Trading

1) Investor :

The investor has to be registered before doing any business in the OTC market. Investor registration form and each of the trading documents will contain instructions advising him as to how to fill up the form and how to proceed. It will also have the terms and conditions which the investor has to follow and comply with, before making use of such documents.

An investor can deal in any scrip by going to any OTC Counter. In case of any grievances against any specific counter, the investor can approach the OTCEI office.

2) Counter :

Counters, operated by members or dealers, will trade in all the scrips listed on the OTC Exchange. They will display the OTC quotes on the PTI-OTC Scan and allow all investors coming to them, to trade during market hours. Counters will use their computer and data communication equipment as per the instructions given in OTCEI's Counter User Manual 'ASTOCS' and as per business rules specified and amended by it from time to time. Counters also have to comply with clauses of the Code of Conduct. At every counter, the investor can see the quotes on the PTI-OTC Scan and can query for all quotes (standard, non-standard or both) and for service. The investor also has a choice to decide to have a deal at either the system price or a negotiated price.

3) Settlor :

All documents generated by counters go to the settlor for record keeping and the settlor monitors the movement of documents. The settlor keeps a record of the signatures of all investors and all counter signatories for all scrips. The settlor verifies the signatures of investor and counter on the CR sent to him by any counter, checks for the genuineness of the CR and sends the confirmation to the respective counter within a fixed time.

In case of a transfer, the settlor receives the CR with the TD, which is verified and passed on to the Registrar, for effecting the -transfer. The application for splitting or consolidation and exchange of CR for share certificates and exchange of Share certificates for CR, are also checked by the settlor and sent to the Registrar/Custodian.

4) Registrar/Custodian :

The registrar is the agent appointed by the company to perform the necessary act in case of allotment, to transfer the shares not exceeding 0.5% of the Company's capital per folio, to maintain a register of members and to keep in custody the share certificates of the company to be exchanged with CRs when the investor requests.

The registrar keeps in its records, signatures and other details of allotees and checks for the records when it receives CR and TD from settlor for effecting a transfer and updates the members register and signature records accordingly. Once the transfer formalities are completed, the Registrar informs the respective counters.

The similar procedure is followed by the Registrar/Custodian for applications for nomination and revocation of nomination, registering Power-of- Attorney, transmission, change of holders name to the extent the register of member is affected.

5) Company :

The company will provide all material information having direct or indirect bearing on the price of shares in the market.

The registrar refers transfers exceeding 0.5% of the capital per folio to the company, for which the company in turn has to effect a transfer within a specified time.

6) Bank :

A central clearing bank on the trading network will clear inter-counter deals. In a short while its services will be extended to investors, to provide automatic bank transfers of funds for their trades on the OTC Exchange.

Steps Involved in Buying and Selling Scrips :

i)   Walk into any convenient OTC counter.

ii)   The PTI-OTC Scan at each dealer's counter continuously displays the best buy and sell quotes offered by market makers and also all other market related information.

      All quotes and transactions ate entered in the Central OTC computer which can be accessed by any dealer's computer, through telephone lines with modems.

iii) See the price of shares on the PTI-OTC scan at the counter.

iv)   Decides to buy/sell.

v)   Ask counter operator to deal on your behalf.

vi)   Deal gets confirmed automatically at the best price.

vii) In case of buying :

      a)   make cheques for payment.

      b)   get the Counter Receipt (CR). The CR is tradeable and contains all information which appears on a share certificate.

      c)   Return CR when cheque is cleared.

      d)   Collect final CR within 7 days.

In Case of Selling :

a)   Give CR and Transfer Deed (TD) to counter.

b)   Receive Sales Confirmation Slip.

c)   Return when CR and TD are cleared and collect cheque.

Various **steps involved in Buying and Selling Scrips** are shown below in Figure 2.9.

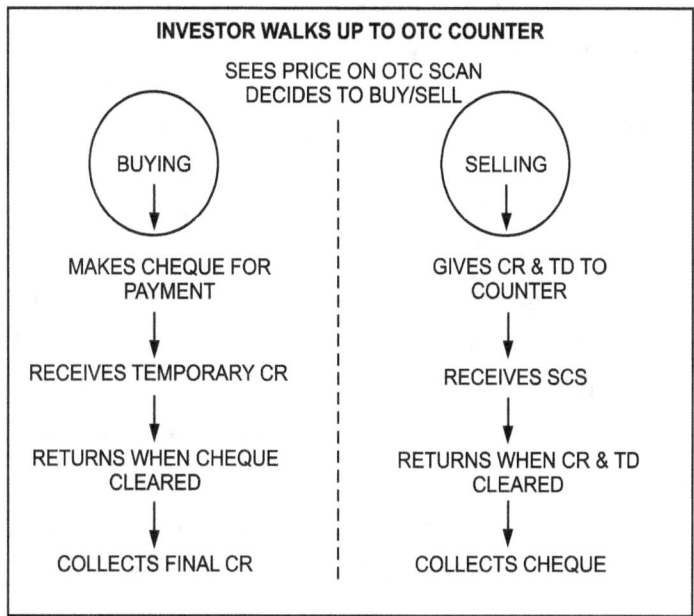

Buying and Selling

Fig. 2.9 : Steps involved in Buying and Selling Scrips

Depository System :

The OTCEI's unique depository system enables convenient and faster settlement for investors. The OTCEI's depositors transfers delivery electronically to the purchaser as soon as the trade is completed. Share certificates are not delivered to the purchaser. Their movement in a national market is wrought with risk and operational delays. The OTCEI's depository system minimises the possibilities of bad deliveries on the exchange by ensuring the validity of the seller's transfer deed at the time of transfer as on the other exchanges. The settlement on the OTC exchange takes place on a rolling basis three days after the day of trade. This means faster payments to the seller and faster deliveries to the buyer.

The OTC Exchange offers a whole lot of investor services, viz. :

i)   Splitting/consolidation of PCRs (Counter Receipt).

ii)   Transfer/nomination.

iii) Change in joint holder's names.

iv)   Exchange of PCR for share certificate and vice-versa.

The OTC Counter is truly a single window for investments. For each of the above services requested by investors, an Application Acknowledgement Slip (AAS) will he issued, nominal service charges may be levied and the services will be completed within reasonable time specified by OTCEI.

Dealership of OTCEI

Corporate bodies, partnership firms, individuals can be its dealers. Corporate bodies should satisfy the following eligibility requirements.

Net worth : Minimum tangible liquid net worth amount will be specified. This should be sufficient to carry on investment, trading, market making in the scrips listed on OTC Exchange.

Infrastructure : Office space; Computers; PTI Scan; Telephones (minimum 2); Telex; Fax; any other data communication equipment specified.

Qualifications : Minimum educational qualification for applicant will be graduation. Additional weightage will be given for additional related professional qualifications.

Experience : Experience in trading, stock valuation, share transfer rules and related laws.

Upcountry services/sub-brokers network : Branch offices; broking arrangements, with details of sub-brokers; developed investor base.

Selection : Advertisement will be released in a newspaper announcing OTCEI's intention of appointing dealers. Prescribed application forms are available at the OTC Exchange of India.

Applications received on or before the specified last date will be processed. Candidates short listed, based on the information available in the respective application forms, may be asked to undertake a written examination. The successful candidates are interviewed by a Selection Panel.

Terms and Conditions for Dealership :

The conditions for OTC dealership are as follows :

i)   If the applicant is a corporate body, the promoters should hold at least 40% of the equity capital.

ii)   In case of change in dealership from individual/partnership firm to corporate body, original individual dealer/partners of the partnership firm should hold atleast 40% of the capital of the new corporate body.

iii) Partnership firms and corporate applicants must nominate one of the authorised signatories whose qualifications will be considered for eligibility and the same person will be required to take a written test and appear for an interview.

iv)   Dealership is not transferable.

v)   If there is a change in the shareholding of a corporate body who is a dealer, resulting in change in ownership/management, OTC Exchange of India reserves the right to review the status of dealership of that dealer.

vi)   Any other conditions stipulated in the advertisement and application form need to be complied with.

Guidelines issued by the SEBI in Connection with the Working of OTCEI

SEBI relaxed norms for listing on the OTCEI during March 1995.

i) Finance and leasing companies were allowed to get listed on OTCEI.

ii) The minimum post issue capital to be offered to the public to enable listing was lowered from 40 percent to 25 percent.

In April, 1995, OTCEI modified its guidelines to allow listing of finance companies with more stringency.

i) The minimum issued capital was increased from ₹ 30 lakh to ₹ 1 crore for finance companies.

ii) A three year track record of profitability was made compulsory before listing took place.

iii) OTCEI sponsor of these companies should hold atleast 10% of the public offer as market making inventory as against 5 percent for other companies.

To facilitate offers for sale of bought out deals, OTCEI changed its guidelines in January 1996. The revised guidelines did away with the requirement of making an offer for sale of the entire bought out deal to the public, except the market making inventory. The offerer can now offer a minimum 25 percent of the bought out deals to the public. At the same time, the ratio of involvement of OTCEI members to non-OTCEI members has been brought down from 60 : 40 to 10 : 90.

The new guidelines issued by the SEBI stated that any company wanting to make a public issue should have a track record of dividend payment, for atleast three years immediately preceeding five years before making the public issue.

If the companies do not satisfy this requirement, then they must atleast get their project appraised by a financial institution or a nationalised bank which would participate in the public issue to the extent of atleast 10 percent of the total outlay in the form of equity or long term debt.

With a view to review the working of the OTCEI and to make recommendations for its further improvement, SEBI appointed an eight member committee under the chairmanship of Dr. S. A. Dave on 17th April, 1996.

The recommendations of the Dave Committee are as follows :

i) The companies which are unable to make public issue as a consequence of the above guidelines be allowed with some checks.

ii) The companies which do not satisfy the criteria should be allowed to get listed on the OTCEI provided they appoint a sponsor and two market makers to the issue.

iii) Companies which get delisted from regional stock exchanges should be allowed to list on OTCEI since shareholders of delisted companies do not have a platform to offload their holdings. These companies should, however, be treated under a special category on the OTCEI.

iv)   The companies discussed above should be allowed listing on the OICEI with a minimum lock in period of three years. After three years, these companies may either choose to remain on the OTCEI or seek listing on other stock exchanges.

v)   The ceiling of ₹ 25 crore on the equity capital of a company seeking listing on the OTCEI be removed.

vi)   The current rolling settlement system of three days should be increased to five years.

vii)   The committee stressed upon the need of increased involvement of the promoters of OTCEI.

Advantages of OTCEI

a) **To the Investors**

The OTCEI offers the following advantages to the investors :

i) **Safety**

Every investor on the OTCEI is provided with an Invest OTC card that comes absolutely free. This card can be obtained at any counter by filling a simple form or when one is allotted shares for OTC issues. The 'Invest OTC' code is given once and is permanent. This code should be used for all transactions and applications for OTC issues. This Invest OTC card ensures the safety and security of one's investment.

ii) **Transparency**

The exact price at which your order was executed along with the 2% brokerage cargo is printed on the confirmation slip. The investors have access to current prices of all scrips being traded on the PTI scan display. This ensures transparency in trading.

iii) **Liquidity**

Every OTC scrip has at least two market makers, for a period of 12 moths from the commencement of trading, who continuously offer buy/sell quotes.

iv) **Quality of Companies**

Every scrip listed on OTCEI has a sponsor from among the OTC members. The sponsor appraises the company for investor worthiness and commits to provide liquidity to the scrip by market making, thus ensuring higher quality of companies.

v) **Access**

Every OTCEI counter acts as a single window to the entire OTC Exchange which means an investor can buy/sell at the nearest counter. The OTC network is spread across 25 cities in India and is rapidly expanding.

OTCEI is an active market and has been receiving a positive response from investors in Indian markets. OTCEI proposes to introduce a vibrant and a well regulated market structure for trading in unlisted securities thereby giving an exit option for venture capital/private equity, offshore Funds and other institutions and corporates. This provides improved investment opportunities in start-up enterprises, especially in the growth sectors with its new initiatives and developments. OTCEI has been setting benchmarks and proving to be of benefit to the corporates and individual investors of India.

b)　The OTCEI offers the following advantages to the company

i)　Small and medium sized companies would be able to raise required capital through OTCEI.

ii)　The cost of public issue is low.

iii)　The company gets high visibility at national level.

iv)　Dependable source of funds through structured bought out deals at reasonable prices.

v)　The companies listed on OTC would be subjected to low income tax.

vi)　The cumbersome process of obtaining the listing of the share may not be there for listing on OTC Exchange.

vii)　Companies which require listing on OTCEI have to offer 10% of the share capital for listing as against 60% being the offer to the public in other stock exchanges.

viii)　Investors preference to deal in transparent and efficient exchange.

ix)　Strong support for the share in secondary market through the presence of committed market makers.

Comparison between Stock Exchange, OTCEI and NSE

Points of Difference	Stock Exchange	OTCEI	NSE
i)　Meaning	Most stocks are traded on exchanges which are placed where buyers and sellers meet and decide on a price. Exchanges are physically locations, where transactions are carried out on a trading floor.	OTC exchange, ushering in a new era in capital markets, has unique features of its own which make it the market of the future. OTCEI was set up in 1992.	NSE is a step to overcome the deficiencies of the existing stock market and to bring Indian financial markets in line with international markets. Incorporated in Nov. 1992.
ii)　Membership	Individuals, firms and corporates.	Corporates only.	Individuals, firms and corporates.
iii)　Method of Training	Floor based	Screen based	Screen based
iv)　System of Trading	Quote-driven manual	Code driven	Order driven
		Computers linked to central OTCEI through telephone lines	Computer inked by satellite through VSAT.
v)　Settlement	T + 14	T + 3 rolling settlement	Same day to T + 5 in WDM Standard Delivery in Equity market
vi)　Transparency	NIL	Ensured	Total transparency
vii)　Intermediary	Jobber needed	Not needed	Not needed

2.2 PRIMARY MARKET

The primary market is where securities created (by means of an IPO) in other words provide the channel for sale of new securities. Primary market provides opportunities to issuers of securities; Government as well as corporates, to raise resources to meet their requirements of investment and/or discharge some obligation.

Corporates may issue the securities at face value, or at a discount/premium and these securities may take a variety of forms such as equity, debt etc. They may issue the securities in domestic market and/or international market.

Primary market or New issue market deals with the issue of new securities to the investors and facilitates the corporate sector in raising funds. Major type of securities issued are equity shares, preference shares and debentures. Equity shares have all along been the most preferred instrument for mobilising resources by the public corporate sector Both existing and new companies raise funds from the new issue market. The primary market is made up of two components: where firms go public for the first time (through initial public offerings or IPOs) and where firms which are already traded raise additional capital (through seasoned, equity offerings or SEOs). Initial capital is raised by issuing only ordinary and preference shares whereas further capital can be raised by selling all the three types of securities. Once the new issues in the primary market are floated and subscribed, these instruments are traded in the secondary market. Secondary market does not play any direct role in making funds available to corporates. Its role in this respect is to provide liquidity to securities issued in the primary market.

Distinction between Primary Market or New Issue Market and Stock Exchange

The new issue market deals with the new securities which were not previously available to the investing public i.e. the securities that are offered to the investing public for the first time. The market, therefore, makes available a new block of securities for public subscription.

The new issue market encompasses all institutions dealing in fresh claim. The forms in which these claims created are equity shares, preference shares, debentures, rights issues, deposits etc. All financial institutions which contribute, underwrite and directly subscribe to the securities are part of new issue market.

The stock exchange is a market for old securities i.e., those which have been already issued and listed on a stock exchange. These securities purchased and sold continuously among investors without involvement of companies. Stock exchange provides not only free transferability shares but also makes continuous valuation of securities traded in the market.

New issue market deals with new securities which are issued for the first time for public subscription. The stock exchange provides a ready market for buying and selling of old securities.

The new issue market provides the issuing company with funds for starting a new enterprise or for either expansion or diversification of an existing one by making direct link between companies which require funds and the investing public. So, the contribution of new issue market is direct. The role of stock exchange in providing capital is indirect as it provides marketability to the shares.

New issue market enjoys neither any tangible form nor any administrative organisational set up nor is subject to any centralised control and administration for the execution of the business. It renders service to the lenders and borrowers of funds at the time of any particular operation and the services are taken up entirely by banks, brokers and underwriters.

The stock exchanges have physical existence and are located in particular geographical areas. Stock exchange is a place where dealers of security meet regularly at appointed time announced by the market. It is a well established organisation with rules and regulations for conduct of the business. The members are supplied with information about companies and daily changes in prices of stocks.

Despite the above mentioned difference, the two markets are complementary in nature and they are inseparably connected to each other.

The two markets act and react upon each other in the same direction. When the stock prices go up in the market, the new issues increase and when the stock prices show a downward trend the new issues decline. The new issue market also depends on the stock exchange to find out price movements and general economic outlook and to forecast the climate for the success of new issues.

The new issues first placed in the new issue market can be disposed off subsequently in the stock exchange. The stock exchange provides the mechanism for regular and continuous purchase and sale of securities. This facility is of immense utility to potential investors who are assured that they will be able to dispose off the allotment of shares at any time. Thus, the two markets are complementary in nature.

2.2.1 FUNCTIONS OF PRIMARY MARKET

Primary Market is a place where securities are introduced as an offer to the public. This offer may be for the first time i.e. New Issue or an issue by an existing listed company.

Every company needs funds for its business. Fund requirements can be for short-term or long-term. Short-term requirement of finds can be met through banks, lenders, institutions etc. Whereas to meet long-term requirements, capital is raised through private placements of shares, rights issue or public issue. These constitute the primary market.

The main, function of new issue market is to facilitate transfer of resources from savers to the users. The savers are individuals, commercial banks, insurance company etc. The users are public limited companies and the government.

Classification of New Issue Market :

The new issue market plays an important role of mobilising the funds from the savers and transfer them to borrowers for production purposes, an important requisite of economic growth. It is not only a platform for raising finance to establish new enterprises but also for expansion/diversification/modernisation of existing units. On this basis, the new **issue market can be classified** as shown in Figure 2.10.

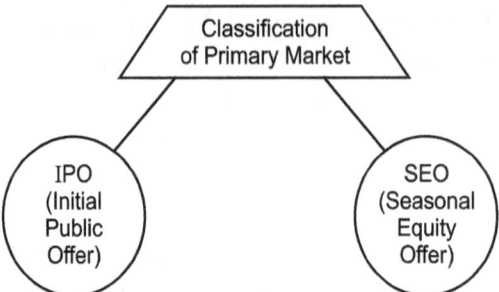

Fig. 2.10 : Classification of Primary Market

i)   Market where firms go to the public for the first time through initial public offering (IPO).

ii)   Market where firms already trade raise additional capital through Seasonal Equity Offering (SEO).

Triple Service Functions of New Issue Market :

The main **functions of new issue market** can be divided into a triple service functions as shown in Figure 2.11.

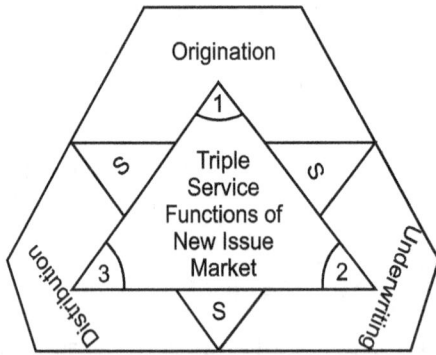

Fig. 2.11 : Triple Service Functions of New Issue Market

1) Origination

The function of origination is done by merchant bankers who may be commercial banks, all India financial institutions or private firms. Initially, this service was provided by specialised division of commercial banks. At present, financial institutions and private firms also perform this service. Though this service is highly important, the success of the issue depends, to a large extent, on the efficiency of the market.

The Two Aspects of Origination Functions are shown in Figure 2.12.

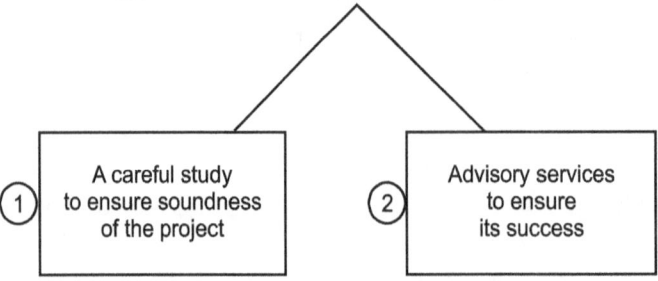

Fig. 2.12 : Two Aspects of Origination Functions

Origination refers to the work of investigation, analysis and processing of new project proposals. Origination starts before an issue is actually floated in the market. There are two aspects in this function :

a)   A careful study of the technical, economic and financial viability to ensure soundness of the project. This is a preliminary investigation undertaken by the sponsors of the issue.

b)   Advisory services which improve the quality of capital issues and ensure its success.

2) Underwriting :

The underwriter of new capital issues may be an individual, a firm or a financial institution involved in a contract with an issuer company to subscribe or agreeing to subscribe or to procure or agreeing to procure subscriptions, whether absolutely or conditionally, for any shares or debentures of the company. Thus, underwriting is an essential process required for marketing of new issues.

Underwriting is an agreement whereby the underwriter promises to subscribe to a specified number of shares or debentures or a specified amount of stock in the event of public not subscribing to the issue. If the issue is fully subscribed then there is no liability for the underwriter. If a part of share issue remains unsold, the underwriter will buy the shares. Thus, underwriting is a guarantee for the marketability of shares.

Methods of Underwriting

An underwriting agreement may take any of the following three forms as shown in Figure 2.13 as **methods of underwriting.**

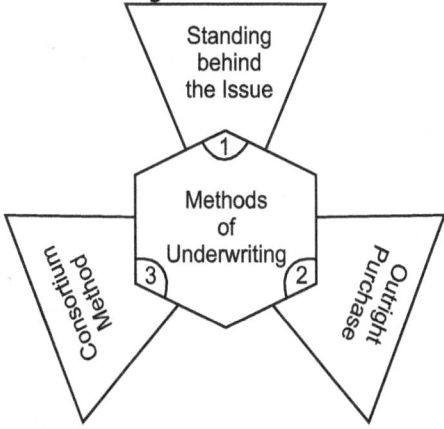

Fig. 2.13 : Methods of Underwriting

a) **Standing behind the Issue :**

Under this method, the underwriter guarantees the sale of a specified number of shares within a specified period. If the public do not subscribe to the specified amount of issue, the underwriter buys the balance in the issue.

b) **Outright Purchase :**

The underwriter, in this method, makes outright purchase of shares and resells them to the investors.

c)   **Consortium Method :**

Underwriting is jointly done by a group of underwriters in this method. The underwriters form syndicate for this purpose. This method is adopted for large issues.

Advantages of Underwriting :

Underwriting offers the following **advantages to the issuing company.**

i)   Underwriters undertake the burden of highly specialised function of distributing securities.

ii)   Provide expert advise with regard to timing of security issue, the pricing of issue, the size and type of securities to be issued etc.

iii) Public confidence on the issue enhances when underwritten by reputed underwriters.

iv)   The issuing company is relieved from the risk of finding buyers for the issue offered to the public. The company is assured of raising adequate capital.

v)   The company is assured of getting minimum subscription within the stipulated time, a statutory obligation to be fulfilled by the issuing company.

3)   Distribution

Distribution is the function of sale of securities to ultimate investors. This service is performed by brokers and agents who maintain regular and direct contact with the ultimate investors.

| Role of SEBI in Primary Market |

i)   Upto 1992, the capital primary market was controlled by the Controller of Capital Issue (CCI) formed under the Capital Issues Control Act. During that period, the pricing of capital issues was controlled by CCI. The premium on issue of equity shares issued through the primary markets was done in accordance with the Capital Issues Control Act.

ii)   The CCI guidelines were abolished with the introduction of Securities & Exchange Board of India (SEBI) formed under the SEBI Act, 1992 with the prime objective of protecting the interests of investors in securities, promoting the development and regulating the securities market and for matters connected therewith or incidental thereto.

iii) The SEBI Act came into force on 30th January, 1992 and with its establishment, all public issues are controlled by the rules and regulations issued by SEBI.

iv)   SEBI was formed to promote fair dealing in issue of securities and to ensure that the capital markets function efficiently, transparently and economically in the better interest of both the issuers and the investors.

v)   The promoters should be able to raise funds at a relatively low cost. At the same time, investors must be protected from unethical practices and their rights must be safeguarded so that there is a steady flow of savings into the market. There must be proper regulation and code of conduct and fair practice by intermediaries to make them competitive and professional.

vi)   Since its formation, SEBI has been instrumental in bringing greater transparency in capital issues. Under the umbrella of SEBI, companies issuing shares are free to fix the premium provided adequate disclosure is made in the offer documents. SEBI has become a vigilant watchdog with the focus towards greater investor protection.

2.2.2 ISSUE MECHANISM

The issue of capital to public by Indian companies is governed by the Disclosure and Investor Protection guidelines prescribed by SEBI. The guidelines provide norms relating to eligibility for companies issuing securities, pricing of issues, listing requirements, disclosure, lock-in period for promoters' contribution, contents of offer documents, pre- and post-issue obligations, etc.

Public Issue means raising funds from the public. The company may require funds to invest in some profitable projects. For this purpose the company may raise funds from the public by the issue of its shares which may later on be listed on my of the stock exchanges.

In order to bring out a Public Issue a company is required to comply with the following laws :

i)   Provisions of Companies Act, 1956.

ii)   Securities Contracts (Regulations) Act, 1956.

iii)   SEBI rules and regulations.

iv)   Compliance of listing agreement with the concerned stock exchanges after the listing of securities.

v)   RBI regulations in case of foreign/NRI equity participation.

Keeping in view investor protection, greater transparency and development of capital market SEBI from time to time, has amended the entry forms for companies to bring out a public issue.

The norms for entry are divided into the following :

*   Unlisted Companies.

*   Listed Companies.

Eligibility :

An unlisted company can make public issue of equity shares or any other security convertible into equity shares, on fixed price basis or on book building basis provided i) it has a net worth of at least ₹ 1 crore in each of the preceding full 3 years, ii) it has a track record of distributable profits for at least 3 out of the preceding 5 years, and iii) the aggregate of the proposed issue and all previous issues made in the same financial year in terms of size does not exceed five times its pre-issue net worth iv) the company has net tangible assets of at least ₹ 3 crore in each of the preceding 3 full years of which not more than 50% of it is held in monetary assets. A listed company is eligible to make a public issue, on fixed price basis or book building basis, if the issue size does not exceed five times its pre-issue net worth. If the company, listed or unlisted does not meet the above criteria, then the following conditions need to be satisfied.

i)   The issue will have to be compulsorily made through book-building route in which 50% of the issue size will have to be allotted to the **Qualified Institutional Buyers** (QIBs), or the project shall at least have 15% participation by financial institutions/ scheduled commercial banks of which at least 10% comes from the appraiser(s). In addition to this, at least 10% of the issue size shall be allotted to QIBs, failing which the full subscription money shall be refunded.

ii)   The minimum post issue face value of the company shall be ₹ 10 crore, or there shall be compulsory market making for at least 2 years from the date of listing of the shares subject to certain conditions.

Pricing of Issues :

The companies eligible to make a public issue can freely price their equity shares or any security convertible into equity at a later date in cases of public/rights issues by listed companies and public issue by unlisted companies. In addition, eligible infrastructure companies can freely price their equity shares subject to compliance of disclosure norms of SEBI. The public and private sector banks can also freely price their shares subject to approval by RBI. A company may issue shares to applicants in the firm allotment category at higher price than the price at which securities are offered to public. Further, an eligible company is free to make public/rights issue in any denomination determined by it in accordance with sub-section (4) of section 13 of the Companies Act, 1956 and SEBI norms.

Promoters Contribution :

The promoters' contribution in case of public issues by unlisted companies and promoters' shareholding in case of 'offers for sale' should not be less than 20% of the post issue capital. In case of public issues by listed companies, promoters should contribute to the extent of 20% of the proposed issue or should ensure post-issue holding to the extent of 20% of the post-issue capital. For composite issues, the promoters' contribution should either be 20% of the proposed public issue or 20% of the post-issue capital. The promoters should bring in the full amount of the promoters contribution including premium at least one day prior to the issue opening date. The requirement of promoters contribution is not applicable in case of i) public issue of securities which has been listed on a stock exchange for at least three years and has a track record of dividend payment for at least three immediate preceding years, ii) companies where no identifiable promoter or promoter group exists, and iii) rights issues.

In case of any issue of capital to the public, the minimum promoter's contribution shall be locked in for a period of three years. The lock-in shall start from the date of allotment in the proposed public issue and the last date of the lock-in shall be reckoned as three years from the date of commencement of commercial production or the date of allotment in the public issue whichever is later. In case of pre-issue share capital of unlisted company, the entire pre-issue share capital, other than that locked in as promoters contribution, is locked for a period of one year from the date of commencement of commercial production or the date of allotment in the public issue, whichever is later.

The lead merchant banker discharges most of the pre- and post-issue obligations. He satisfies himself about all aspects of offering and adequacy of disclosures in the offer document. He issues a due diligence certificate stating that he has examined the prospectus, he finds it in order and that it brings out all the facts and does not contain anything wrong or misleading. He also takes care of allotment, refund and despatch of certificates.

Options to bring out of Public Issue :

In case of unlisted companies there are two options to bring out a public issue :

Option-1

- The company should have a track record of distributable profits for atleast three out of five preceding years and;
- The pre-issue net worth should be at least ₹ 1,00,00,000 in three out of five years with the minimum net worth in the immediately preceding two years.

The issue size including offer to public, firm allotment, promoters contribution through offer document should not exceed five times its pre-issue net worth as per the last available audited accounts.

Option-II

Earlier, it was considered that if a company cannot satisfy the first option then it can come out with a public issue provided the project is appraised by any bank or public financial institution with at least 10% of project cost financed by such appraiser.

But w.e.f. 4th August, 2000; SEBI has amended its guideline stating that if the company is unable to satisfy the first option or if the issue size is more than 5 times of its pre-issue net worth then the second option to come out with the issue is through book building process only. The issue can come out through book building process provided 60% of the issue size is allotted to Qualified Institutional Buyers (QIB's). In case it is not so, the money so received shall be refunded.

Book Building :

According to SEBI guidelines, **book building** is defined as a process undertaken by which a demand for the securities proposed to be issued by a corporate body is elicited and built up and the price for such securities is assessed for the determination of the quantum of such securities to be issued by means of a notice, circular, advertisement or information memoranda or offer document.

Book building is basically a process used in Initial Public Offer (IPO) for efficient price discovery. It is a mechanism where, during the period for which IPO is open, bids are collected from investors at prices which are above or equal to the floor price. The offer price is determined after the bid closing date.

As per SEBI guidelines, an issuer company can issue securities through prospectus in the following manner :

i)   100% of the net offer to the public through book building process.

ii)   75% of the net offer to the public through book building process and 25% at the price determined through book building. The Fixed Price portion is conducted like a normal public issue after the Book Built portion, during which the issue price is determined.

In Book Building, securities are offered at prices above or equal to the floor price as compared to a public issue in which they are offered at a fixed price. So in book building demand can be known everyday as the book is built while in case of public issue demand is known at the close of the issue.

Procedure of Book Building :

Book building is carried out by a well developed online trading network which is a fully automated screen based bidding system which enables the members to enter bids directly from their offices through a sophisticated telecommunication network.

i)   The Book Running Lead Manager will give the list of trading members who are eligible to participate in the book building process to the exchange. Members have to submit a one time undertaking to the Exchange. Eligible trading members are required to give in the prescribed Format details of the user Ids that they would like to use.

ii)   Subscribers call approach any of the trading members for submitting bids. Online transaction registration slips are generated automatically after entering the bids into the system which act as a proof of the registration of each Bid option.

Thus, the Book Running Lead Manager gets the quotations regarding the acceptable price of the issue and this method helps in pricing the issue in such a way that it increases the acceptability of the issue and also lives an idea about the issue, which will be subscribed.

Green Shoe Option :

Green shoe option (GSO) means an option of allocating shares in excess of the shares included in the public issue and operating a post listing stabilising mechanism, which is granted to a company. In case, an issuer company is making an IPO through book building mechanism, it can avail of the GSO subject to certain conditions. It shall, in the resolution of the general meeting authorising the public issue seek authorization, also for the possibility of allotment of further shares to the stabilising agent at the end of the stabilising period. A lead book runner shall be appointed as the stabilising agent (SA) and shall be responsible for the price stabilisation process, if required. The SA shall also enter into an agreement with the promoter who shall lend their shares specifying the maximum number of shares that may be borrowed from the promoters which shall not be more than 15% of the total issue size. The allocation of these shares shall be pro-rata to all the applicants.

Buy-Back of Shares :

Buy-back of shares is a device which facilitates capital restructuring of a company. It helps in arresting wide fluctuation in share prices and paves the way for efficient allocation of resources. Earlier, buy back of shares was prohibited in India by the Companies Act, 1956. However, buy back was allowed in India through an amendment ordinance in 1998. Now, Indian companies are free to buy their own shares and other securities up to 25 percent of their net worth out of its free reserves, or securities premium account, or proceeds of an earlier issue other than a fresh issue made specifically for buy back purposes. In another development, companies are given the option to issue shares of any denomination without a uniform par value.

Issue through Prospectus :

Prospectus is the most important document for the company to come out with a public issue. As per Section 2(36) of the Companies Act, "Prospectus" means any document described or issued as a prospectus and includes any notice, circular, advertisement or other document inviting deposits from the public or inviting deposits from public for the subscription or purchase of any shares in, or debentures of, a body corporate.

Prospectus is a document by way of which the investor gets all the information pertaining to the company in which they are going to invest. It gives the detailed information about the Company, Promoter or Directors, Group Companies, Capital Structure, Terms of the present issues, details of proposed project, particulars of the issue etc. There are certain mandatory disclosures which have to be made in the prospectus. SEBI has issued guidelines, SEBI (Disclosure for Investor and Protection), Guidelines, 2000 which gives details about the contents of prospectus.

Regulations regarding Issue of Prospectus :

a)   A company cannot come out with public issue unless a draft prospectus is filed with SEBI.

b)   A company cannot file prospectus directly with SEBI. It has to be filed through a merchant banker. After the preparation of prospectus, the merchant banker along with the due diligence certificates and other compliance sends the same to SEBI.

c)   SEBI on receiving the same scrutinises it and may suggest changes within 21 days of receipt of prospectus. (Earlier, the situation was that the company was required to obtain Acknowledgement Card from SEBI).

d)   If the issue size is upto ₹ 20 crores then the merchant bankers are required to file prospectus with the regional office of SEBI falling, under the jurisdiction in which registered office of the company is situated.

e)   If the issue size is more than ₹ 20 crores, merchant bankers are required to file prospectus at SEBI, Mumbai office.

f)   Prospectus is also required to be filed with the concerned stock exchanges along with the application for listing its securities. Presently, companies approaching the stock exchange for public issue should obtain in-principal approval from such stock exchanges.

After making changes, if any made by SEBI/Stock Exchanges, the final Prospectus duly signed by all the Directors (or by Authorised representatives through its Power of Attorney) must be filed with the Registrar of Companies (ROC) along with the copy of all material documents.

The Registrar of Companies may suggest changes which should also be reported to SEBI/Stock Exchanges. The date on which ROC Card is obtained is the date of the prospectus.

Provisions Regarding Promoter's Contribution and Lock-in Requirement :

Some specific provisions have been inserted with regard to the contribution of the promoters in the capital of the company.

In case of public issues by listed companies, the promoter's contribution should be either 20% of the proposed issue or 20%, then the excess of 20% shall attract the provisions of the guidelines on preferential allotment, if the issue price is lower than the price as determined on the basis of said preferential allotment guidelines.

Promoters Contribution to be Brought in Before the Issue :

Promoters are required to bring the full amount of the promoter's contribution at least one day prior to the opening of the public issue and should be kept in an escrow account with a scheduled Bank.

Exemption from Requirement of Minimum Promoters' Contribution :

If the company is a listed company for at least three years and has a track record of dividend payment for at least 3 immediately preceding years, the requirement of promoter's contribution will not be applicable.

Lock-in Requirements :

i)   The eligible promoter's contribution is locked-in for three years.

ii) The entire pre-issue share capital, other than that locked-in as promoter's contribution, shall be locked-in for a period of one year.

iii) All the securities issued on firm allotment basis shall be locked in for a period of one year.

iv) The date of the lock-in shall be reckoned from the date of commencement of commercial production or the date of allotment in the public issue, whichever is later.

Other Lock-in Requirement :

i)   The shares that are held by promoters and are locked-in may be pledged with banks or financial institutions for loans, provided the pledge of shares is one of the terms of the sanction of loan.

ii) The locked-in shares held by promoters can he transferred between the promoters provided they are disclosed as promoters in the prospectus and there would be no change in the period of lock-in.

iii) The Share Certificates issued for lock-in shares should inscribe the word 'Non-Transferable up to ... 'or' 'Lock-in' upto to ....

Rules Regarding Reservations and Firm Allotment :

i)   In case of an unlisted company, Public Issue should be at least 25% of the post issue capital.

ii) In case of listed company, Public Issue should be at least 25% of the issue size.

iii) The above is relaxed in case of a public issue of unlisted companies in information technology sector where at least 10% of the securities may be offered to public; subject to i) 20 lakhs securities are offered to public and ii) issue size is minimum ₹ 50 crores.

iv) The company can reserve shares in the issue on competitive basis wherein allotment of shares is made in proportion to the shares applied for by the concerned reserved categories.

v) Company is allowed to make firm allotment to the following :
   - Indian and Multilateral Development Financial Institutions
   - Indian Mutual Funds
   - FII
   - Permanent/regular employees of the company Scheduled Banks
   - Merchant Bankers (subject to 5% of the issue size)

vi) The aggregate of **reservations and firm allotment** for employees cannot exceed 10% of the issue size.

vii) For shareholders, it cannot exceed 10% of the issue size.

Pre-Issue Obligation (i.e. before the opening of issue) :

i) Board Resolution for approving the draft prospectus and related resolutions.

ii) Shareholder's Resolution pursuant to Section 81 (1 A) of the Companies Act, 1956.

iii) Filing of form 23 with ROC for passing special resolution for issuing shares as above.

iv) Appointment of intermediaries and entering into MOU with them.

v) Due diligence by a merchant banker.

vi) Submission of all required papers/documents with merchant bankers.

vii) Preparation of draft prospectus in consultation with the merchant banker and submitting the same with SEBI alongwith the fees and other requirements and submitting the same with stock exchanges as per guidelines.

viii) Receipt of queries from SEBI/stock exchanges, if any and make changes in prospectus, if required.

ix) Reply to SEBI / stock exchanges in connection with changes in prospectus.

x) Obtaining in-principle approval from stock exchanges.

xi) File final prospectus with SEBI/stock exchanges/ROC.

xii) Statutory Advertisements.

xiii) Submission of 1% Security Deposit with the Regional Stock Exchange.

xiv) Depositing Promoter's Contribution in the issue in a separate bank account.

Post-Issue Obligation (i.e. after the closure of issue) :

i) Collection of Application forms and processing the same at the Registrar and Share Transfer Agent in consultation with the Merchant Banker.

ii) Separate account to be opened for the applications received from public.

iii) Submitting a 3-day post issue monitoring report with SEBI by merchant banker.

iv) Basis of allotment in consultation with the regional stock exchange.

v) Post-Issue Advertisement.

Different Kinds of Issues :

A **public issue** is an offer to the public to subscribe to the share capital of a company. Once this is done, the company allots shares to the applicants as per the prescribed rules and regulations laid down by SEBI. **Different Kinds of Issues** are shown below in Figure 2.14.

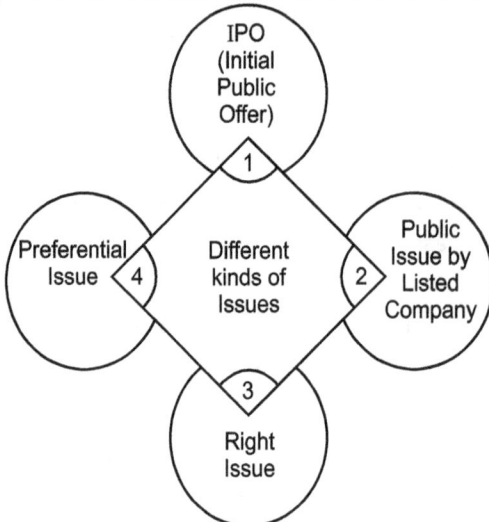

Fig. 2.14 : Different Kinds of Issues

1)   Initial Public Offering (IPO) :

Initial Public Offering is when an unlisted company makes either a fresh issue of securities or an offer for sale of its existing securities or both for the first time to the public. This paves way for listing and trading of the issuer's securities.

The market design for primary market is provided in the provision of the Companies Act, 1956, which deals with issues, listing and allotment of securities. In addition, DIP guidelines of SEBI prescribe a series of disclosures norms to be complied about by issuer, promoter, management, project, risk factors and eligibility norms for accessing the market.

A company making a public issue of securities has to file a draft prospectus with SEBI, through an eligible merchant banker, at least 2l days prior to the filling of prospectus with the Registrar of Companies (ROCs).

An unlisted company can make public issue of equity shares or any other security convertible into equity shares, on fixed price basis or on book building basis, provided –

i)   It has a pre-issue net worth of not less than ₹ 1 crore in 3 out of the preceding 5 years and has minimum net worth in immediately preceding two years.

ii)   It has a track record of distributable profits in terms of section 205 of the Companies Act, 1956, for at least 3 out of immediately preceding 5 years.

iii)   The issue size (offer through offer document + firm allotment + promoters contribution through the offer document) does not exceed five times its pre-issue net worth. A listed company is eligible to make a public issue, on fixed basis or on book building basis, if the issue size does not exceed five times its pre-issue net worth.

2) Public Issue by Listed Companies :

It is when an already listed company makes either a fresh use of securities to the public or an offer for sale to the public through an offer document.

The procedure for a public issue by a listed company is similar to that of an IPO. A Company sends application form similar to IPO to existing share holder to accept the right issue is to the destination of share holder.

3) Right Issue :

Rights Issue involves selling of securities in the primary market by issuing right to the existing shareholder. When a Company issues additional equity capital, is has to be offered in the first instance to the existing shareholders on a pro-rata basis and this enables the company to issue additional capital to public and raise funds. The number of rights that a shareholder gets is equal to the number of shares held by the existing share holder.

This is required under section 81 of the Companies Act 1956. The shareholder, however, may, by a special resolution forfeit this right, partially or fully, to enable the company to issue additional capital to public.

4) Preferential Issue :

Preferential Issue is issue of equity by a listed company to selected investors at a price which may or may not be related to the prevailing market price is referred to as preferential issue in the India Capital Market.

Preferential issue in India is given mainly to promoters, or friendly investors, toward off the threat of take over.

Foreign Capital Issuance (ADR/GRD) :

Indian companies are permitted to raise foreign currency resources through two main resources :

i)   Issue of foreign currency convertible bonds, more commonly known as 'Euro' Issues; and

ii) Issue of ordinary shares through depository receipts namely **American Depository Receipt (ADR) and Global Depository Receipt (GDR)**.

An **American Depository Receipt ("ADR")** is a physical certificate evidencing ownership of American Depository Shares, ("ADSs"). An American Depository Share ("ADS") is a U.S. dollar denominated form of equity ownership in a non-U.S. company. It represents the foreign shares of the company held on deposit by a custodian bank in the company's home country and carries the corporate and economic rights of the foreign shares, subject to the terms specified on the ADR certificate.

ADSs provide U.S. investors with a convenient way to invest in overseas securities and to trade non-U.S. securities in the U.S. ADSs are issued by a depository bank, such as JP Morgan Chase Bank. They are traded in the same manner as shares in U.S. companies, on the New York Stock Exchange (NYSE) and the American Stock Exchange (AMEX) or quoted on NASDAQ and the over-the-counter (OTC) market.

Global Depository Receipts (GDRs) is similar to ADR, which can be used to raise capital simultaneously in two or more markets through a global offering. GDRs may be used in public or private markets inside or outside US.

Other Methods of issuing Securities

Issue of bonus shares, offer to the employees, offer to the creditors and offer to the customers offer for sale and placement are other methods of issuing securities.

i)   **Issue of Bonus Shares.**

ii) **Offer to the Employees :** The issue of shares may be offered to employees. This helps promote better industrial relations and higher productivity. Public sector organisations and joint sector organisation offer shares to their employees.

iii) **Offer to the Creditors :** At the time of reorganisation of capital, creditors may be asked to buy shares in full settlement of their loans or advances.

iv) **Offer to the Customers :** Public utility undertakings offer shares to their customers. Shareholding by customers give them say in the affairs and functioning of the concern.

v)   **Offer for Sale :** This method of sale consists in outright sale of securities through the intermediary of Issue Houses or sharebrokers. In other words, the shares are not offered to the public directly. This method consists of two stages : The first stage is a direct sale by the issuing company to the Issue House and brokers at an agreed price. In the second stage, the intermediaries resell the above securities to the ultimate investors. The Issue Houses or stock brokers purchase the securities at a negotiated price and resell at a higher price. The difference in the purchase and sale price is called turn or spread.

vi) **Placement :** Under this method, the Issue Houses or brokers buy the securities outright with the intention of placing them with their clients afterwards. Here, the brokers act as almost wholesalers selling them in retail to the public. The brokers would make profit in the process of reselling to the public. The Issue Houses or brokers maintain their own list of clients and through customer contact sell the securities.

This method of private placement is used to a limited extent in India. The promoters sell the shares to their friends, relatives and well-wishers to get minimum subscription which is a precondition for issue of shares to the public.

2.2.3 PARTICIPANTS OF PRIMARY MARKET

The Primary Market has essentially three categories of participants viz. the **issuers of security, investors in security** and the **intermediaries**. The products in the market include equities, bonds and derivatives.

The primary market is the channel for creation of new securities through financial instruments by public limited companies as well as government agencies. The resources in the primary market are mobilised either through the public issues or through private placement. It is a public issue if anybody and everybody can subscribe for it, whereas, if the issue is made available to a selected group of persons it is termed as private placement. The **Participants of Primary Market** are shown below in Figure 2.15.

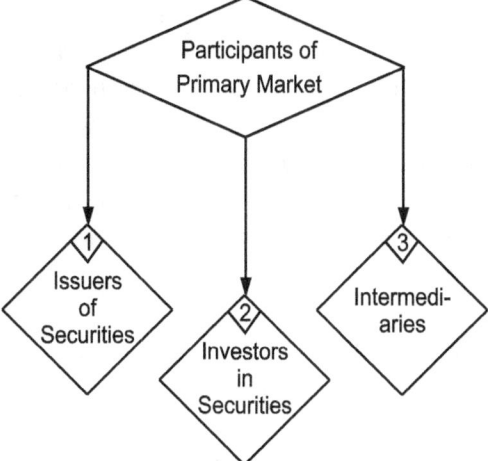

Fig. 2.15 : Participants of Primary Market

1) Issuers of Securities :

Primary market provides opportunity to issuers of securities, Government as well as corporates, to raise resources to meet their requirements of investment and/or discharge some obligation.

Corporates may issue the securities at face value, or at discount/premium and these securities may take a variety of forms such as equity, debts, etc. They may issue the securities in domestic market and/or international market.

Most companies are usually started privately by their promoter(s). However, the promoters' capital and the borrowings from banks and financial institutions may not be sufficient for setting up or running the business over a long term. So companies invite the public to contribute towards the equity and issue shares to individual investors.

The nominal or stated amount (in ₹) is assigned for security purposes by the issuer. For shares, it is the original cost of the stock shown on the certificate; for bonds, it is the amount paid to the holder at maturity, also known as par value or simply par. For an equity share, the face value is usually a very small amount (₹ 5, ₹ 10) and does not have much bearing on the price of the share, which may quote higher in the market at ₹ 100 or ₹ 1000 or any other price. For a debt security, face value is the amount repaid to the investor when the bond matures (usually, Government securities and corporate bonds have a face value of ₹ 100). The price at which the security trades depends on the fluctuations in the interest rates in the economy.

Issuers of new securities include agencies concerned with the floatation of initial issues and those concerned with floatation of existing issues. The agency, which performs the function of forming a company and floating its initial security issues is, generally known as promoter. The promoter conducts detailed investigation about the company to be set up, formulates financial plan, prepares prospectus for capital issues, approaches underwriting and brokerage firms for underwriting the issues and makes arrangements for advertising and circulating the prospectus to procure subscriptions. Thus, promoter is the issuer or supplier of new companies in the market. In case of existing companies, the companies are themselves supplier of new issues when they float further issues. When the existing companies offer new security issues only to their existing stockholders, they will not constitute the suppliers of new issues in the new issue market. On the contrary, if they offer issues to public through prospectuses, they are regarded as the suppliers of new issue in the market. In the case of existing companies, it is the Board of Directors, who take decisions as to why, how and when new issues will be floated. They also enter into agreements with underwriters and brokers before floating public issues.

2) **Investors in Securities**

The **Investors in Securities** are shown below in Figure 2.16.

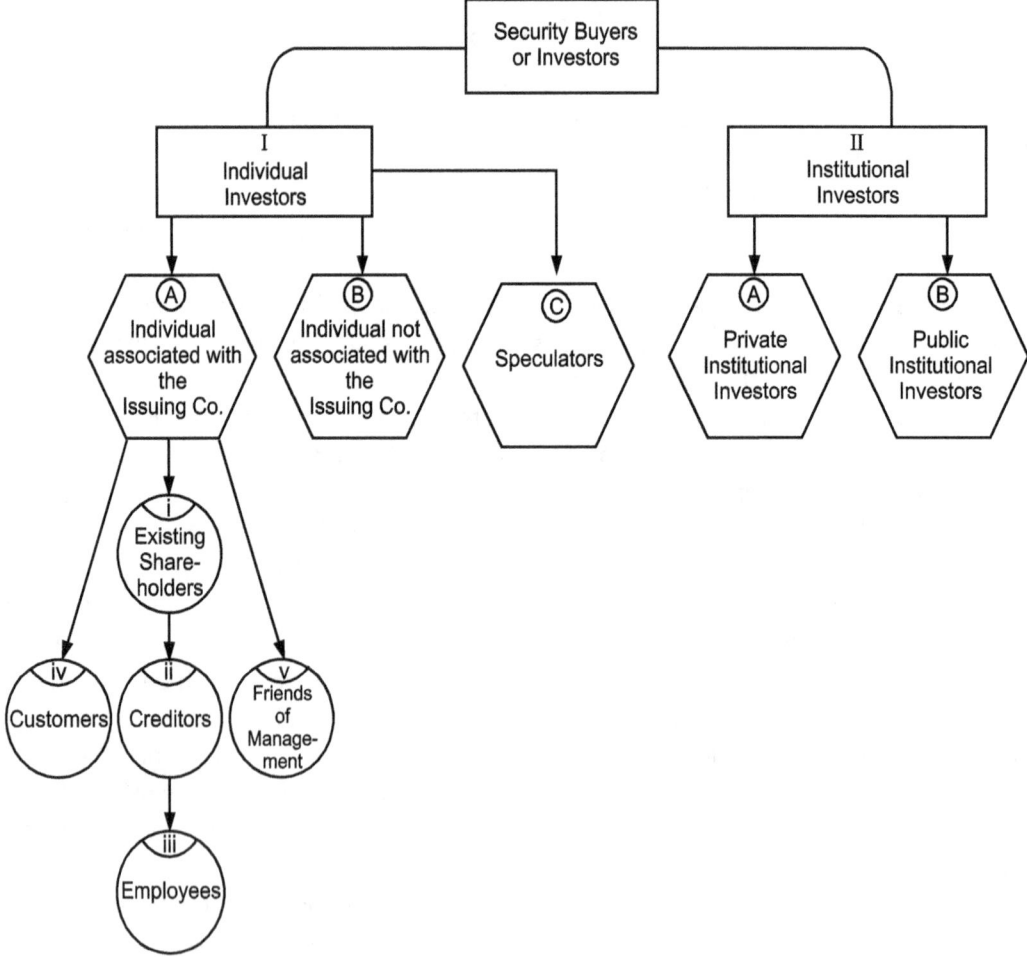

Fig. 2.16 : Investors in Securities

The security buyers maybe classified into two broad categories, viz., (I) Individual investors, and (II) Institutional investors.

(I) Individual Investors

Individual investors include buyers of securities who invest their own funds. They represent the whole gamut of investment temperaments. Investment decision of individual investors is governed by their expectations about the future earnings and the prevailing rate of interest at which claims to resources may be obtained. Expected future earnings, in turn, are a function of the state of industry and the economy, its potential of development and future expectations about it, the existing stock of capital, technological innovation, government policies, etc.

Individual investors may be of varied types which can conveniently be classified into three main groups : a) Individuals associated with the issuing company; b) Individuals not associated with the issuing company; and c) Speculators.

A) Individuals Associated with the Issuing Company.

This group of investors comprises i) Existing shareholders, ii) Creditors, iii) Employees of the issuing company, iv) Customers and v) Friends of the management.

i) Existing Shareholders :

Existing shareholders of the company are important buyers of its new security issue. Because of the pre-emptive rights of the shareholders the company is under legal obligation to offer new shares to the existing equity shareholders before placing them in the market for public subscription. Thus, the existing shareholders have the privilege to subscribe to new security issues of the company so as to preserve their proportionate ownership in the corporation.

ii) Creditors :

Creditors of the established company sometimes buy its securities as a demonstration of their goodwill towards the concern or in order to retain its patronage. In case of convertible bonds, the bondholders who are initially the creditors of the company turn out to be shareholders after sometime when shares are offered to them in exchange of the bonds.

iii) Employees :

In their bid to raise capital, companies have been found selling securities to their employees. In most of the cases, stock offered to employees made no distinction as to purchasers, giving an opportunity to share in the ownership of the company. In a few instances, special types of securities are offered to employees.

iv) Customers :

Sometimes, a company offers shares to its customers who after buying shares become owners of the company. This kind of sale of securities not only helps the company in securing funds economically but also solicits the cooperation of customers in many respects.

Customer-ownership has been very popular in the USA particularly in public utility concerns.

v)   **Friends of Management :**

In the case of newly set-up organisations having no old stockholders, creditors or employees and limited access to capital market agencies, the management finds it easier to approach their friends for procuring the required funds.

B)   Individuals not associated with issuing company

In society, there may be extra cautious investors who are more keen in safety of their capital and liquidity of investors even though return on investments is low. These investors are buyers of highest grade investment securities promising great safety of principal, ready marketability and a definite minimum rate of income. Such investors assume a minimum risk and, in return, sacrifice control in the corporation, a high rate of income or both.

C)   Speculators

Speculators are not real investors. They make investment in securities in the hope of earning income from anticipated changes in value of securities. Their intention is to make a profit out of the fluctuations in security prices.

(II) Institutional Investors

Institutional investors can be categorised on the basis of ownership and extent of control in two groups, viz., a) Private Institutional investors and b) Public Institutional Investors.

A)   Private Institutional Investors :

Private institutional investors comprise such institutions are owned by private business enterprises. In this category, all institutions such as non-nationalised banks, general insurance companies and industrial concerns are included which invest on their own account.

B)   Public Institutional Investors :

Public institutional investors comprise institutions which are owned by Central and State Governments, and have been set up to satisfy financial needs of business enterprises of the country. Industrial Financial Corporation of India, Life Insurance Corporation, Industrial Development Bank of India. State Financial Corporations, State Industrial Development Corporations and Unit Trust of India are state owned agencies presently operating in Indian capital market and Supplying funds to corporate enterprises through various ways including purchase of corporate securities.

3) Intermediaries :

Many intermediaries are involved in connection with the public issue. Following are the intermediaries who have to be registered with SEBI and must have valid certificate from SEBI to act as intermediaries :

i)   **Merchant Bankers** play the most vital role amongst all intermediaries. They assist the company right from preparing prospectus to the listing of securities at the stock exchanges. Merchant bankers have to satisfy themselves about the correctness and propriety of all the information provided in the prospectus. It is mandatory for them to carry due diligence for all the information provided in the prospectus and they must issue a certificate to this effect to SEBI. A Company may appoint more than one merchant banker provided *inter se* allocation of responsibilities between the Merchant bankers is properly structured.

ii)   **Underwriters** are those intermediaries who underwrite the securities offered to the public. In case there is under subscription (in short, the company does not receive good response from public and amount received from is less than the issue size), underwriters subscribe to the unsubscribed amount so that the issue is successful.

iii) **Registrar and Share Transfer Agents** process all applications received from the public and prepare the basis of allotment. The dispatch of share certificates/refund orders are handled by them.

iv)   **Bankers to the Issue** are banks which accept applications from the public on behalf of the company. These applications are then forwarded to Registrar and Share Transfer Agents for further processing.

v)   **Stock Brokers and Sub-Brokers** are those intermediaries who through their contacts/sources invite the public for subscribing shares for which they get commission.

vi)   **Depositories** are the intermediaries who hold securities in dematerialised form on behalf of the shareholders.

2.3 SECONDARY MARKET

The market where existing securities are traded is referred to as the **secondary market or stock market**. In a stock market, purchases and sales of securities whether of Government or Semi-Government bodies or other public bodies and also shares and debentures issued by joint stock companies are effected. The securities of government are traded in the stock market as a separate component, called guilt edged market. Government securities are traded outside the trading wing in the form of over the counter sales or purchases. Another component of the stock market deals with trading in shares and debentures of limited companies.

2.3.1 OBJECTIVES OF SECONDARY MARKET I.E. STOCK EXCHANGE

Like any other organisation, the stock exchange management should be guided by its obligation. The following are the major **Objectives of Stock Exchange**.

i)   Arrangements for listing of companies.

ii)   Control and regulation of trading in securities, settlement and clearance.

iii) Regulation of members activities.

    a) Disputes with other members.

    b) Disputes with client.

    c) Regulation of members activities.

iv)   Other services to members and public, such as spread of information, corporate disclosures etc.

The management policy originates from i) The government and SEBI guidelines. ii) Bye-laws of the exchange. iii) Decisions of the governing board. Administration of policies is through committees and implemented by the executive director.

2.3.2 FUNCTIONS OF SECONDARY MARKET I.E. STOCK MARKET

Stock market provides an efficient market place to its members where they buy and sell securities and organised and regulate transactions in them. It is an indispensable institution where principal objectives are to provide marketability to existing securities and to facilitate the acquisition of new capital by newly set-up ventures. In order to accomplish such type of objectives, the stock market performs the following important functions :

1) To provide for Regular Market

'Stock market' provides a continuous market "where a security may be bought and sold during the business hours at comparatively small variations from the last quoted price". As a continuous and ready market it provides liquidity, price, continuity and negotiability to capital locked up in investments. Marketability is that quality of a security which enables its owner to dispose it to the best advantage in the shortest time. A security exchange provides a meeting place for buyers and sellers, or their representatives.

This enables investors to liquidate their investments quickly and with the least possible loss. Without stock markets, purchasers of new issues would have to hold their securities to maturities or in the case of common stocks, indefinitely. This may be enough to discourage a large group of investors. High marketability of securities increases their value and facilitates the use of these securities as collateral for loan. The creditors know the worth of listed securities on the basis of the price quotations of securities on the stock exchange.

The computer records the data on prices and volume of trade on a daily basis. These data are fed memberwise and scripwise. The changes in prices and trade volumes thus recorded are used for the management decision on trade regulation. The control measures are as follows :

a) Margins on daily purchases and sales, scripwise, at a rate varying upto 50% of the value of deals to be deposited with the exchange as non-interest bearing deposits; as also the margins on the outstanding position of brokers.

b) Margins on carry forward deals at the time of settlement to be deposited by members until these deals are squared up.

c) adhoc margins on members, if their turnover increases over a permitted level.

d) Price band fixation if there is high volatility in price of any scrip or stoppage of trade in any scrip, if its price change is beyond a limit with the help of circuit breakers (at say 10% or 20%).

The management has to keep a watch on the price and volume trends scripwise and memberwise as trading takes place during the day and to help impose margins on members/scrips and to regulate trading in an orderly manner.

2) To ensure continuity and stability in share prices

A well regulated and efficient stock market determines, through its continuous process of evaluation, price for securities as close as possible to their investment values based on present and future income-yielding prospects of the various enterprises. The efficiency of the market must be measured by its efforts in enabling securities to be quickly and cheaply bought and sold at prices as close as possible to their true values. Bulls and bears, bankers and brokers, speculators and investors, all over the world bid and offer against each other by cable and telegraph and record the epitomised result of their bidding in the prices current on the stock exchange.

Stockbrokers render useful services in equalising prices of securities of different markets. They make heavy buyings in the market where share prices are ruling low and thereby increase pressure of demand of securities which would in consequence raise share prices. Where share prices are high the stock brokers would tend to depress the rise when they will increase the supply by substantial sale of securities. Thus, through the mechanism of regular purchase and sale of securities, the stock exchanges ensure continuity and stability in share prices.

3) To provide safety in dealings

A well organised and regulated stock market ensures a greater measure of safety and fair dealings to the average investors because transactions are made publicly under well-defined rules, regulations and bye-laws of the exchange.

Performance of this function necessitates the working of a stock market under a code of well defined rules and regulations so as to minimise the danger inherent in speculative dealings and manipulations. Moreover, a high standard of commercial honesty and integrity among its members is necessary to promote and inculcate just and equitable principles of trade and business.

4) To help in mobilization of surplus of funds of investors

The stock exchange helps in mobilisation of surplus funds of individuals, business firms, and corporations for investment in corporate securities, otherwise such funds would either remain idle or be deposited in commercial or savings banks where the interest return would be substantially lower.

By providing regular market for securities and correct evaluation of securities and ensuring adequate safeguards to innocent investors against unscrupulous practices of stock brokers, the stock market instils confidence, in the minds of savers who are encouraged to save more and to invest these savings in securities promising high return.

5) To allocate funds among productive channels

The stock market facilitates the process of distributing capital among different industries, among different plants in a given industry and among different countries or regions of the world. In a particular country, the stock exchange directs and allocates the flow of savings into the most productive channels. "It serves to allocate just enough funds for any time for industries and checks the flow of capital just when an industry begins to show diminishing or uneconomic return."

A permanent rising trend in share price of particular industry suggests that more capital can be absorbed by the industry with advantage. On the contrary, if share price in the industry registers continued fall, this suggests that the industry cannot absorb the capital profitably. Through price mechanism the stock market prevents gluts and scarcities of capital as between different industries and avoids misalignments between, supply of capital and the demands of industry and affects economies in the use of capital.

6) To ensure wide distribution of securities

A stock market ensures wide distribution of securities. If a company's securities are listed in different stock markets of the country, its securities will be bought and sold by persons scattered all over the country and ownership of securities is widely diffused. With the help of the stock markets not only new sources of new capital could be tapped but more and more people can also be made to share some direct interest in the tools of production and the net results therefrom.

Trading Mechanism on a Stock Exchange i.e. Trading Functioning of Stock Market :

The following are the steps of buying and selling Securities on a stock exchange –

a)   Choice of a Broker :

An individual buys or sells securities directly so he/She has to appoint a broker for this purpose. The broker may be chosen on the basis of accessibility, references, repute etc.

b)   Placement of Order :

Once a broker has been appointed next step is to place an order with him for buying/selling securities.

The various types of orders are –

i)   Market Order : It is an order to buy a certain number of securities at the best prevailing market price within a certain time period. For e.g. "Buy 100 CIPLA at best".

ii)   Limit Order : It is an order for purchase or sale of securities at a fixed price i.e. the client places a price limit which should not be crossed e.g. "Buy 100 CIPLA @ ₹ 150".

iii)   Discretionary Order : Here the client leaves the decision to buy/sell at the discretion of the broker i.e. whatever time and price he thinks the best.

iv)   Immediate or Cancel Order i.e. to buy/sell securities immediately quoted prices or cancel the order e.g. Buy 100 CIPLA @ 150 immediately.

v)   Stop Loss Order : It is an order to buy as soon as the price of securities rises to a particular level and sell as soon as it falls to a particular level to avoid any loss.

As soon as the order is place, it is recorded in an 'Order Book'.

c)   Execution of Order :

After the order is entered matching bids are required. The buying and selling bids should match the order to be executed. The buyer and seller may negotiate with each other and come to a mutually agreed price acceptable to both. As soon as order is executed a confirmation memo is prepared and given to the client.

d)   Preparation of Contract Note :

After issue of confirmation memo, a contract note is signed between the broker and the client stating the transaction fees (commission of broker), number of' shares bought or sold, price at which they are brought or sold etc.

e)   Settlement of Transaction :

Earlier there was a system of account settlement in which settlement cycle was 'T + 7' or weekly settlement cycle which was Monday to Friday in BSE and Wednesday to Tuesday in NSE. But now both the exchanges have entered into compulsory rolling settlement which is 'T + 2' cycle of settlement.

The Cycle is

T	–	Day of trade
T + 1	–	Confirmation of order, preparation of contract note
T + 2	–	Pay-in/Pay-out
T + 3	–	Auction for Shortages
T + 4	–	********
T + 5	–	Pay-in/Pay-out of auctioned securities

f)   Transfer of Ownership :

Once the trading is complete the buyer holds the possession of securities given by the seller along with a transfer deed which specifies the number of shares to be transferred in the buyer's name. The buyer then lodges these shares with the Registrar and Transfer Agent of' the company and then requisite action is taken to transfer tile shares in the name of tile buyer.

Internet Trading :

Since June 2000, internet trading has gained popularity over physical trading. For tile purpose of internet trading a brokerage firm provides a platform e.g. ICICI securities. KOTAK MAHINDRA.

A unique 'User ID' and password I5 given to the client and the client has to open a cash account and DEMAT account with the firm. Quotes can be put by the client using the ID and password and then as soon as the order is confirmed and finalized, cash or securities are debited or credited from the respective accounts.

Carry Forward Badla :

Badla or carry forward is a deal between the Bull and the Bear in which the bull asks the Bear to carry forward the settlement of securities to the next cycle. Bull may buy securities in anticipation of price rise but the price may not actually rise towards the end of settlement cycle. So he may enter into an agreement with the seller to delay the settlement till the next cycle. For this he pays an interest on the amount due to the seller or badla financer.

In case the transaction is initiated from seller's side, it is called 'ulta badla' or 'backwardation'.

Badla was allowed till 1993 but in January 1994 it was banned by SEBI. Later in 1994 (March), SEBI received a proposal to modify Badla but it rejected the same. In February 1995, a three member committee was appointed by SEBI to review Badla and its report was submitted in 1997. According to the report carry forward or badla is allowed only till 90 days. After the 75th, day it was necessary to take delivery of shares. Total value of transaction per broker in the settlement badla cannot exceed ₹ 20 crores. Although the stocks in which badla is allowed was to he decided by exchange, however, SEBI has laid restrictions that this trading should he done only in liquid stocks.

Risk Management :

The various Margins are required to be deposited with the broker to ensure liquidity and safety of trades in the market. It helps in reducing speculative transactions and liquidity.

2.3.3 STOCK BROKING

A broker is none other than a commission agent who transacts business in securities on behalf of his clients who are non-members of a stock exchange. Thus, a non-member can purchase and sell securities only through a broker who is a member of the stock exchange. To deal in securities on recognised stock exchanges, the broker should register his name as a broker with the SEBI, stock-broker can deal in the new issues (primary market), existing securities (secondary market), government securities, P.S.U. bonds and money market etc. Brokers are members of stock exchanges.

Qualifications for Membership :

The qualifications for membership of stock exchanges in respect of individuals are as follows :

i) He must be a citizen of India, of an age not less than 21 years and education of not less than 10 + 2.

ii) He must be having a minimum networth which varies from exchange to exchange, and a minimum experience of two years in this business.

iii) He should not have been convicted of any offence involving fraud, dishonesty, cheating etc., and not compounded with creditors or declared insolvent.

iv) He should not be doing any other business except that of agent or broker.

v) Not connected with any company or corporation as employee/director etc.

vi) Not a defaulter on any other exchange.

Code of Conduct for Stock Brokers (As per SEBI Regulation)
Securities and Exchange Board of India (Stock Brokers and Sub-Brokers) Regulations, 1992
Code of Conduct for Stock Brokers (Regulation 7)

A. **General**

(1) *Integrity* : A stock broker, shall maintain high standards of integrity, promptitude and fairness in the conduct of all his business.

(2) *Exercise of due skill and care* : A stock broker, shall act with due skill, care and diligence in the conduct of all his business.

(3) *Manipulation* : A stock broker shall not indulge in manipulative, fraudulent or deceptive transactions or schemes or spread rumours with a view to distorting market equilibrium or making personal gains.

(4) *Malpractices :* A stock broker shall not create false market either singly or in concert with others or indulge in any act detrimental to the investors interest or which leads to interference with the fair and smooth functioning of the market. A stock broker shall not involve himself in excessive speculative business in the market beyond reasonable levels not commensurate with his financial soundness.

(5) *Compliance with statutory requirements :* A stock broker shall abide by all the provisions of the Act and the rules, regulations issued by the Government, the Board and the Stock Exchange from time to time as may be applicable to him.

B. Duty to the Investor

(1) *Execution of Orders :* A stock broker, in his dealings with the clients and the general investing public, shall faithfully execute the orders for buying and selling of securities at the best available market price and no: refuse to deal with a small investor merely on the ground of the volume of business involved. A stock broker shall promptly inform his client about the execution or non-execution of an order, and make prompt payment in respect of securities at the best available market price and not refuse to deal with a small investor merely on the ground of the volume of business involved. A stock broker shall promptly inform his client about the execution or non-execution of an order, and make prompt payment in respect of securities sold and arrange for prompt delivery of securities purchased by clients.

(2) *Issue of Contract Note :* A stock broker shall issue without delay to his client a contract note for all transactions in the form specified by the stock exchange.

(3) *Breach of Trust :* A stock broker shall not disclose or discuss with any other person or make improper use of the details of personal investments and other information of a confidential nature of the client which he comes to know in his business relationship.

(4) *Business and Commission*

    (a) A stock broker shall not encourage sales or purchases of securities with the sole object of generating brokerage or commission.

    (b) A stock broker shall not furnish false or misleading quotations or give any other false or misleading advice or information to the clients with a view of inducing him to do business in particular securities and enabling himself to earn brokerage or commission thereby.

(5) *Business of Defaulting Clients :* A stock broker shall not deal or transact business knowingly, directly or indirectly or execute an order for a client who has failed to carry out his commitments in relation to securities with another stock broker.

(6) *Fairness to Clients :* A stockbroker, when dealing with a client, shall disclose whether he is acting as a principal or as an agent and shall ensure at the same time, that no conflict of interest arises between him and the client In the event of a conflict of interest, he shall inform the client accordingly and shall not seek to gain a direct or

indirect personal advantage from the situation and not seek to gain a direct or indirect personal advantage from the situation and shall not consider clients' interest inferior to his own.

(7) *Investment Advice :* A stock broker shall not make a recommendation to any client who might be expected to rely thereon to acquire, dispose of, retain any securities unless he has reasonable grounds for believing that the recommendation is suitable for such a client upon the basis of the facts, if disclosed by such a client as to his own security holdings, financial situation and objectives of such investment. The stock broker should seek such information from clients, wherever he feels it is appropriate to do so.

(8) *Competence of Stock Broker :* A stock broker should have adequately trained staff and arrangements to render fair prompt and competent services to his clients.

C. Stock brokers vis-a-vis other Stock Brokers

(1) *Conduct of Dealings :* A stock broker shall co-operate with the other contracting party in comparing unmatched transactions. A stock broker shall not knowingly and willfully deliver documents which constitute bad delivery and shall co-operate with other contracting party for prompt replacement of documents which are declared as bad delivery.

(2) *Protection of Clients Interests :* A stock broker shall extend fullest co-operation to other stock brokers in protecting the interests of his clients regarding their rights to dividends, bonus shares, right shares and any other right related to such securities.

(3) *Transactions with Stock Brokers :* A stock broker shall carry out his transactions with other stock brokers and shall comply with his obligations in completing the settlement of transactions with them.

(4) *Advertisement and Publicity :* A stock broker shall not advertise his business publicly unless permitted by the stock exchange.

(5) *Inducements of Clients :* A stock broker shall not resort to unfair means of inducing clients from other stock brokers.

(6) *False or Misleading Returns :* A stockbroker shall not neglect or fail or refuse to submit the required returns and not make any false or misleading statement on any returns required to be submitted to the Board and the stock exchange.

Code of Conduct for Sub-Brokers

(REGULATION 15)

A. General

(1) *Integrity :* A sub-broker, shall maintain high standards of integrity, promptitude and fairness in the conduct of all investment business.

(2) *Execution of Orders :* A sub-broker, shall act with due skill, care and diligence in the conduct of all investment business.

B.   Duty to the Investor

(1) *Execution of Orders :* A sub-broker, in his dealings with the clients and the general investing public, shall faithfully execute the orders for buying and selling of securities at the best available market price. A sub-broker shall promptly inform his client about the execution or non-execution of an order and make payment in respect of securities sold and arrange (or prompt delivery of securities purchased by clients.

(2) *Issue of Purchase of Sale Notes*

    (a)   A sub-broker shall issue promptly to his clients purchase or sale notes for all the transactions entered into by him with his clients.

    (b)   A sub-broker shall issue promptly to his clients scrip-wise split purchase or sale notes and similarly bills and-receipts showing the brokerage separately in respect of all transactions in the specified form.

    (c)   A sub-broker shall only split the contract notes client-wise and scrip-wise originally issued to him by the affiliated broker into different denominations.

    (d)   A sub-broker shall not match the purchase and sale orders of his clients and each order must invariably be routed through a member-broker of the stock exchange with whom he is affiliated.

(3) *Breach of Trust :* A sub-broker shall not disclose or discuss with any other person or make improper use of the details of personal investments and other information of a confidential nature of the client which he comes to know in his business relationship.

(4) *Business and Commission*

    (a)   A sub-broker shall not encourage sales or purchases of securities with the sole object of generating brokerage or commission.

    (b)   A sub-broker shall not furnish false or misleading quotations or give any other false or misleading advice or information to the clients with a view of inducing him to do business in particular securities and enabling himself to earn brokerage or commission thereby.

    (c)   A sub-broker shall not charge from his clients a commission exceeding one and one-half of one percent of the value mentioned in the respective sale or purchase notes.

(5) *Business of Defaulting Clients :* A sub-broker shall not deal or transact business knowingly, directly or indirectly or execute an order for a client who has failed to carry out his commitments in relation to securities and is in default with another broker or subbroker.

(6) *Fairness to Clients :* A sub-broker, when dealing with a client, shall disclose that he is acting as an agent and shall issue appropriate purchase/sale note ensuring at the same time, that no conflict of interestarises between him and the client In the event

of a conflict of interest, he shall inform the client accordingly and shall not seek to gain a direct or indirect personal advantage from the situation and shall not consider clients interest inferior to his own.

(7)   *Investment Advice :* A sub-broker shall not make a recommendation to any client who might be expected to rely thereon to acquire, dispose of, retain any securities unless he has reasonable grounds for believing that the recommendation is suitable for such a client upon the basis of the facts, if disclosed by such a client as to his own security holdings, financial situation and objectives of such investment. The sub-broker should seek such information from clients, wherever they feel it is appropriate to do so.

(8)   *Competence of Sub-broker :* A sub-broker should have adequately trained staff and arrangements to render fair, prompt and competence services to his clients and continuous compliance with the regulatory system.

C.   Sub-Brokers vis-a-vis Stock Brokers

(1)   *Conduct of Dealings :* A sub-broker shall co-operate with his broker in comparing unmatched transactions. A sub-broker shall not knowingly and willfully deliver documents which constitute bad delivery. A sub-broker shall co-operate with other contracting party for prompt replacement of documents which are declared as bad delivery.

(2)   *Protection of Clients Interests :* A sub-broker shall extend fullest cooperation to his stock broker in protecting the interests of their clients regarding their rights to dividends, right or bonus shares, or any other rights relatable to such securities.

(3)   *Transactions with Brokers :* A sub-broker shall not fail to carry out his stock-broking transactions with his broker nor shall he fail to meet his business liabilities or show negligence in completing the settlement of transactions with them.

(4)   *Legal Agreement between Brokers :* A sub-brokers shall execute an agreement or contract with his affiliating brokers which would clearly specify the rights and obligations of the sub-broker and the principal broker.

(5)   *Advertisement and Publicity :* A sub-broker shall not advertise his business publicly unless permitted by the stock exchange.

(6)   *Inducement of Clients :* A sub-broker shall not resort to unfair means of inducing clients from other brokers.

D.   Sub-Brokers vis-a-vis Regulatory Authorities

(1)   *General Conduct :* A sub-broker shall not indulge in dishonourable, disgraceful or disorderly or improper conduct on the stock exchange nor shall he willfully obstruct the business of the stock exchange. He shall comply with the rules, bye-laws and regulations of the stock exchange.

(2)   *Failure to give Information :* A sub-broker shall not neglect or fail or refuse to submit to the Board or the stock exchange with which he is registered, such books, special returns, correspondence, documents, and papers or any part thereof as may be required.

(3) *False or Misleading Returns :* A sub-broker shall not neglect or fail or refuse to submit the required returns and not make any false or misleading statement on any returns required to be submitted to the Board or the stock exchanges.

(4) *Manipulation :* A sub-broker shall not indulge in manipulative, fraudulent-or deceptive transactions or schemes or spread rumours with a view to distorting market equilibrium or making personal gains.

(5) *Malpractices :* A sub-broker shall not create false market either singly or in concert with others or indulge in any act detrimental to the public interest or which leads to interference with the fair and smooth functions of the market mechanism of the stock exchanges. A sub-broker shall not involve himself in excessive speculative business in the market beyond reasonable levels not commensurate with his financial soundness.

(Regulation 10)

I. Fees to be Paid by the Stock Broker

1. Every stock broker shall subject to paragraphs 2 and 3 of this Schedule pay registration fees in the manner set out below:

    (a) where the annual turnover does not exceed rupees one crore during any financial year, a sum of rupees five thousand for each financial year; or

    (b) where the annual turnover of the stock broker exceeds rupees one crore during any financial year, a sum of rupees five thousand plus one hundredth of one percent of the turnover in excess of rupees one crore for each financial year;

    (c) after the expiry of five financial years from the date of initial registration as a stock broker, he shall pay a sum of rupees five thousand for a block of five financial years commencing from the sixth financial year after the date of grant of initial registration to keep his registration in force.

2. Fees referred to in clauses (a) and (b) of paragraph 1 above shall be paid –

    (a) in respect of the financial year 1992-93 within one month of the commencement of these regulations;.

    (b) in respect of the financial year beginning on the 1st day of April, 1993 and the following financial years, on or before the 1st day of October of the financial year to which such payment relates, and such fees shall be computed with reference to the annual turnover relating to the preceding financial year.

3. Every remittance of fees referred to in clauses (a) and (b) of paragraph 1, shall be accompanied by a certificate as to the authenticity of turnover on the basis of which fees have been computed duly signed by the stock exchange of which the stock broker is a member or by a qualified auditor as defined in Section 226 of the Companies Act, 1956.

Explanation : For the purposes of paragraphs 1, 2 and 3, "annual turnover" means the aggregate of the sale and purchase prices of securities received and receivable by the stock broker on his own accounts as well as on account of his clients in respect of sale and purchase or dealing in securities during any financial year.

II. Fees to be Paid by Sub-Broker

(a) A sub-broker shall pay a fee of rupees one thousand for each financial year for an initial period of five years.

(b) After the expiry of the five years mentioned above, the sub-broker shall pay a fee of rupees five hundred for each financial year as long as the Certificate remains in force.

III. Manner of Fees to be Paid

The fees indicated above shall be paid on or before the 1st day of October each year payable by a cheque, draft or other instrument in favour of "The Securities and Exchange Board of India" at Bombay.

Types of Brokers in Stock Exchange

The following are the kinds of brokers operating in a stock exchange –

i)   Jobbers or Tarawanwiwallas : These brokers are also called Market Makers in London Stock Exchange and Specialists in New York Stock Exchange while in India they are popular as Jobbers. Jobbers give two way quotes or prices at which they are ready to buy a security as well as selling, quote or price at which they are ready to sell the same security. Both the quotes are given by the Jobber to sell or buy in his own name. So a Jobber buys or sells securities in his own name and earns a profit margin in turn. He specializes in a few securities and does not get any commission as he operates on his own behalf. A Jobber may strike a deal with a broker operating oil behalf of, a client or another Jobber. In BSE every company with a market capitalisation greater than 3 crores must appoint a Jobber to increase market liquidity of its stocks.

A Tarawaniwala is an active member in the Bombay Stock Exchange. He is very similar to a jobber in the London Stock Exchange particularly with regard to the method of transacting business. But, a tarawaniwala can act both as a broker as well as a jobber. Basically he is a jobber. At the same time, he is not prohibited from acting as a broker. The drawback of this system is that a tarawaniwala can act against the interest of investors by purchasing securities from them in his own name at lower prices and selling the same securities to them at higher prices. Hence, many committees have pointed out the questionable practices being adopted by a tarawaniwala.

ii)   Commission Brokers : They are simply brokers who operate on behalf of their clients i.e. buy and sell securities not on their behalf (as a Jobber) but on behalf of their clients. A broker on getting order from the client executes it on behalf of the client and settles the deal. He charges a commission for this purpose and this may range from 0.75% to 1%.

iii)   Sub-Brokers : As broker cannot be present everywhere so on behalf of these sub-brokers deal with the clients. So these sub-brokers bring the clients in contact of the broker.

But they cannot buy or sell securities on clients behalf. They are registered with stock exchange. They charge commission for bringing the client in contact of the broker and this commission is paid out of the commission received by the broker from the client. However, the maximum commission received by a sub-broker can be 40% of the total commission paid by the client.

iv) Authorized Clerks : They are appointed by a broker to act on his behalf in his absence. So they have the power of attorney and can sign documents or buy and sell shares on broker's behalf and in his absence. Brokers are liable for any action of the authorized clerks and have to pay entrance as well as annual subscription fee for them. He can also remove them at any time after prior information to the exchange.

Activity of Brokers :

Stock brokers can operate in the capital market in the following capacities.

a) New issue marketing, underwriting, etc.

b) Client and institutional brokering business for earning brokerage.

c) Jobbing business giving two way quotations and earning profit through margin between bid and offer rates.

d) Arbitrage business - trading as between two or more stock exchanges to take advantage of price differential as profit.

e) Badla financing - financing of the carry forward purchases or sales and earning interest on the finance. (Badla trading was balanced w.e.f. March 1994 by SEBI).

f) Investment advice and consultancy to clients and investors before putting through their deals.

g) Portfolio management of the clients funds on discretionary or non-discretionary basis.

For stock brokers to act as underwriters the stock exchange authorities have to give permission, which is normally given, if the underwriting liability is less than 5% of the total issue. For acting as investment advisors and portfolio managers, there are separate criteria to be satisfied for getting their licence from SEBI. Without SEBI permission, these two functions cannot be undertaken by the brokers.

The functions of brokers in the capital market encompass a wide variety of services. As they are registered members of stock exchange, their activities however, are governed bye-laws and bye-laws of the stock exchange. Permitted Activities of Brokers are as shown in the following Figure 2.17.

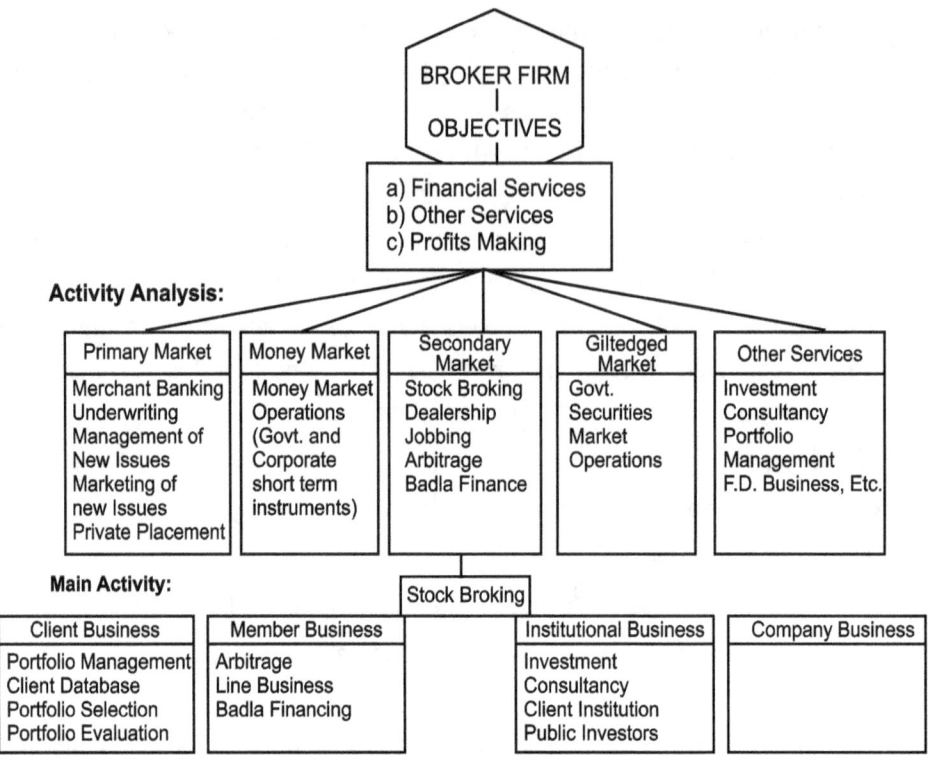

Fig. 2.17 : Permitted Activities of Brokers

The two major functions of brokers are client and institutional business which may involve investment consultancy, and portfolio management also. The other activities of broker firms are of special categories. Thus, jobbing is trading with brokers on wholesale basis, quoting bid and offer rates. The differential between the buying and selling rates is his profit. So is the trading on own account, which may result in profit or loss.

Arbitrage business is buying in one market and selling in another to take advantage of differences in prices. This again leads to speculative gain or loss.

In addition to the above special categories, there is another business that brokers may undertake namely badla finance, which involves lending of money or shares for facilitating carry forward business of shares in the stock market, since prohibited by SEBI.

Client - Broker Relations :

Recently SEBI has given guidelines for brokers to keep all the accounts of their clients separately.

i)   Members have to show and distinguish their own business from that of clients.

ii) They have to pay money into clients' accounts if it is to be paid to them or received from them.

iii) Clients' accounts have to be separately opened and operated either in one consolidated account or in the name of each client separately.

iv) Similarly accounts of securities of clients have to be shown separately from that of the member's own. Such accounts may be kept client wise or for each client separately.

v)   Clients' money and their securities should not be clubbed with that of the member's own.

vi) Members should pass the contract notes on the same day as the deal is executed and show brokerage separately and get the duplicate copy of the contract note signed by the client for record.

vii) Members should get the details from clients regarding the other members with whom they are also dealing and make enquiries with such members about the client's standing.

viii) Members avoid receipt of cash and payment in cash to clients and all dealings should be in A/c Payee Cheques with the clients.

ix) Members should exercise caution for big orders such as ₹ 1 lakh and above particularly from new members.

x)   Margin money may also be collected from clients, if they are buy orders and earnest deposit/securities for sell orders etc.

2.3.4 E-BROKING

NSE launched internet trading in early February 2000. It is the first exchange in the country to provide web-based access to investors to trade directly on the exchange. The orders originating from the PCs of the investors are routed through the internet to the trading terminals of the designated brokers with whom they are connected and further to the exchange for trade executions. Soon after these orders get matched and result into trades, the investors get confirmation about them on their PCs through the internet route.

Wireless Application Protocol (WAP)

SEBI has approved trading through wireless medium on WAP platform. WAP is introduced in November 2000. This provides access to its order book through the hand held devices which use WAP technology. This serves primarily retail investors who are mobile and want to trade from any place when the market prices for stocks at their choice are attractive.

2.3.5 DEPOSITORY SYSTEM

Meaning

A Depository (NSDL & CDSL) is an organisation like a Central Bank where the securities of a shareholder are held in the electronic form at the request of the shareholder through the medium of a Depository Participant.

Definition

The term depository is defined as 'a central location for keeping securities on deposit. It is also defined as 'a facility for holding securities, either in certificated or uncertificated form to enable book entry transfer of securities'.

It is understood from the above two definitions that the depository is a place where securities are stored, recorded in the books on behalf of the investors.

In recent times, the volume of securities and the size of the business handled have increased manifold. Hence, the present day depositories are fully automated to serve the customers faster and accurate.

Therefore, a depository can be defined as, "an institution which transfers the ownership of securities in electronic mode on behalf of its -members".

Similar to the brokers who trade oil behalf of investors in and outside the Stock Exchange, a Depository Participant (DP) is the representative (agent) of the investor in the depository system providing the link between the Company and investor through the Depository. Depository Participants maintain the securities account balances of the investors and intimate them the status of their holding from time to time. According to SEBI guidelines, Financial Institutions like banks, custodians, stock brokers etc. can become depository participants. A DP is one with whom an investor needs to open an account to deal in electronic form. While the Depository can be compared to a Bank, DP is like a branch of the bank with which an investor can have an account.

A Depository is a securities "bank," where dematerialised physical securities are held in custody, and from where they can be traded. This facilitates faster, risk-free and low cost settlement. A Depository is similar to a bank and performs activities similar in nature.

An analogy between a bank and a depository may be shown as follows :

Bank	Depository
• Holds funds in account.	• Holds funds in an account
• Transfers funds between accounts on the instruction of the account holder	• Transfers funds between accounts on the instruction of the account holder
• Facilitates transfers without having to handle money	• Facilitates transfer of ownership
• Facilitates safekeeping of money	• Facilitates safekeeping of shares

Depositories in India

There are two Depositories in India, CDSL and NSDL. CDSL was promoted by Bombay Stock Exchange Limited (BSE) jointly with leading banks such as State Bank of India, Bank of India, Bank of Baroda, HDFC Bank, Standard Chartered Bank, Union Bank of India and Centurion Bank in 1999.

NSDL National Securities-Depository Limited (NSDL) and Central Depository Services (CDS). NSDL was the first Indian Depository. It was inaugurated in November 1996. NSDL was set up with an initial capital of ₹ 124 crore, promoted by Industrial Development Bank of India (IDBI), Unit Trust of India (UTI), National Stock Exchange of India Ltd. (NSEIL) and die State Bank of India (SBI).

Demat, Dematerialisation and Rematerialisation

Demat :

Demat is a commonly used abbreviation for the word Dematerialisation, which is a process whereby securities like shares, debentures are converted from the Material (paper document) form into electronic data and stored in the computers of an electronic depository.

Dematerialisations :

It is a process by which the physical certificates of an investor are take Mack-by the company / registrar, and actually destroyed, and an equivalent number of securities are credited to the shareholders account. This is done at the request of the investor.

Rematerialisation :

It is a term used for converting electronic holdings back into certificates. The registrar will print new certificates with a new range of certificate numbers.

SEBI as on June 07, 1996, granted a certificate of Registration as Depository to the National Securities Depositories Limited (NSDL) under SEBI (Depository and Participants) Regulation 1996. NSDL was inaugurated on November 08, 1996 and since, then, has commenced its operations.

The setting up on depositor is in India for handling transfer of securities, is a major step in moving towards paper less trading, consistent with international practices. SEBI has made trading in 50 scrips for institutional investors mandatory in the dematerialised form, and has stipulated that dematerialised delivery will be valid in the paper-based settlement system.

2.3.5.1 FUNCTIONS OF DEPOSITORY SYSTEM

The **Depository System Functions** Very much like the banking system. A hank holds funds in accounts whereas a Depository holds securities in accounts for its clients. A Bank transfers funds between accounts whereas a Depository transfers securities between accounts. In both systems, the transfer of funds or- securities happens without- the actual.-handling of funds or securities. Both the Banks and the Depository arc accountable for the safe keeping of funds and securities respectively.

The process of opening an account with a Depository Participant is similar to the opening of a bank account.

i)   First, the investor has to open an account with a Depository Participant (DR) of his choice by filling up an Account Opening Form and signing a "Participant-Client Agreement". The investor will be then given a unique client ID number, which must be quoted in all correspondence with the DP.

ii)   Thereafter, the investor will have to fill up and submit a Dematerialization Request Form (DRF) provided by the DP dully signed by all the holders and surrender the physical shares intended to be dematted to the DP.

iii)   Tile DP upon receipt of the shares and the DRF, will issue to him an acknowledgement and will send an electronic request to the Company/Registrars and Transfer Agents of the Company through the Depository for confirmation of demat.

iv) The DP will simultaneously surrender the DRF and the shares to the Company/ Registrars and Transfer Agents of the Company with covering letter requesting the Company to confirm demat.

v) The Registrars and Transfer Agents of' the Company, after necessary verification of' the documents received from the DP, will cancel the physical shares and confirm demat to the Depository.

vi) This confirmation will be passed on by the Depository to tile DP which holds the account of the investor. A item receiving this confirmation from the Depository, the DP will credit investor's account with the number of shares dematerialized. The DP will hold the shares in the dematerialized form thereafter on investor's behalf. And he will become the beneficial owner of these dematerialized shares.

vii) When tile investor submits the shares for dematerialization, his DP will deface the share certificates with the stamp "SURRENDERED FOR DEMAT'ERIALISATION". This ensures that his shares are not lost in transit or misused till credit is received by the investor ill his demat account.

Charges to be-paid for opening an account and to demat one's physical share :

Each DP can levy charges by way of account opening fees, transaction fees, custody fees and so on and these charges differ from Depository Participant to Depository Participant.

Dividend of Dematted Shares :

The Depositories will give the list of demat account holders and the number of shares held by them in electronic form on the Record date to the Registrars and Transfer Agents of the Company (known as BENPOS). On the basis of BENPOS, the Company will issue dividend warrants in favour of the demat account holders.

The rights of the shareholders holding shares in demat form are at par with the holders in physical form. Hence the investor will be eligible to get the Annual Report and will have the right to attend the AGM as a shareholder.

Conversion of Dematted Shares back into Physical Shares : (Process of Rematerialisation)

If the investors wish to get their securities in the physical form all they have to do is to :

(i) Submit a re-materialisation of Request Form (RRF) through their DP in the same manner as Dematerialization.

(ii) The Depository Participant will forward their request to the Depository after verifying that they have the necessary securities in balance.

(iii) The Depository in turn will intimate the Registrar and Transfer Agents of the Company who will print and dispatch to them the share certificates for the number of shares so rematerialized and the investors' account will be debited by the Depository and credited with the Company.

(iv) The Registrar and Transfer Agents will print new certificates with a new range of certificate numbers and provide them to the investor.

One demat account with one D.P. only

Earlier there were absolutely no restrictions on the number of DPs an investor can open accounts with. Opening an account with a DP is very similar to opening a bank account. Just as a person can have savings or current accounts with more than one bank, in the same way he can open accounts with more than one Depository Participant. But w.e.f. 2006 due to frauds in allotment of shares in IPOs, SEBI has issued new guidelines where in investor cannot have more than one Demat account and can open it with one Depository Participant only.

How do you trade in electronic shares ?

Buying and selling electronic shares is just like buying and selling physical shares, the only difference is trading in electronic shares is simpler and safer.

- If you wish to sell your electronic share, you place an order with your broker and instruct your participant by way of a Delivery Instruction (Which is a cheque-like instrument) to debit your account with the number of shares sold by you.
- When you buy electronic shares you must inform your broker about your depository account number so that the electronic shares bought by you are credited into your account and instruct your participant by way of Receipt Instruction to receive credit in your account.
- Payment for the electronic shares either bought or sold is made in the same way as in case of physical securities.
- The shares you have bought are transferred in your name the very next day of pay out with no fear that the shares may turn out to be bad deliveries or fake! No formalities of filling transfer deeds, affixing share transfer stamps and applying to the Company for registering the shares in your name.

In recent days, most of the brokers have D.P A/C with them. So try to choose the broker who has DT A/C. In this case, if you give power of attorney of transferring of your sold shares then you can did not give instruction slip.

Note : Keep one thing in mind. See that your broker should not keep in his pool account the scrip you have purchased. Inform your broker that it must be transferred immediately to your demat account. On line trading automatic systems is followed as broker takes the power of authority when he gives this facility and no need to give delivery instruction slip when you sell. (while you do on line trading)

Facilities Offered by-Depository System :

i)   Dematerialisation i.e., converting physical certificates to electronic form;

ii) Rematerialisation i.e., conversion of securities (such as shares, debentures, bonds and units) in demat form into physical certificates;

iii) Electronic settlement of trades in stock exchanges connected to NSDL.

iv) Pledging/hypothecation of dematerialised securities against bank loan.

v)   Electronic credit of securities allotted in public issues, rights issue and splitting of securities.

vi) Receipt of non-cash corporate benefits such as bonus, in electronic form.

vii) Other services viz. holding debt instruments in the same account, availing stock lending/borrowing facility, etc.

Following two depositories providing 'demat' services in India :
i)   National Securities Depository Limited (NSDL)
ii) Central Depository Services (India) Limited (CDSL)

NSDL was formed and registered under the Companies Act, 1956 during December 1995 and commenced operations during November 1996.

NSDL was promoted by Industrial Development Bank of India (IDBI) the largest Development Bank of India, Unit Trust of India (UTI) the largest Mutual Fund in India and Natioal Stock Exchange (NSE) the largest Stock Exchange in India. Some of the prominent banks in the country also have a stake in NSDL.

Central Depository Services (India) Limited which commenced operating during February 1999. CDSL was promoted by Stock Exchange, Mumbai in association with Bank of Baroda, Bank of India, State Bank of India and HDFC Bank.

2.3.5.2 BENEFITS OF DEPOSITORY SYSTEM

Benefits to investors by opting for dematerialisation (Conversion of Physical holding into Electronic) and Consolidation of' Folios :

A) **Benefits of Dematerialisation :**
   i)   **Trading of securities in compulsory dematerialised form :** Trading of securities at the Stock Exchanges is predominant in dematerialised form. Practically there is no trading of securities in physical form.
   ii) **Holding of different investments in one account:** Holding investments in equity and debt instruments units of mutual funds, Government of India Bonds, Post Office Saving Schemes in a single account.
   iii) **Non stamp duty :** No stamp duty is levied for transfer of any kind of securities in the depository. The water extends to equity shares, debt instruments and units of mutual funds.
   iv) **SMS Alert facility :** Depositories not provide SMS Alert facility whereby investors can obtain alerts of any debits or credits due to a corporate action in your demat account.
   v)   **Faster disbursement of non-cash corporate benefits like** rights, bonus, etc. Depositories provide for direct credit of non-cash corporate entitlements to an investors account thereby ensuring faster disbursement and avoiding risk of loss of certificates in transit.
   vi) **Ease in portfolio monitoring,** since the statement of account gives a consolidated position of investments in all instruments.
   vii) **Periodic Status Reports :** Periodic Status Report on holdings and transactions are forwarded to the shareholders from their depository participants.
   viii) **Freeze or lock of accounts by the investor :** Investors can freeze or lock their accounts for any given period of time, if so desired. Accounts can be frozen for debits (preventing transfer of securities out of accounts) or for credits (preventing any movements of hindrances into accounts) or for both.

ix) **Elimination of all risks associated with physical certificates :** Dealing in physical securities have associated security risks of theft of stocks, mutilation of certificates loss of certificates during movements through and from the registrars, thus exposing the investor to the cost of obtaining duplicate certificates etc. This problem does not arise in the depository environment.

x) **Immediate transfer and registration of securities :** In the depository environment, once the securities are credited to the investors account on pay out, he becomes the legal owner of the securities. There is no further need to send it to the company's registrar for registration. Having purchased securities in the physical environment, the investor has to send it to the company's registrar so that the change of ownership can be registered.

xi) **Faster settlement cycle :** The settlement cycle follow rolling settlement on T + 1 basis i.e. the settlement of trades will be on the next working day from the trade day. This will enable faster turnover of stock and more liquidity with the investor.

xii) **End of problems related to change of address of investor :** In case of change of address, investors are saved from undergoing the entire change procedure with each company or registrar. Investors have to only inform their DP with all relevant documents and the required changes are effected in the database of all the companies, where the investor is a registered holder of securities.

xiii) **Elimination of problems related to transmission of demat shares :** In case of dematerialised holdings, the process of transmission is more convenient as the transmission formalities for all securities held in a demat account can be completed by submitting documents to the DP whereas, in case of physical securities the surviving joint holder(s) legal heirs/nominee has to correspond independently with each company in which shares are held.

B) **Benefits of Consolidation of Folios :**

i) The present day scenario provides the investor with a lot of convenience in maintaining the portfolios through dematerialisation. Investors need to open multiple demat accounts in case the shares are held in different Combinations. Consolidation of the folios would minimize the necessity to open multiple demat accounts and thereby maintenance costs can be reduced.

ii) Consolidation of folios would also help in shareholder(s) getting a single share certificate for all the shares held by them thereby reducing dematerialisation costs if the shareholder(s) opt for converting the shares into electronic mode.

iii) Maintenance of multiple folios would result in payment of dividend amounts through multiple warrants, resulting in higher chances of pilferage/misplacement in postal transit. Consolidation of folios would lead to payment of dividend through a single warrant and hence the shareholder is assured of receiving the dividend of all the shares held by him.

iv) In case of dividend being credited directly to the hunk accounts of the investor, the requirement tar the investor to verify his bank account to ensure that dividend for all the shares has been credited does not arise. The dividend for all the shares held by him would be credited as a single, transaction.

2.3.6 STOCK MARKET TRADING

Most stocks are traded on exchanges, which are places where buyers and sellers meet and decide on a price. Some exchanges are physical locations where transactions are carried on a trading floor. The other types of exchange is virtual, composed of a network of computers where trades are made electronically.

The purpose of a stock market is to facilitate the exchange of securities between buyers and sellers, reducing the risks of investing. There are two types of security markets i.e. primary and secondary market. The primary market is where securities are created (by means of an IPO) while in secondary market, investors trade previously-issued securities without the involvement of the issuing companies. The secondary market is what people are referring to when they talk about the stock market. It is important to understand that the trading of a company's stock does not directly involve that company.

When much of the trading is done face-to-face on a trading floor is also referred as listed exchange. In this trading, orders come in through brokerage firms that are members of the exchange and flow down to floor brokers who go to a specific spot on the floor where the stock trades. At this location known as the trading post, there is a specific person known as the specialist whose jobs is to match buyers and sellers. Prices are determined using an auction method where the current price is the highest amount any buyer is willing to pay and the lowest price at which someone is willing to sell. Once the process of a trade has been completed, the details are sent back to the brokerage firm, who then notifies the investor, who place the order. Other stocks (other than listed) may trade "over the counter" that is, through dealer. A large company will usually have its stock listed on many exchanges across the world.

In short, 'trade in stock markets' means the transfer of money of a stock or security from seller to buyer. This requires these two parties to agree on a price. Equities (stocks or shares) confer on ownership interest in a particular company.

The purpose of a stock exchange is to facilitate the exchange of securities between buyers and sellers, thus providing a market place (virtual or real). The exchanges provide real time trading information on the listed securities, facilitating price discovery.

The New York Stock Exchange (NYSE) is a physical exchange, with a hybrid market for placing orders both electronically and manually on the trading floor. Orders executed on the trading floor enter by way of exchange members and flow down to a floor broker, who goes to the floor trading post specialist for that stock to trade the order.

The 'NASDAQ' is a virtual listed exchange, where all of the trading is done over a computer network. The process is similar to the New York Stock Exchange. However, buyers and sellers are electronically matched. One or more NASDAQ market makers will always provide a bid and ask price at which they will always purchase or sell their stock.

Participants in stock market range from small individual stock investors to larger traders investors, who can be based anywhere in the world and include banks, insurance companies or pension fund and hedge funds. Their buyer or sell orders may be executed on their behalf by a stock exchange trader.

2.3.7 DERIVATIVES TRADING

The derivative markets are for those assets or instruments, which are synthetic financial products derived from the real assets or stocks or commodities. These new financial products have combinations of features of the existing real products and can be traded separately independent of the instruments or stocks, from which they are derived.

The major derivative products have been classified as options, futures and hybrids, which are all widely used in developed countries and in some developing countries. These products are increasingly becoming popular and traded volumes in these products are increasing, year after year :

Derivatives are financial instruments/contracts whose value depends upon the value of an underlying. Since their value is essentially derived out of an underlying, they are financial abstractions whose value is derived mathematically from the changes in the value of the underlying.

The underlying can be an agricultural commodity like wheat, barley or tea; individual stocks like Microsoft, Daimler-Chrysler, Infosys and Zee Telefilms; stock indexes like Standard & Poor 500, Nikkei-225, BSE Sensex or NSE Nifty; financial instruments like T. bills, notes and-bonds; currencies like the Dollar, Euro, Pound; or even interest rates and literally anything. Since derivatives today, are being written on any type of underlying, and not necessarily on an asset, the underlying can be a widget a hypothetical thing which is used for the purpose of an example.

Meaning

As the word implies, a derivative instrument is derived from "something" backing it. This something may be a loan, an asset, an interest rate, a currency flow, a stock trade, a commodity transaction, a trade flow etc. Derivatives enable a company to hedge 'this something without changing the flow associated with the business operation.

Derivative is financial instruments that are linked to a specific financial instrument or indicator or commodity and through which specific financial risks can be traded in financial markets in their own right. The value of a financial derivative derives from the price of an underlying item, such as an asset or index. Unlike debt securities, no principal is advanced to be repaid and no investment income accrues.

In a strict sense, derivatives are based upon all those major financial instruments which are explicitly traded like equities, debt instruments, forex instruments and commodity based contracts. Thus, when we talk about derivatives, we usually mean only financial derivatives, namely, forwards, futures, options, swaps etc. The peculiar features of these instruments are that :

i) they can be designed in such a way so as to cater to the varied requirements of the users either by simply using any one of the above instruments or by using a combination of two or more such instruments.

ii) they can be designed and traded on the basis of the expectations regarding the future price movements of underlying assets.

iii) they are all off-balance sheet instruments and

iv) they are used as a device for reducing the risks of fluctuations in asset values.

Definitions

It is very difficult to define the term derivatives in a comprehensive way since many developments have taken place in this field in recent years. However, some attempt have been made by the experts to define the term "derivatives".

"Derivative is a product whose value is derived from the value of one or more basic variables, called bases (underlying asset, index, or reference rate), in a contractual manner. The underlying asset can be equity, forex, commodity or any other asset. For example, rice farmers may wish to sell their harvest at a future date to eliminate the risk of a change in prices by that date Such a transaction is an example of a derivative. The price of this derivative is driven by the spot price of rice which is the underlying".

According to one expert, "Derivatives involve payment/receipt of income generated by the underlying asset on a notional principal".

According to another definition, "Derivatives are a special type of off-balance sheet instruments in which no principal is ever paid".

Yet another definition runs as follows: "Derivatives are instruments which make payments calculated using price of interest rates derived from on balance sheet or cash instruments, hut do not actually employ those cash instruments to fund payments".

All these definitions point out the fact that transactions are carried out on a notional principal, transferring only the income generated by the underlying asset.

The emergence of the market for derivative products,, most notably forwards, futures and options, can be traced back to the willingness of risk: averse economic agents to guard themselves against uncertainties arising out of fluctuations in asset prices. By their very nature, the financial markets are marked by a very high degree of volatility. Through the use of derivative products, it is possible to partially or fully transfer price risks by locking in asset prices. As instruments of risk management, these generally do not influence the fluctuations in the underlying asset prices. However, by locking-in asset prices, derivative products minimize the impact of fluctuations in asset prices on the profitability and cash flow situation of risk averse investors.

Derivative products initially emerged as hedging devices against fluctuations in commodity prices and commodity linked derivatives. The financial derivatives came into spotlight due to growing instability in the financial market. In recent years, the market for financial derivatives has grown tremendously both in terms of variety of instruments available, their complexity and also turnover.

Participants

Derivative contracts have several variants. The most common variants are forwards, futures, and options. The following three broad categories of participant's hedgers, speculators, and arbitrageurs trade in the derivatives market.

Hedgers face risk associated with the price of an asset. They use futures or options markets to reduce or eliminate this risk.

Speculators wish to bet on future movements in the price of an asset. Futures and options contracts can give them an extra leverage; that is, they can increase-both the potential losses in a speculative venture.

Arbitrageurs are in business to take advantage of a discrepancy between prices in two different markets. 1f, for example, they se the futures price of an asset getting out of line with cash price, they will take offsetting positions in the two markets to lock in a profit.

Functions of Derivatives Market

The **derivatives market** performs a number of **economic functions** such as,

i)   Prices in an organized derivatives market reflect the perception of market participants about the future and lead the prices of underlying to the perceived future level. The prices of derivatives converge with the prices of the underlying at the expiration of the derivative contract. Thus, derivatives help in discovery of future as well as current prices.

ii) An important incidental benefit that flows from derivatives trading is that it acts as a catalyst for new entrepreneurial activity. The derivatives have a history of attracting many bright, creative and well-educated people having an entrepreneurial attitude. They often energize others to create new businesses, new products and new employment opportunities, the benefit of which are immense,

iii) Derivatives markets help increase savings and investment in the long run. Transfer of risk enables market participants to expand their volume of activity.

iv) The derivatives market helps to transfer risks from those who have them but may not like them to those who have an appetite for them.

v)   Derivatives, due to their inherent nature, are linked to the underlying cash markets. With the introduction of derivatives, the underlying market witness higher trading volumes because of participation by more players who would not otherwise participate for lack of an arrangement to transfer risk.

vi) Speculative trades shift to a more controlled environment of derivatives market in the absence of an organized derivatives market, speculators trade in the underlying cash markets. Margining, monitoring and surveillance of the activities of various participants become extremely difficult in these kinds of mixed markets.

Kinds of Financial Derivatives

The important Kinds of Financial Derivatives are shown below in Figure 2.18.

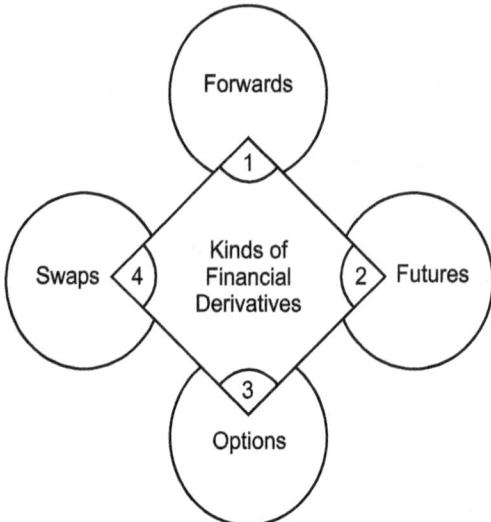

Fig. 2.18 : Kinds of Financial Derivatives

1) Forwards :

A forward contract is a customized contract between two entities, where settlement takes place on a specific date in the future at today's pre-agreed price.

2) Futures :

A futures contract is an agreement between two parties to buy or sell an asset at a certain time in the future at a certain price. Futures contracts are special types of forward contracts in the sense that the former are standardised exchange-traded contracts.

3) Options :

Options are of two types - calls and puts. Calls give the buyer the right but not the obligation to buy a given quantity of the underlying asset, at a given price on or before a given future date. Puts give the buyer the right but not the obligation to sell a given quantity of the underlying asset at a given price on or before a given date.

4) Swaps :

Swap is yet another exciting trading instrument. In fact, it is a combination of forwards by two counterparties. It is arranged to reap the benefits arising from the fluctuations in the market either currency market or interest rate market or any other market for that matter.

Futures :

A futures contract is an agreement between two parties to buy or sell an asset at a certain time in the future at a certain price. But unlike forward contracts, the futures contracts are standardised and exchange traded, to facilitate liquidity in the futures contracts, the exchange specifies certain standard features of the contract. It is a standardised contract with standard underlying instrument, a standard quantity and quality of the underlying instrument that can be delivered, (or which can be used for reference purposes in settlement) and a standard timing of such settlement. A futures contract may be offset prior to maturity by entering into an equal and opposite transaction. More than 99% of futures transactions are offset this way.

The standardised items in a futures contract are:

i)   Quantity of the underlying.

ii) Quality of the underlying.

iii) The date and the month of delivery.

iv) The units of price quotation and minimum price change.

v)   Location of settlement.

Futures Terminology :

i)   Spot Price

The price at which an asset trades in the spot market.

ii) Futures Price

The price at which the futures contract trades in the futures market.

iii) Contract Cycle

The period over which a contract trades. The index futures contracts on the NSE have one month, two-month and three month expiry cycles which expire on the last Thursday of the month. Thus a January expiration contract expires on the last Thursday of January and a February expiration contract ceases trading on the last Thursday of February. On the Friday following the last Thursday, a new contract having a three-month expiry is introduced for trading.

iv) Expiry Date

It is the date specified in the futures contract. This is the last day on which the contract will be traded, at the end of which it will cease to exist.

v) Contract Size

The amount of asset that has to be delivered under one contract. For instance, the contract size/lot size on NSE's futures market is 50 Nifties.

vi) Basis

In the context of financial futures, basis can be defined as the futures price minus the spot price. There will be a different basis for each delivery month for each contract. In a normal market, basis will be .positive. This reflects that future prices normally exceed spot prices.

vii) Cost of Carry

The relationship between futures prices and spot prices can be summarized in terms of what is known as the cost or carry. This measures the storage cost plus the interest that is paid to finance the asset less the income earned on the asset.

viii) Initial Margin

The amount that must be deposited in the margin account at the time a futures contract is first entered into is known as initial margin.

ix) Marking-to-Market

In the futures market, at the end of each trading day, the margin account is adjusted to reflect the investor's gain or loss depending upon the futures closing price. This is called marking-to-market.

x) Maintenance Margin

This is somewhat lower than the initial margin. This is set to ensure that the balance in the margin account never becomes negative. if the balance in the margin account bills below the maintenance margin, the investor receives a margin call and is expected to top up the margin account to the initial margin level before trading commences on the next day.

Options :

Options are fundamentally different from forward and futures contracts. An option gives the holder of the option the right to do something. The holder does not have to exercise this right. In contrast, in a forward or futures contract, the two parties have committed themselves to do something. Whereas it costs nothing (except margin requirements) to enter into a futures contract, the purchase of an option requires an upfront payment.

Options Terminology :

i) Index Options

These options have the index as the underlying.

ii) Stock Options:

Stock options are options on individual stocks. A contract gives the holder the right but no obligations to buy or sell shares at the specified price.

iii) Buyer of an Option

The buyer of an option is the one who by premium buys the right but clot the obligation lo exercise his potion on the seller/writer.

iv) Writer of an option

The writer of a call/put option is the one who receives the option premium and is there by obliged to sell/buy the asset if the buyer wishes to exercise his option.

v) Types of options

There are two basic types of options, call options and put options.

    a) Call Options : A call option gives the holder the right but not the obligation to buy an a-set by a certain date for a certain price.

b) Put option : A put option gives the holder the right but not the obligation to sell an asset by a certain date for a certain price.

vi) Option Price

Option price is the price which the option buyer pays to the option seller. It is also referred to as the option premium.

vii) Expiration Date

The date specified in the options contract is known as the expiration date, the exercise date, the strike date or the maturity.

viii) Strike Price

The price specified in the options contract is known as the strike price or the exercise price.

Difference between Futures and Forwards Contracts :

Forward contracts are often confused with futures coat-acts. The confusion is primarily because both serve essentially the same economic functions of allocating risk in the presence of future price uncertainty. However futures are a significant improvement over the forward contracts as they eliminate counterparty risk and offer more liquidity.

Futures	Forwards
• Trade on an organised exchange	• OTC in nature
• Standardised contract terms	• Customised contract terms
• More liquid	• Less liquid
• Requires margin payment	• Doesn't require margin payment
• Follows daily settlement	• Settlement happens at end of period

Difference between Futures and Options :

Options are different from futures in several senses. At a practical level, the option buyer faces an interesting situation. He pays for the option in full at the time it is purchased. After this, he only has an upside. There is no of possibility of the options position generating any further losses to him (other than the funds already paid for the option). This is different from futures, which is free to enter into, but can generate very large losses/Profit. This characteristic makes options attractive to many occasional market participants, who cannot put in the time to closely monitor their futures positions.

More generally, options offer 'non-linear payoffs' whereas futures only have 'linear payoffs'. By combining futures and options, a wide variety of innovative and useful payoff structures can be created.

Futures	Options
• Exchange traded	• Same as futures
• Exchange defines the product	• Same as futures
• Price is zero, strike price moves	• Strike price is fixed, price moves
• Price is zero	• Price is always positive
• Linear payoff	• Non-linear payoff
• Both long and short at risk	• Only short at risk

Procedure of Derivative Trading :

Order matching is essentially on the basis of security, its price, time and quantity. All quantity fields are in units and price in rupees. The lot size on the futures and options market is 50 for Nifty. The exchange notifies the regular lot size and tick size for each security traded on this segment from time to time. Orders, as and when they are received, are first time stamped and then immediately processed for potential match. When any order enters the trading system, it is an active order. If it finds a match, a trade is generated. If a match is not found, then the orders are stored in different 'books'.

Orders are stored in price - time priority in various books in the following sequence :

i)   Best Price.

ii) Within Price

iii) By time priority.

Derivative Products

The F & O segment of NSE provides trading facilities for the following derivative products/instruments.

i)   Index Futures

NSE trades Nifty futures contracts having one month, two month and three month expiry cycles. All contracts expire on the last Thursday of every month. Thus a January expiration contract would expire on the last Thursday of January and a February expiry contract would cease trading on the last Thursday of February, incase of holiday, contract shall exchange on preceding day. On the Friday following the last Thursday, a new contract having a three - month expiry would be introduced for trading. Depending on the time period for which you want to take an exposure in index futures contracts, you can place buy and sell orders in the respective contracts.

The Instrument type 'FUTIDX' refers to 'Futures contracts on index' and Contract symbol – 'NIFTY' denote a 'Futures contract on Nifty index' and the expiry date represents the last date on which the contract will be available for trading. Each futures contract has a separate limit order book. All passive orders are stacked in the system in terms of price time priority and trades take place at the passive order price (similar to the existing capital market trading system). The best buy order for a given futures contract will be the order to buy the index at the highest index level whereas the best sell order will be the order to sell the index at the lowest index level. Trading for NIFTY is for a-minimum lot size of 50 units.

ii) Index Options :

On NSE's index options market, contracts at different strikes, having one-month, two-month and three-month expiry cycles are available for trading. There are typically one-month, two-month and three-month options, each with five different strikes available for trading.

iii) Stock Futures :

Trading in stock futures commenced on the NSE from November 2001.These contracts are rash settled on a T + 1 basis. The expiration cycle for stock futures is the same as for index futures, index options and stock options. A new contract is introduced on the trading day following the expiry of the near month contract.

iv) Stock Options :

Trading in stock options commenced on the NSE from July 2001. These contracts -are American style and are settled in cash. The expiration cycle for stock option is the same as for index futures and index options. A new contract is introduced on the trading day following the expiry of the near month contract. NSE provides a minimum of seven strike prices for every option type (i.e. call and put) during the trading month. There are at least three in-the-money contracts, three out-of-the-money contracts and one at the money contracts available for trading.

Open Interest :

Open interest is the total number of outstanding contracts that are held by market participants at the end of each day. Putting it simply, open interest is a measure of how much interest is there in a particular option or future. Increasing open interest means that fresh funds are flowing in the market, while declining open interest means that market is liquidating.

Contract Expiry and Introduction of New Contract :

All future and option contracts expire on last Thursday of the expiry month. Incase of holiday, contract shall expire on preceding day.

Future and Option contracts have three months expiration cycle. On expiry of contract, an new contract is introduced on the trading day following the expiry of a contract. The new contract is introduced for three months duration. This way, at any point of time, there will be three contracts, available for trading in the market.

Customer Margins :

In order to avoid unhealthy competition among clearing members in reducing margins to attract customers, a mandatory minimum margin is obtained by the members from the customers. Such a step insures the market against serious liquidity crisis arising out of possible defaults by the clearing members owing to insufficient margin retention.

In order to secure their own interest as well as that of the entire system responsible for the smooth functioning of the market, which comprises of the stock exchanges, clearing houses and the Links involved, the member collect ma, gins from their clients as may be stipulated by the stock exchanges from time to time. The members pass on the margins to the clearing house on the net basis, i.e. at a stipulated percentage of die net of purchase and sale position while they collect the margins from clients on gross basis, i.e. separately on purchases and sales.

The stock exchange imposes margins as follows :

Initial margins on the both buy as well as the sell.

The accounts of buyers and sellers are marked to the market on daily basis.

The concept of margin here is the same as that for any other trade, i.e., to introduce a financial stake of the client, to ensure performance of contract and cover day to day adverse fluctuation in the prices of securities bought. The margins paid by the investor are placed at the disposal of the clearing house through the brokerage firms. The clearing house gets the protection against possible business risks through the margins placed with it in this manner and by the process of 'marking to market :

The margins for futures contracts has two components :

Initial margin, and Mark-to-market.

i) Initial Margin :

In a futures contract both the buyers & seller are required to perform the contract. Accordingly both the buyers & the seller are required to put in the Initial margins. The initial margin is knows as performances margin and is usually 10 to 25 % of the purchase price of the contract. The margin is set by the stock exchange keeping in view the volumes of tile business and size of transaction as well as operative risks of the market in general.

The concept being used by NSE to compute initial margin on the futures transaction is called Value-at-Risk (VAR) whereas the options markets has a SPAN based margins system. Through the VAR methodology, the possible erosion in the value of a stock or portfolio, on an average, during a day is evaluated and accordingly initial margins are prescribed. Initial margin is to be paid up-front and can be given by way of cash, bank guarantee or other acceptable collateral.

ii) Marking to Market :

Marking to the market means, debiting or crediting the clients equity accounts with the losses or gain of the day, based on which, margins are sought or released. It is import-ant to note that through Marking to market process, the clearing house substitutes each existing futures contracts with a new contracts that has the settle price or the base price (as referred to by NSE). Base price shall be the pervious day's closing Nifty value. Settle price (as reported in the financial. press as well as the BHAVCOPY issued by NSE on-line) is the purchase price in the new contract for the next trading day.

Settlement Mechanism :

Futures contracts have two types of settlements, the MTM settlement which happens on a continuous basis at the end of each day, and the final settlement which happens on the last trading day of the futures contract.

MTM Settlement :

All futures contracts for each member are mark-to-market (MTM) to the daily settlement price of the relevant futures contract at the end of each day.

The CMs who have a loss are required to pay the mark-to-market (MTM) loss amount in cash which is in turn passed on the CMs who have made a MTM profit. This is known as daily mark-to-market settlement. CMs are responsible to collect and settle the daily MTM profits/losses incurred by the TMs and their clients clearing and settling through them. Similarly, TMs ARE responsible to collect/pay losses/profits from/to their clients by the next day. The pay-in and pay-out of the mark-to-market settlement are affected on the day, following the trade day (T + 1). The mark to market losses or profits are directly debited or credited to the CMs clearing bank account.

After completion of daily settlement computation, all the open position are reset to the daily settlement price. Such positions become the open positions for the next day.

Final Settlement for Futures :

On the expiry day, of the futures contracts, after the close of trading hours, NSCCL marks all positions of a CM to the final settlement of future contracts, after the close of trading hours, NSCCL marks all positions of a CM to the final settlement price and the resulting profit/loss is settled in cash. Final settlement of future contracts is similar to the daily settlement process except for the method of computation of final settlement price. The final settlement profit/loss is computed as the difference between trade price or the previous day's settlement price, as case may be, and the final settlement price of the relevant futures contract, Final settlement loss/profit amount is debited/ credited to the relevant CM's clearing bank account on the day following expiry day of the contract. Open positions in futures contracts cease to exist after their expiration day.

Derivatives Trading in India

Derivatives are traded in India both on BSE and NSE since June 2000. First index futures were introduced in June 2000 and Index options in June 2001. Stock options were allowed in July 2001 and Stock Futures in November 2001, both on the BSE and NSE. But interest rate futures were introduced on NSE in June 2003.

By legislative amendments, options and futures were made tradeable by treating them as securities, by Amendment to the Securities Contracts (Regulation) Act. Derivative trading has picked up faster on NSE than on the BSE, due to institutional support there and better regulatory framework. Secondly, the turnover in derivatives has far surpassed the turnover in the cash market, due to larger speculative fervour and greater participation by FIIs and MFs in the derivative market for hedging and speculation.

Presently traded derivatives are Index Futures, Index Options, Stock Futures and Stock Options and Daily quotations of them are published in the Financial Dailies. They give data on open, high, low, close, for each of the Contracts - Open position and number of contracts in each of the instruments - Index and Stocks, etc. The data on total turnover is also published by BSE and NSE and on a monthly basis, by the RBI in their Handbook of Statistics.

In terms of volume of turnover, the most widely-traded are the Index Futures and Stock Futures followed by Index Options and Stock Options. But in terms of hedge, as seen earlier, in this chapter options provide a better hedge, covering both the long and short positions of traders. In terms of stocks traded, only most widely traded securities like ACC, Tisco, Reliance etc, are included for derivative trading. Contracts upto three months are now available for trading in the Index Futures.

At present, derivatives trading is allowed in 31 stocks in both BSE and NSE. Most of the derivatives trading is concentrated in the NSE futures and options segment, which clocks an average daily turnover of over ₹ 2000 crore while turnover on BSE is less than ₹ 10 crore. Trading has shot up from 21,295 contracts per day in December 2001 to 26,496 in March 2002 and touched 40,806 in October 2002. The daily derivatives volume eventually crossed the 50,000 contracts a day mark in December 2002, which happens to be the highest in the world. SEBI has now allowed trading in 31 additional scrips on the NSE taking the total to 62 stocks and that is exciting news.

QUESTIONS FOR SELF STUDY

I. Theory Questions :

1. Define 'Stock Market' and state the important characteristics of stock market.
2. What is 'Stock Exchange' ? Explain the organizational set-up of a typical stock exchange.
3. State the qualifications required to become a member of a recognized stock exchange.
4. Define the term 'Stock Market'. State the services rendered by the stock market.
5. What is 'Stock Market Indices' ? State the important determinants of Stock Index.
6. Explain the important features of Bombay Stock Exchange.
7. State the organizational structure of Bombay Stock Exchange.
8. What are the eligibility criteria for trading membership of National Stock Exchange.
9. State the important objectives of National Stock Exchange.
10. What is over the counter exchange of India ? State the need of over the Counter Exchange of India.
11. State the important features of 'Over the Counter Exchange of India'.
12. Explain the advantages of 'Over the Counter Exchange of India' to the investors and to the company.
13. What is 'Primary Market' ? Explain the functions of Primary Market.
14. State the role of SEBI in Primary Market.
15. What is 'Issue Mechanism' ? State the options available to bring out a public issue of unlisted companies.
16. What is 'Public Issue" ? State the different kinds of issues.
17. What is 'Secondary Market' ? State the objectives of secondary market.
18. Explain the term 'Secondary Market'. Explain the important functions of secondary market.
19. What is 'Depository System' ? Explain the important functions of Depository System.
20. What is 'Derivatives Trading' ? State the functions of Derivatives Market.
21. Differentiate between :
    i) Stock Exchange and over the Counter Exchange of India, ii) Primary Market and Secondary Market, iii) Futures and Forwards Contrasts, iv) Futures and Options.
22. Write short notes on :
    i) Membership of Stock-Exchanges, ii) Powers of Governing Boards of Stock Exchanges, iii) Services rendered to the Corporation by the Stock Exchanges, iv) Stock Market Indices, v) Objectives of Bombay Stock Exchanges, vi) Basket Trading System, vii) Ownership and Management of National Stock Exchange, viii) Wholesale Debt Market, ix) National Stock Exchanges Indices, x) Triple Service Functions of New Issue Market, xi) Book-Building, xii) Right Issue, xiii) Participants of Primary Market, xiv) Trading Functioning of Stock Market, xv) Stock Broking, xvi) Types of Brokers in Stock Market, xvii) E-Broking, xviii) Benefits of Dematerialisation, xix) Kinds of Financial Derivatives, xx) Derivatives Trading of India.

3...

Financial Services

Contents ...

FINANCIAL SERVICES

The Indian financial infrastructure is unquestionably one of the strongest among the developing countries, both in terms of **hardware, i.e. financial institutions and instruments and software, i.e. financial services.**

Recently, there have been many exciting and unprecedented developments in the Indian capital market in general, and that of the stock exchanges in particular is attracting the attention of every one not only in India, but also abroad.

There are three types of players, whose interests need to be safeguarded in the securities market. They are **firstly**, the corporate entities issuing equity and other instruments, **secondly**, financial intermediaries including brokers and institutions and **thirdly**, the investors contributing savings for deriving benefits.

Financial Services represents the software portion of the financial environment. A variety of services is rendered by the public and private sector institutions engaged in financial services.

In general, all types of activities which are of a financial nature could be brought under the term 'financial services'. The term "Financial Services" in a broad sense means "mobilising and allocating savings". Thus, it includes all activities involved in the transformation of saving into investment. In the present day financial markets, investment has become complicated and is both an art and a science. One makes investments for a return higher than what he can get by keeping the money in a commercial or cooperative Bank or even in an investment Bank. In the finance field, it is a common knowledge that money or finance is scarce and that investors try to maximise their return. But the return is higher, if the risk is also higher. Return and Risk go together and they have a trade off. All investments are risky, to some degree or other. The art of investment is to see that the return is maximised with the minimum of risk, which is inherent in investments.

The **'financial service'** can also be called 'financial intermediation' Financial intermediation is a process by which funds are mobilised from a large number of savers and make them available to all those who are in need of it and particularly to corporate customers. Thus, financial services sector is a key area and it is very vital for industrial developments. A well developed financial services industry is absolutely necessary to mobilise the savings and to allocate them to various investable channels and thereby to promote industrial development in a country.

Classification of Financial Services

Financial Services can be broadly classified into two activities as shown below in Figure 3.1.

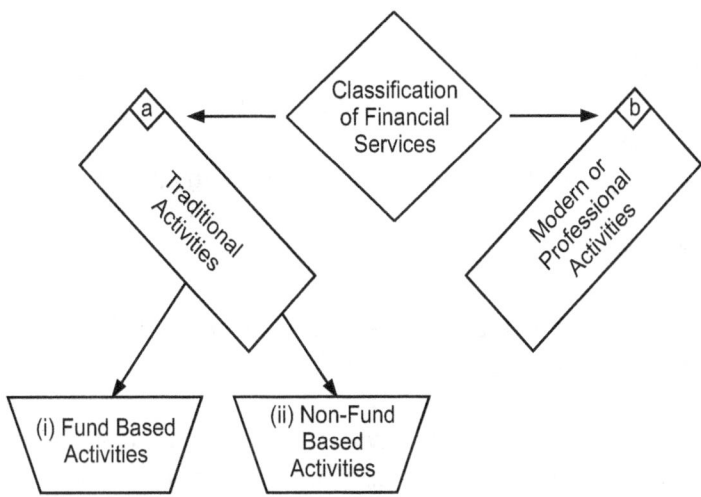

Fig. 3.1 : Classification of Financial Services

a) Traditional Activities

Traditionally, the financial intermediaries have been rendering a wide range of services encompassing both capital and money market activities. They can be grouped under two heads viz. i) Fund based activities and ii) Non-fund based activities.

i) Fund Based Activities :

The traditional services which come under fund based activities are the following.

- Underwriting of or investment in shares, debentures, bonds etc. of new issues (primary market activities).
- Dealing in secondary market activities related to securities.
- Participating in money market instruments like commercial papers, certificate of deposits, treasury bills, discounting of bills etc.
- Involving in equipment leasing, hire purchase, venture capital, seed capital etc.
- Dealing in foreign exchange market activities.

ii) Non-fund Based Activities :

Financial intermediaries provide services on the basis of non-fund activities also. This can also be called "fee based" activity.

A wide variety of services, are being provided under this head. They include the following :

- Making arrangements for the placement of capital and debt instruments with investment institutions.
- Arrangement of funds from financial institutions for the clients' project cost or his working capital requirements.
- Assisting in the process of getting all Government and other clearances, certifications, permits etc.

- Managing the capital issues – i.e. management of pre-issue and post-issue activities relating to the capital issue in accordance with the SEBI guidelines and thus enabling the promoters to market their issues.

b) Modern Activities

Besides the above traditional services the financial intermediaries render following fund based as well as non-fund based activities.

i) Issue Management

Also so known as merchant banking or investment banking. This service is witnessing a boom with the number and amount of public/right issues increasing by leaps and bounds after the abolition of CCI.

ii) Loan Syndication

Finance companies organise loan syndications for both rupee and foreign currency loans by negotiating the best possible loan packages acceptable to the borrowers and the leaders.

iii) Credit Rating

The credit worthiness of the borrower has to be measured before granting him a loan. CRISIL was set up as the first credit rating agency. After the ICRA and CARE have also been set up a provide credit rating services. Government has made it mandatory to have a notified credit rating before issuing debentures, fixed deposits and commercial paper.

iv) Portfolio Management

These are specialist agencies which manage the portfolios of individuals and institutions to suit the needs of the owners.

v) Securities Broking

Brokers and sub-brokers provide the service of buying and selling of securities in the stock exchanges for their clients.

vi) Issue Underwriting

It is an arrangement between the issuing company and the underwriter whereby the underwriter agrees to take up the shares/debentures if they are not fully subscribed by the public.

vii) Education and Training

Education and training in the areas of financial services is offered by institutions like the Institute of Chartered Financial Analysts of India (ICFAI). The UTI Institute of Capital Markets also offers short term and long term seminars and courses in these areas.

Other than above, some of the modern services provided by financial intermediaries are as under :

i) Rendering project advisory services right from the preparation of the project report till the raising of funds for starting the project with necessary Government approval.

ii) Planning for mergers and acquisitions and assisting for their smooth carry out.

iii)   Guiding corporate customers in capital restructuring.

iv)   Acting as Trustees to the debentureholders.

v)   Recommending suitable changes in the management structure and management style with a view to achieving better results.

vi)   Structuring the financial collaboration/joint ventures by identifying suitable joint venture partner and preparing joint venture agreement.

vii)   Rehabilitating and reconstructing sick companies through appropriate scheme of reconstruction and facilitating the implementation of the scheme.

viii)   Hedging of risks due to exchange rate risk, interest rate risk, economic risk and political risk by using swaps and other derivative products.

ix)   Undertaking services relating to the capital market such as :
   - Clearing services,
   - Registration and transfers,
   - Safe-custody of securities,
   - Collection of income on securities.

x)   Undertaking risk management services like insurance services, buy-back options etc.

xi)   Advising the clients on the question of selecting the best source of funds taking into consideration the quantum of funds required, their cost, lending period etc.

xii)   Guiding the clients in the minimisation of the cost of debt and in the determination of the optimum debt-equity mix.

3.1 MERCHANT BANKING

3.1.1 MEANING

A "**Merchant Banker**" could be defined as "an organisation that acts as an intermediary between the issuers and the ultimate purchasers of securities in the primary security market".

Merchant Banker has been defined under the **Securities and Exchange Board of India (Merchant Bankers) Rules, 1992** as "any person who is engaged in the business of issue management by making arrangements regarding corporate advisory service in relation to such issue management".

The term merchant banking is used differently in different countries and so there is no precise definition for it. In London, merchant banker refers to those who are members of British Merchant Banking and Securities House Association who carry on consultation, leasing, portfolio services, assets management, euro credit, loan syndication etc. In America, merchant banking is concerned with mobilising savings of people and directing the funds to business enterprise.

There is no universal definition for merchant banking. It assumes diverse functions in different countries. So merchant banking may be defined as, "an institution which covers a wide range of activities such as management of customer services, portfolio management, credit syndication, acceptance credit, counselling, insurance etc."

The Notification of the Ministry of Finance defines **a Merchant Banker** as, "any person who is engaged in the business of issue management either by making arrangements regarding selling, buying or subscribing to the securities are manager, consultant, adviser or rendering corporate advisory service in relation to such issue management".

Origin of Merchant Banking

Merchant banking originated through the entering of London merchants in financing foreign trade through acceptance of bill. Later, the merchants assisted the Government of under developed countries in raising long term funds through flotation of bonds in London money market. Over a period, they extended their activities to domestic business of syndication of long term and short term finance, underwriting of new issues, acting as registrars and share transfer agents, debenture trustees, portfolio managers, negotiating agents for mergers, take over etc. The post war period witnessed the rapid growth of merchant banking through the innovative instrument like Euro dollar and the growth of various financial centres like Singapore, Hong Kong, Baharain, Kuwait, Dubai etc.

Merchant Banking, as a commercial activity, took shape in India through the management of Public Issues of Capital and Loan Syndication. It was originated in 1969 with the setting up of Merchant Banking Division by ANZ Grindlays Bank. The main service offered at that time to the corporate enterprises by the merchant banks included the management of Public issues and some aspects of financial consultancy. The early and mid-seventies witnessed a boom in the growth of merchant banking organisations in the country with various commercial banks, financial institutions, broker's firms entering into the field of merchant banking.

Merchant Banking in India

In India prior to the enactment of Indian Companies Act, 1956, managing agents acted as issue houses for securities, evaluated project venture capital, for new firms. Few share broking firms also functioned as merchant bankers.

The need for specialised merchant banking service was felt in India with the rapid growth in the number and size of the issues made in the primary market. The merchant banking services were started by foreign banks, namely the National Grindlays Bank in 1967 and the City Bank in 1970. The Banking Commission in its report in 1972 recommended the setting up of merchant banking institutions by commercial banks and financial institutions. This marked the beginning of specialised merchant banking in India.

The main function of merchant banking is issue management. The issued can be public issue through prospectus, offer of sale, private placements, etc. Thus, the merchant banks offer 'commercial banking services' as well as various 'consultancy services', for which they charge fees or service charges. Canara Bank, Grindlay's Bank, Citibank, Bank of Baroda, Indian Bank Syndicate Bank, Indian Overseas Bank, ICICI, IDBI, SBI etc. have separate 'Merchant Banking Division'.

Various types of services include preparation, planning and execution of new projects and techno-commercial, managerial advice. Since 1972, most commercial banks have created merchant banking divisions. Growth of merchant banks has taken place because of the following factors :

i)   Industrialisation on large-scale.

ii)   Liberalisation of Indian economy.

iii)   Growth and increase in small/medium scale industries due to greater encourage-ment from government.

iv)   Growing complexity in government rules and regulations.

v)   Growing specialisation.

vi)   Increasing need for massive funds.

vii)   Top quality services rendered by the merchant banks.

The issue function may be both broadly divided into pre-issue management and post-issue management. In both stages legal requirements have to be complied with and since several agencies are involved, activities connected with issue have to be coordinated. For convenience of treatment pre-issue management is divided into :

1)   issue through prospectus, offer for sale and private placement,

2)   marketing and underwriting and

3)   pricing of issues; and post-issue management dealing with stock exchange and collection of subscriptions, allotment and dispatch of shares/refund orders through registrar to the issue.

To begin with merchant banking services were offered along with other traditional banking services. In the mid-eighties, the Banking Regulations Act was amended permitting commercial banks to offer a wide range of financial services through the subsidiary rule. The State Bank of India was the first Indian Bank to set up Merchant Banking Division in 1972. Later, ICICI set up its Merchant Banking Division followed by Bank of India, Bank of Baroda, Canara Bank, Punjab National Bank and UCO Bank. The merchant banking gained prominence during 1983-84 due to new issue boom. During this period, new issue boom is considered as service banking, a banking department rendering non-fund based services/services of arranging funds rather than providing them. The Indian concept of a merchant bank is of a merchant banking department, a department of a commercial bank or the satellite of such a bank. Globally, merchant banks have grown independently of commercial banking sometimes giving the latter a head on competition although the trends are towards the integration of the two. Further, Indian merchant banking has, by and large, been synonymous with issue management whereas outside the country it is much more than that.

The merchant bankers have been performing a wide variety of services. They have become innovative, creative and pathsetters in the capital market, but SEBI wants them to be much more responsive to investors responsible for all that the companies do and be know all and end all for the capital market. They have to act as leaders and coordinators for all intermediaries in the new issue market and certify to the SEBI as to the genuineness of the facts stated in the draft prospectus and related materials issued by the companies.

To act as merchant banker, it has become necessary to take a licence from the SEBI since May 1992. Now only merchant bankers both private and public who are registered with SEBI can act in that capacity.

A code of conduct is laid down for them and violation of the provisions of the code will attract penal points and finally insulting in the cancellation of their licence.

Reform measures were initiated in the capital market from 1992, starting with the conferring of statutory powers on the Securities and Exchange Board of India (SEBI) and the repeal of Capital Issues Control Act and the abolition of the office of the Controller of Capital Issues. These have brought about significant improvement in the functional and regulatory efficiency of the market, enabling the Merchant Bankers to shoulder greater legal and moral responsibilities towards the investing public. Commercial banks and foreign development finance institutions have organised them through formation divisions, nationalised banks have formed subsidiaries companies and share brokers and consultancies constituted themselves into public limited companies or registered themselves as private limited companies. Some merchant banking outfits have entered into collaboration having merchant bankers abroad with several branches.

In addition to Indian Merchant Bankers, a large number of reputed international Merchant Bankers like Merrill Lynch, Morgan Stanley, Goldman Sachs, Jardie Fleming, Kleinwort Benson etc. are operating in India under authorisation of SEBI. As a result of proliferation, Indian Merchant Bankers are faced with severe competition not only among themselves but also with the well developed global players.

The Narasimham Committee on Financial Sector Reforms (1991) foresaw considerable potential for the widespread operation of merchant banks in India, in view of a deregulated industrial economy of India. Therefore the Committee, held the view that the Indian merchant banks should be further strengthened by encouraging them to form joint ventures with well-reputed international merchant and investment banks. In due course the Committee felt, the merchant banks can be allowed to have access to the market for deposits and borrowed funds, subject to the prudential norms prepared to suit the special needs of their functions.

Merchant banking has now been brought under the statutory regulation of SEBI and has to be authorised to do business by it. Merchant banking has to observe stipulated capital adequacy norms and abide by a code of conduct very carefully.

Registration of Merchant Bankers

SEBI Registration :

The Categories of Merchant Bankers, which are licensed by the SEBI are shown in Figure 3.2 as follows.

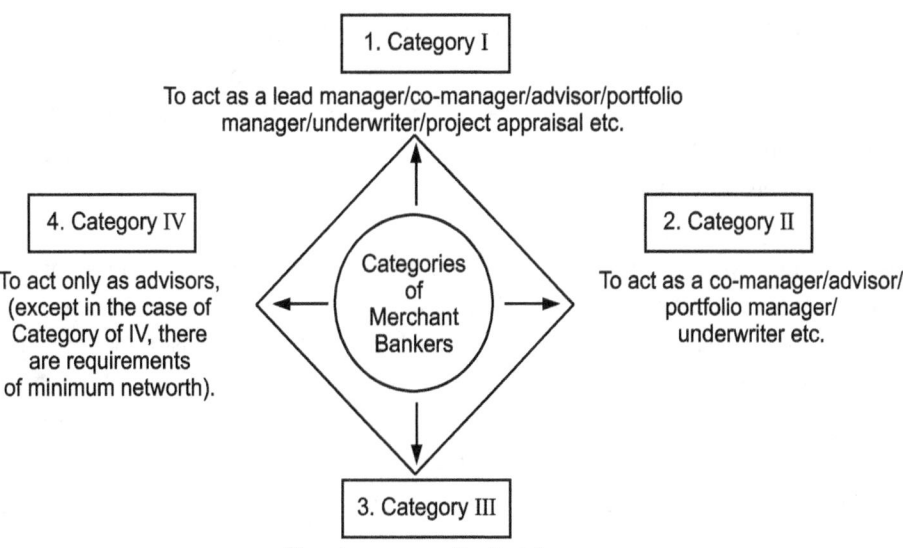

Fig. 3.2 : Categories of Merchant Bankers

The required networth and initial licence fee are set out below.

Category	Minimum Networth	Initial Licencee Fee
Category I	₹ 1 crore	₹ 5 lakhs
Category II	₹ 50 lakhs	₹ 3 lakhs
Category III	₹ 20 lakhs	₹ 1 lakh
Category IV	Nil	–

Criteria for Authorisation :

Merchant banking has been statutorily brought within the framework of the Securities and Exchange Board of India under SEBI (Merchant Bankers) Regulations, 1992.

In terms of the guidelines issued during April 1990, all merchant bankers will require authorisation by SEBI to carry out business.

The criteria for authorisation include :

i) Professional qualification in finance, law or business management;

ii) Infrastructure like adequate office space, equipment and manpower;

iii) Employment of two persons who have the experience to conduct business of merchant bankers;

iv) Capital adequacy;

v) Past track of record, experience, general reputation and fairness in all transactions.

The merchant bankers are closely observed by the SEBI, their activities monitored and their performance, in terms of investor service is assessed. A minimum of 5% commitment to new issues is insisted on merchant bankers, if they have to prove their involvement in the issue. They can also accept underwriting obligation. The sponsors on OTCEI have also got an obligation of 5% commitment to new issues offered to public to prove their involvement in it.

Classification of Activities of Merchant Bankers (Categories) :

SEBI issued further guidelines classifying the merchant bankers into four categories based on the nature and range of activities and their responsibilities to SEBI investors and issuers of securities. SEBI has issued revised guidelines on 22nd December, 1992 classifying the activities of merchant bankers as follows :

The first category consists of merchant bankers who carry on any activity of issue management which will *inter alia* consist of preparation of prospectus and other information relating to the issue, determining financial structure, tie-up of financiers and final allotment and refund of subscription and to act in the capacity of managers, advisors or consultants to an issue, portfolio manager and underwriter.

The second category consists of those authorised to act in the capacity of co-manager/advisor, consultant, underwriter to an issue or portfolio manager.

The third category consists of those authorised to act as underwriter, advisors or consultant to an issue.

The fourth category consists of merchant bankers who act as advisor or consultant to an issue.

Minimum networth for the first category is ₹ 1 crore, second category ₹ 60 lakhs, third category ₹ 20 lakhs and fourth category is nil.

Registration Procedure :

The authorisation is for a period of three years and the licensing fees and annual fees payable are fixed by the SEBI. Only two managers are permitted to manage for issues of the size of ₹ 50 crores and a maximum of 4 managers for mega issues of above ₹ 100 crores.

The SEBI has laid the responsibility on merchant bank for the true disclosures and factual statements made on the prospectus and the authenticity of such statements.

All draft prospectuses are to be submitted to SEBI before public issue. These prospectuses are rated by the SEBI based on the disclosures, facts of highlights, and risk factors and objective assessment of business prospects and profitability etc.

SEBI has also developed a system of awarding grades to the prospectus in recognition of its merit or penal points for faults, non compliance of SEBI directives, or any type of defaults.

The merchant banks are also ordained to send quarterly reports on the public and right issues on hand, the names of companies, the size of issue, likely dates of opening of issues, stock exchanges where they are to be listed and other details regarding these issues. These reports are to be sent to SEBI at the beginning of every quarter. These data are consolidated and the SEBI releases it to the press for public information, as part of it services for investor protection.

The SEBI was also critical of the sale of unsubscribed portion of the new issues at discounts to mutual funds and financial institutions. This has happened in the case of a few companies which have flopped but the companies have resorted to this practice to cover up and maintain their public image. The impression given to the stock exchange would show that their issues are fully subscribed. The concerned merchant bankers were warned by the SEBI not to resort to such practices and the institutions and public should get the Securities at the same price and discounts and all underneath dealings are prohibited as per the SEBI guidelines and directives issued to merchant bankers.

An application should be submitted to SEBI in Form A of the SEBI (Merchant Bankers) Regulations, 1992. SEBI shall consider the application and on being satisfied issue a certificate of registration in Form B of the SEBI (Merchant Bankers) Regulations, 1992. ₹ 5 lakhs which should be paid within 15 days of date of receipt of intimation regarding grant of certificate.

Validity period of Certificate of Registration :

The validity period of certificate of registration is three years from the date of issue. For renewal of registration three months before the expiry period, an application should be submitted to SEBI in Form A of the SEBI (Merchant Bankers) Regulations, 1992. SEBI shall consider the application and on being satisfied renew certificate of registration for a further period of 3 years. A renewal fee of ₹ 2.5 lakhs should be paid within 15 days of date of the receipt of intimation regarding renewal of certificate. The person whose registration is not current shall not carry on the activity as merchant banker from the date of expiry of validity period.

Further requirements by the SEBI for Registration :

i) The Securities and Exchange Board of India (SEBI) has stated that merchant bankers, must be involved more closely in the market making process as share brokers do not have the requisite expertise to evaluate the fundamentals of the scrips before taking over the role of market makers. Further, share brokers generally being partnership firms, do not have the financial clout which is necessary for market making activity. Resultantly, the SEBI has suggested that any member of the stock exchange, along with one merchant banker registered with SEBI could act as a market maker.

ii) The SEBI has felt that to ensure liquidity of scrips, it was necessary to facilitate greater movement, which could only be achieved through the institution of market makers. Market makers would also create a market for the scrips by offering two-way quotes to the investors. A minimum of ten scrips have been proposed by SEBI for the market makers.

iii) An initial authorisation fee, an annual fee and renewal fee may be collected by SEBI.

iv) All issues must be managed at least at one authorised banker, functioning as the sole manager or the lead manager. Ordinarily not more than two merchant bankers should be associated as lead managers. But, for issues over ₹ 100 crores and above, the number of lead managers may go upto a maximum of four. The specific responsibilities of each lead manager must be submitted to SEBI prior to the issue.

v) The lead merchant banker holding a certificate under category I shall accept a minimum underwriting obligation of 5% of the total underwriting commitment or ₹ 25 lakhs whichever is less.

vi)   Each merchant banker is required to furnish to the SEBI half yearly unaudited financial results when required by it with a view to monitor the capital adequacy of the merchant banker.

vii) SEBI has prescribed a code of conduct to the merchant bankers. The banker must perform his duties with highest standards of integrity and fairness in all his dealings. He will render at all times high standards of service, exercise due diligence, ensure proper care and exercise independent professional judgement. The merchant banker and his personnel will act in an ethical manner in all his dealings with the investors, clients and fellow bankers. All merchant bankers must adhere to the code of conduct.

viii) The above guidelines will be administered by SEBI and it will supervise the activities of merchant bankers.

ix)   SEBI has been vested with power to suspend or cancel the authorisation in case of violation of the guidelines.

x)   To ensure transparency and accountability in the operation of merchant bankers and to protect the investors, a number of obligations and responsibilities have been imposed on them. It has been decided to ask merchant bankers to enter into agreement with corporate body setting out their mutual rights, liabilities and obligations relating to an issue particularly on disclosure, allotment and refund, maintenance of books of accounts and submission of half yearly exports to SEBI.

xi)   Inspections will be conducted by SEBI to ensure that provisions of the regulations are properly complied with and to investigate the complaints from customers. It is obligatory on the part of merchant bankers to furnish all the details sought by the investigating team. The regulations, however, indicate that the Board would give reasonable notice to merchant bankers before undertaking inspection. On the basis of the inspection report, the Board will communicate the contents of the report to the concerned merchant banker to give him/her an opportunity to put forth his/her submissions. On receipt of the explanations, if any of the merchant bankers, the SEBI would advise merchant bankers to take any measures that it may deem fit, and to comply with the provisions of the regulations.

Details of additional information for renewal of registration as Merchant Banker is given in Annexure I.

The format of half yearly report to be submitted by merchant bankers is given in Annexure II.

Changes in SEBI Rules and Regulations :

In September, 1997, SEBI brought about some major changes in SEBI (Merchant Bankers) Rules and Regulations, 1992. Accordingly, only Corporate bodies will be allowed to function as merchant bankers. Moreover, the multiple categories of merchant bankers shall be abolished and there will be just one entity viz., Merchant Banker. The merchant bankers presently functioning as Merchant Bankers Category II, III and IV shall have an option to either upgrade themselves as Merchant Bankers (presently Merchant Banker Category I) or seek separate registration as underwriters or Portfolio Managers under the respective regulations. The merchant bankers will be prohibited from carrying out fund based activity other than those related exclusively to the capital markets. In effect, the activities undertaken by NBFCs such as accepting deposits, leasing and bill discounting would not be allowed to be undertaken by a merchant banker.

Merchant Bankers Commission

As determined by the Finance Ministry, Government of India, Merchant Bankers are eligible to charge commission/fee from their clients as detailed below :

i)   Merchant Banker can charge 0.5% as the maximum as commission for whole of the issue.

ii) They can charge project appraisal fees.

iii) A lead manager can claim a commission of 0.5% upto ₹ 25 crore and 0.2% in excess of ₹ 25 crore.

iv) Underwriting Commission.

(Percent)

Type of Security	On amount devolving on underwriters	On amount subscribed by public
1. Equity shares	2.50	2.50
2. Preference shares/debentures		
a) upto ₹ 5 lakh	2.50	1.50
b) excess of ₹ 5 lakh	2.00	1.00

v)   Brokerage commission 1.5%.

vi) Other expenses like advertising, printing, Registrar's expenses, stamp duty etc., in connection with the issue can be reimbursed from its clients.

Qualities required for Merchant Banking Activities

Merchant bankers play a significant role as a catalyst to transform the project idea into industrial ventures. To perform these activities effectively the merchant bankers are expected to possess certain qualities which are as under :

i)   Innovative approach in developing capital market instruments to satisfy the ever changing needs of investing public.

ii) Integrity and maintenance of high professional standards are the essential requisites for the success of merchant bankers present scenario.

iii) Ability to analyse various aspects such as technical, financial and economic aspects concerning the formation of an industrial project.

iv)   Knowledge about the various aspects of capital markets, trends in stock exchange, psychology of investing public, change in the economic and technological environment in the country.

v)   Ability to build up the bank-client relationship and live upto the clients expectations with total involvement in the project assigned to them.

Action against defaulting Merchant Bankers

The notification procedure relating to action to be initiated against merchant banks in case of default has been detailed out. The regulations empower SEBI to take action against defaulting banker such as suspension/cancellation of registration. In case of deliberate manipulation, or price rigging or cornering activities or deterioration in the financial position, the Board is empowered to cancel the registration of the merchant banker. Under the regulation, the SEBI is empowered to suspend a registration of a member banker in case the merchant banker furnishes wrong or false information, fails to resolve the complaints of the investors, etc. The penalty or suspension or cancellation of registration can be imposed by SEBI only after holding an enquiry and giving sufficient opportunities to the merchant banker of being heard. Any merchant banker aggrieved by an order of SEBI, can, however, appeal to the Union Government.

3.1.2 FUNCTIONS

Traditionally, merchant banks have been concerned with the acceptance of credit for the financing of international trade and the raising of loans for overseas borrowers by new capital issues. However, they have now extended their interests to domestic financing, particularly to advising on amalgamations and takeovers and to investment management, hire-purchasing and leasing finance. At present, **merchant banks** are carrying out the following **functions** :

i)   **Promotional Function :**

Merchant bankers act as a promoter of various industrial enterprises. They help an entrepreneur in the conception of an idea, identification of projects. Its location, obtaining many sanctions/approval from various State and Central Government departments including license and registration under Industrial Development and Regulation Act and many other enactments, preparation of project feasibility reports, ensuring availability of raw materials, skilled labour, tax incentives and concessions.

A merchant bank has to provide advice and liasion in obtaining the consent of the Central and State Governments, for the project, where necessary. It has to undertake pre-investment surveys and market studies. It has to find out and advise as to how the rupee resources can be raised from financial institutions and banks. It has to spell out what it can do in raising foreign exchange resources for imports of machinery, technical know-how, raw materials etc. It has to explore the possibilities of foreign collaboration and advise on setting up of turn-key projects in foreign countries.

ii) Issue Management :

A) Pre-issue Management :

Merchant banker's main function, in India, is issue management, which involves the following functions in respect of issue through prospectus. This 'function' involves many activities as under :

a) Merchant bankers have to ensure that the information required by companies act is furnished in the prospectus. They arrange for drafting of prospectus and vetting thereof by reputed solicitors. The merchant bank is expected to exercise due diligence ensuring compliance by company in regard to prospectus and after the prospectus is ready it has to be sent to SEBI for vetting. It is only after clearance by SEBI that it is filed with the registrar office.

b) Members of recognised stock exchange are appointed as brokers to issue. They can canvass subscription by mailing the literature to clients and undertaking wide publicity. The appointment brokers is similar to appointment of underwriters. A profile of the project is sent to brokers to the issue. Appointment is made on the preference of the management of the company (issuers) they ensure wide geographical distribution, reputation of the brokers, inspire confidence among the investors and track record in the securing subscriptions to issue early.

c) Principal brokers assist merchant bankers to devise strategy for success of the public issue, keep liaison between merchant banker and stock exchange and canvass support for the issue among the stockbrokers. Sometimes they centralise mailing of prospectus, applications forms and other publicity materials at the insistence of the merchant banker.

d) Bankers to the issue accept application with the subscriptions tender at their designated branches and forward them to the register. Bankers to the issue also undertake publicity to the issue by distributing publicity, materials, application forms and prospectus. There are eligible for brokerage on shares allotted against application bearing their stamps.

e) An outside agency is employed when merchant banker cannot attend issue house work. Merchant bankers have a panel of issue house and help the issuing company in finalising the terms and conditions of appointment.

f) The merchant bankers should arrange a meeting with company representatives and advertising agents to finalise arrangements relating to –

- Date of opening and closing issue.
- Registration of the prospectus.
- Launching publicity campaign.
- Fixing the date of board meeting to approve and sign prospectus and pass the necessary resolution.

g) Pricing of issues is done by companies themselves in consultation with merchant bankers. If a premium is too low the issue gets over subscribed and fails. The merchant bankers apart from taking into account earning per share, book value and average market price for two or three years have to take into account future prospects of the company and assess whether the market can absorb the premium on issue.

h) Publicity campaign covers the preparation of all publicity materials and brochures, prospectus, announcement, advertisements in the press, radio, TV, conferences, and hoardings. Success of an issue depends on the size of the publicity materials. Merchant bankers play a key role by helping them in the choice of media, size, and publications in which advertisement should appear. Publicity is a function of size of issue, image of issuer and company location. Effective marketing include arrangements of conferences at potential centers to explain nature and strength of the project to various cross section of investors and their counselors.

i) Co-ordinating all the activities concerned, including printing, publicity, advertisement, work of registrar receipt and processing of application, formalising the basis of allotment, negotiating it with stock exchanges and preparing the Resister of allotment.

j) In the case of debentures, as managers to the issue the merchant banks, have to perform the following functions :

- Laying down certain terms and conditions in order to make the issue attractive.
- Assisting finalisation of the relative security or mortgage deeds and to obtain approval for the same from the solicitors/trustees etc. of the company.

B) Post-Issue Management :

Post-management consist of collection of application forms from bankers and the statement of amounts are received, screening applications and deciding allotment procedure in consultation with stock exchange. Post-management concludes with the mailing of allotment letters/share certificates and refund orders.

Registrars to the issue management play a major role in post issue-management. They work in collaboration with bankers to issue. The registrar to issue gets the application forms together, sorts them, and arranges them in order. Merchant banks assist the company by coordinating this activity till final allotment is made and allotment letters and refund orders are posted.

After the basis of allotment is approved by the stock exchange and allotted by the Board, the auditor/company secretary has to certify that the allotment has been made by the company as per the basis of allotment approved by the exchange. Registrars have to ensure that the applications are processed and allotment/refund orders are sent within 70 days of the close of the issue. The time limit of 70 days has been proved to be difficult to adhere and applicants have to wait for anytime between 90 to 180 days. Merchant bankers assist the company by co-ordinating the above activities.

iii) Loan Syndication :

These financial intermediaries arrange loans for their clients, by analysing their cash flow pattern so that the terms of borrowing meet the client's cash requirements. They also offer assistance in loan documentation procedures. In the case of a new enterprise, availability of working capital is a problem. For the promoters, the merchant bank arranges the short-term or medium-term credit syndication. For existing companies merchant banks in India have successfully tapped non-traditional sources like issue of debentures.

Merchant Banks help clients approach financial institutions for term loans. The decisions as to which financial institution should be approached depends on industry, location of the unit and size of project cost. The Merchant Bankers, first, make an appraisal of the project to satisfy that it is viable. The next step is designing capital structure, determining the promoter's contribution and arriving at a figure of approximate amount of term loan to be raised. The Merchant hanker has to ensure that the project adheres to the guidelines for financing industrial projects. After verifications that the project would be eligible for term loan, a preliminary meeting is fixed with financial institution. If the financial institution agrees to consider the proposal, the application is filled in and submitted along with other documents.

iv) Restructuring Strategies :

Merchant bankers assist the management of the client company to successfully restructure various activities, which include mergers and acquisitions, divestitures, management buyouts, joint venture among others. To help companies achieve the objectives of these restructuring strategies, the merchant banker participates in different activities at various stages which include understanding the objectives behind the strategy (objectives could be either to obtain financial, marketing, or production benefits), and help in searching for tile right partner in the strategic decision and financial valuation of the proposal.

v) Mergers and Acquisitions :

Merchant banks often represent firms in mergers, acquisitions, and divestitures. Example projects include the acquisition of a specific firm, the sale of a company or a subsidiary of the company, and assistance in and executing a merger or joint venture. In each case, the merchant bank should provide a thorough analysis of the entity, bought or sold, as well as a valuation range and recommended structure.

vi) Investment Management :

The corporate investors as well as individuals like the NRIs are interested in exploring suitable areas for investment. Many foreign companies may also have such interest.Merchant banks render expert advice on matters pertaining to investment decisions; for example, they assess the effects of taxation and inflation on gilt-edged and other securities. They also tender advice on investment in government securities to trusts, charitable institutions and companies. They undertake to buy and sell securities for their client companies.

vii) Arranging Fixed Deposits :

Merchant banks help companies to raise finance by way of public deposits. For this purpose, they provide not only the required guidance but but act as brokers for the mobilisation of public deposits. The management of new deposit accounts is also undertaken by them.

viii) Servicing of Issue :

Many merchant banks are prepared to act as paying agents for the service of the long-term loans issued in the past for foreign governments, municipalities and other institutions, to keep a register of shareholders and debenture-holders for companies to act as paying agents for their dividends and debenture issues; to arrange for the investment of funds and for the safe custody of securities on account of clients in the country and abroad.

ix) Underwriting and Consultancy :

In the case of new issues, the functions of underwriting and consultancy achieve importance which is performed by merchant banks. In this case also issue management involves all the steps noted above, in respect of a public issue. In fact, underwriting is considered to be the main work of merchant banks which is of prime importance for new issues and raising of new capital for the corporate sector. Out of the amount underwritten, a part devolves on the merchant bank as the underwriter - how much or what percentage depends upon the mood of the capital market and the genuine worth of the project. The SEBI has made underwriting obligatory for all issues offered to the public.

x) Help in Financial Management and in Designing Proper Capital Structure :

Merchant bank helps in financial management and in designing proper capital structure and debt-equity ratio etc. for the company. It provides advice on restructuring of capital amalgamation, mergers take-over etc. Wherever need be, it also undertakes, the management of investment trusts, charitable trusts. It provides management aid and entrepreneurial aid regarding management audit providing designs of the complete system operational research and management consultancy.

xi) Assistance in Providing Project Finance :

Industrial concerns are often facing the issues of expansion modernisation, rationalisation or embarking upon a new project. Once the company decides, the merchant bank can provide assistance in working out a comprehensive plan of finding for the project as well as the pattern of financing. It works in close liaison with the client firm, its technical consultants, its finding institutions and then prepares and furnishes a complete dossier. It goes further for arranging various sources of finance.

xii) Portfolio Management :

Portfolio refers to investment in different kinds of securities such as shares, debentures or bonds issued by different companies and securities issued by the government. It is not merely a collection of unrelated assets but a carefully blended asset combination within a unified framework. Portfolio management refers to maintaining proper combination of securities in a manner that they give maximum return with minimum risk. Merchant bankers provide portfolio management service to their clients.

xiii) Other functions of Merchants Bankers :

a) Project appraisal - technical and financial feasibility studies as desired by the company. Many times companies will get a project appraised by an agency before going public or for rights and the actual responsibility for lead manager may be given to another party.

b) Corporate counselling and reporting. This includes counselling on financial structure, operational efficiency or assist a sick unit with a package of solutions or render technical advice.

c) Some merchant banking units like Can Bank Financial Services and Ind Bank Financial Services have also membership of stock exchanges, sponsership of OTCEI and incidental activities like investment advice counselling, brokerage and dealership in the stock market, etc., are also performed by them.

d) A few merchant banks are also found to be undertaking, management of NRI investments, portfolio management, bill discounting and money market operations, which were drastically curtailed after the security scam revelations and subsequent RBI curbs. Fixed deposit broking, lease finance, venture capital financing, foreign Currency finance etc., are some of the additional functions which they may undertake.

e) Of all the functions corporate counselling is the most widely practiced by the Indian merchant banks. This includes guidance to companies in areas of diversification, product lines and their appraisal and rejuvenating of the sick and ailing companies. Corporate counselling is a wide spectrum service including project counselling, capital restructuring and investment management, preinvestment studies etc.

3.1.3 SERVICES RENDERED

Merchant banking is normally considered to be related only to the services associated with public issue management, but they also offer domestic project finance syndication. Larger merchant banks in the country offer a wide range of services. Generally, the **Merchant banks** offer the following **services** :

i) Managers, Consultants or Advisors to the Issue :

The managers to the issue assist in the drafting of prospectus, application forms and completion of formalities under the Companies Act, appointment of Registrar for dealing with share applications and transfer and listing of shares of the company on the stock exchange. Companies are free to appoint one or more agencies as managers to the issue. SEBI guidelines insist that all issues should be managed by atleast one authorised merchant banker. Ordinarily, not more than two merchant bankers should be associated as lead managers, advisers and consultants to a public issue. In issues of over ₹ 100 crores, upto a maximum of four merchant bankers could be associated as managers.

ii) Financial Feasibility Explorations :

These are in the nature of financial feasibility explorations in selected areas of interest of the client. They include such studies for foreign companies wishing to participate in joint ventures in India, and often involve a package covering advice on the nature of participation anal Government regulatory factors.

iii) Off Shore Finance :

The merchant bankers help their clients in the following areas involving foreign currency.

i)   Long-term foreign currency loans

ii)   Joint venture abroad

iii)   Financing exports and imports and

iv)   Foreign collaboration arrangements.

The bankers render other financial services such as appraisal, negotiations and compliance with procedural and legal aspects.

iv) Non-Resident Investment :

The services of merchant bankers include investment advisory services to NRI in terms of identification of investment opportunities, selection of securities, investment management etc. They also take care of the operational details like purchase and sale of securities, securing necessary clearance from RBI for repatriation of interest and dividend.

The non-resident themselves for investment will have to follow many rules and regulations which are complicated. In this regard merchant bankers should help the NRI in selecting right type of securities and offering expertise guidance in fulfilling government regulations. By this service to NRI account holders merchant bankers can mobilise more resources for the corporate sector.

v) Advisory services relating to Mergers and Takeovers :

Merchant bankers are the middlemen in setting negotiation between the offeree and offeror. Being a professional expert they are apt to safeguard the interest of the shareholders in both the companies. Once the merger partner is proposed, the merchant banker appraises merger/takeover proposal with respect to financial viability and technical feasibility. He negotiates purchase consideration and mode of payment. He gets approval from the government/RBI, drafts scheme of amalgamation and obtains approval from financial institutions.

vi) Project Finance :

Merchant banks undertake the preparation of project files, loan applications for financial assistance on behalf of promoters from various financial institutions for term-loans, working capital finance for new projects, etc. They also arrange finance for projects from foreign countries.

vii) Sponsor of Issue :

Merchant bankers act as sponsors or issues rather than as sources of finance. In this capacity, they obtain current consent/acknowledgement from the SEBI for the issue of capital, preparation of the prospectus, engage in tying-up arrangements for underwriting, for the appointment of brokers and bankers to the issue, for press publicity and compliance with stock exchange listing requirement.

viii) Useful Services to Entrepreneurs :

Merchant Bankers render useful services to entrepreneurs insetting up and managing projects. Various promotional activities such as conception of project ideas, feasibility studies, market surveys, choice of suitable location for the enterprise, and its size, preparation of various legal documents and obtaining the consent of the relevant authorities, etc. require expertise knowledge and skill which small and medium entrepreneurs hardly possess. By performing these tasks merchant banker helps particularly the smaller entrepreneurs in overcoming the complex problems of promotion of an enterprise.

Not only that a merchant banker is helpful in flotation of the enterprise he helps the entrepreneurs during the course of operations. He renders professional guidance to the entrepreneurs in regard to choice of capital mix, management of public issues, credit syndication, investment counseling and many other related matters. He helps the management in raising desired amount of funds from different sources.

ix) Advice on Financial Structuring and Syndication :

In the case of many joint enterprises and overseas ventures in the Middle-East, South-East Asia and Africa, etc, advice on the financial structuring of these projects, as well as assistance in syndication of the finance itself is now increasingly available through the Indian merchant banks.

x) Lease Assistance in Acquisition and Mergers :

Besides these wide range of services some of the larger banks are also involved in areas such as the arrangement of lease and assistance in acquisitions and mergers, etc.

xi) Diversified Activities :

Earlier banks confined most of their operations to deposit mobilisation and credit dispensation. But in India, they have diversified their activities in line with their counterparts in the developed countries, and gone into merchant banking also. This innovating banking has helped many young entrepreneurs who lacked sufficient experience and had a little capital to invest to enter the field of industrial enterprise. This has led to the need for some agency which can protect their interest from planning to execution of the projects.

xii) Quick Implementation of Projects :

Companies require the service of these experts to tackle problems in technical, financial, managerial and organisational fields. It has been revealed by the Reserve Bank that insufficient project preparation, defective technical planning, inefficient or indifferent management and financial bottlenecks faced by promoters were primarily responsible for delayed implementation of projects. Merchant banks have a role to play in overcoming these shortcomings.

Recent Trends in Merchant Banking

As part of the marketing techniques, the management which is highly professional for most merchant banks, plan new issues to be managed well in advance. There is a wide range of services which flow to them as companies find their services efficient and cost effective.

There is an association of merchant banks, of which the ICICI is the coordinator and leader. Among institutions, the leading merchant bankers are IDBI, ICICI and IFC and all public sector banks have merchant banking departments or merchant bank subsidiaries. Over the last few years a number of private sector merchant banks have also come into existence and some have increased their market share in the business. There are at present about 300 authorised merchant bankers as per the SEBI data.

Since May, 1992, the government has allowed the free entry into the capital market of all companies for raising fresh capital. The pricing of shares for such issues is also left to the companies which means that the premium fixation is in the hands of merchant bankers. Since June 1992 many merchant bankers have brought out issues at exorbitant premiums, some of which have flopped when investors have realised that they are over priced. The responsibility of supporting them and making them a success of such issues fell on the merchant banker either through underwriters or by outright investment of financial institutions like IDBI, IFCI, etc. Some issues even when they are overpriced were initially sold off in the flush of boom psychology. But subsequently, the investors have become scared by the falling quotations of high priced issues. They turned very discretionary and cautious. The lessons learnt by merchant bankers are firstly to price issues at fairly reasonable levels and to time them properly, if particularly the issues are big ones. The SEBI has also come out with a heavy hand on merchant bankers asking them to follow the CCI's earlier guidelines for fixing premium and justification of the pricing by the criteria followed.

Merchant banking in India has a very bright future in view of considerable demand of financial, technical and managerial services by new as well as existing enterprises going in the stock market on a massive scale for raising large amount of funds to meet their requirements. The growing popularity of the services of merchant bankers is a clear indication of the vast scope that lies ahead of them.

The prospects for merchant banking activity are increasing fast. The activities and functions that they can perform have also widened in the last couple of years, with increasing deregulation and financial sophistication the growth of non-bank financial services is going to be enormous. It is in this context that merchant banks will increase in number and competition among themselves will also grow. The profits and profitability of the merchant banking activity thus has vast potential. With the growth of capital market, merchant banking activity and that of new issues are bound to grow in an exponential order in the years to come.

✳✳✳

ANNEXURE I

ADDITIONAL INFORMATION FOR RENEWAL OF REGISTRATION AS MERCHANT BANKER (As per SEBI Guidelines)

1.0 Key personnel

1.1 Detailed bio-data clearly giving following information for the key personnel who joined merchant banking division after the previous registration :

(a)   Name :

(b)   Qualification :

(c)   Designation in tile, applicant company;

(d)   Experience details giving information about : Name of the organisation, duration, area of work [including of applicant company, if any].

1.2 A copy of experience certificate from previous employers, copy of appointment letter, acceptance letter, copy of experience certificates and copy of salary slip in the applicant company.

2.0 Details of directors

2.1 If any of the Directors are wholetime directors the same to be indicated.

3.0 Details of membership of stock exchange

3.1 If the applicant company/associate company/group company/subsidiary   company of these are member of any recognised stock exchange, the following be submitted :

i)   A conduct certificate from the concerned stock exchange regarding its functioning as member;

ii)   Details regarding payment of fees and also whether the member is facing any charges/disciplinary action or if in past any such action has been taken by the concerned stock exchange/Board;

iii) NOC from the stock exchange for functioning as a merchant banker (in case applicant company holds a corporate membership)/Director/full time employee.

4.0 Final accounts

4.1 A copy of audited annual accounts (including Auditors' report and schedules) as on ...... (latest F.Y.)/as on date of meeting the net worth criteria.

5.0 State whether issuer company is registered as a Non-Banking Finance Company with RBI. If yes, state the place where it is registered and give the registration number and details about any comment of RBI for their inspection for latest three financial years.

6.0 Declarations to be furnished : (to be signed by two Directors)

"We hereby declare and undertake as under :

i) That the applicant company, its promoter, director, partner or employee has not at any time been convicted for any offence involving moral turpitude or has been found guilty of any economic offence.

ii) That the applicant company/ associate company, its promoters, directors, partners or employees are not involved in any litigation connected with the securities market and there are no charges against them as on date.

iii) That none of the associate, subsidiary, interconnected or group company of the applicant company has applied or has been granted registration by the Board to undertake merchant banking activities.

iv) That the applicant company/ associate company, its directors, partners are not facing any Charges/disciplinary action from any stock exchange.

v) That the applicant company, its associates, its director, partner or principal officer is not involved in the securities scam and are not named in the Janakiraman Committee Report/JPC Report. (If involved, detailed comments may be forwarded).

vi) That all investments indicated in the certified annual accounts are held in the name of the company only". (If not, details of such holdings may be forwarded).

***

ANNEXURE II

FORMAT FOR HALF YEARLY REPORT TO BE SUBMITTED BY MERCHANT BANKERS (As per SEBI Guidelines).

For the period ending September/March, 20......)

1. Name/Category of registration.
2. SEBI Registration No.
3. Name of the Compliance Officer.
4. Addition/deletion/change in address, etc. of branch offices from last submitted report.
5. Change, if any, in constitution of the organisation (private limited, public limited, partnership, merger, acquisition, etc.)
6. Change, if any, in directorship details since the last report :

Name	Induction / Retirement / Resignation	Reasons	Effective qualification date	Brief experience (in case of induction)	Share in the company

7. Change in the key management personnel since last report (since grant of registration in case of first report).

Name	Date of App./ Registration / Termination	Qualification	Experience

8. Change including addition to/in associate concerns :

Name of Co. / Firm	Nature of change	Activities handled	Nature of interest with merchant banker

9. New activities undertaken / discontinuation of any existing activities :

Activity	When commenced / discontinued reasons for discontinuation	Object of the new activities	

10. Details of all pending litigations involving the merchant banker.

11. Issue management activities (Attach separate sheet if required) :

Name of issuer companies	Type of issue (public/rights/composite)	Instrument
Offer amount (₹ in lakhs) Issue closing date Stock Exchanges where instruments were to be listed Opening trading price at respective SEs	Issue price/ Conversion price Number of times oversubscribed Reasons for delay in listing Current market price	Issue opening date Functional responsibility First date of trading in respective SEs Remarks

12. Penalty/warnings given by SEBI, if any.
13. Underwriting activities.
13.1 Total number of issues underwritten during the period.
13.2 Total amount underwritten during the period (₹ in lakhs).
13.3 Outstanding underwriting commitment at the close of the period (₹ in lakhs).
13.4 Details of disputed/devolved cases.

Sr. No.	Name of the issuer	Instrument	Amount under-written (₹ in lakhs)	Amount devolved (₹ in lakhs)	Development yes/no	If not met, the reasons thereof and how dispute was settled	Penalty / warning if any issued by SEBI

14. Redressal of investor grievances.
14.1 System of redressal of investor grievances (a brief write up) –
    i)   Number of investor grievances received during the period;
    ii)   Nature of grievances;
    iii) Number of grievances resolved;
    iv) Number of grievances pending;
    v)   The date of oldest grievance.
15. Financial information

Capital structure	Year ended (₹ in lakhs)	Previous year ended (₹ in lakhs)
i) Paid-up capital ii) Free reserves iii) Secured loan iv) Unsecured loan v) Others TOTAL i) Fixed Assets (net block) ii) Quoted investment at cost/market price		

whichever is lower		
iii) Unquoted investment		
iv) Current Assets		
v) Misc. Expenses not written off		
vi) Others		
TOTAL		

(Please enclose the copy of latest audited financial results along with schedules).

16. Changes, if any, in major shareholding (more than 5%).

Name of the shareholder	Investment/Disinvestment	Percentage of total paid-up capital

17. Name of the major shareholders holding more than 5%.

18. Any capital issue (rights or public) during the period. If yes, details thereof inclusive of status of complaints from investors and their redressal.

19. Indictment or involvement in any economic offence by the merchant banker or their directors or principal, officer, if any, during the period.

Place :

Date :   Authorised Signatory

3.2 MUTUAL FUNDS

Different investment avenues are available to investors. Mutual funds also offer good investment opportunities to the investors. Like all investments, they also carry certain risks. The investors should compare the risks and expected yields after adjustment of tax on various instruments while taking investment decisions. The investors may seek advice from experts and consultants including agents and distributors of mutual funds schemes while making investment decisions.

3.2.1 MEANING

Mutual fund is an American Concept and the terms 'Investment Trust', 'Investment Company', 'Mutual Fund', 'Money Fund' etc., are being used interchangeably in American literature. Investment company as defined in the US Investment Company Act of 1940 is any issuer that is or holds out as being engaged primarily or proposes to engage primarily in the business of investing, reinvesting or trading in securities, is engaged or proposes to engage in the business of issuing face amount of certificates of the instalment type or has been engaged in such business and has any such certificates outstanding; is engaged or proposes to engage in the business of investing, reinvesting, owning, holding or trading in securities and owns or proposes to acquire investment securities having a value exceeding 40% of the value of such issuer's total assets (exclusive of Government Securities and Cash items) on an unconsidered basis.

To state in simple words, a mutual fund collects the savings from small investors, invest them in Government and other corporate securities and earn income through interest and dividends, besides capital gains. It works on the principle of 'small drops of water make a big ocean'. For instance, if one has ₹ 1,000 to invest, it may not fetch very much on its own But when it is pooled with ₹ 1,000 each from a lot of other people, then, one could create a 'big fund' large enough to invest in a wide varieties of shares and debentures on a commanding scale and thus, to enjoy the economies of large scale operations, Hence, a mutual fund is nothing but a form of collective investment.

The Securities and Exchange Board of India (Mutual Fund, Regulations, 1993 defines a **Mutual Fund** as "a fund established in the form of a trust by a sponsor, to raise monies by the trustees through the sale of units to the public, under one or more schemes, for investing in securities in accordance with these regulations".

These mutual funds are referred to as Unit Trusts in the U.K. and as open end Investment companies in the U.S.A. Therefore, Kamm, J.O. defines an **Open End Investment Company** as "an organisation formed for the investment of funds obtained from individuals and institutional investors who in exchange for the funds receive shares which can be redeemed at any time at their underlying asset values".

According to **Weston J. Fred and Brigham Eugene F, Unit Trusts** are "Corporations which accept dollars from savers and then use these dollars to buy stocks, long term bonds, short term debt instruments issued by business or government units; these corporations pool funds and thus reduce risk by diversification".

Thus, mutual funds are corporations which pool funds by selling their own shares and reduce risk by diversification.

Mutual fund is a mechanism for pooling the resources by issuing units to the investors and investing funds in securities in accordance with objectives as disclosed in offer document. Investments in securities are spread across a wide cross-section of industries and sectors and thus the risk is reduced. Diversification reduces the risk because all stocks may not move in the same direction in the same proportion at the same time. Mutual fund issues units to the investors in accordance with quantum of money invested by them. Investors of mutual funds are known as unitholders. The profits or losses are shared by the investors in proportion to their investments. The mutual funds normally come out with a number of schemes with different investment objectives which are launched from time to time. A mutual fund is required to be registered with Securities and Exchange Board of India (SEBI) which regulates securities markets before it can collect funds from the public.

A Mutual Fund is a trust that pools the savings of a number of investors who share a common financial goal. The money thus collected is then invested in capital market instruments such as shares, debentures and other securities. The income earned through these investments and the capital appreciation realised are shared by its unit holders in proportion to the number of units owned by them. Thus a Mutual Fund is the most suitable investment for the common man as it offers an opportunity to invest in a diversified, professionally managed basket of securities at a relatively low cost. The flow diagram below describes broadly the working of a mutual fund.

The **Mutual Fund Operation Flow Diagram** as shown below in Figure 3.3 describes broadly the working of a Mutual Fund.

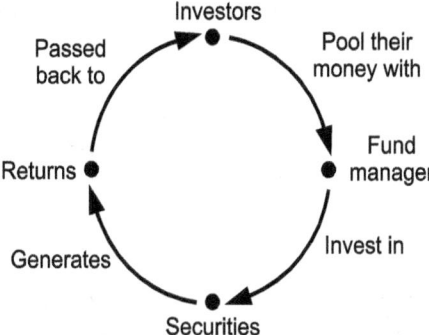

Fig. 3.3 : Mutual Fund Operation Flow Diagram

Concept of Mutual Fund

The flow chart as shown below describes broadly the working of a Mutual Fund.

Many investors with common financial objectives pool their money

⇓

Investors on a proportionate basis, get mutual fund units for the sum contributed to the pool

⇓

The money collected from the investors in invested into shares, debentures and other securities by fund managers

⇓

The fund manager realises gain or losses and collect dividends or interest income

⇓

Any capital gain or loss from such investors are passed onto the investors in the proportion of number of units held by them.

Organisation of Mutual Fund

There are many entities involved and the structure of a Mutual Fund may be shown as under :

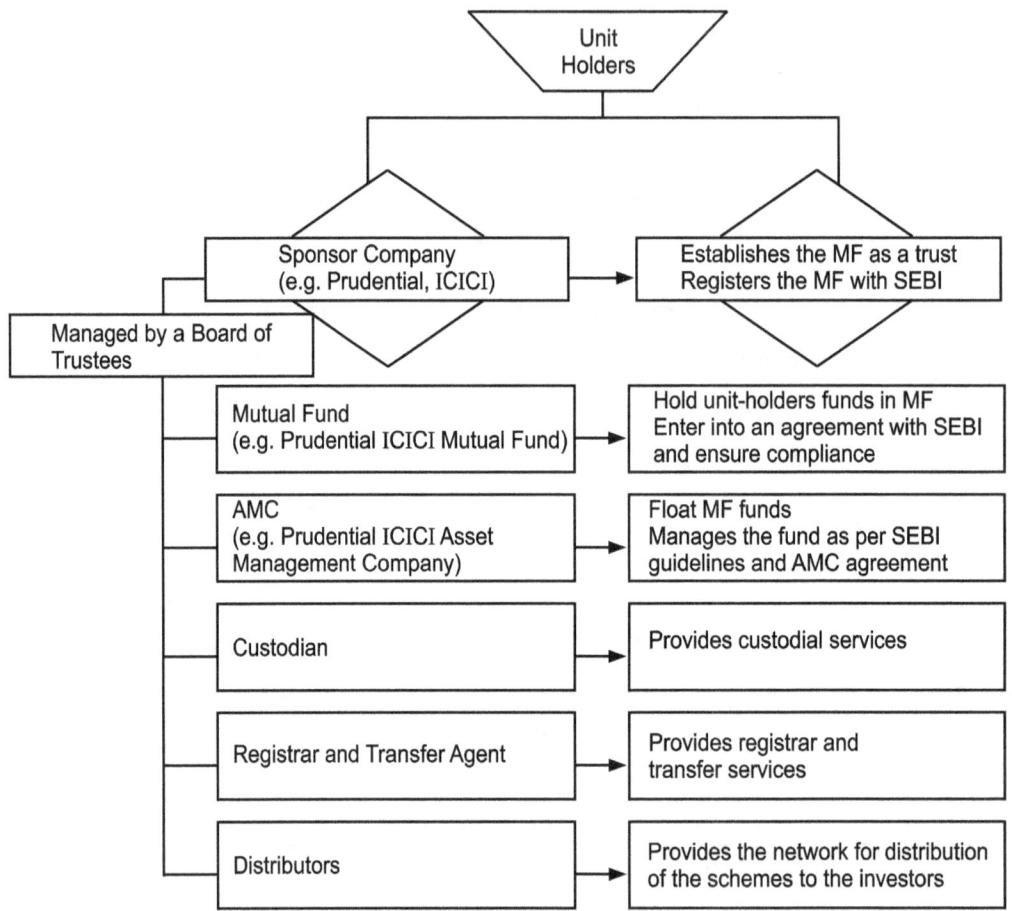

Mutual Funds :

Mutual fund is a vehicle that facilitates a number of investors to pool their money and have it jointly managed by a professional money manager.

Sponsor :

A sponsor is the person who acting alone or in combination with another body corporate establishes a mutual fund. The Sponsor is not responsible or liable for any loss or shortfall resulting from the operation of the Schemes beyond the initial contribution made by it towards setting up of the Mutual Fund.

Trustee :

Trustee is usually a company (Corporate body) or a Board of Trustees (Body of individuals). The main responsibility of the Trustee is to safeguard the interest of the unit holders and ensure that the AMC functions in the interest of investors and in accordance with the Securities and Exchange Board of India (Mutual Funds) Regulations, 1996.

Asset Management Company (AMC)

The AMC is appointed by the Trustee as the Investment Manager of the Mutual Fund. At least 50% of the directors of the AMC are independent directors who are not associated with the Sponsor in any manner. The AMC must have a net worth of at least 10 crores at all times.

The Registrar and Transfer Agent

The AMC if so authorised by the Trust Deed appoints the Registrar and Transfer Agent to the Mutual Fund. The Registrar processes the application form, redemption requests and dispatches account statements to the unit holders. The Registrar and Transfer agent also handles communications with investors and updates investor records.

Custodian : Often an independent organisation, it takes custody of securities and other assets of a mutual fund. Among public sector mutual funds, the sponsor or trustee generally also acts as the custodian. A custodian's responsibilities include receipt and delivery of securities, collecting income, distributing dividends, safekeeping of units and segregating assets and settlements between schemes. Their charges range between 0.15-0.2 percent of the net value of the holding. Custodians can service more than one fund. SEBI's regulations specify each constituent's role clearly.

Along with this there are distributors who sell the schemes to the investors for which they are paid an incentive in the form of commission.

Regulatory Authorities

To protect the interest of the investors, SEBI formulates policies and regulates the mutual funds. It notified regulations in 1993 (fully revised in 1996) and issue guidelines from time to time. MF either promoted by public or by private sector entities including the one promoted by foreign entities is governed by these Regulations.

SEBI approved Asset Management Company (AMC) manages the funds by making investments in various types of securities. Custodian, registered with SEBI, holds the securities of various schemes of the fund in its custody.

According to SEBI Regulations, two thirds of the directors of Trustee Company or board of trustees must be independent.

The Association of Mutual Funds in India (AMFI) reassures the investors in units of mutual funds that the mutual funds function within the strict regulatory framework. Its objective is to increase public awareness of the mutual fund industry.

AMFI is also engaged in upgrading professional standards and in promoting best Industry practices in diverse areas such as valuation, disclosure, transparency etc.

History and Growth of Mutual Funds in India

The mutual fund industry in India Started in 1963 with the formation of Unit Trust of India, at the initiative of the Government of India and Reserve Bank. The evolutionary history of mutual funds in India can be broadly divided into four distinct phases

First Phase 1964-87

The beginning of mutual fund industry in India was marked by the establishment of Unit Trust of India (UTI) in 1963 by an Act of Parliament. It was set-up by the Reserve Bank of India and functioned under the Regulatory and Administrative Control of the Reserve Bank of India. In 1978, UTI was delinked from RBI and the Industrial Development Bank of India (IDBI) took over the regulatory and administrative control. UTI launched the first Unit scheme in 1964 called US-64. At the end of 1988, UTI had ₹ 6,700 crores of assets under management.

Second Phase - 1987-1993 (Entry of Public Sector Funds

In 1987, non-UTI, public sector mutual funds set-up by public sector banks and Life Insurance Corporation of India (LIC) and General Insurance Corporation of India (GIC), entered the Indian market. SBI Mutual Fund was the first non-UTI mutual fund established in June 1987, followed by Canbank Mutual Fund (Dec 87), Punjab National Bank Mutual Fund (Aug 89), Indian Bank Mutual Fund (Nov 89), Bank of India (Jun 90), Bank of Baroda Mutual Fund (Oct 92). LIC established its mutual fund in June 1989 while GIC had set-up its mutual fund in December 1990.

At the end of 1993, the mutual fund industry had assets under management of ₹ 47,004 crores.

Third Phase - 1993-2003 (Entry of Private Sector Funds)

A new era started in the Indian mutual fund industry in 1993, when private sector funds entered the market giving the Indian investors a wider choice of funds for investment. Also, 1993 was the year in which the first Mutual Fund Regulations came into being, under which all mutual funds, except UTI were to be registered and governed. The erstwhile Kothari Pioneer (now merged with Franklin Templeton) was the first private sector mutual fund registered in July 1993.

The 1993 SEBI (Mutual Fund) Regulations, were substituted by a more comprehensive and revised Mutual Fund Regulations in 1996. The industry now functions under the SEBI (Mutual Fund) Regulations, 1996.

The recent trend in the mutual fund industry is to go for tie-up arrangements with foreign collaborators. We find Tatas tying up with Kleinworth Benson; GIC with George Soros; Credit Capital with Lazard Brothers; Kothari with Pioneer; ICICI with JP Morgan; 20th Century with Morgan and so on. Of course, these tie-ups would bring in new perspective, systems and technology and this very foreign tag may add credit to the institution.

The private sector which entered the arena in 1993 is concentrating on the primary market. It is so because investments in new shares fetch appreciation between 30 and 1500 percent in a very short period. Promoters too give preferential treatment to mutual funds because it reduces their marketing cost. Again, they go for fund-participation in a venture even before it goes public. They see potential for immense appreciation in unlisted securities which intend to go to public with a short period of one year.

In India, mutual funds have been preferred as an avenue for investment by the household savers only from 1990s. The sales of units of UTI which were ₹ 890 crores in 1985-86 rose to ₹ 4100 crores in 1990-91 and ₹ 9500 crores in 1993-94. The public sector mutual funds were able to collect ₹ 3800 crores in 1990-91. However, they could collect only ₹ 400 crores in 1993-94. The private sector mutual funds mobilised ₹ 1700 crores in 1993-94. On the whole, the mutual fund industry was able to mobilise approximately ₹ 12000 crores in

1993-94 which amounts to 8% of the gross domestic householding savings in the country. It is a good going indeed.

The number of mutual fund houses went on increasing, with many foreign mutual funds setting-up funds in India and also the industry has witnessed several mergers and acquisitions.

At the end of January 2003, there were 33 mutual funds with total assets of ₹ 1,21,805 crores. The Unit Trust of India with ₹ 44,541 crores of assets under management was way ahead of other mutual funds.

Fourth Phase - since February 2003

In February 2003, following the repeal of the Unit Trust of India Act 1963, UTI was bifurcated into two separate entities. One became the Specified Undertaking of the Unit Trust of India with assets under management of ₹ 29,835 crores as at the end of January 2003, representing broadly, the assets of US 64 scheme, assured return and certain other schemes. The specified undertaking of Unit Trust of India, functions under an administrator and under the rules framed by Government of India and does not come under the purview of the Mutual Fund Regulations.

The second is the UTI Mutual Fund Ltd, sponsored by SBI, PNB, BOB and LIC. It is registered with SEBI and functions under the Mutual Fund Regulations. With the bifurcation of the erstwhile UTI which had in March 2000, more than ₹ 76,000 crores of assets under management and with the setting up of a UTI Mutual Fund, conforming to the SEBI Mutual Fund Regulations, and with recent mergers taking place among different private sector funds, the mutual fund industry has entered its current phase of consolidation and growth. At the end of September 2004, there were 29 funds, which managed assets of ₹ 1,53,108 crores under 421 schemes. The following graph describes the growth in assets of mutual fund industry since inception till.

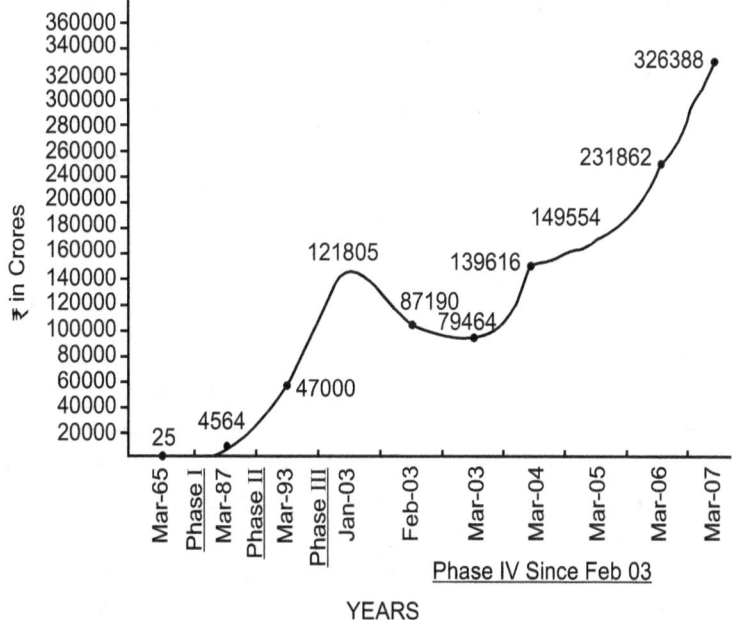

Graph showing Growth in Assets of Mutual Fund Industry

Role of SEBI in Mutual Fund Industry

Unit Trust of India was the first mutual fund set up in India in the year 1963. In early 1990s, Government allowed public sector banks and institutions to set up mutual funds. In the year 1992, Securities and Exchange Board of India (SEBI) Act was passed. The objectives of SEBI are-to protect the interest of investors in securities and to promote the development of and to regulate the securities market. As far as mutual funds are concerned, SEBI formulates policies and regulates the mutual funds to protect the interest of the investors. SEBI notified regulations for the mutual funds in 1993. Thereafter, mutual funds sponsored by private sector entities were allowed to enter the capital market. The regulations were fully revised in 1996 and have been amended thereafter from time to time. SEBI has also issued guidelines to the mutual funds from time to time to protect the interests of investors. All mutual funds whether promoted by public sector or private sector entities including those promoted by foreign entities are governed by the same set of Regulations. There is no distinction in regulatory requirements for these mutual funds and all are subject to monitoring and inspections by SEBI. The risks associated with the schemes launched by the mutual funds sponsored by these entities are of similar type. It may be mentioned here that Unit Trust of India (UTI) is not registered with SEBI as a mutual fund.

A mutual fund is set up in the form of a trust, which has a sponsor, trustees, asset management company (AMC) and a custodian. The trust is established by a sponsor or more than one sponsor who is like the promoter of a company. The trustees of the mutual fund hold its property for the benefit of the unitholders. Asset Management Company (AMC) approved by SEBI manages the funds by making investments in various types of securities. Custodian, who is registered with SEBI, holds the securities of various schemes of the fund in its custody. The trustees are vested with the general power of superintendence and direction over AMC. They monitor the performance and compliance of SEBI Regulations by the mutual fund. SEBI Regulations require that at least two thirds of the directors of trustee company or board of trustees must be independent i.e. they should not be associated with the sponsors. Also, 50% of the directors of AMC must be independent. All mutual funds are required to be registered with SEBI before they launch any scheme.

Net Asset Value (NAV) of a scheme

The performance of a particular scheme of a mutual fund is denoted by Net Asset Value (NAV). Mutual funds invest the money collected from the investors in securities markets. In simple words, Net Asset Value is the market value of the securities held by the scheme. Since market value of securities changes every day, NAV of a scheme also varies on day to day basis. The NAV per unit is the market value of securities of a scheme divided by the total number of units of the scheme on any particular date. For example, if the market value of securities of a mutual fund scheme is Re. 200 lakhs and the mutual fund has issued 10 lakhs units of ₹ 10 each to the investors, then the NAV per unit of the fund is ₹ 20. NAV is required to be disclosed by the mutual funds on a regular basis daily or weekly - depending on the type of scheme.

SEBI and Mutual Funds

The following are the guidelines for mutual funds.

Mutual funds have become a major vehicle for mobilisation of savings particularly from the small and household sectors for investment in the stock market. In view of their growing importance in the capital market, their expanding investor base and the decision to allow Mutual funds to be set up in the joint and private sectors it has become necessary to evolve a comprehensive set of prudential guidelines for the all-round development and regulation of mutual funds and for ensuring investor protection. These guidelines are laid down below.

Scope

These guidelines shall be applicable to all mutual funds which invest primarily in the capital market and also partly in money market instruments subject to the following :

i)   Money market mutual funds that would invest exclusively in money market instruments would be regulated by the Reserve Bank of India on the basis of specified guidelines to be laid down by the RBI. However, money market schemes of other mutual funds would be regulated by the Securities and Exchange Board of India. These regulations will be in conformity with the guidelines to be issued by the Reserve Bank for money market mutual funds investing exclusively in money market instruments.

ii) Offshore funds which have non-residential investors and are regulated by the provisions of the countries where these are registered shall be outside the purview of these guidelines. These funds shall continue to be governed by the rules and procedures laid down for the purpose of approving and monitoring their performance by the department of economic affairs, ministry of finance and the government's/RBI's directives on this subject.

iii) Mutual funds with special characteristics, e.g., funds dealing with assets other than securities may be specifically exempted by the government from the purview of these guidelines.

Existing mutual funds should conform to these guidelines within a period of 6 months from the date of issue of these guidelines.

Establishment

Mutual funds shall be authorised for business by the Securities and Exchange Board of India (SEBI).

Mutual funds shall be sponsored by the registered companies with a sound track record, general reputation and fairness in all their business transactions.

Mutual funds shall be established in the form of trusts under the Indian Trusts Act. The sponsoring institution will be free to work out the details regarding the constitution of the rest.

The trust shall then be authorised to float one or several different schemes under which units shall be issued to the investors.

Mutual funds shall be operated only by separately established asset management companies.

Asset Management Company (AMC)

Authorisation for Business

AMC shall be authorised for business by SEBI on the basis of the following criteria :

i)   AMCs which are already existing should have a sound track record, general reputation and fairness in all their business transactions.

ii)   The directors of AMCs should be persons of high repute and standing, having at least 10 years of professional experience in the relevant fields such as portfolio management, investment analysis, financial administration, etc.

iii) At least 50% of the board of AMC should be independent directors not connected with the sponsoring organisation.

iv)   The AMC should at all times have a minimum networth of ₹ 5 crore.

SEBI shall approve the memorandum and articles of association of the AMC.

The names of the directors and any subsequent changes must be intimated to SEBI.

SEBI may lay down additional selection criteria or change them from time to time for regulating the expansion of mutual funds in the larger interest of mutual funds industry and healthy growth of capital market.

Except in the case of bank sponsored AMCs where the prior concurrence of RBI would be required, SEBI may withdraw the authorisation granted to any AMC if it is found to be not serving the best interests of investors or of mutual funds industry or of capital market. The board of trustees of a mutual fund in such cases should reappoint another AMC or liquidate the mutual fund as may be necessary within 3 months of withdrawal of authorisation of the existing AMC and distribute the proceeds to unit holders.

Restrictions on Business Activities

AMC should not be allowed to act as the trustee of a unit trust. In other words, the AMC and the trustee should be two separate legal entities.

AMC should not be permitted to undertake any other business activity other than management of mutual funds and such other activities as financial services consultancy, exchange of research and analysis on commercial basis as long as these arc not in conflict with the fund management activity itself.

An AMC or its affiliate acting for a fund cannot act as the AMC for any other fund. For this purpose, a company is considered as an affiliate if it is a company :

i)   Which directly or indirectly and by itself, or in combination with other persons exercises a significant control over the AMC.

ii)   Over which the AMC, directly or indirectly and by itself or in combination with other persons exercises a significant control.

iii) Over which significant control is exercised directly or indirectly by person or persons or the relatives of such person or persons whether by themselves or in combination, as are the same person or persons or the relative of such person or persons whether by themselves or in combination who exercise significant control over the AMC.

iv) In which any director, officer or employee of the AMC is a director, officer or employee.

v) Without prejudice to the generality of the above restriction, significant control shall be deemed to exist. In relation to a company, where any person or combination of persons directly or indirectly own, control or hold with power to vote 3 percent or more of the voting share of such company.

vi) In between two companies if the same person or combination of persons directly or indirectly own, control or hold with power to vote 3 percent or more of the voting shares of each the two companies.

No person should be a director of more than one AMC.

No person who is a director of an AMC should hold the position of a trustee, or director in a trust company of funds operated by the same AMC.

No person should be a director/trustee in more than one trust company/ board of trustees.

Trustee and Trust Companies

Trusteeship functions should be carried out by separately established trust companies. Until such companies are formed, existing debenture trustees, banks and financial institutions may be allowed to act as mutual fund trustees, or a separate board of trustees consisting of individuals of sufficient repute and experience may act as mutual fund trustees.

At least 50 percent of the board of trustees shall be independent outside members. They shall not have any affiliation with the sponsoring institution or any of its subsidiaries.

The trust company and/or the composition of the board of trustees including the eligibility of each member should be intimated to SEBI.

The trustees should have the responsibility to ensure that managers comply with the guidelines and reports periodically to the investors in the fund that this is the case. This should entail, interalia, the following checks :

- that investments are of the permitted kind and within set limits; that the fund's assets are duly protected;
- that transaction in units are properly executed by the manager which may include spot checks;
- pricing of units;
- payments into and out of the fund;
- internal controls, (e.g., for capital adequacy);
- the income due to the fund is properly accounted for;
- that all expenses and charges to the funds arc as permitted;
- that distributions from the fund are properly made.

In order to effect these checks the trustees should have the right to obtain from the AMC all information concerning the operations of the trust.

The AMC should submit a quarterly report on the functioning of the mutual funds to the trustees. The trustees in turn should submit a six monthly report to the SEBI, and an annual report to the investors in the fund.

Trust Deeds

The sponsor should submit the trust deed to SEBI for prior approval.

The trust deed should include all safeguards considered to be essential for investor protection.

Custodian

The mutual funds shall use the services of a custodian registered with SEBI.

It should be ensured that the custodian should be totally delinked from the AMC.

Each authorised unit trust should be allowed to float different schemes as long as the asset management company concerned meets the required capital adequacy criteria and whose authorisation has not been withdrawn by SEBI for any reason, whatsoever.

Each schemes floated by a mutual fund should have prior registration with SEBI. The asset management company should prepare a prospectus/letter of offer for each scheme and should get it vetted by SEBI before inviting public participation. SEBI shall decide each proposal within 30 days of its receipt, failing which the scheme may be floated by the fund presuming SEBI's clearance.

Mutual funds should be allowed to start and operate both closed-end and open-end schemes.

The closed-end scheme shall be considered for approval as per the procedures applicable to capital issues by companies.

For each closed-end scheme, the mutual fund should be required to raise at least ₹ 20 crore and for each open-end scheme, at least ₹ 50 crore. The entire subscription should be refunded to the investors, if a) the minimum amount of ₹ 20 crore or 60% of the targeted amount, whichever is higher, is not raised for a closed-end scheme, or b) the minimum amount of ₹ 50 crore or 60% of the targeted amount, whichever is higher, is not raised for an open-end scheme.

Mutual funds should not be permitted to keep close-end schemes open for subscription for more than 45 days. For open-end schemes, the first 45 days of the subscription period should be considered for determining the target figure or minimum size. Mutual funds should provide continuous liquidity. Closed-end schemes should be listed on exchanges. For open-end schemes, mutual funds shall sell and repurchase units at predetermined prices based on net asset value and such prices should be published at least once in a week.

Each scheme under the same management should have a clearly identified and responsible fund manager.

Investment Limitations

Mutual funds will be allowed to invest only in transferable securities either in the money market or in the capital market, including any privately-placed debentures or scrutinised debt.

i) Privately placed debentures, scrutinised debt and other unquoted debt instruments holdings shall not exceed 10% in case of growth funds, and 40% in case of income funds.

ii) All debt instruments must have been rated as investment grade by an approved credit rating agency. If not rated, the specific approval of the board of AMC should be taken to become eligible for holding in the portfolio.

Mutual funds should not be allowed to give term loans for any purpose.

No individual scheme of the mutual funds should invest more than five percent of its corpus in any one company's shares.

No mutual fund under all its schemes should own more than five percent of any company's paid-up capital carrying voting rights.

No mutual fund under all its schemes taken together should invest more than 10% of its funds in the shares or debentures or other securities of a single company.

No mutual fund under all its schemes taken together should invest more than 15% of its funds in the shares and debentures of any specific industry (such as cotton, textile, tea, tyres etc.). This provision will not, however, apply to a scheme which has been floated for investments in one or more specified industries and a declaration to that effect has been made in the offer letter.

No scheme should invest in or lend to another scheme under the same AMC.

Mutual funds must take delivery of scrips purchased and give delivery in the case of scrips sold and in no case shall engage in short selling or carry-forward transactions or badla finance. The scrips purchased should be transferred to the fund's name and scheme also.

Transfers from one scheme to another in the same mutual fund should be allowed only if –

i) Such transfers are done at the prevailing market price for quoted instruments on spot basis,

ii) The securities so transferred would be in accordance with the investment objective of the transferee scheme,

iii) Transfer of unquoted instruments should be done only with specific approval of the board of trustees,

iv) The registration and accounting of the transaction is completed and is ratified in the next meeting of the board of trustees.

Winding up

Each closed-end scheme should have a duration fixed in number of years, at the end of which, it should be wound up or extended with the permission of SEBI.

An open-end scheme shall be wound up if the total number of units outstanding after repurchases at a point of time falls below 50% of the originally issued number of units.

Expenses

The asset management company may charge the mutual fund with investment management and advisory fees which should have been disclosed fully in the prospectus subject to the following ceiling :

i)   1.25% of the weekly average net assets outstanding in the current year for the scheme concerned as long as the net assets do not exceed ₹ 100 crore, and

ii)   1% of the excess amount over ₹ 100 crore, where net assets so calculated exceed ₹ 100 crore.

In addition, the asset management company may charge the mutual fund with the following expense :

i)   Mutual funds issue costs of sponsoring the funds and its schemes, recurring expenses including, marketing and selling expenses including agent's commission, if any, brokerage and transaction costs, registrar services for transfer of shares sold or redeemed.

The asset management company should be expected to meet all its expenses and responsible to provide the following :

i)   Offices pace, supplies and personnel including analysts and portfolio managers,

ii)   Regulatory compliance and reporting services,

iii) Preparation and distribution of the fund's prospectus, annual and periodic reports and other investor communications,

iv)   Advertising and other sales material,

v)   Accounting, service and preparation of tax returns,

v)   Insurance coverage and other services.

The fees payable to the trustees shall be charged to the mutual fund.

The fees payable to the custodian for safekeeping of fund assets and related matters shall be charged to the mutual fund.

The initial issue expenses should not exceed 6% of the funds raised under each scheme.

In any case, the total of all the expenses charged to the fund except the initial issue expenses should not exceed 3% of the weekly average net assets outstanding during the current year and the same shall be disclosed through advertisements, accounts, etc.

All expenses should be clearly identified and appropriately attributed 60 the individual schemes.

Income Distribution

All mutual funds must distribute a minimum of 90 percent of their profits in any given year.

Rights of the Parties

The asset management company can be changed by either the trustee company/board or by 75% of the investors in the fund.

If a change in the asset management company is recommended by the trustee company/board, it should be subject to scrutiny and approval of SEBI.

SEBI should have the right to review a mutual fund's role in takeovers.

Accounting Requirements

Mutual funds should be required to segregate their earnings as current income, short-term capital gains and long-term capital gains.

Accounting for all the schemes should be required to be done for the same year-ending.

For all quoted instruments, mutual funds must calculate weekly NAV at the last available closing market prices. For unquoted investments, the valuation may be done once weekly either at cost or by any other method authorised by SEBI. For investments considered doubtful, the directors' best estimate may be accepted, subject to the auditors' certificate of reasonability.

Disclosure and Reporting

SEBI will have the right to call for any information regarding the operations of the mutual funds and any of its schemes from the mutual funds, asset management company, custodian, sponsor or any other person associated with the mutual fund.

SEBI will require from every mutual fund at least the following periodic reports, in addition to any others it may see fit.

i)   Copies of the duly audited annual statements of accounts including the balance sheet and the profit and loss account for the fund and for each scheme, once a year.

ii)   Six-monthly unaudited accounts as above.

iii) A statement of movements in net assets for each of the schemes of the fund, every quarter.

iv)   A portfolio statement, including changes from the previous periods, for each scheme, every quarter.

SEBI shall also lay down the accounting policies to be complied with by all mutual funds and the format and contents of the financial statements and other reports.

SEBI shall require all mutual funds to adopt a written code of ethics designed to deal with the potential conflicts of interest that may arise from transactions by the affiliated persons or companies, disclosing all reportable transactions as determined by SEBI in a format prescribed by SEBI.

SEBI shall lay down a common advertising code for all mutual funds to comply with. All mutual funds will be expected to submit to SEBI the texts of the marketing literature and advertisements issued to the investors.

The marketing and publicity brochures for each scheme shall properly disclose the investment objectives, the method and periodicity of valuation of investment, the exact method and periodicity of sales and purchases and other details considered by SEBI to be essential for investors.

SEBI can, after due investigation, impose penalties on mutual funds for violating the guidelines as may be necessary. However, for cases of penalties of suspension or de-authorisation of mutual funds entities, prior concurrence of RBI and the government shall be taken.

Appeals against decisions of SEBI lie to the Department of Economic Affairs, Ministry of Finance.

The SEBI has recently allowed the Mutual Funds to invest 100% of funds in Money Market upto 6 months from the date of collection and thereafter 30% of funds for 5 months to one year and later only 25% in Money Market and again 100% of funds in Money Market, 6 months prior to repayment to investors.

Duties and Obligations of the Trustees

In accordance with Securities and Exchange Board of India (Mutual Funds) Regulations, 1996 and the Trust Deed constituting the Mutual Fund, the Trustees are required to fulfill several duties and obligations, including the following :

- The Trustee and the Asset Management Company shall with the prior approval of Securities and Exchange Board of India (SEBI) enter into an Investment Management Agreement (IMA).

- The Investment Management Agreement shall contain such clauses as are mentioned in the Fourth Schedule of the SEBI (MFs) Regulations, 1996 and other such clauses as are necessary for the purpose of making investments.

- The Trustees shall have a right to obtain from the Asset Management Company such information as is considered necessary by the Trustees.

- The Trustee shall ensure that the Asset Management Company has been diligent in empanelling the brokers, in monitoring securities transactions with brokers and avoiding undue concentration of business with any broker.

- The Trustee shall ensure that the Asset Management Company has not given any undue or unfair advantage to any associate or dealt with any of the associates of the Asset Management Company in any manner detrimental to interest of unit holders.

- The Trustee shall ensure that the transactions entered into by the Asset Management Company are in accordance with the SEBI (Mutual Funds) Regulations, 1996 and the Scheme.

- The Trustee shall ensure that the Asset Management Company has been managing the Mutual Fund Scheme independent of other activities and have taken adequate steps to ensure that the interest of investors of one Scheme are not compromised with those of any other scheme or of other activities of the Asset Management Company,

- The Trustee shall ensure that all the activities of the Asset Management Company are in accordance with the provisions of SEBI (Mutual Funds) Regulations, 1996.

- Where the Trustees have reason to believe that the conduct of the business of the Mutual Fund is not in accordance with the Regulations and the Scheme, they shall forthwith take such remedial steps as deemed necessary by them and shall immediately inform SEBI of the violation and the action taken by them.

- The Trustees shall be accountable for and be the Custodian of the funds and property of the respective Schemes and shall hold the same in trust for the benefit of the unit holders in accordance with the SEBI (Mutual Funds) Regulations, 1996 and the provisions of the Trust Deed.

- The Trustees shall be responsible for the calculation of any income due to be paid to the Mutual Fund and also of any income received in the Mutual Fund for the unit holders of any Scheme in accordance with the SEBI (Mutual Funds) Regulations, 1996 and the Trust Deed.

- The Trustees shall ensure that no change in the fundamental attributes of any Scheme or the Trust or fees and expenses payable or any other change which would modify the Scheme and affects the interest of unit holders, shall be carried out unless :

  - A written communication about the proposed change is sent to each unit holder and an advertisement is given in one English daily newspaper having nationwide circulation as well as in a newspaper published in the language of the region where the head office of the Mutual Fund is situated; and

  - The unit holders are given an option to exit at the prevailing net asset value without any exit load.

- The Trustee shall call for the details of transactions in securities by the key personnel of the Asset Management Company in his own name or on behalf of the Asset Management Company and shall report to SEBI, as and when required.

- The Trustee shall quarterly review all transactions carried out between the Mutual Fund, Asset Management Company and its associates.

- The Trustee shall quarterly review the net worth of the Asset Management Company and shall ensure that the same is in accordance with the clause (f) of sub-regulation (1) of regulation 21 of SEBI (Mutual Funds) Regulations, 1996.

- The Trustee shall periodically review all service contracts such as custody arrangements, transfer agency of the securities and satisfy itself that such contracts are executed in the interest of the unit holders.

The Trustee shall exercise due diligence as under :

- The Trustees shall be discerning in the appointment of the directors on the Board of the Asset Management Company.

- The Trustees shall review the desirability or continuance of the Asset Management Company if substantial irregularities are observed in any of the Schemes and shall not allow the Asset Management Company to float new Schemes.

- The Trustee shall ensure that the trust property is properly protected, held and administered by proper persons and by a proper number of such persons.
- The Trustee shall ensure that all the service providers are holding appropriate registrations from SEBI or concerned regulatory authority.
- The Trustees shall arrange for test checks of service contracts.
- The Trustees shall immediately report to SEBI of any special developments in the Mutual Fund.

3.2.2 FUNCTIONS

Mutual Fund is a form of collective investment brought in by a large group of investors for the mutual benefit of savers as well as investors. Each fund is divided into equal-portions or units. Anyone investing in the fund is allocated units in proportion to the size of one's investment. The price of these units is governed principally by value of the underlying investments held by the fund. Following functions and services are rendered by mutual fund industry.

i) Mobilising Savings :

Mutual funds are financial intermediaries concerned with mobilising savings of those who have surplus income and channelisation of these savings in those avenues where there is demand of funds. These institutions employ their resources in such a manner as to afford for their investors the combined benefits of low risk, steady return, high liquidity and capital appreciation through diversification and expert management.

ii) Investment Vehicle :

A mutual fund is an institutional device through which the investors pool funds of the savers to invest in a diversified portfolio of securities, thus spreading and reducing risk. Thus, it is an investment vehicle through which small and large investors pool their funds under the direction of an investment manager. These funds are invested in wide variety of securities in such a way as to minimise risk while ensuring steady return.

iii) Reduce the burden of industrial sector :

Savings pooled by mutual funds are invested largely in industrial securities. They usually finance long-term business requirements largely by way of direct subscription to share capital of industrial enterprise. Mutual funds, while themselves raising resources from a large number of small savers, make funds available to industrial concerns in relatively bigger lots and thus reduce their burden and botheration involved in raising finance directly from individual savers.

iv) Salutary impact on the stock market :

By playing the role of financial intermediation mutual funds provide a convenient and effective link between savings and investment. Well managed mutual funds would be mutually beneficial arrangement. While, on the one hand, they help the investing community by offering a share of corporate growth, on the other they have a salutary impact on the stock markets. By blending caution with aggression and analysis with intuition, the funds can successfully convert market opportunities into lucrative returns for the investors.

v) Attract foreign capital :

Role of the mutual funds is not limited to domestic sphere only. In addition to attracting domestic savings, these funds can offer their units abroad and attract foreign capital just as UTI has recently done by offering India Fund India Growth Fund schemes. Similarly, they may serve as useful institutions for securing profitable investment avenues abroad for domestic savings.

vi) Solving the problems of savers :

a)   Savers of moderate means in the underdeveloped regions are generally reluctant to invest in corporate securities because of their lack of adequate knowledge about complicated investment affairs. Moreover, their sources being small, they can at best hold securities of one or two or just a few industrial concerns only and as such the fate of their savings and prospects of earnings therefrom are tied to the fate of such unit or units. Investment in securities of mutual funds take care of both these problems, for such investment, in effect, represents a parts of the funds' entire portfolio diversified in terms of securities, units, industries and geographical regions.

b)   Investment in foreign industrial securities requires fairly detailed knowledge of the state of the foreign economy in general and of industries in particular as also of fiscal and monetary policies, state of the money and capital markets and of the financial position of industrial enterprises and their future prospects. As a result, despite attractive investment prospects abroad for surplus domestic savings. individual investors would find it an extremely difficult task to make foreign investment

vii) Providing Research Service :

A mutual fund is able to command vast resources and hence it is possible for it to have an indepth study and carry out research on corporate securities. Each Fund maintains a large research team which constantly analyses the companies and the industries and recommends the fund to buy or sell a particular share. Thus, investments are made purely on the basis of a thorough research. Since research involves a lot of time, efforts and expenditure, an individual investor cannot take up this work. By investing in a mutual fund, the investor gets the benefit of the research done by the Fund.

viii) Offering Tax Benefits :

Certain funds offer tax benefits to its customers. Thus, apart from dividends, interest and capital appreciation, investors also stand to get the benefit of tax concession.

The mutual funds themselves are totally exempt from tax on all income on their investments. But, all other companies have to pay taxes and they can declare dividends only from the profits after tax. But, mutual funds do not deduct tax at source from dividends. This is really a boon to investors.

ix) Introducing Flexible Investment Schedule :

Some mutual funds have permitted the investors to exchange their units from one scheme to another and this flexibility is a great boon to investors. Income Units can be exchanged for growth units depending upon the performance of the funds. One cannot derive such a flexibility in any other investments.

x) Providing Greater Affordability and Liquidity :

Even a very small investor can afford to invest in Mutual Funds. They provide an attractive and cost effective alternative to direct purchase of shares. In the absence of MFs, small investors cannot think of participating in a number of investments with such a meagre sum. Again, there is greater liquidity. Units can be sold to the Fund at any time at the Net Asset Value and thus quick access to liquid cash is assured.

xi) Acting as a Substitute for Initial Public Offerings (IPOs) :

In most cases investors are not able to get allotment in IPOs of companies because they are often oversubscribed. Moreover, they have to apply for a minimum of 500 shares which is very difficult particularly for small investors. But, in mutual funds, allotment is more or less guaranteed. Mutual Funds are also guaranteed a certain percentage of IPOs by companies. Thus, by participating in MFs, investors are able to get the satisfaction of participating in hundreds of varieties of companies.

xii) Reducing the Marketing Cost of New Issues :

Moreover the mutual funds help to reduce the marketing cost of the new issues. The promoters used to allot a major share of the Initial Public offering to the mutual funds and thus they are saved from the marketing cost of such issues.

xiii) Keeping the Money Market Active :

An individual investor cannot have any access to money market instruments since the minimum amount of investment is out of his reach. On the other hand, mutual funds keep the money market active by investing money on the money market instruments. In fact, the availability of more money market instruments itself is a good sign for a developed money market which is very essential for the successful functioning of the central bank in a country.

3.2.3 TYPES OF MUTUAL FUNDS

As per the government guidelines, there are three types of mutual funds permitted by the government 1) Capital Market Mutual Funds whose investments in stock and capital markets constitute the bulk of the funds and are regulated by SEBI, 2) Money Market Mutual Funds which are to be authorised by the RBI and whose investment are mostly in Money Market Instruments and 3) Offshore investments which are governed by the guidelines of RBI and Ministry of Finance.

Types of Mutual Fund Schemes are shown below in Figure 3.4.

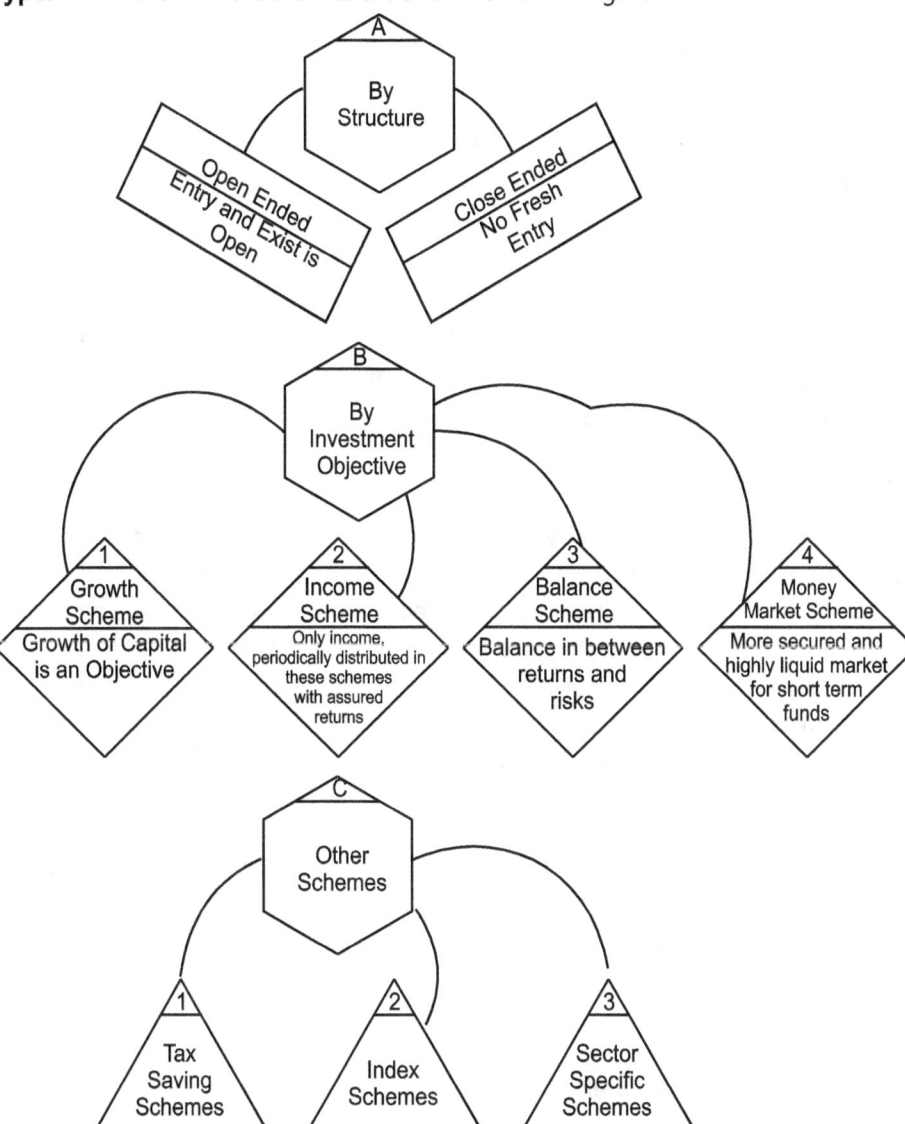

Fig. 3.4 : Types of Mutual Fund Schemes

Different Schemes available under Mutual Funds are :

A) By Structure

1) Open - Ended Funds

2) Close - Ended Funds

B) By Investment Objective

1) Growth Schemes

2) Income Schemes

3) Balanced Schemes

4) Money Market Schemes

C) Other Schemes

1) Tax Saving Schemes

2) Index Schemes

3) Sector Specific Schemes

A) By Structure, Mutual Fund Schemes can broadly classified into two schemes

i) Open-ended Schemes and ii) Close-ended Schemes.

3.2.3.1 OPEN ENDED FUNDS

Meaning

Open ended schemes have no fixed duration. They will continue to exist till the fund decides to terminate the scheme as per regulations with the consent of its investors. Majority of the schemes offered these days are open ended schemes. Like all mutual fund schemes, open ended schemes have an initial offer period when the scheme is launched. Investors can subscribe to the scheme at face value at the time of the initial offer. Once the initial offer closes, new investors can purchase units on any working day at the prevailing value, commonly called the net asset value or NAV, of the units. The funds will repurchase the units from investors, any time, at the prevailing NAV. Open ended schemes are required to declare their NAV on a daily basis.

An open-ended fund or scheme is one that is available for subscription and repurchase on a continuous basis. These schemes do not have a fixed maturity period. Investors can conveniently buy and sell units at Net Asset Value (NAV) related Prices which are declared on a daily basis. The key feature of open-end schemes is liquidity.

Features

The main **features of the Open-Ended Funds** are :

i)   The main objective of this fund is income generation. The investors get dividend, rights or bonuses as rewards for their investment.

ii) Since the units are not listed on the stock market, their prices are linked to the Net Asset Value (NAV) of the units. The NAV is determined by the Fund and it varies from time to time.

iii) Generally, the listed prices are very close to their Net Asset/ Value. The Fund fixes a different price for their purchases and sales.

iv) The fund manager has to be very careful in managing the investments because he has to meet the redemption demands at any time made during the life of the scheme.

v)   There is complete flexibility with regard to one's investment or disinvestment. In other words, there is free entry and exit of investors in an open-ended fund. There is no time limit. The investor can join in and come out from the Fund as and when he desires.

vi)   These units are not publicly traded but, the Fund is ready to repurchase them and resell them at any time.

vii) The investor is offered instant liquidity in the sense that the units can be sold on any working day to the Fund. In fact, the Fund operates just like a bank account wherein one can get cash across the counter for any number of units sold.

Drawback of an Open Ended Funds

One major drawback of an open ended scheme is that a large number of investors may try to redeem their units in the event of a negative economic event. Such large scale redemptions would force the fund managers to exit their investment positions at less than optimum value, in order to repay the investors.

The fund mangers will have a problem in the event of a major positive economic event as well. For example, if the stock markets are doing well many investors would purchase mutual fund units. The fund managers will be forced to deploy the large inflow of funds when the markets are peaking and stock prices are high. This could affect the overall performance of the fund in the longer term, if the stock prices are to go down in the future.

3.2.3.2 CLOSE ENDED FUNDS

Meaning

Close ended schemes have a fixed duration which will be specified at the time of the initial offer. The fund can change the duration with the consent of the investors, subject to relevant rules and regulations.

Unlike open ended schemes, close ended schemes are available for purchase only during the initial offer period. The fund will not issue units to investors after the initial offer period.

As per SEBI guidelines, investors in close ended schemes must be offered a convenient exit route at all times. Such schemes should be listed for trading in one or more stock exchanges unless the fund offers regular buybacks at the prevailing values.

A cose-ended fund or scheme has a stipulated maturity period e.g. 5-7 years. The fund is open for subscription Only during a specified period at the lime of launch of the scheme. Investors can invest in the scheme at the time of the initial public issue and thereafter they can buy or sell the units of the scheme on the stock exchanges where the units are listed. In order to provide an exit route to the investors, some close-ended funds give an option of selling back the units to the mutual fund through periodic repurchase at NAV related prices. SEBI Regulations stipulate that at least one of the two exit routes is provided to the investor i.e. either repurchase facility or through listing on stock exchanges. These mutual funds schemes disclose NAV generally on weekly basis.

Under this scheme, the corpus of the fund and its duration are prefixed. In other words, the corpus of the fund and the number of units are determined in advance. Once the subscription reaches the pre-determined level, the entry of investors is closed. After the expiry of the fixed period, the entire corpus is disinvested and the proceeds are distributed to the various unit holders in proportion to their holdings. Thus, the fund ceases to be a fund, after the final distribution.

Features

The main **features of the close-ended funds** are :

i)   The main objective of this fund is capital appreciation.

ii)   The whole fund is available for the entire duration of the scheme and there will not be any redemption demands before its maturity. Hence, the fund manager can manage the investments efficiently and profitably without the necessity of maintaining an liquidity.

iii)   At the time of redemption, the entire investment pertaining to a closed-end scheme is liquidated and the proceeds are distributed among the unit holders.

iv)   From the investor's point of view, it may attract more tax since the entire capital appreciation is realised in total at one stage itself.

v)   The period and/or the target amount of the fund is definite and fixed beforehand.

vi)   Once the period is over and/or the target is reached, the door is closed for the investors. They cannot purchase any more units.

vii)   These units are publicly traded through stock exchange and generally, there is no repurchase facility by the fund.

viii) If the market condition is not favourable, it may also affect the investor since he may not get the full benefit of capital appreciation in the value of the investment.

Since the quantum of funds under management is fixed and there will be no periodic redemption pressures if it is an exchange traded scheme.

Overall returns of a close ended scheme may be affected by the market conditions at the time of closure of the scheme. Therefore, such schemes are more suited for investing in relatively shorter term opportunities like stocks of a particular industrial sector which is in its growth phase. In such a case, the scheme can be launched when the industry is at its infancy and can be closed when the industry matures and growth rate flattens.

B) Schemes according to Investment Objective

A scheme can also be classified as growth scheme, income scheme or balanced scheme considering its investment objective. Such schemes may be open-ended or close-ended schemes as described earlier. Such schemes may be classified mainly as follows :

3.2.3.3 Income Funds

Meaning

Income Schemes are also known as debt schemes or bond schemes. The aim of these schemes is to provide regular and steady income to investors. These schemes generally invest in fixed income securities such as bonds and corporate debentures. Capital appreciation in such schemes may be limited. Such funds are less risky compared to equity schemes. These funds are not affected because of fluctuations in equity markets. However, opportunities of capital appreciation are also limited in such funds. The NAVs of such funds are affected because of change in interest rates in the country. If the interest rates fall, NAVs of such funds are likely to increase in the short run and vice versa. However, long term investors may not bother about these fluctuations.

Unlike equities, prices of fixed income investments like government securities are less volatile. Their prices depend on the prevailing interest rates and changes in the interest rate outlook for the future.

When interest rates in the economy moves up; prices of existing bonds or bonds issued in the past go down as the income offered by them becomes less attractive. Their prices move up when interest rates go down. Unless a major economic change occurs, changes in interest rates are modest and gradual.

Income funds concentrates more on the distribution of regular income and it also sees that the average return is higher than that of the income from bank deposits.

Features

The main features of the Income Funds are :

i)   The investor is assured of regular income at periodic intervals, say half-yearly or yearly and so on.

ii)   The main objective of this type of Fund is to declare regular dividends and not capital appreciation.

iii)   The pattern of investment is oriented towards high and fixed income yielding securities like debentures, bonds etc.

iv)   This is best suited to the old and retired people who may not have any regular income.

v)   It concerns itself with short run gains only.

Income funds also invest in equities, but the proportion of equities to the overall portfolio would be relatively low. Even when they invest in equities, income schemes generally consider for investment only the large, less volatile stocks which pay high dividends. The maximum allowed percentage of equity investments in the overall portfolio would be specified at the time of launch of the scheme. This percentage is kept low to keep the overall portfolio risk to the minimum.

By reducing the risks, income funds also reduce the possibility of long term capital appreciation to a large extent. Hence, returns are generally lower than growth funds.

3.2.3.4 BALANCED FUNDS

This is otherwise called "income-cum-growth" fund. It is nothing but a combination of both income and growth funds. It aims at distributing regular income as well as capital appreciation. This is achieved by balancing the investments between the high growth equity shares and also the fixed income earning securities.

The aim of balanced funds is to provide both growth and regular income as such schemes invest both in equities and fixed income securities in the proportion indicated in their offer documents. These are appropriate for investors looking for moderate growth. They generally invest 40-60% in equity and debt instruments. These funds are also affected because of fluctuations in share prices in the stock markets. However, NAVs of such funds are likely to be less volatile compared to pure equity funds.

The objective of these funds is to provide a balanced mixture of safety, income and capital appreciation. The strategy of balanced funds is to invest in a combination of fixed income and equities. A typical balanced fund might have a weighting of 60% equity and 40% fixed income. The weighting might also be restricted to a specified maximum for each asset class. A similar type of fund is known as an asset allocation fund. Objectives are similar to those of a balanced fund, but these kinds of funds typically do not have to hold a specified percentage of any asset class. The portfolio manager is therefore given freedom to switch the ratio of asset classes as the economy moves through the business cycle.

No specific asset class receives a higher weight in the targeted investment portfolio of a balanced scheme. Most often, the portfolio will be equally balanced between equity and fixed income securities. However, as in the case of other funds, investments in equities may go up when the stock markets are in good shape and vice versa. Such allocations are again done within the acceptable risk levels for the scheme and also within the target percentages for each asset class specified at the time of launch of the scheme.

Money Market Schemes or Liquid Funds

These funds are also income funds and their aim is to provide easy liquidity, preservation of capital and moderate income. These schemes invest exclusively in safer short-term instruments such as treasury bills, certificates of deposit, commercial paper and inter-bank call money, government securities, etc.

These instruments are called money market instruments. They take the place of shares, debentures and bonds in a capital market. They pay money market rates of interest. These funds are called 'money funds' in the U.S.A. and they have been functioning since 1972. Investors generally use it as a "parking place" or "stop gap arrangement" for their cash resources till they finally decide about the proper avenue for their investment i.e., long term financial assets like bonds and stocks. Returns on these schemes fluctuate much less compared to other funds. These funds are appropriate for corporate and individual investors as a means to park their surplus funds for short periods. These funds go for safe and liquid investment. Frequent realisation of interest and redemption of Fund at short notice are the special features of this Fund. The funds will not be subject to reserve requirements. The re-purchase could be subject to a minimum lock in period of 3 months.

Since the RBI has fixed the minimum amount of investment as ₹ One lakh, it is out of the reach of many small investors. In the U.S.A. the minimum amount is only $ 100. Recently, the private sector funds have been permitted to deal in money market mutual funds. Generally, it is best suited only to institutional investors like banks and other financial institutions.

Money market usually refers to the market for very short term borrowings mostly by banks and other financial institutions to meet immediate requirements. The maturity of such borrowings can be as short as one day. Interest rates will depend on the overall liquidity position in the financial system. In other words, interest rates will be high when sufficient funds are not available in the market and vice versa. Money market transactions are highly secure as the borrowers are the best banks and financial institutions.

Retail investors cannot participate in money market transactions as the value of individual transactions is very high. Money market schemes offer an opportunity for retail investors to participate in this relatively more secure and highly liquid market for short term funds. Money market schemes are also known as liquid schemes.

3.2.3.5 Growth Funds

Growth Schemes are also known as equity schemes. The aim of these schemes is to provide capital appreciation over medium to long term. These schemes normally invest a major part of their fund in equities and are willing to bear short-term decline in value for possible future appreciation.

Such funds have comparatively high risks. These schemes provide different options to the investors like dividend option, capital appreciation etc. and the investors may choose an option depending on their preferences. The investors must indicate the option in the application form. The mutual funds also allow the investors to change the options at a later date. Growth schemes are good for investors having a long-term outlook seeking appreciation over a period of time.

Growth Funds concentrate mainly on long run gains i.e., capital appreciation. They do not offer regular income and they aim at capital appreciation in the long run. Hence, they have been described as "Nest Eggs" investments.

Growth schemes offer potentially the best possible returns among all mutual fund schemes but carry the highest risk as well.

With their large exposure to the stock markets, growth funds are among the most popular among small investors. When the stock markets do well most growth funds offer returns which are often better than overall market returns.

Features

The main features of the Growth Funds are :

i) The Fund tries to get capital appreciation by taking much risks and investing on risk bearing equities and high growth equity shares.

ii) The fund may declare dividend, but its principal objective is only capital appreciation.

iii) This is best suited to salaried and business people who have high risk bearing capacity and ability to defer liquidity. They can accumulate wealth for future needs.

iv)   The growth oriented fund aims at meeting the investors need for capital appreciation.

v)   The investment strategy therefore, conforms to the fund objective by investing the funds predominantly on equities with high growth potential.

While observing the results of growth fund, it is clear that, the large exposure to stock markets also means that risks involved are also higher. Returns from growth schemes are often very volatile as they trace stock market performance. Growth fund returns may look very spectacular when the stock markets are doing well. They will look quite dismal when the markets go through a downtrend.

Generally, growth funds are not pure equity schemes unless they are specified so. A smaller portion of the portfolio is invested in fixed income securities like bonds. The targeted percentage of each asset class like equities, bonds, etc would be specified when the scheme is launched. The actual investments in each of these would depend on the prevailing market conditions. In other words, when the stock markets are not doing well the scheme would invest more in bonds and vice versa.

C) Other Schemes

Other sources are as under :

Tax Saving Funds

These schemes offer tax rebates to the investors under specific provisions of the Income Tax Act, 1961 as the Government offers tax incentives for investment in specified avenues. e.g. Equity Linked Savings Schemes (ELSS). Pension schemes launched by the mutual funds also offer tax benefits. These schemes are growth oriented and invest pre-dominantly in equities. Their growth opportunities and risks associated are like any equity-oriented scheme.

Under Indian tax laws, investment in specified mutual fund schemes qualify for a deduction from the taxable income. Eligible mutual fund schemes should be predominantly equity oriented and investors have a lock in period of three years. In other words, investors cannot exit the scheme within three years from the date of investment. Such schemes are called Equity Linked Savings Scheme or ELSS in India.

Section 80 C of the Income Tax Act, which is the relevant section for ELSS, provides for a deduction of up to ₹ 1 lakh every year. The limit of ₹ 1 lakh under the section is for all eligible investments specified and can be claimed for a Single Investment or many.

Though tax saving schemes is no different from general equity oriented schemes, many investors in India consider them with the objective of tax management rather than as an investment.

3.2.3.6 INDEX FUNDS

Index Funds invest in all the stocks which form part of a stock market index. They aim to trace the performance of the index. In other words, the returns from an index fund and the gain or loss in the stock market index it is based on would be the same for any given time frame.

A stock market index is like a portfolio of stocks with different weights for each stock based on its relative importance. Index funds invest in stocks in the same proportion of their relative weights on the index.

Index Funds replicate the portfolio of a particular index such as the BSE Sensitive index, S&P NSE 50 index (Nifty), etc. These schemes invest in the securities in the same weightage comprising an index. NAVs of such schemes would rise or fall in accordance with the rise or fall in the index, though not exactly by the same percentage due to some factors known as "tracking error" in technical terms. Necessary disclosures in this regard are made in the offer document of the mutual fund scheme. There are also exchange traded index funds launched by the mutual funds which are traded on the stock exchanges.

Sector Specific Funds :

These are the funds/schemes which invest in the securities of only those sectors or industries as specified in the offer documents. e.g. Pharmaceuticals, Software, Fast Moving Consumer Goods (FMCG), Petroleum stocks. etc. The returns in these funds are dependent on the performance of the respective sectors/industries. While these funds may give higher returns, they are more risky compared to diversified funds. Investors need to keep a watch, on the performance of those sectors/industries and must exit at an appropriate time. They may also seek advice of an expert.

Sector specific schemes invest in stocks belonging to a specific category, industry etc. Such schemes aim to capitalise on the opportunities available in certain categories of stocks which may have attracted or have the potential to attract market attention. Sector funds try to achieve returns which are superior to the overall market returns. Such funds carry relatively high risks since the portfolio is not well diversified and is concentrated only on one sector or category.

The reasons for sector specific investments could be many. Some industries may be experiencing tremendous growth opportunities because of specific economic developments and most companies in that industry would have the potential to do well. In some other cases, the industry may be at a beginning stage and it would be difficult to pick the companies that would do well in future from the handful available. Therefore, it may make sense to invest in all the significant companies in the sector. The telecom and textile export industries in India are examples of sectors which offer tremendous growth opportunities to most of the companies in those sectors.

It may happen that due to some competitive advantages enjoyed by the country, certain sectors of the economy would have huge export potential and opportunities to expand globally. Sector funds targeted to capitalise on such sectors would invest in major companies across all the identified sectors. Another fund may target investments in Indian companies who are having a significant global presence or are planning to expand abroad.

Sector Funds are targeted at specific sectors of the economy such as financial, technology, health, etc. Sector funds are extremely volatile. There is a greater possibility of big gains, as well as big losses in such a fund. For e.g. Magnum IT Fund (technology sector), JM auto sector fund (automobiles sector), Reliance Pharma Fund (pharmaceutical sector) etc.

International Mutual Funds

1)   Global/International Funds : International mutual funds are those funds that invest in non-domestic securities market throughout the world. Investing in international markets provides greater portfolio diversification and lets investor capitalise on some of the world's best opportunities. If investments are chosen carefully, international mutual fund may be profitable when some markets are rising and others are declining. However, fund managers need to keep close watch on foreign currencies and world markets as profitable investments in a rising market can lose money if the foreign currency rises against the dollar. For example UTI MNC Fund, Kotak MNC Fund etc.

2)   Offshore Funds : Offshore funds are mutual funds with investments source abroad. In other words, the subscription to these funds is mobilised from international financial markets for investment in the economics and capital markets of specific country(ies). Thus, these funds are cross-border investments facilitating capital movement of investible surpluses from cash rich countries to high growth or potentially high growth economies of the world.

In other words, the sources of investments for these funds are from abroad. So, they are regulated by the provisions of the foreign countries where those funds are registered. These funds facilitate flow of funds across different countries, with free and efficient movement of capital for investment and repatriation. Off-shore funds are preferred to direct foreign investment, since, it does not allow foreign domination over host country's corporate sector. However, these funds involve much currency and country risk and hence they generally yield higher return.

In India, these funds are subject to the approval of the Department of Economic Affairs, Ministry of Finance and the RBI monitors such funds by issuing directions then and there. In India, a number of offshore funds exist. 'India Fund' and India Growth Fund' were floated by the UTI in U.K. and U.S.A. respectively. The State Bank of India floated the India Magnum Fund in Netherlands. 'The Indo-Suez Himalayan Fund N.V' was launched by Canbank Mutual Fund in collaboration with Indo-Suez Asia Investment Services Ltd. It also floated 'Commonwealth Equity Fund'.

Classification of Mutual Fund by Nature

By nature, mutual funds are classified as under :

i)   Equity fund

These funds invest a maximum part of their corpus into equities holdings. The structure of the fund may vary different for different schemes and the fund manager's outlook on different stocks. The Equity Funds are sub-classified depending upon their investment objective, as follows :

- Diversified Equity Funds.
- Mid-Cap Funds.
- Sector Specific Funds.
- Tax Savings Funds (ELSS).

Equity investments, are meant for a longer time horizon, thus Equity funds rank high on the risk-return matrix.

ii) Debt funds

The objective of these Funds is to invest in debt papers. Government authorities, private companies, banks and financial institutions are some of the major issuers of debt papers. By investing in debt instruments, these funds ensure low risk and provide stable Income to the investors.

iii) Gilt Funds

Invest their corpus in securities issued by Government, popularly known as Government of India debt papers. These Funds carry zero Default risk but are associated with Interest Rate risk. These schemes are safer as they invest in papers backed by Government.

iv) MIPs

Invests maximum of their total corpus in debt instruments while they take minimum exposure in equities. It gets benefit of both equity and debt market. These scheme ranks slightly high on the risk-return matrix when compared with other debt schemes.

v) Short-term Plans (STPs)

Meant for investment horizon for three to six months. These funds primarily invest in short term papers like Certificate of Deposits (CDs) and Commercial Papers (CPs). Some portion of the corpus is also invested in corporate debentures.

Advantages of Investing in Mutual Funds

The **main advantages of investing capital in Mutual Funds** are as follows :

i) **Professional Management :** The basic advantage of funds is that, they are professionally managed, by well qualified persons. Investors purchase funds because they do not have the time or the expertise to manage their own portfolio. A mutual fund is considered to be relatively less expensive way to make and monitor their investments.

ii) **Diversification :** Purchasing units in a mutual fund instead of buying individual stocks or bonds, the investors risk is spread out and minimised up to certain extent. The idea behind diversification is to invest in a large number of assets so that a loss in any particular investment is minimised by gains in others.

iii) **Economies of Scale :** Mutual fund buys and sells large amounts of securities at a time, thus help to reduce transaction costs, and help to bring down the average cost of the unit for their investors.

iv) **Liquidity :** Just like an individual stock, mutual fund also allows investors to liquidate heir holdings as and when they want.

v) **Simplicity :** Investments in mutual fund is considered to be easy, compared to other available instruments in the market, and the minimum investment is small. Most AMCs also have automatic purchase plans which is as little as ₹ 2000, where SIP starts with just ₹50 per month.

vi) **Safety of Investments :** Besides depending on the expert supervision of fund managers, the legislation in a country (like SEBI in India) also provides for the safety of investments. Mutual funds have to broadly follow the laid down provisions for their regulations, SEBI acts as a watchdog and attempts whole heatedly to safeguard investors interests.

vii) **Tax Shelter :** Depending on the scheme of mutual fund, tax shelter is also available to the investor.

Disadvantages of Investing Mutual Funds

The **disadvantages of investing in Mutual Funds** are as follows :

i) **Professional Management :** Some funds does not perform in neither the market, as their management is not dynamic enough to explore the available opportunity in the market, thus many investors debate over whether or not the so-called professionals are any better than mutual fund or investor himself, for picking up stocks.

ii) **Costs :** The biggest source of AMC income, is generally from the entry and exit load which they charge from investors, at the time of purchase. The mutual fund industries are thus charging extra cost under layers of jargon.

iii) **Dilution :** Because funds have small holdings across different companies, high returns from a few investments often don't make much difference on the overall return. Dilution is also the result of a successful fund getting too big. When money pours into funds that have had strong success, the manager often has trouble finding a good investment for all the new money.

iv) **Taxes :** When making decisions about your money, fund managers don't consider your personal tax situation. For example, when a fund manager sells a security, a capital-gain tax is triggered, which affects how profitable the individual is from the sale. It might have been more advantageous for the individual to defer the capital gains liability.

3.3 PORTFOLIO MANAGEMENT

3.3.1 MEANING

As the investor acquire different sets of assets of financial nature, such as gold, silver, insurance policy, post office certificates, NSC or NSS, building, real estate etc. they are making provisions for the future. The risk of each of such investment is to be understood before hand. Many times the investors go on acquiring these assets in an ad-hoc and unplanned manner and the result is high risk, how return profit which they may face. All such assets would constitute his portfolio and the wise investor not only plans his portfolio as per his risk return profile or preferences but manages his portfolio efficiently so as to secure the highest return for the lowest risk possible at the level of investment. This is the portfolio management.

Objective

The objective of portfolio management is to maximise the return and minimise risk. A portfolio is a basket of investments or assets held by the individual or a corporate body. The **basic objectives of Portfolio Management** are shown in Figure 3.5 as under.

Fig. 3.5 : Basic Objectives of Portfolio Management

i)   **Risk :** Risk is inherent in any investment. This risk may relate to loss or delay In repayment of the principal capital or loss or non-payment of interest or variability of returns. While some investments arc almost riskless like Government securities bank deposits, others are more risky.

ii)   **Return :** Yield or return differs from the nature of the instruments, maturity period and the creditor or debtor nature of the instrument and a host of other factors. The most important factor influencing return is risk. Normally, the higher the risk, the higher is the return. The return is the income plus capital appreciation in the case of ownership instruments and only yield an interest in the case of debt instruments like debentures or bonds.

Portfolios are combinations of assets held by the investors. These combinations may be of various asset classes like equity and debt or of different issues like Govt. bonds and corporate debt or of various instruments like discount bonds, warrants, debenture, and Blue chip equity, or scrips of emerging blue chip companies.

A combination of such securities with different risk-return characteristics will constitute the portfolio of the investor. Thus a portfolio is a combination of various assets and/or instruments of investments. The combination may have different features of risk and return, separate from those of the components. The portfolio is also built up out of the wealth or income of the investor over a period of time, with a view to suit his risk or return preferences to that of the portfolio that he holds. The portfolio analysis is thus an analysis of the risk - return characteristics of individual securities in the portfolio and changes that may take place in combination with other securities due to interaction among themselves and impact of each one of them on others.

Traditional and Modern Approach :

The traditional Portfolio Theory aims at the selection of such securities that would fit in well with the asset preferences, needs and choices of the investor. Thus a retired executive invests in fixed income securities for a regular and fixed return. A business executive or a young aggressive investor on the other hand invests in new and growing companies and in risky ventures. Modern Portfolio Theory postulates that maximisation of return and minimisation of risk will yield optimal returns and the choice and attitudes of investors are only a starting point for investment decision and that vigrous risk return analysis is necessary for optimisation of returns.

Important Aspects of Portfolio Management

Basically, Portfolio Management involves :

i) A proper Investment decision-making of what to buy and sell;

ii) Proper Money Management in terms of investment in a basket of assets so as to satisfy the asset preferences of Investors;

iii) Minimise risk and maximise returns.

The **important Aspects of Portfolio Management** are shown in Figure 3.6.

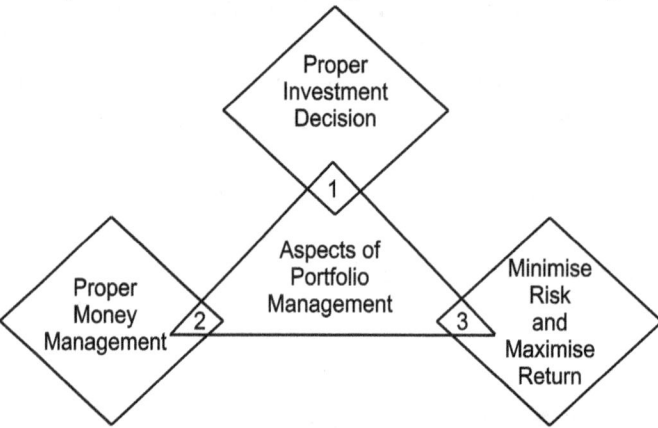

Fig. 3.6 : Aspects of Portfolio Management

1) Proper Investment Decision

Investment is parting with one's fund, to be used by another party, user of fund, for productivity activity. It can mean giving an advance or loan or contributing to the equity (ownership capital) or debt capital of a corporate or non-corporate business unit. Generalised, investment means conversion of cash or money into a monetary asset or a claim on future money for a return. This return is for saving (as abstaining from present consumption), parting with saving or liquidity (to be rewarded for waiting for a consumption) and for taking a risk involving the uncertainty about the actual return, time of waiting and cost of getting back funds, safety of funds and risk of the variability of the return.

2) Proper Money Management

The primary goal of money management in the investment process is to stick trade-off between liquidity and profitability in order to maximise long-term gain. This is possible only when the investor aims at optimising the use of money in operations. Portfolio management makes proper money management in terms of investment in a basket of assets so as to satisfy the asset preference of investors.

3) Minimise risk and Maximise returns

Risk comprises of two components i) **Systematic market related** and ii) **Unsystematic risk or Company specific risk.**

The **Types of Risk** are shown in Figure 3.7 as follows :

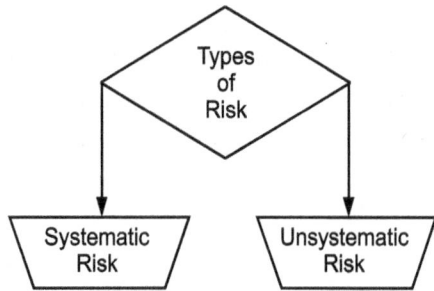

Fig. 3.7 : Types of Risk

Specific Risk : If risk is company specific risk it can be reduced by diversification into different industries and companies of different types and nature and whose covariances are different and whose performances arc disparate.

Types of Risk

Systematic Risk		Unsystematic Risk
Market related risk due to demand problems, interest rates, inflation, raw materials, import and export policy, Tax policy etc., Business-Risk, Market-Risk, Financial-Risk, Interest Rate Risk, Inflation-Risk, etc.		Company related risks due to higher cost, mismanagement, detective sales or inventory, strategy, insolvency, fall in demand and company specific recession, labour problems etc.

The company specific risk or unsystematic risks can be reduced by diversifying into a few companies belonging to various industry groups assets groups or different types of capital instruments like equity shares, bonds, debentures etc. Thus, asset groups are gold, silver, land, real estate, bank deposits, deposits with company, sugar, paper, plastic, electricity, electronics etc. Each of them have their own risk-return characteristics and accordingly investments are to be made, based on individual risk preferences. In this way, unsystematic risk can be reduced. The systematic risk can be managed by the use of 'Beta' of different company shares. However, systematic risk cannot be eliminated but managed with the help of Beta (β), which is explained as follows :

$$\beta = \frac{\% \text{ age change of Scrip return}}{\% \text{ age change of Market return}}$$

If $\beta = 1$, the risk of the company is the same as that of the market and if $\beta > 1$, the company's risk is more than the market risk. If $\beta < 1$, the position is reversed.

Beta : In a simple language, Beta is percentage in the script return dividend by the percentage change in market return. Here, the appreciation in the script price relative to the market price index is considered.

Time Value of Money :

In Portfolio Management and investment decision-making, time element and time value of money are very relevant. Savings are automatic or induced. If induced, it requires a return enough to induce them to part with liquidity. Thus, savings and liquidity will be parted by the investors if only their time preference is satisfied by a proper return.

Money has time value. Because of following reasons, a rupee today is more valuable than a rupee a year hence.

   i)   Individuals, in general, prefer current consumption to future consumption.

   ii)   Capital can be employed productively to generate positive returns. An investment rupee today would grow to $(1 + r)$ a year hence (r is the rate of return earned on investment).

   ii)   In an inflationary period a rupee today represents a greater real purchasing power a rupee a year hence.

Many financial problems involve cash flows occurring at different points of time. For evaluating such cash flows an explicit consideration of time value of money is required.

"Time Value of Money" Concept of Valuation :

The recognition of the time value of money is extremely important in financial decision-making. Most of the financial decisions affect firm's cash flow in different time periods. Purchase of a fixed asset results in immediate outflow of cash and will also generate future cash inflows during the life of the fixed asset. Similarly, borrowing funds from banks or financial institutions results in inflow of cash, but, creates an obligation on the part of the firm to pay interest and return principal sum in future period.

If the firm raises funds by issuing equity shares, there will be inflow of cash at the time of issuing shares for cash, but, as the firm pays dividends in future, the firm will have to meet the outflow of cash. Sound capital budgeting decision-making requires logical comparison of the present cash outflows with the future cash inflows. Absolute cash flows which differ in magnitude and timing, do not render themselves comparable. The comparison becomes meaningful only when it recognises the time value of money and makes appropriate adjustment for time.

"Time Preference for Money" :

An individual's preference for possession of a given amount of cash now, rather than the same amount at some future time is called "time preference for money." An individual's lime preference for money could be traced to the following reasons :

   a)   Since the future is uncertain, an individual prefers receiving cash now,

   b)   Most people have subjective preference for present consumption over future consumption of goods and services.

   c)   Most individuals prefer present cash to future cash because they like to employ present funds to tap the available existing investment opportunities.

The justification for corporate time preference for money lies only in the availability of investment opportunities. In financial decision-making, a firm has to compare cash inflows of one investment opportunity with that of the other.

Time Preference Rate :

Time Preference rate is also known as, discount rate. It is generally expressed by an interest rate. If an individual's time preference is 18%, it means that he is prepared to forego the opportunity of receiving ₹ 100 now if he is offered ₹ 118 after one year. Thus, the individual is indifferent between ₹ 100 now and ₹ 118 after one year as he considers these two amounts equivalent in value. Discount rate enables a firm to translate different amounts received at different times to amounts of equivalent value to the firm in the present at common point reference.

Discounting :

Discounting is a popular technique used in evaluation of capital projects which meets the financial goal of maximisation of present wealth of the firm. Selection of projects under discounting method involves basically, the use of a discount rate calculating the present value of future cash inflows allows us to isolate differences in the timing of these cash inflows.

In an economy wherein capital has value, a rupee today is worth more than a rupee to be received 1 year, 2 years or 3 years from now. Therefore, we need a means for standardising differences in timing of cash flows so that the time value of money is properly recognised.

Example

A firm has an opportunity to receive with complete certainty ₹ 1,000 at the end of each of the next 2 years. If the firm's opportunity cost of funds is 10% per annum, what is this proposal worth to the firm today ?

Answer

In this case, we have the terminal value (future value) as well as the required interest rate, we must solve for the appropriate beginning value.

Consequently, we divide the future value by the required rate of interest and this operation is called "Discounting."

Present value of ₹ 1,000 to be received at the end of 1 year

$$PV = \frac{₹\,1,000}{(1.1)} = ₹\,909.09$$

Present value of ₹ 1,000 to be received at the end of 2 years is,

$$PV = \frac{₹\,1,000}{(1.1)^2} = ₹\,826.45$$

Thus, ₹ 1,000 received 2 years from now, has a lower present value than ₹ 1,000 received year from now.

Therefore, the opportunity is worth ₹ 909.09 + ₹ 826.45 = ₹ 1735.54 to the Firm today.

In solving present value problems, it is useful to express the interest factor separate from the amount to be received in the future

Present value of ₹ 1,000 to be received at the end of 1 year.

$$PV = ₹\,1,000 \left[\frac{1}{(1.1)}\right] = ₹\,909.09$$

Present value of ₹ 1,000 to be received at the end of 2 years, is

$$PV = ₹\,1,000 \left[\frac{1}{(1.1)^2}\right] = ₹\,826.45$$

In this way, we are able to isolate the interest factor, and this isolation facilitates present value calculation. In such calculations, the interest rate is known as the discount rate.

The general formula for finding the present value of Xn to be received at the end of year n (where K is the discount rate) is,

$$PV = X_n \left[\frac{1}{(1 + K)^n}\right]$$

Note : Using present value tables we can calculate the present value of various future streams of cash flows. The present value of an amount of money to be received in the future decreases at a decreasing rate, as the discount rate increases.

Present value, when interest is compounded more than once a year. When interest is compounded more than once a year, the formula for calculation present values will be :

$$PV = \frac{X_n}{\left(1 + \dfrac{k}{m}\right)^{mn}}$$

where,

i) X_n is the cash flow at the end of year n.

ii)   m is the number of times in a year interest is compounded.

iii) k is the discount rate.

Annuities

An annuity maybe defined as a series of uniform receipts occurring over a specified number of years, which result from an initial deposit. Present value of an annuity is given by the following formula :

$$PV = \frac{A}{i}\left[1 - \frac{1}{(1 + i)^n}\right]$$

Where, A represents an annuity

$$i = \frac{r}{100} \text{ where r = rate of interest}$$

$$n = \text{Number of years}$$

Example

An equipment requires an initial investment of ₹ 6,000. Annual cash inflow is estimated at ₹ 2,000 for 5 years. Cost of capital is 20%.

    i)   Calculate present value of Cash inflows.

    ii)   What is NPV of the project ?

Answer

$$= PV = \frac{A}{i}\left[1 - \frac{1}{(1 + i)^n}\right]$$

$$= ₹\,\frac{2,000}{\frac{20}{100}}\left[1 - \frac{1}{\left(1 + \frac{20}{100}\right)^5}\right]$$

$$= ₹\,\frac{2,000}{0.2}\left[1 - \frac{1}{(1.2)^5}\right]$$

$$= ₹\,10,000\left[1 - \frac{1}{2.48832}\right]$$

$$= ₹\,10,000\,[1 - 0.4018775]$$

$$= ₹\,10,000 \times 0.5981225$$

$$= ₹\,5,981.23$$

Net present value = PV of cash inflow − PV of Cash outflows

(i.e., initial investment)

$$= ₹\,5,981.23 - 6,000$$

$$= ₹\,-18.77$$

The period for which an annuity is payable is called "status". The person who receives the annuity is called "Annuitant."

When an annuity is payable for a fixed number of years, it is called "annuity certain." Annuity which is payable till the happening of a certain event is called "annuity contingent."

An annuity is a "perpetual annuity" when payments are to continue forever.

When payments are made at the end of each period, it is known as Immediate Annuity or Ordinary Annuity.

When payments are made at the beginning of each period, it is known as "Annuity Due." Unless specifically stated, it is taken as Immediate Annuity.

An annuity that is to take effect after a certain number of years is known as Deferred Annuity. An Immediate Annuity deferred for n years implies that its first payment is due at the end of (n + 1) years.

Present value of an annuity is present worth of various payments.

A freehold estate is one that yields a perpetuity known as rent.

Future Value of Annuities

Amount of any annuity is the total sum of unpaid instalments together with the stipulated compound interest at the end of the given number of years.

Symbols used :

$$A = \text{Annuity}$$
$$M = \text{Amount of Annuity A left unpaid for n years or period}$$
$$PV = \text{Present value of an annuity A for n years or periods}$$
$$C = \text{Interest on unit sum for 1 year (unit sum means one rupee)}$$

Amount of n immediate Annuity certain.

$$M = \frac{A}{i}\left[(1 + i)^n - 1\right]$$

Amount of an Annuity Due

$$M = (1 + i)\left(\frac{A}{i}\right)\left[(1 + i)^n - 1\right]$$

Present value of an Immediate Annuity

$$PV = \frac{A}{i}\left[1 - \frac{1}{(1 + i)^n}\right]$$

Present value of an Annuity Due

$$PV = (1 + i)\left(\frac{A}{i}\right)\left[1 - \frac{1}{(1 + i)^n}\right]$$

Concept of "time Value of Money"

The concept of time value of money deals with the fact that an amount of money received in the future is not as valuable as the same amount of money received in the present. This is because :

i)   The future is uncertain;

ii)   Individuals prefer current to future consumption;

iii)   The opportunity exists to invest the amount received in the present at a specific rate of interest;

iv)   Inflationary trends are a common feature reducing the value of money in the future.

All this means that future benefits should include some compensation for waiting. In other words, the future benefits should be equal to the sum of the present benefits and an amount equivalent to the compensation for waiting. Suppose a person get 10% per annum as interest on a savings bank deposit. He would be indifferent between the two options of getting ₹ 100 today and receiving ₹ 110 after a year. Here the sum :

i)   ₹ 100 is the present value of the receipt.

ii)   ₹ 10 the compensation for waiting.

iii)   ₹ 110 is the future value of the receipt.

It can also be said that the future value is the sum of the present value compounded at a given rate of interest. The present value is therefore calculated by reverse compounding. It is the formula used to compute compound interest, and not the one used to compute simple interest, that is involved in computing the future value of a receipt. The reason for this is that it is not only the original amount that earns interest but also the earned interest that earns further interest.

SEBi Guidelines for Portfolio Managers

The SEBI has given permission to Merchant Bankers of Category I and II to do Portfolio Management. As per the guidelines of September, 1991 a separate category of Portfolio Managers is also licensed by SEBI for which guidelines were given in January 1993.

Annexure I and II provide SEBI Rules and Regulations governing portfolio managers and the code of conduct to be observed by them.

***

ANNEXURE – I

SECURITIES AND EXCHANGE BOARD OF INDIA (PORTFOLIO MANAGERS) RULES, 1993[1]

G.S.R.4(E) – In exercise of the powers conferred by Section 29 of the Securities and Exchange Board of India Act, 1992 (15 of 1992), the Central Government hereby makes the following rules, namely :

1. **Short title and commencement**

   (1) These rules may be called the Securities and Exchange Board of India (Portfolio Managers) Rules, 1993.

   (2) They shall come into force on the date of their publication in the Official Gazette.

2. **Definitions**

   In these rules, unless the context otherwise requires :

   (a) "Act" means the Securities and Exchange Board of India Act, 1992 (15 of 1992);

   (b) "Body corporate" shall have the meaning assigned to it in or under clause (7) of Section 2 of the Companies Act, 1956 (1 of 1956);

   (c) "Certificate" means a certificate of registration issued by the Board;

   (d) "Portfolio" means the total holdings of securities belonging to any person;

---

[1] Published in the Gazette of India Extraordinary, Part-II, Section 3, sub-section (i), dated 7.1.1993.

(e)   "Portfolio manager" means any person who pursuant to a contract or arrangement with a client, advises or directs or undertakes on behalf of the client (whether as a discretionary portfolio manager or otherwise) the management or administration of a portfolio of securities or the funds of the client, as the case may be;

(f)   "Discretionary portfolio manager" means a portfolio manager who exercises or may, under a contract relating to portfolio management exercises any degree of discretion as to the investments or management of the portfolio of securities or the funds of the client, as the case may be;

(g)   "Regulations" means the Securities and Exchange Board of India (Portfolio Managers) Regulations, 1993.

3.   No person to act as portfolio manager without certificate

No person shall carry on any activity as a portfolio manager unless he holds a certificate granted by the Board under the regulations.

Provided that such person, who was engaged as portfolio manager prior to the coming into force of that Act, may continue to carry on activity as portfolio manager, if he has made an application for such registration, till the disposal of such application;

Provided further that nothing contained in this rule shall apply in case of a merchant banker holding a certificate granted by the Board under the Securities and Exchange Board of India (Merchant Banker) Regulations, 1992 as Category I or Category II merchant banker, as the case may be.

4.   Conditions for grant or renewal of certificate to portfolio manager

The Board may grant or renew a certificate to a portfolio manager subject to the following conditions, namely :

(a)   the portfolio manager in case of any change in the status and constitution, shall obtain the prior permission of the Board to carry on its activities.

(b)   he shall pay the amount of fees for registration or renewal, as the case may be, in the manner provided in the regulations;

(c)   he shall take adequate steps for redressal of grievances of the clients within one month of the date of the receipt of the complaint and keep the Board informed about the number, nature and other particulars of the complaints received;

(d)   he shall abide by the rules and regulations made under the Act in respect of the activities carried on by the portfolio manager.

5.   Period of validity of the certificate

The certificate of registration or its renewal, as the case may be, shall be valid for a period of three years from the date of its issue to the portfolio manager.

ANNEXURE II

SECURITIES AND EXCHANGE BOARD OF INDIA (PORTFOLIO MANAGERS) REGULATIONS, 1993[2]

SEBI/LE/92/III-In exercise of the powers conferred by Section 30 of the Securities and Exchange Board of India Act, 1992(15 of 1992), the Board with the previous approval of the Central Government, hereby makes the following regulations, namely :

CHAPTER 1
PRELIMINARY

1. **Short title and commencement**

   (1) These regulations may be called the Securities and Exchange Board of India (Portfolio Managers) Regulations, 1993.

   (2) They shall come into force on the date of their publication in the Official Gazette.

2. **Definitions**

   In these regulations, unless the context otherwise requires :

   (a) "enquiry officer" means any officer of the Board, or any other person, having experience in dealing with the problems relating to the securities market, who is authorised by the Board under Chapter V;

   (b) "form" means a form specified in Schedule I;

   (c) "inspecting authority" means one or more persons appointed by the Board to exercise powers conferred under Chapter IV;

   (d) "principal officer" means

   (i)   proprietor, in case of a proprietory concern;

   (ii) partner, in the case of a partnership firm;

   (iii) director, in the case of a body corporate;

Who is mainly responsible for the activities of the portfolio manager and has been designated as principal officer by the portfolio manager;

   (e) "rules" means Securities and Exchange Board of India (Portfolio Managers) Rules, 1993;

   (f) words and expressions used and not defined in these regulations but defined in the Act and the rules shall have the meanings respectively assigned to them in the Act or the rules as the case may be.

---

2   Published in the Gazette of India, Extraordinary Part-III, Section 4, dated 7th January, 1993.

CHAPTER II

REGISTRATION OF PORTFOLIO MANAGERS

3. Application for grant of certificate

(1) An application by a portfolio manager for grant of a certificate shall be made to the Board in Form A.

(2) Notwithstanding anything contained in sub-regulation (1), any application made by a portfolio manager prior to coming into force of these regulations containing such particulars or as near thereto as mentioned in Form A shall be treated as an application made in pursuance of subregulation (i) and dealt with accordingly.

4. Application to conform to the requirements

Subject to the provisions of sub-regulation (2) of regulation 3, any application, which is not complete in all respects and does not conform to the instructions specified in the form, shall be rejected:

Provided that, before rejecting any such application, the applicant shall be given an opportunity to remove within the time specified such objections as may be indicated by the Board.

5. Furnishing of further information, clarification and personal representation

(1) The Board may require the applicant to furnish further information or clarification regarding matters relevant to his activity of a portfolio manager for the purposes of disposal of the application.

(2) The applicant or its principal officer shall, if so required, appear before the Board for personal representation.

6. Consideration of application

The Board shall take into account for considering the grant of a certificate, all manners which are relevant to the activities relating to portfolio manager and in particular whether the applicant complies with the following requirements namely :

(a) the applicant has the necessary infrastructure like adequate office space, equipments, and manpower to effectively discharge his activities;

(b) the applicant has in his employment minimum of two persons who have the experience to conduct the business of portfolio manager;

(c) a person directly or indirectly connected with the applicant has not been granted registration by the Board in case of the applicant being a body corporate;

Explanation : For the purposes of this clause the expression "directly or indirectly connected" means any person being an associate, subsidiary, interconnected or group company of the applicant being a body corporate;

(d) the applicant fulfils the capital adequacy requirements specified in   regulation 7;

(e) the applicant, his partner, director or principal is not involved in any litigation connected with the securities market and which has an adverse bearing on the business of the applicant;

(f)   the applicant, his director, partner or principal officer has not at any time been convicted for any offence involving moral turpitude or has been found guilty of any economic offence;

(g)   the applicant has the professional qualification from an institution recognised by the Government in finance, law, accountancy or business management

(h)   grant of certificate to the applicant is in the interest of investors.

7.   Capital Adequacy Requirement

(1)   The capital adequacy requirements referred to in sub-regulation (d) of regulation 6 shall not be less than net worth of Rupees fifty lacs of the person making the application;

Explanation : For the purpose of this regulation, "net worth" means in the case of an applicant which is a partnership firm or a body corporate, the value of the capital contributed to the business of such firm or the paid up capital of such body corporate and plus free reserves as the case may be at the time of making application under sub-regulation (1) of regulation 3.

8.   Procedure for Registration

The Board on being satisfied that the applicant fulfils the requirements specified in regulation 6 shall send an intimation to the applicant and on receipt of the payment of fees as specified in Schedule II then grant a certificate in Form B.

9.   Renewal of certificate

(1)   A portfolio manager may, three months before the expiry of the validity of the certificate, make an application for renewal in Form A.

(2)   The application for renewal, under sub-regulation (1) shall be dealt with in the same manner as if it were an application for grant of a certificate made under regulation 3.

(3)   The Board on being satisfied that the applicant fulfils the requirements specified in regulation 6 for renewal of certificate shall grant a certificate in Form B and send an intimation to the applicant.

10. Procedure where registration is not granted

(1)   Where an application for grant of a certificate under regulation 3 or of renewal under regulation 9 does not satisfy the requirements set out in regulation 6, the Board may reject the application, after giving an opportunity of being heard.

(2)   The refusal to grant registration shall be communicated by the Board within thirty days of such refusal to the applicant stating therein the grounds on which the application has been rejected.

(3)   Any applicant may, being aggrieved by the decision of the Board under sub-regulation (1) apply within a period of thirty days from the date of receipt of such intimation, to the Board for reconsideration of its decision.

(4)   The Board shall reconsider an application made under subregulation (3) and communicate its decision as soon as possible in writing to the applicant

11. Effect of refusal to grant certificate

Any portfolio manager whose application for a certificate has been refused by the Board shall on and from the date of the receipt of the communication under sub-regulation (2) of regulation 10 cease to carry on any activity as portfolio manager.

12. Payment of fees and the consequences of failure to pay fees

(1)   Every applicant eligible for grant of a certificate shall pay fees in such manner and within the period specified in Schedule II.

(2)   Where a portfolio manager fails to pay the fees as provided in Schedule II, the Board may suspend the certificate, whereupon the portfolio manager shall forthwith cease to carry on the activity as a portfolio manager for the period during which the suspension subsists.

CHAPTER III
GENERAL OBLIGATIONS AND RESPONSIBILITIES

13. Code of Conduct

Every portfolio manager shall abide by the code of conduct as specified in Schedule III.

14. Contract with Clients

(1)   (a)   Every portfolio manager shall before taking up an assignment of management of portfolio on behalf of a client, enter into an agreement with such client clearly defining the *inter se relationship*, and setting out their mutual rights, liabilities and obligations relating to management of the portfolio of the client

(b)   The contract shall, *inter alia*, contain

(i)   the investment objectives and the services to be provided;

(ii)   areas of investment and restrictions, if any, imposed by the client with regard to investment in a particular company or industry;

(iii)   attendant risks involved in the management of the portfolio;

(iv)   period of the contract and provision of early termination, if any,

(v)   amount to be invested;

(vi)   procedure   of   setting   client's   account   including   form   of repayment on maturity or early termination of contract;

(vii)   fees payable to the portfolio manager;

(viii)   custody of securities.

(2)   The funds of all clients shall be placed by the portfolio manager in a separate account to be maintained by him in a scheduled commercial bank.

Explanation : For the purposes of this sub-regulation "scheduled bank" means any bank included in the Second Schedule to the Reserve Bank of India Act, 1934 (2 of 1934).

(3)   The portfolio manager shall charge an agreed fee from the client for rendering portfolio management services without guaranteeing or assuring; either directly or indirectly any return and such fee shall be independent of the return to the client and shall not be on a return sharing basis.

15. General responsibilities of a Portfolio Manager

(1) The discretionary portfolio manager shall individually and independently manage the funds of each client in accordance with the needs of the client in a manner which does not partake character of a mutual fund, whereas the non-discretionary portfolio manager shall manage the funds in accordance with the directions of the client

(2) The portfolio manager shall act in a fiduciary capacity with regard to the client's funds.

(3) The portfolio manager shall transact in securities within the limitation placed by the client himself with regard to dealing in securities under the provisions of the Reserve Bank of India Act 1934 (2 of 1934);

(4) The portfolio manager shall not derive any direct or indirect benefit out of the client's funds or securities.

(5) The portfolio manager shall not pledge or give on loan securities held on behalf of clients to a third person without obtaining a written permission from his client.

(6) The portfoilo manager shall ensure proper and timely handling of complaints from his clients and take appropriate action immediately.

16. Investment of Client's Money

(1) (a) The portfolio manger shall not accept money or securities from his client for a period of less than one year :
Provided that in the case of placement of funds for portfolio management by the same client on more than one occasion or on a continual basis each placement shall be for a minimum period of one year.

(b) Any renewal of portfolio fund on maturity of the initial period shall be deemed as a fresh placement and shall be for a minimum period of one year.

(2) Notwithstanding anything contained in the agreement between a portfolio manager and his client referred to in regulation 14 hereof, the portfolio funds can be withdrawn or taken back by portfolio client at his risk before the maturity date of the contract under the following circumstances, namely :

(a) voluntary or compulsory termination of portfolio management services by the portfolio manager;

(b) suspension on termination of registration of portfolio manager by the Board;

(c) bankruptcy or liquidation in case the portfolio manager is a body corporate;

(d) permanent disability, lunacy or insolvency in case the portfolio manager is an individual.

(3) The portfolio manager shall invest funds of his clients in money market instruments or as specified in the contract.
Provided that the portfolio manager shall not deploy the clients funds in bill discounting, badla financing or for the purpose of lending or placement with corporate or non-corporate bodies.

Explanation : For the purposes of this sub-regulation:

"money market instruments" includes commercial paper, trade bill, treasury bills, certificate of deposit and usance bills.

(4)   The portfolio manager shall not while dealing with clients funds indulge in speculative transactions, that is, he shall not enter into any transaction for purchase or sale of any security in which transaction is periodically or ultimately settled otherwise than by actual delivery or transfer of security. The portfolio manager may enter into transactions on behalf of client for the specific purpose of meeting margin requirements only if the contract so provides and the client is made aware of the amendment risks of such transactions.

(5)   The portfolio manager shall, ordinarily purchase or sell securities separately for each client. However, in the event of aggregation of purchases or sales for economy of scale, *inter se* allocation shall be done on a pro rata basis and at weighted average price of the day's transactions. The portfolio manager shall not keep any open position in respect of allocation of sales or purchases effected in a day.

(6)   Any transaction of purchase or sale including that between the portfolio manager's own accounts and client's accounts or between two clients' accounts shall be at the prevailing market price.

(7)   The portfolio manager shall segregate each clients' funds and portfolio securities and keep them separately from his own funds and securities and be responsible for safe-keeping of clients' funds and securities.

(8)   The portfolio manager may hold the securities belonging to the portfolio account in his own name on behalf of his clients only if the contract so provides and in such an event the records of the portfolio manager and his report to the client should clearly indicate that the securities are held by him on behalf of the portfolio account.

17. Maintenance of books of accounts, records etc.

(1)   Every portfolio manager shall keep and maintain the following books of accounts, records and documents namely:

(a)   a copy of balance sheet at the end of each accounting period;

(b)   a copy of the profit and loss account for each accounting period;

(c)   a copy of the auditors' report on the accounts for each accounting period;

(d)   a statement of financial position; and

(e)   records in support of every investment transaction or recommendation which will indicate the data, facts and opinions leading to that investment decision.

(2)   Every portfolio manager shall intimate to the Board the place where the books of accounts, records and documents are maintained.

(3)   Without prejudice to sub-regulation (1) every portfolio manager shall, after the end of each accounting period, furnish to the Board carries of the balance sheet, profit and loss account and such other documents as are mentioned in any of the

regulations under this chapter for any other preceding five accounting years when required by the Board.

18. Submission of half-yearly results

Every portfolio manager shall furnish to the Board half-yearly unaudited financial results when required by the Board with a view to monitor the capital adequacy of the portfolio manager.

19. Maintenance of books of accounts, records and other documents

The portfolio manager shall preserve the books of account and other records and documents mentioned in any of the regulations mentioned under this chapter for a minimum period of five years.

20. Accounts and audit

(1) (a) The portfolio manager shall maintain separate client-wise accounts.

   (b) The funds received from the clients, investments or disinvestments and all the credits to the account of the client like interest, dividend, bonus, or any other beneficial interest received on the investment and debits, for expenses, if any, shall be properly accounted for and details thereof shall be properly reflected in the client's account

   (c) The tax deducted atsource as required under the provisions of the Income-tax Act, 1961 (43 of 1961) shall be recorded in the portfolio account

(2) The books of account will be audited yearly by qualified auditor to ensure that the portfolio manager has followed proper accounting methods and procedures and that the portfolio manager has performed his duties in accordance with the law. A certificate to this effect shall, if so specified, be submitted to the Board within six months of close of portfolio manager's accounting period.

21. Reports to be furnished to the client

(1) The portfolio manager shall furnish periodically a report to the client, agreed in the contract, but not exceeding a period of six months and such report shall contain the following details, namely :

   (a) the composition and the value of the portfolio, description of security, number of securities, value of each security held in the portfolio, cash balance and aggregate value of the portfolio as on the date of report.

   (b) transactions undertaken during the period of report including date of transaction and details of purchases and sales.

   (c) beneficial interest received during that period in respect of interest, dividend, bonus shares, rights shares and debentures.

   (d) expenses incurred in managing the portfolio of the client.

   (e) details of risk foreseen by the portfolio manager and the risk relating to the securities recommended by the portfolio manager for investment or disinvestment.

(2) The portfolio manager shall also furnish to the client documents and information relating only to the management of a portfolio.

(3) On termination of the contract, the portfolio manager shall give a detailed statement of accounts to the client and settle the account with the client as agreed in the contract.

(4) In the event of any dispute between the portfolio manager and his clients, the client shall have the right to obtain details of his portfolio from portfolio manager.

22. Report on steps taken on Auditor's Report

Every portfolio manager shall within two months from the date of the auditors report take steps to rectify the deficiencies made out in the auditors report.

23. Disclosures to the Board

A portfolio manager shall disclose to the Board as and when required the following information, namely:

(i) particulars regarding the management of a portfolio;

(ii) any change in the information or particulars previously furnished, which have a bearing on the certificate granted to him;

(iii) the names of the clients whose portfolio he has managed;

(iv) particulars relating to the capital adequacy requirement as specified in regulation 7.

CHAPTER IV

INSPECTION AND DISCIPLINARY PROCEEDINGS

24. Right of inspection by the Board

(1) The Board may appoint one or more persons as inspecting authority to undertake the inspecting of the books of account, records and documents of the portfolio manager for any of the purposes specified in sub-regulation.

(2) The purposes referred to in sub-regulation (1) may be as follows, namely :

(a) to ensure that the books of account are being maintained in the manner required;

(b) that the provisions of the Act, rules and regulations are being complied with;

(c) to investigate into the complaints received from investors, other portfolio managers or any other person on any matter having a bearing on the activities of the portfolio manager; and

(d) to investigate *suo moto* in the interest of securities business or investors' interest into the affairs of the portfolio manager.

25. Notice before Inspection

(1) Before undertaking an inspection under regulation 24 the Board shall give a reasonable notice to the portfolio manager for that purpose.

(2) Notwithstanding anything contained in sub-regulation (1) where the Board is satisfied that in the interest of the investors no such notice would be given, it may be an order in writing direct that the inspection of the affairs of the portfolio manager be taken up without such notice.

(3)   During the course of inspection the portfolio manager against whom an inspection is being carried out shall be bound to discharge his obligations as provided under regulation 26.

26. Obligations of portfolio manager on inspection

(1)   It shall be the duty of every director, proprietor, partner, officer and employee of the portfolio manager who is being inspected to produce to the inspecting authority such books, accounts and other documents in his custody or control and furnish him with the statements and information relating to his activities as a portfolio manager within such time as the inspecting authority may require.

(2)   The portfolio manager shall allow the inspecting authority to have a reasonable access to the premises occupied by such portfolio manager or by any other person, on his behalf and also extend reasonable facility for examining any books, records, documents and computer data in the possession of the documents or other material which in the opinion of the inspecting authority are relevant for the purposes of the inspection.

(3)   The inspecting authority shall in the course of inspection, be entitled to examine or record statements of any principal officer, director, partner, proprietor and employee of the portfolio manager.

(4)   It shall be the duty of every director, proprietor, partner, officer or employee of the portfolio manager to give to the inspecting authority all assistance in connection with the inspection which the portfolio manager may reasonably be expected to give.

27. Submission of report to the Board

The inspecting authority shall, as soon as may be possible, submit an inspection report to the Board.

28. Communication of findings etc., to the Portfolio Manager

(1)   The Board shall after consideration of the inspection report communicate the findings to the portfolio manager to give him an opportunity of being heard before any action taken by the Board on the findings of the inspecting authority.

(2)   On receipt of the explanation, if any, from the portfolio manager the Board may call upon the portfolio manager to take such measures as the Board may deem fit in the interest of the securities market and for due compliance with the provision of the Act, rules and regulations.

29. Appointment of auditor

The Board may appoint a qualified auditor to investigate into the books of account or the affairs of the portfolio manager :

Provided that the auditor so appointed shall have the same powers of the inspecting authority as are mentioned in regulation 24 and the obligation of the portfolio manager and his employees in regulation 26 shall be applicable to the investigation under this regulation.

Explanation : For the purposes of sub-regulation (2) of regulation 20 and under this regulation, the expression "qualified auditor" shall have the same meaning as given to it in Section 226 of the Companies Act, 1956 (1 tons of 1956).

CHAPTER V
PROCEDURE FOR ACTION CASE OF DEFAULT

30. Liability for action in case of default

(1)   A portfolio manager who –

     (a)   fails to comply with any conditions subject to which certificate has been granted;

     (b)   contravenes any of the provisions of the Act, rules or regulations; shall be liable to any of the penalties specified in sub-regulation (2).

(2)   The penalties referred to in sub-regulation (1) may be either :

     (a)   suspension of registration; or

     (b)   cancellation of registration.

31. Suspension of registration

(1)   A penalty of suspension of registration of a portfolio manager may be imposed where –

     (a)   the portfolio manager violates the provisions of the Act, rules or regulations;

   (i)   the Portfolio manager –

     (a)   fails to furnish any information relating to his activity as portfolio manager as required by the Board;

     (b)   furnishes wrong or false information;

     (c)   does not submit periodical returns as required by the Board;

     (d)   does not co-operate in any enquiry conducted by the Board;

   (ii)   the portfolio manager fails to resolve the complaints of the investors or fails to give a satisfactory reply to the Board in this behalf;

   (iii)   the portfolio manager indulges in manipulating or price rigging or cornering activities;

   (iv)   the portfolio manager is guilty of misconduct or improper or unbusiness like or unprofessional conduct which is not in accordance with the Code of Conduct specified in Schedule III;

   (v)   the portfolio manager fails to maintain the capital adequacy requirement in accordance with the provisions of regulation 7;

   (vi)   the portfolio manager fails to pay the fees;

   (vii)   the portfolio manager violates the conditions of registration;

   (viii)   the portfolio manager does not carry out his obligations as specified in the regulation.

32. Cancellation of registration

A penalty of cancellation of registration of a portfolio manager may be imposed where –

   (i)   the portfolio manager indulges in deliberate manipulation or price rigging or cornering activities affecting the securities market and the investors interest;

(ii)   the financial position of the portfolio manager deteriorates to such an extent that the Board is of the opinion that his continuance as portfolio manager is not in the interest of investors;

(iii)   the portfolio manager is guilty of fraud, or is convicted of a criminal offence;

(iv)   the portiolio manager is guilty of repeated defaults of the nature mentioned in regulation 31 provided that the Board furnishes the reasons for cancellation in writing.

33. Manner of making order of suspension and cancellation

No order of penalty of suspension or cancellation, as the case may be, shall be imposed except after holding an enquiry in accordance with the procedure specified in regulation 34.

34. Manner of holding enquiry before suspension or cancellation

(1)   For the purpose of holding an enquiry under regulation 33, the Board may appoint an enquiry officer.

(2)   The enquiry officer shall issue to the portfolio manager a notice at the registered office or the principal place of business of the portfolio manager.

(3)   The portfolio manager may, within thirty days from the date of receipt of such notice, furnish to the enquiry officer a reply together with copies of documentary or other evidence relied on by him or sought by the Board from the portfolio manager.

(4)   The enquiry officer shall, give a reasonable opportunity of hearing to the portfolio manager to enable him to make submissions in support of his reply made under sub-regulation (3).

(5)   Before the enquiry officer, the portfolio manager may either appear in person or through any person duly authorised by the portfolio manager:

Provided that no lawyer or advocate shall be permitted to represent the portfolio manager at the enquiry:

Provided further that where a lawyer or an advocate has been appointed by the Board as a presenting officer under sub-regulation (6), it shall be lawful for the portfolio manager to present its case through a lawyer or advocate.

(6)   If it is considered necessary, the enquiry officer may ask the Board to appoint a presenting officer to present its case.

(7)   The enquiry officer shall, after taking into account all relevant facts and submissions made by the portfolio manager, submit a report to the Board and recommend the penalty to be imposed as also the grounds on the basis of which the proposed penalty is justified.

35. Show cause notice and order

(1)   On receipt of the report from the enquiry officer, the Board shall consider the same and issue a show cause notice as to why the penalty as proposed by the enquiry officer should not be imposed.

(2) The portfolio manager shall within twenty-one days of the date of the receipt of the show-cause notice send a reply to the Board.

(3) The Board after considering the reply to the show cause notice, if received, shall as soon as possible but not later than thirty days from the receipt of the reply, if any, pass such order as it deems fit

(4) Every order passed under sub-regulation (3) shall be self-contained and give reasons for the conclusions stated therein including justification of the penalty imposed by that order.

(5) The Board shall send a copy of the order under sub-regulation (3) to the portfolio manager.

36. Effect of suspension and cancellation of registration of portfolio manager

(1) On and from the date of the suspension of the portfolio manager he shall cease to carry on any activity as a portfolio manager during the period of suspension.

(2) On and from the date of cancellation, the portfolio manager shall with immediate effect cease to carry on any activity as a portfolio manager.

37. Publication of order of suspension

The order of suspension or cancellation of certificate passed under subregulation (3) of regulation 35, shall be published in atleast two daily newspapers by the Board.

38. Appeal to the Central Government

Any person aggrieved by an order of the Board may prefer an appeal to the Central Government.

SCHEDULE II
SECURITIES AND EXCHANGE BOARD OF INDIA (PORTFOLIO MANAGERS) REGULATIONS, 1993
(Regulation 12)
Fees

1. Every portfolio manager shall subject to paragraphs 3 and 4 of this Schedule, pay a sum of ₹ 2.50 lakhs every year for the first two years and thereafter a sum of ₹ 1 lakh for the third year.

2. Every portfolio manager shall, to keep his registration in force, pay renewal fee of ₹ 75,000 per annum from the fourth year from the date of initial registration.

3. Fee specified in paragraphs (1) and (2) above shall be paid in the following manner –

    (a) First instalment is to be paid within 15 days from the date of intimation from the Board under regulation 8.

    (b) Subsequent instalments including the renewal fee to be paid on or before expiry of 12 months of each year of registration beginning from the date of grant of such registration.

4. The fees specified in paragraphs (1) and (2) above, shall be payable by a cheque or draft in favour of "The Securities and Exchange Board of India" at Bombay.

SCHEDULE III
SECURITIES AND EXCHANGE BOARD OF INDIA (PORTFOLIO MANAGERS) REGULATIONS, 1993
(Regulation 13)

Code of Conduct Portfolio Manager

1. A portfolio manager shall, in the conduct of his business, observe high standards of integrity and fairness in all his dealings with his clients and other portfolio managers.

2. The money received by a portfolio manager from a client for an investment purpose should be deployed by the portfolio manager as soon as possible for that purpose and money due and payable to a client should be paid forthwith.

3. A portfolio manager shall render at all times high standards of service, exercise due diligence, ensure proper care and exercise independent professional judgement. The portfolio manager shall either avoid any conflict of interest in his investment or disinvestment decision, or where any conflict of interest arises, ensure fair treatment to all his customers. He shall disclose to the clients, possible sources of conflict of duties and interests, while providing unbiased services. A portfolio manager shall not place his interest above those of his client.

4. A portfolio manager shall not make any statement or become privy to any act, practice or unfair competition, which is likely to be harmful to the interests of other portfolio managers or is likely to place such other portfolio managers in a disadvantageous position in relation to the portfolio manager himself, while competing for or executing any assignment.

5. A portfolio manager shall not make any exaggerated statement, whether oral or written, to the client either about the qualification or the capability to render certain services or his achievements in regard to services rendered to other clients.

6. At the time of entering into a contract, the portfolio manager shall obtain in writing from the client, his interest in various corporate bodies which enables him to obtain unpublished price-sensitive information of the body corporate.

7. A portfolio manager shall not disclose to any clients, or press any confidential information about his client, which has come to his knowledge.

8. The portfolio manager shall where necessary and in the interest of the client take adequate steps for registration of the transfer of the clients securities and for claiming and receiving dividends, interest payments and other rights accruing to the client. He shall also take necessary action for conversion of securities, and subscription/renunciation of/or rights in accordance with the clients instruction.

9. A portfolio manager shall endeavour to –

   (a) ensure that the investors are provided with true and adequate information without making any misguiding or exaggerated claims and are made aware of attendant risks before any investment decision is taken by them;

(b)   render the best possible advice to the client having regard to the client's needs and the environment, and his own professional skills;

(c)   ensure that all professional dealings are effected in a prompt, efficient and cost effective manner.

10. (1)   A portfolio manager shall not be a party to –

    (a)   creation of false market in securities;

    (b)   price rigging or manipulation of securities;

    (c)   passing of price sensitive information to brokers, members of the stock exchanges and any other intermediaries in the capital market or take any other action which is prejudicial to the interest of the investors.

(2)   No portfolio manager or any of its directors, partners or managers shall either on their respective accounts or through their associates or family members, relatives, enter into any transaction in securities of companies on the basis of unpublished price sensitive information obtained by them during the course of any professional assignment.

3.3.2 PORTFOLIO MANAGEMENT SERVICES

It refers to professional services rendered for management of portfolio of others namely clients or customers with the help of experts in investment advisory services. The latter involves the advice regarding the worthwhileness of any particular investment or advice of what to buy and sell. The former on the other hand involves continuing relationship with client to manage investments with or without discretion for the client as per his requirements.

Method of Operation

The professional portfolio manager can be approached by any individual or organisation with a minimum amount of investible funds of ₹ 1 lakh or two lakhs. If the manager is willing to accept him as his client, a contract is entered into for management of his funds either on discretionary basis or non-discretionary basis, specifying the objectives, risk to be tolerated, composition of assets/securities in the portfolio and their relative proportion, fees payable and time period of management, as per the preference of the client.

SEBI Norms

SEBI has prohibited the portfolio manager to assume any risk on behalf of the client. Portfolio manager cannot also assure any fixed return to the client. The investments made or advised by him are subject to risk which the client has to bear. The investment consultancy and management has to be charged at rates which are fixed and transparent as per the contract. No sharing of profits or discounts or cash incentives to client are permitted.

The portfolio manager is prohibited to do lending, badla financing and bills discounting as per SEBI norms. He cannot put the clients funds in any investment, not permitted by the contract, entered into with the client. Normally, investment can be made in both capital market and money market instruments.

Clients' money has to be kept in a separate account with a public sector bank and cannot be mixed up with his own funds or investments. All the deals done for a client's account are entered in his name and contract notes, bills etc., are all passed in his name. A separate ledger account is maintained for all purchases/sales on client's behalf, which should be done at the market price. Final settlement and termination of contract is as per the contract and for the time period agreed upon. Notice of termination of contract is also as per the contract. During the period of contract, portfolio manager is only acting on a contractual basis and on a fiduciary basis. No contract for less than a year is permitted by the SEBI.

Only those who arc registered and pay the required licence fee are eligible to operate as Portfolio Managers. An applicant for this purpose should have necessary infrastructure with professionally qualified persons and with a minimum of two persons with experience in this business and a minimum net worth of ₹ 50 lakhs. The Certificate once granted is valid for three years. Fees payable for registration are ₹ 2.5 lakhs every year for two years and ₹ 1 lakh for the third year. From the fourth year onwards, renewal fees per annum are ₹ 75,000.

Professional Portfolio Management, backed by competent research staff became the order of the day. After the success of Mutual Funds in Portfolio Management, a number of brokers and Investment Consultants some of whom are also professionally qualified have become Portfolio Managers. They have managed the funds of client on both discretionary and non-discretionary basis. It was found that many of them, including Mutual Funds have guaranteed a minimum return or capital appreciation and adopted all kinds of incentives which arc now prohibited by SEBI.

They resorted to speculative overtrading and insider trading, discounts, etc., to achieve their targetted returns to the clients, which are also prohibited by SEBI.

The return on equity investments in the capital market particularly if proper investment strategy is adopted would satisfy the investor's objectives and the real returns would be higher than any other saving instruments. It is in this context, the art and science of investment and of Portfolio Management become the *sine-qua-non* of success.

3.4 CREDIT RATING

3.4.1 MEANING

A Credit Rating is like a measuring device that measures the safety of an avenue of investment. Which includes financial products such as corporate bonds, debentures, short-term debt instruments like commercial papers, fixed deposits, and the like are given credit ratings by certain companies like CRISIL, ICRA, CARE and Fitch. The primary aim of credit ratings is to review the capacity of the issuer to repay his debt in a timely fashion.

'Credit Rating' defined by well known rating agencies are as follows :

According to **CRISIL,**

"Credit rating is an unbiased and independent opinion as to issuer's capacity to meet its financial obligations. It does not constitute a recommendation to buy/sell or hold a particular security."

According to **ICRA**,

"Ratings art opinions on the relative capability of timely servicing of corporate debt and obligations. These are not recommendations to buy or sell....neither the accuracy nor the completeness of the information is guaranteed."

Moodys :

"Ratings are designed exclusively for the purpose of grading bonds according to their investment qualities".

Australian Ratings

A Corporate Credit rating provides lenders with a simple system of gradation by which the relative capacities of companies to make timely repayment of interest and principal on a particular type of debt can be noted.

The Credit Rating concept originated in the USA. In 1860, Henry Vannum, started publishing financial statistics of railroad companies. In 1909. Moody's Investors Agencies started rating Railroad giving more thrust to the concept. Since then the importance has grown extensively in the global market. System of ratings got institutionalised following the Great Depression. In 1933, the US controller of currency enacted a rule that banks could purchase securities rated only BBB/Baa or above. In 1970, Penn Central, the then largest Railroad company in the world went bankrupt with just under $ 100 million in outstanding commercial paper. This forced the investors to ask for rating for commercial paper. Consequently, today, almost 100% of the commercial paper volume and 99% of the corporate bond volume are rated in the U.S.A.

Features of Credit Rating

Following are the important features of Credit Rating.

i) The ratings are expressed in code number which can be easily comprehended even by the lay investors. The ratings are the quickest way of understanding a company's financial standing without going into the complicated financial reports. Credit rating is only a guidance to the investors and not a recommendation to a particular debt instrument.

ii) Credit rating is an assessment of the capacity of an issuer of debt security, by an independent agency, to pay interest and repay the principal as per the terms of issue of debt. A rating agency collects the qualitative as well as quantitative data from a company which has to be rated and assesses the relative strength and capacity of company to honour its obligations contained in the debt instrument throughout the duration of the instrument.

iii) A credit rating does not create a fiduciary relationship between the rating agency and the users of rating since there is no legal basis for such relationships.

iv) Credit rating, as it exists in India, is done for a it specific debt security and not for a company as a whole. No rating agency tells that it is an indicator of the financial status of the company. All that a rating agency claims is that the rating symbols indicate the capacity of the company to honour the terms of contract of a debt instrument.

3.4.2 Need

The Indian capital market has been growing considerably for the past several years. The market has been very competitive and offering a wide variety of choices for investors. Most of the companies are relaying increasingly on the capital market for expansion, diversification and modernisation. Since 1991, the country has been embarking on liberalisation and globalisation by initiating certain economic reforms which include deregulation, privatisation, foreign investment participation, public sector undertakings (PSUs) disinvestment, abolition of FERA, changes in economy, fiscal, monetary and trade policies, industrial policy reforms, financial sector reforms, abolition of office of the controller of capital issues, etc.

Many companies are raising money in the capital market and each company intends to raise capital through different types of securities and debt instruments. Hence, it is difficult for the investor to judge which investment is safer and more reliable. Some investors feel that some companies have not paid dividends for the past several years and some others complain that certain scrips have not been traded on the floors of stock exchanges and their investment is dead and blocked.

In this regard, SEBI's consultative paper in 1984-85 reveals that out of 3401 equity scrips listed on all the stock exchanges only 217 scrips (6%) were actively traded every day. In the rest, about 390 scrips (12%) traded once in a fortnight, 954 (28%) traded once a month, 959 (28%) were not traded for more than a year. In the same way as per the analysis of capital mark journal in July 1993, out of the sample 2275 companies listed on the Bombay stock exchange during 1988-89, only 36% were traded between 50-90% of the days, of which only 20% were traded almost daily. The balance 74% were traded irregularly, of which about 51% were traded on less than 10% of the three years back. The situation is not very much different now. As a token of service in this regard to investors, SEBI is contemplating to introduce 'market makers' who will provide liquidity to shares.

Salaried people usually put their savings in fixed deposits of companies to get a slightly higher return than they would from banks. But a look at the investor's grievance columns in several news papers and magazines makes it clear that several companies do default in paying interest and even in returning capital. But till recently, investors had little information on which to base their investment decisions. Hence there is a need for credit rating system in India. Credit rating agencies have been established in more than 25 countries to serve the needs of investors and corporate borrowers.

Credit rating is a symbolic indicator of the current opinion of rating agency of the relative capability and willingness of an issuer of a debt programme to service the debt obligations as per the terms of the contract between it and the investor. It is, however, neither a general purpose evaluation of a corporate entity nor an overall assessment of the credit risk likely to be involved in all debts contracted or to be contracted by an issuer.

A rating is specific to a debt instrument and is intended to grade different and specific instrument in terms of credit risk associated with the particular instruments. A rating does not amount to any recommendation to buy, hold or sell an instrument as it does not take into consideration factors such as market prices, personal risk preferences of an investor and such other considerations which may influence an investment decision.

The ratings are so devised that they provide an investor with a simple and easily understood indicator expressing the underlying credit quality and the risks associated with an instrument of debt. It also establishes a link between risk and return, which is what the investor needs to understand while investing his money.

Functions supported by the credit rating firms are as follows. Because of these functions services of credit rating firms are essential.

i) Superior Information

Rating by an independent and professional firm offers a superior and more reliable source of information on credit risk for three inter related risks :

a)   it provides unbiased opinion.

b)   due to professional resources, a rating firm has greater ability to assess risks.

c)   it has access to lot of information which may not be publicly available.

ii) Formulation of Public Policy Guidelines on Institutional Investment

The public policy on the kinds of securities that are eligible for inclusion in different kinds of institutional portfolios can be developed with great confidence if securities are rated professionally by independent agencies.

iii) Low Cost Information

Credit rating is a source of low cost information to investors. The collection processing and analysis of relevant information is done by a specialised agency which a group of investors can trust.

iv) Basis for a Proper Risk-Return Trade Off

If debt securities are rated professionally and if such ratings enjoy widespread investor acceptance and confidence, a more rational risk - return trade off would be established in the capital market.

v) Investors Protection

Hiring of credit agency implies that the management of the company is ready to show its operations for independent scrutiny. So, the investors who are not provided with confidential information can have overall assessment based on ratings. The creditable and objective rating agency can provide increased disclosure, better accounting standard and improved investor protection.

vi) Sources of Additional Certification

Credit rating agency provides additional information to the issue of debt/financial instrument. A highly rated firm can enter the market with great confidence. Indian experience shows that use of rating, benefit a great deal by getting larger amount of money from a wider audience at a lower cost.

vii) Forewarns Risks

Credit rating acts as a guide to companies which get a lower rating. It forewarns the management of the perception of risk in the market and prompts to take steps on their operating and marketing risks and thereby changes the perception in the market.

Credit Rating is Mandatory

Public issue of corporate bonds and debentures by companies, the SERT (Securities and 'Exchange Board of India) has made it mandatory for the company to obtain a rating for the instrument. Also, in case of an issue of ₹ 100 crore and more, the SEBI requires the company to obtain two ratings from two different rating companies so as to ensure complete transparency in the ratings.

Risks taken care while Rating a Company

Ratings cover various feature like financial risks, industry risks, instrument specific risks and business risks.

i)   Financial risks comprise a detailed analysis of the fundamental strengths of the company, taking with in its purview the financials of the company, such as the Profit and Loss A/c, balance sheet, cash flow statements its accounting policies and practices. This would include the company's current risk structure and its leverage.

ii) Then the rating company would look into the specific instrument for which the rating is sought. This entails a specific analysis of its maturity, coupon rate, repayment terms; options etc.

iii) Industry risks mainly weigh up the characteristics of the industry in which the company operates. This would include the tariff structure import duties, competition factors, political factors etc.

iv) Business risks assess the peculiarities of the particular company, such as its locational advantage, marketing arrangement, technology etc.

Credit Rating Codes

Each rating company has various codes to depict the rating result. Which differ as per the nature of the instrument, for instance, there is a separate code for fixed deposits, short term instrument, long term instrument etc, even though, the interpretation of the codes is the same for all instruments over all companies.

The codes that depict the rating result are broadly classified into 8 categories which basically describe the risk structure of the instruments are as follows :

i)   Highest safety

The top most rating "AAA for Crisil" is that of 'highest safety'. This indicates a fundamentally strong position with negligible risk factors.

ii) High Safety

The second safest is that of 'high safety' "AA for CRISIL".

iii) Adequate Safety

The adequate safety code "A for Crisil" essentially means that risk factors are modest and the strength differs only marginally from 'AAA'. In the case of 'A', the risk factors are more acute in periods of economic stress.

iv) **Moderate Safety**

This code depicts Moderate safety "BBB for Crisil", and considerable variability of risk factors with protective factors being below average. Up to this code, the risk element may be absorbable for an average risk appetite.

v) **Inadequate Safety**

This code of inadequate safety "BB for Crisil" hints at a slide in the risk factor and indicates that any present or prospective changes in the business are likely to affect the repayment obligations of the instrument.

vi) **Prone to Risk**

The third last code, Prone to risk "B for Crisil", represents speculative instruments.

vi) **Substantial Risk**

The second last of the codes, substantial risk "C for Crisil", similar to the previous code, indicates that even a slight change in economic or business conditions may result in the company's inability to service the debt.

vii) **Default**

The last of the eight codes, the default "D for Crisil" indicates a very high level of speculation. An instrument with that rating may have already defaulted on its repayment before or is expected to default.

Risk Level	CARE	CRISIL	ICRA	FITCH
High Safety	CARE AAA	AAA	LAAA	AAA
Highest Safety	CARE AA	AA	LAA	AA
Adequate Safety	CARE A	A	LA	A
Moderate Safety	CARE BBB	BBB	LBBB	BBB
Inadequate Safety	CARE BB	BB	LBB	BB
Risk Prone	CARE B	B	LB	B
Substantial Risk	CARE C	C	LC	C
Default	CARE D	D	LD	D

Methodology of Rating

The main aim of rating is a search for valuing the fundamentals and the probabilities for changes in the fundamentals. The methodology includes extensive meetings, interaction and visits. A team of rating analysts meets and interacts with executive of the company at different levels including chief executives. It also meets the external professionals like Bankers, Auditors, Appraising institutions, suppliers, customers, etc. The team visits the location of manufacturers facilities, some representative offices and corporate offices of the issuing companies. Prior to all this the credit rating agency receives the basic information about the companies business as well as the audited annual accounts of the company for the last three to five years and analyse them.

Methodology of Rating is shown below in Figure 3.8 as follows.

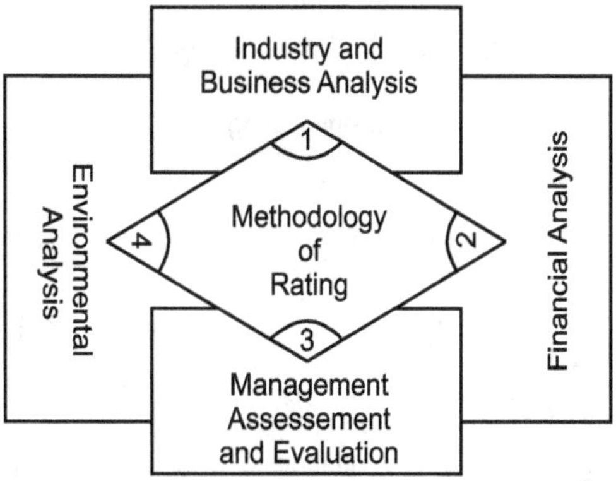

Fig. 3.8 : Methodology of Rating

The information and data collected through the above methodology will be used broadly to analyse the following aspects;

1) Industry and Business Analysis

Industry characteristics (nature, basis of competition, market share, structure, Government policies, etc.) distribution system, product and customer diversity, technological aspects, locational advantages, labour-management relationship, cost structure, business cycles, size and capacity intensity.

2) Financial Analysis

Capital structure, liquidity position, financial flexibility (Alternative financing plans in times of stress, ability to raise funds, asset redeployment potential, etc.) cash flow adequacy (to meet debt and fixed and working capital needs), profitability, leverage, interest coverage, projections, with particular emphasis on the components of cash flow and the claims thereon, accounting policies and practices, depreciation policies, inventory valuation, overstatement/understatement of profits, off balance sheet claims and liabilities, amortisation of intangible assets, foreign currency transactions, etc.

3) Management Assessment and Evaluation

Historical background, planning, control systems, managerial talent and quality, corporate strategy and philosophy, organisational structure, management capabilities under stress, personnel and HRD policies including succession planning.

4) Environmental Analysis

Regulatory environment (Structure and regulatory framework and their impact on the company, trends in regulation/deregulation and their impact on the company) operating environment, national economic outlook areas of special significance to the company, pending litigation, tax status, possibility of default risk under a variety of future scenarios.

3.4.3 CREDIT RATING AGENCIES

The **Credit Rating Agencies** in India are shown below in Figure 3.9.

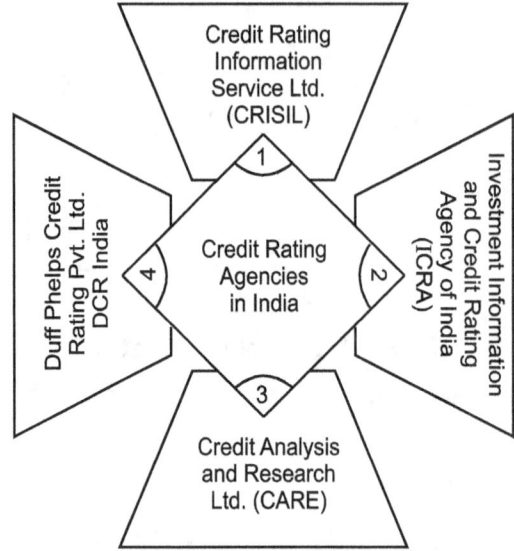

Fig. 3.9 : Credit Rating Agencies in India

Currently there are four credit rating agencies in India viz.

1)   Credit Rating Information Service Ltd. (CRISIL).
2)   Investment Information and Credit Rating Agency of India (ICRA).
3)   Credit Analysis and Research (CARE).
4)   Duff Phelps Credit Rating Pvt. Ltd. (DCR India).

1)   Credit Rating Information Services Limited

Credit Rating Information Services Limited (CRISIL) the first credit agency was floated on 1st January, 1988. It was started jointly by ICICI and UTI with an equity capital of ₹ 4 crores. Each of them holds 18% of the capital. The other promoters are Asian Development Bank (15%), the LIC and General Insurance Corporation and its subsidiaries and the SBI (5% each), the Housing Finance Development Corporation (6.2%), nine public sector and private sector banks (19.25%) and 10 foreign banks (7.55%).

The principal objective of crisil is to rate the debt obligations of Indian Companies. Its rating guides investors about the risk of timely payment of interest and principal on a particular debt instrument.

Crisil has five offices one each in Mumbai, Delhi, Kolkata, Chennai and Bengaluru. Its majority shareholder is Standard and Poor's, the world's foremost provider of independent credit ratings, indices, risk evaluation, investment research and data.

CRISIL is India's leading Ratings, Research, Risk and Policy Advisory Company.

CRISIL offers domestic and international customers a unique combination of local insights and global perspectives, delivering independent information, opinions and solutions that help them make better informed business and investment decisions, improve the efficiency of markets and market participants, and help shape infrastructure policy and projects. Its integrated range of capabilities includes credit ratings and risk assessment; research on India's economy, industries and companies; global equity research; fund services; risk management and infrastructure advisory services more.

Crisil employs a multi-layered decision-making process in assigning ratings. When it receives a request for rating, it assigns two teams on the job. The first team meets the officials and makes an assessment of the industry, company and management. The second team is also required to make its own study of the industry. Then the first team interacts with the backup team. The findings of the interactions are presented simultaneously in a detailed note to the Branch Internal Committee comprising atleast three senior analysts of CRISIL and an Internal Committee of six senior executives and thereafter the note is presented with the recommended ratings to the Rating Committee comprising six directors of the company who are not connected with any shareholders of CRISIL. The Rating Committee members are chosen carefully so that they do not have any links with industries or investment agencies connected with the units being rated. This multi-layered process ensures that no individual decides on rating and that prejudices and biases are eliminated.

The evaluation of the company is made on a confidential basis. The rating process ensures complete confidentiality of information that may be provided by the company.

Credit rating Symbols

CRISIL uses the conventional rating symbols used in the USA and widely accepted in many other countries.

The following table shows the investment-wise rating symbols assigned by CRISIL and the meaning of each rating from the angle of safety to the investors.

CRISIL Debenture Rating Symbols

High Investment Grades	
AAA (Triple A)	: Highest Safety
AA (Double A)	: High Safety
Investment Grades	
A	: Adequate Safety
BBB (Triple B)	: Moderate Safety
Speculative Grade	
BB (Double B)	: Inadequate Safety
B	: High Risk
C	: Substantial Risk
D	: Default

Notes :

i)   CRISIL may apply '+' (plus) or '−' (minus) sign for ratings from AA to C to reflect comparative standing within the category.

ii) The contents within parenthesis are a guide to the pronunciation of the rating symbols.

iii) Preference shares rating symbols are identical to debenture rating symbols except that the letters 'pf' are prefixed to the rating symbols. e.g. pf AAA ("pf Triple A").

CRISIL Fixed Deposit Rating Symbols

Investment Grades	
FAAA (F-Triple A)	: Highest Safety
FAA (F-Double A)	: High Safety
FA : Adequate Safety	
Speculative Grades	
FB	: Inadequate Safety
FC	: High Risk
FD	: Default

Note :

i)   CRISIL may apply '+' (plus) or '−' (minus) sign for ratings from FAAA to FC to indicate the relative position within the rating category.

ii) The contents within parenthesis are a guide to the pronounciation of the rating symbols.

Credit Rating for Short Term Instruments

Rating Symbol	Indication
	(Each rating indicates that the degree of safety regarding timely payment on the instrument is shown against the symbol).
P_1	Very Strong
P_2	Strong
P_3	Adequate
P_4	Minimal
P_5	Expected to be in default on maturity or in default

Note :

CRISIL may apply "+" signs for ratings from P_1 to P_3 to reflect a comparatively higher standing within the category.

Crisil monitors the ratings it assigns constantly. The ratings may be upgraded, downgraded or withdrawn depending upon new information or developments concerning the company whose debt obligation is rated. It has the right to widely disseminate the ratings through the media, through its own publications or through any other methods.

2) Investment Information and Credit Rating Agency of India Ltd. (ICRA).

ICRA has been set up in 1991 as an independent and professional credit rating agency, promoted by Industrial Finance Corporation of India jointly with other leading investment institutions, commercial banks and Financial service companies like SBI, UTI, LIC, GIC, Exim Bank, Housing Development Finance Corporation Ltd., City Bank, Infrastructure Leasing and Financial Services Ltd., 20th Century Finance Corporation Ltd., Andhra Bank, Canara Bank, etc.

Its major shareholders include Moody's Investors Service and leading Indian financial institutions & banks. ICRA is a leading provider of investment information and credit rating services in India. With the growth and globalisation of the Indian capital markets leading to an exponential surge in demand for professional credit risk analysis, ICRA has been proactive in widening its service offerings, executing assignment including credit ratings, equity gradings, specialised performance gradings and mandated studies spanning diverse industrial sectors. In addition to being a leading credit rating agency with expertise in virtually every sector of the Indian economy, and has broad-based its services for the corporate and financial sectors, both in India and overseas.

Currently, ICRA offers its services under the following manners :

i)   Rating Services
ii)   Information, Grading and Research Services
iii)   Advisory Services
iv)   Economic Research
v)   Outsourcing

IICRA Rating Scale

Long-term including Debentures Bonds and Preference Shares

LAAA	:	High Safety
LAA	:	High Safety
LA	:	Adequate Safety
LBBB	:	Moderate Safety
LBB :		Inadequate Safety
LB	:	Risk Prone
LC	:	Substantial Risk
LD	:	Default, Extremely Speculative

Medium-term including Deposits Fixed

MAAA	:	Highest Safety
MAA	:	High Safety
MA	:	Adequate Safety
MB	:	Inadequate Safety
MC	:	Risk Prone
MD	:	Default

Short-term including Commercial Paper

A-1	Highest Safety
A-2	High Safety
A-3	Adequate Safety
A-4	Risk Prone
A-5	Default

Notes :

i)   The rating symbols group together similar (but not necessarily identical) concerns of terms of their relative capability of timely servicing of debts/obligations, as per terms of contracts, i.e., the relative degree of safety/risk.

ii)   The sign (+) or (−) may be used after the rating symbol to indicate the comparative position of the company within the group covered by the symbol.

iii) The letter 'P' in parenthesis after the rating symbol indicates that the debt instrument is being used to raise resources by a new company for financing a new project and the rating assumes successful completion of the project.

iv)   The rating symbols for different instruments of the same company need not necessarily be the same.

IICRA Fixed Deposit Rating Symbols		IICRA Credit Assessment Symbols	
MAAA	Highest Safety	1.	Very Strong Capacity
MAA+		2.	
MAA	High Safety	3.	Strong Capacity
MAA−		4.	
MA+		5.	
MA	Adequate Safety	6.	Adequate Capacity
MA−		7.	
MB+		8.	
MB	Inadequate Safety	9.	Inadequate Capacity
MB−		10.	
MC+	High Risk	11.	Poor Capacity
MC		12.	
MC −		13.	
MD	Default	14.	Default

3) Credit Analysis and Research Ltd. (CARE)

CARE is a credit rating and information services company promoted by financial institutions, banks and private sector companies. While IDBI took the initiative in promoting the company, other organisations including Canara Bank, UTI, two private sector banks and ten companies in the financial services sector have joined CARE as share-holders. CARE received RBI accreditation for rating commercial paper in September 1993 and announced its first rating in November 1993. All agencies do the rating for long-term debt instruments including debentures, bonds, and preference shares, medium-term debt instruments including fixed deposits and short-term debt instruments including commercial paper. It is a credit rating, information and advisory services . CARE assigned its first rating in November 1993, and upto 31st March, 2006. CARE's ratings were recognised by the Government of India and all regulatory authorities including the Reserve Bank of India (RBI), and the Securities and Exchange Board of India (SEBI).

The rating coverage has extended beyond industrial companies, to include public utilities, financial institutions, infrastructure projects, special purpose vehicles, state governments and municipal bodies. CARE's clients include some of the largest private sector-manufacturing and financial services companies as well financial institutions of India. CARE is well equipped to rate all types of debt instruments like Commercial Paper, Fixed Deposit, Bonds, Debentures and Structured Obligations.

CARE's Information and Advisory services group prepares credit reports on specific requests from banks or business partners, conducts sector studies and provides advisory services in the areas of financial restructuring, valuation and credit appraisal systems. CARE was retained, by the Disinvestment Commission, Government of India, for assistance in equity valuation of a number of state owned companies and for suggesting divestment strategies for these companies.

'CARE' Rating Scale

Sr. No.	Investment Grade	CARE
For Long-term debt instruments		
1	Highest Safety	CARE AAA
2	High Safety	CARE AA
3	Adequate Safety	CARE A
4	Inadequate Safety	CARE BB
5	High Risk	CARE B
For Medium-term debt instruments		
1	Highest Safety	CARE AAA
2	High Safety	CARE AA
3	Adequate Safety	CARE A
4	Inadequate Safety	CARE BB
5	High Risk	CARE C
For Short-term debt instruments		
1	Highest Safety	PR1
2	High Safety	PR2
3	Adequate Safety	PR3
4	Inadequate Safety	PR4
5	High Risk	

4) Duff Phelps Credit Rating Pvt. Ltd. (DCR India)

Duff and Phelps Co. promoted by Duff and Phelps, the world's 4th largest rating agency. The larger credit rating agency engaged in traditional, fundamental credit analysis generally approach the rating with systematic procedures and organisational structures. Organisationally, this rating agency divided the rating universe into separate categories by industry (e.g. energy or banking) and type of instrument (e.g. corporate debt, government securities, structure and finance). At the core of the rating process is the rating committee. Rating committees are generally formed ad-hoc to initiate, withdraw or change a rating.

Credit rating process adopted by DCR India is shown below in Figure 3.10.

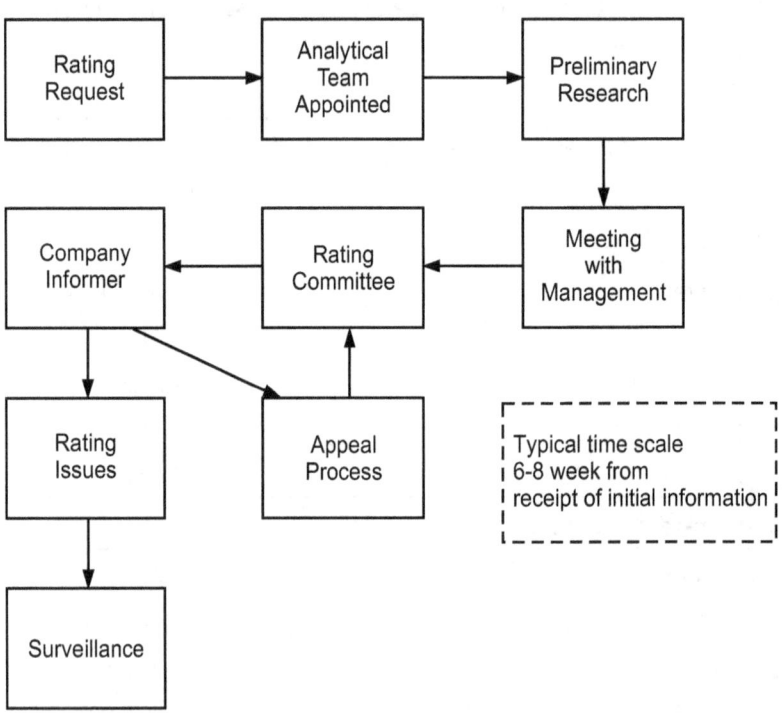

Fig. 3.10 : Credit Rating Process adopted by DCR, India

Rating Symbols of Agencies

Credit rating agencies have developed the conventional rating system prevailing in the advanced countries. Table 4.1 shows the rating symbols of debt securities and their meanings.

Table 3.1
Rating Symbols of Different Agencies

Debt category	Debt instrument	Rating symbols				Remarks
		CRISIL	ICRA	CARE		
Long-term instrument	Debenture bonds, preference shares	AAA	LAAA	CARE	AAA	High safety
		*AA	*LAA	*CARE	AA	Highest safety
		*A	*LA	*CARE	A	Adequate safety
		*BBB	*LBBB	*CARE	BBB	Moderate safety
		*BB	*LBB	*CARE	BB	Inadequate safety
		*B	*LB	*CARE	B	Risk prone
		C	*LC	*CARE	C	Substantial risk
		D	LD	CARE	D	Default
Medium-term instrument	Fixed deposit	FAAA	MAAA	CARE	AAA	Highest safety
		*FAA	*MAA	*CARE	AA	High safety
		*FA	*MA	*CARE	A	Adequate safety
		*FB	*MB	*CARE	BBB	Inadequate safety
				*CARE	BB	-do-
				*CARE	B	-do-
		*FC	*MC	*CARE	C	Risk prone
		*FD	MD	CARE	D	Default
Short-term instrument	Commercial paper	*P1	*A1	*PR-1		High safety
		*P2	*A2	*PR-2		Highest safety
		*P3	*A3	*PR-3		Adequate safety
		*P4	*A4	*PR-4		Risk prone
		*P5	A5	PR-5		Default

* The suffix of "+" (plus) or "−" (minus) signs are used with the rating symbols to indicate the comparative positions of the instrument within the group covered by the symbol.

SEBI Guidelines 1999

i)   No credit rating agencies shall rate a security issued by its promoters.

ii) It has barred rating agencies from rating securities issued by any borrower, subsidiary or associate of the promoter if it has a chairman, director. employee of any such firm.

iii) Dual rating is compulsory for public and rights issue of debt instruments of ₹ 100 crore or more.

iv)   SEBI has decided to incorporate a clause in the listing agreement of stock exchanges requiring companies to cooperate with agencies by providing correct information. Refusal to do so may lead to breach of contract between rating agencies and client.

v)   The issues would be required to incorporate an undertaking in their offer documents promising necessary cooperation with the rating agency in providing factual information.

vi)   It is also suggested that a penal clause be introduced in the listing agreement of the information provided is proved to be incorrect at a later stage, to protect investors' interest.

vii) The net worth of rating agencies has been fixed at ₹ 5 crore.

viii) Rating agencies can choose their methodology of operation but self regulatory mechanism will give a better maturity status for agencies.

ix)   No chairman, director or employee of the promoters shall be a chairman, director or employee of the CRA or its rating committee. Promoter of a CRA is a person who holds more than 107 of holdings of the CRA.

x)   Period of validity of registration shall be 3 years.

Future of Credit Rating

Credit ratings are guide posts to investors. Rating agencies, which evaluate companies issuing debt instruments, can help reduce investment risks substantially: These agencies ensure scientific investment decision-making by the investors. Rating agencies should broad-base their activities by rating mutual funds, equity instruments, chit funds and real estate developers. At present rating is done only to debt instruments. There are several investment opportunities like equity shares, mutual funds, chit funds, real estates, etc. These investments are not rated by any credit agency. Several private mutual funds companies are approaching public for funds. Several chit funds companies and real estate developers are playing in the market. Hence, rating should be made mandatory for all the investors so as to guide and protect the investor community.

Limitations of Rating Agencies

The ratings are not recommendations to invest. They do not take into account many aspects which influence an investment decision. The ratings do not evaluate the reasonableness of the issue price, possibilities for capital gains or take into account the liquidity in the secondary market.

Though ratings give a fair indication of credit worthiness of the issuer, but there are certain limitations to these ratings. Ratings are done purely on the bases of historic data and past trends. This does not comprehensively cover all aspects of the business and economy. Investor should realise that a credit rating is not the final declaration of the company's risk and that he should use the rating as a reference and base point for his own discretion.

3.5 FOREIGN DIRECT INVESTMENT

International Financial Management has assumed an important role of Indian economy, with FDI's, FFIs and FIIs playing a key role in the stock and capital market. The recent estimate is that FIIs hold about 25% of market capitalisation of the listed companies in the Stock Exchanges in India. Many Indian corporates are listed and traded on Foreign Stock Exchanges. Many foreign banks were permitted to operate in India and Indian banks have become more globalised in their operations. India has emerged as a creditor country among the IMF of members. World Bank is reported to be planning to issue Rupee bonds in India to raise rupee resources. Indian rupee has shown strength and resilience that it was in demand in International Finance Markets.

The past two decades have witnessed a process of accelerating change in the global financial markets. Driven by an interacting process of liberalisation and innovation, regulations have been removed, new financial products have emerged and old boundaries between financial intermediaries have been blurred. Risk management tools have become increasingly sophisticated. Global economies have found new ways to mobilise domestic and international savings.

Meaning

The international form of capital has facilitated development of the world's natural resources and has been instrumental in transmitting the direct effect of the industrial revolution from one region to another. A number of presently more advanced countries owe a good deal of their earlier industrial development to the influx of foreign capital. In fact, nearly every developed country had to rely on external sources to supplement its own meager savings during the early stage of development. Foreign Capital combined with skill and enterprise is essential for the development of economic potentialities in under-developed or developing regions where the opportunities for the accumulation of capital are unequally distributed. Thus, the "expanding world economy" cannot be fully realised without a continuous international flow of investment funds. Different countries are at different stages of economic development – some are more profusely equipped with savings available for investment while others have large and more urgent opportunity for the profitable investment of savings.

Need of Foreign Direct Investment

International finance has now become an important source of funds of both short-term and long-term nature for the corporates in India, due to Current Account convertibility of the Rupee, introduced in 1994 and globalisation of the Indian markets. The decision to raise funds in India or abroad is a question of cost and easy availability and the capital structure requirements of the corporates. International finance has become an alternative to domestic sources. The access and entry into foreign capital markets and the rates at which one can borrow and whether one can borrow or not depends on the credit rating of the company and the country, capacity to service that debt as measured by its export earnings or foreign exchange earnings, the timing and the state of the domestic and foreign markets. The actual decision to resort to foreign finance, the extent and terms of borrowing, repayment schedule etc., will vary from company to company and country to country. A company which becomes eligible to raise funds abroad achieves a global status and recognition of institutional investors abroad and they are mostly MNCs. The foreign institutions and pension funds etc. supply the funds for various reasons, such as diversification of their asset portfolio due to differences in country risks, potential for capital appreciations and gain in Return On Investment (ROI). But their investments are made after an indepth study of the country and currency risk and fundamentals of the company, under question. The investors abroad are again of different categories; namely, foreign security firms, pension funds, provident funds, country offshore funds, mutual funds and foreign financial institutions.

In India, with the recent economic and financial reforms, markets have become free, competitive and globalised. The FIIs and FFIs, including foreign security firms are allowed to operate in Indian Financial markets. The convertibility of the rupee on Current Account facilitated the inflows and outflows of funds. The policy of Foreign Direct Investment has been liberalised in India so as to promote the investment both in equity and debt subject to some limits, in the Indian corporates. These policy changes widened the avenues or sources of funds as also the instruments through which they can raise funds from abroad.

The Indian business markets play a crucial role in economic development through saving-investment process, also known as capital formation. A vibrant and competitive financial market is necessary concommitment of trade and industrial policy liberalisation to sustain the ongoing reform in the structural aspects of the real economy. Many financial reforms were taken to improve the efficiency and stability of the financial system, internal and external development which made it increasingly difficult to maintain a tightly regulated financial system.

The process of liberalisation initiated by the Government has not been new, but prior piecemeal efforts were not stable and widespread. The structural reforms initiated during last 5 years have had a positive impact on the investment climate of the country. The new economic policies aimed at liberalisation and globalisation are all embracing, consistent and appear to be irreversible. The country has pursued conservative inward looking policies for almost four decades. The positive effects of these policies may be many but they are outweighed by their negative impact of inefficiency, corruption, delays and noncompetitive nature of industrial/economic environment. Many mighty socialist economies have crumbled under their dead weight and India could very well imagine what is in store for it, if it does not change the course. The whole nation is in a mood for change and manmohanomics is getting a fair trial inspite of scams and corruption charges.

In its bid to open up the country's economy, the government of India has geared up the investment sector to meet the challenges, which economy is likely to face. As such Indian financial markets are undergoing a process of rapid change which has transformed the entire complexion of financial system.

FOREIGN DIRECT INVESTMENT IN INDIAN CAPITAL MARKET

The liberalisation of the financial sector throws up the need for several financial markets and services. The Indian financial services such as leasing, hire purchase, financing for take over and loan syndication and non-fund based services, such as portfolio management, investment advice, financial engineering and restructuring and issue management have grown substantially.

India is better placed to attract FDIs compared to several countries because of the following reasons :

i)   Availability of abundant supply of skilled as well as semi-skilled labour many of whom know English language;

ii) Availability of good infrastructure facilities like transportation, telecommunications, networks of banking institutions, etc.;

iii) A huge market of about 850 million people of whom 250 million belong to the middle and high income group. Even if one takes into account just 1% of this population, it would mean 8.5 million consumers, which is equal to the combined population of Singapore and Hong Kong;

iv) Free and independent judicial system and press;

v)   Availability of several unexploited natural resources; and

vi) Above all Government's sincerity in its intention to attract FDI is genuine.

FDI decisions depend upon the risk perceptions of the firm. In order to protect its long-term interests a firm may behave or show responses in different ways. Apart from risk, strategic and operational factors may influence FDI decisions. Strategies pursued by a firm operating in foreign markets may be defensive or aggressive. A firm deciding in favour of FDI has to take decisions regarding location of its facilities, plant or business. Relative labour cost, production and marketing infrastructure, cost of maintaining, expatriates, transport costs, etc., will influence the location decision. Choice of location is largely determined by the corporate strategy pursued by the firm viz., market strategy, production strategy and supply strategy.

The major effort of the Govt. to attract foreign direct investment in India was outlined in the Industrial Policy Statement of 1991. Since then there was a sustained growth of direct investment inflows from U.5. $ 97 million in 1990-91 to U.S. $ 3904 million in 2001-02 and U.S. $ 4660 million in 2002-03. Companies registered in Mauritius, U.S.A., U.K., Germany and Japan account for the bulk of the foreign direct investment. Industry-wise, the major areas or industry groups are Computers, Engineering and Services.

Table 3.2: Total Foreign Direct Investment

Year	Amount in million of U.S. $
1994-95	1,314
1995-96	2,133
1996-97	2,821
1997-98	3,557
2000-01	4,029
2001-02	3,904
2002-03	4,660
2003-04	4,675

Source : RBI Report on Currency and Finance.

INDIAN DIRECT INVESTMENT ABROAD

"Direct Investment" shall mean investment by an Indian party in the equity share capital of the foreign concern with a view to acquiring a long-term interest in that concern. Besides the equity stake, such long-term interest may be reflected through representation on the Board of Directors of the foreign concern and in the supply of technical know-how, capital goods, components, raw materials, etc. and managerial personnel to the foreign concern.

Meaning of Important terms related to Direct Investment Abroad :

i) **"Host Country",**

shall mean the country in which the foreign concern receiving the direct investment is formed, registered or incorporated.

ii) **"Indian Party",**

shall mean a private or public limited company incorporated in accordance with the laws of India. When more than one Indian body corporate make a direct investment in a foreign concern, all the bodies corporate shall together constitute the "Indian Party".

iii) **"Joint Venture" (JV),**

shall mean a foreign concern formed, registered or incorporated in accordance with the laws and regulations of the host country in which the Indian party makes a direct investment, whether such investment amounts to a majority or minority shareholding;

iv) **"Wholly Owned Subsidiary" (WOS),**

shall mean a foreign concern formed, registered or incorporated in accordance with the laws and regulations of the host country whose entire equity share capital is owned by the Indian Party.

RBI Guidelines for Indian Direct Investment Abroad

A) The Need for Guidelines

The Need for RBI Guidelines is shown below in Figure 3.11.

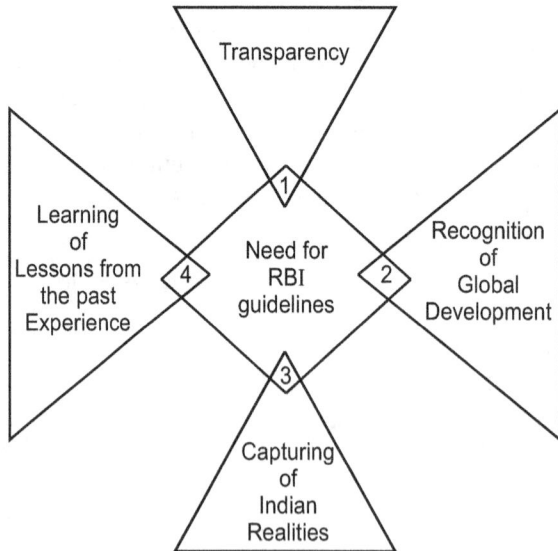

Fig. 3.11 : Need for RBI Guidelines

Guidelines for Indian Direct Investment in Joint Ventures (JV) and Wholly Owned Subsidiaries (WOS) Abroad, reflect the need for transparency, recognition of global development, capturing of Indian realities and learning of lessons from the past experience.

1)   Firstly, there is a need for **a transparent policy** framework to enable Indian businessmen to plan their business and to be able to react to potential collaborators outside the country. Such transparency is also required to enable the financial institutions and banks to assess their support through professional judgment in the context of financial sector reforms. Further, the Non-Resident Indian community, which is expecting to play a strong role in globalising the Indian economy, is seeking a transparent policy.

2)   Secondly, there is a need for a **formal recognition of the changing global reality**. These include close relationship between flow of investment and trade, increasing role of medium sized units; success in the domestic economy as a precursor to success in the international arena; the importance of continuously updating the technology through cross investments; more dynamic relation between market seeking and resource seeking investments and tendency for skill and service intensity rather than material intensity in the international flows; the importance of going behind the tariff walls erected by the emerging regional blocks; the trend towards multi-country ownership of enterprises and finally, the emerging significance of ethnic links in international investment and trade. It is also necessary to recognise that there can be a massive outflow of foreign investment by companies if not monitored carefully.

3)   Thirdly, the **Indian realities** relate to the new economic policies. These   include : strengthening globalisation of Indian economy by allowing the Indian entrepreneurship to go global; being a capital importing country, the need to avoid large capital outflow; visualising the global economic relationship well beyond physical exports; ensuring that Indian industry and business attain strategic positions in certain areas or regional blocks; increasing attention to Joint Ventures abroad in third countries while finalising bilateral trade and economic relationships and the need for a more dynamic approach towards access to world technology through all means including overseas investment.

4)   Fourthly, **the lessons of experience** have to be captured and a clear signal given about the new policy framework. The lessons of past experience include the low return on investment; large incidence of mortality after approval; low return on investment in the form of dividends; limited coverage and capital intensity of overseas investment, perhaps because they were linked with physical exports; inadequate coverage of trading and the service sector till recently; difficulties for cash borrowing and guarantees by the parent company in India resulting in cash crunch experienced by the overseas venture; inadequate interaction between Embassies and investors; lack of self-regulatory mechanism; a regulatory approach instead of facilitator or strategic approach to overseas investment; procedural bottlenecks with clearance being required from multiple agencies and finally the impression that approval of the Government includes clearance from the commercial viability angle also and consequently implying directed lending by banking institutions resulting in defaults to Indian banks.

Liberalised outward investment procedures of 1992 have had a positive impact and approvals have increased in number, range and innovativeness.

B) Basic Objectives of a Transparent Policy

The basic objectives of a transparent policy towards overseas investment from India through these guidelines are :

i)   recognising the link between trade and investment flows, to provide a framework for Indian Industry and Business to access global networks;

ii) to ensure that such flows, though determined by commercial interests, are consistent with the macro-economic and balance of payment compulsions of the country, particularly in terms of the magnitude of the capital flows;

iii) to provide a transparent mechanism of knowing the priorities of the Government in regard to the overseas investment, so as to influence the stakeholders including financial institutions/banking sector and Embassies so that there is an understanding and alignment between macro-economic objectives and the individual business decisions;

iv) to give liberal access to Indian business for technology-sourcing or resource-seeking or market-seeking as strategic responses to the emerging global opportunities for trade in goods or services;

v)   to give a signal that there is a qualitative change in the approach of the Government, from one of the regulator or controller to one of the facilitator;

vi) to encourage the Indian industry to adopt a spirit of self-regulation and collective effort for improving the image of Indian industry abroad.

In the light of the above, the following guidelines are issued to elaborate the policy framework in the EXIM Policy. The Reserve Bank of India (RBI) will accord all necessary approvals, and monitor the progress by prescribing the reporting obligations.

C) Applicability

These guidelines shall apply to Direct Investment by Indian parties in Joint Ventures (JV) and Wholly Owned Subsidiaries (WOS) abroad (hereinafter referred to as "Foreign Concerns"). They apply to direct investment by Indian parties in newly promoted foreign concerns, to make initial or additional direct investment by Indian parties in existing foreign concerns and to investments for acquisitions of overseas business.

The foreign concern in which the direct investment is proposed to be made may be engaged in industrial, commercial, trading or service activity including hotel or tourism industry. This includes financial service such as insurance, mutual funds, etc.

These guidelines do not apply to –

i)   portfolio investment by Indian parties in foreign concerns;

ii) direct investment in foreign concerns engaged in the banking sector;

iii) Overseas direct investment funded out of Exchange Earners' Foreign Currency (EEFC) balances upto a maximum of US $ 15 million permitted by authorised dealers; and

iv) Overseas direct investment funded out of Global Depository Receipts (GDRs) upto a maximum of 50% of GDRs raised, permitted by Ministry of Finance, Department of Economic Affairs.

Cases under Sl. No.(i) to (iv) above shall be considered in terms of separate procedures as prescribed by the Reserve Bank/Department of Economic Affairs (Ministry of Finance).

D) Categories of Applications processed by the Reserve Bank

There shall be two categories or applications for setting up overseas JVs and WOSs viz. Category "A" : Fast Track and Category "B" : Normal Cases. All applications are to be made to and processed by the Reserve Bank.

Category 'A' - Fast Track

An application for direct investment in a Joint Venture/Wholly Owned Subsidiary abroad from a private/public limited company will be eligible for automatic approval by RBI provided:

i) the total value of the investment by the Indian party does not exceed US $ 4 (four) million, and in respect of Indian Rupee investments in Nepal, the total value of the investment does not exceed Rs.25 (twenty five) crores;

ii) the amount of investment is upto 25% of annual average export/ foreign exchange earnings of the Indian party (other than equity exports to existing JVs/WOSs abroad) in the preceding three years (not applicable to Indian Rupee investments in Nepal); and

iii) the amount of investment (net of that amount of EEFC/GDR funding which would have been eligible for clearance under the EEFC/GDR Fast Track) should be repatriated in full by way of dividends, royalty, technical services fee, etc. within a period of five years with effect from the date of first remittance of equity to the foreign concern or the date of first shipment of equity exports or the due date for receipt of entitlements which are to be capitalised, whichever is earlier.

The investment may, besides cash remittance at the discretion of the Indian party, be contributed by the capitalisation in full or in part of :

i) Indian made plant, machinery, equipment and components supplied to the foreign concern;

ii) The proceeds of goods exported by the Indian party to the foreign concern;

iii) Fees, royalties, commissions or other entitlements from the foreign concern for the supply of technical know-how, consultancy, managerial or other services.

In cases where the applicant company is a new company and does not have the requisite export performance/exchange earnings, credit may be given to the parent company's exports/exchange earnings, provided the applicant company is either a wholly owned subsidiary of the exporting/exchange earning company, or the latter owns at least 51% shares in the former. In case of exports being routed through subsidiaries set up exclusively for international business, credit may be given to the parent company for the exports/exchange earnings of its subsidiaries.

Apart from the above requirements, the following shall apply to applications for overseas direct investment in the financial sector :

i)   Financial services companies proposing to set up JV/WOS overseas should have a good track record of minimum 3 years and should either be registered with SEBI as Category-I Merchant Banker or as an NBFC under the Non-Banking Finance Companies (Reserve Bank) Directions, 1977 issued by the Reserve Bank from time to time.

ii)   In all cases at (a) above, the company should have a minimum net worth (paid-up capital + free reserves) of ₹ 15 crores.

iii)   Financial companies seeking to make overseas investments should have fulfilled the prudential norms relating to capital adequacy ratio of 8%.

iv)   Subsidiaries of Indian financial institutions which are conforming to the above said norms will also be permitted to make overseas direct investment in the financial services sector.

Within the overall limit of US $ 4.00 million, the Indian party, may opt for –

i)   cash remittance,

ii)   capitalisation of export proceeds towards equity, or

iii)   giving loans or corporate guarantees to/on behalf of Indian JVs/ WOSs.

Guarantees shall be taken at 50% of the face value for determining the overall limit of investment.

For loans/guarantees from banks/financial institutions from India to/on behalf of Indian JVs/WOSs abroad, requisite clearances from commercial banking angle for loans and guarantees as required would need to be taken as normally prescribed.

Where the Reserve Bank, in its judgment, feels that a proposal under automatic route is predominantly real estate-oriented, such proposals shall be remitted to the Special Committee.

All applications under the automatic route will be eligible for approval within 21 days of receipt of complete application by the Reserve Bank, which shall include a broad feasibility study, a statement of credit-worthiness from a bank and statement from a Chartered Accountant verifying the ratios, projections made, etc. In considering applications on the automatic route the Reserve Bank shall give due regard to the criteria laid down for the same (which is given below.)

In case the application is for takeover or participation in an existing unit, the basis of share valuation shall be certified by a Chartered Accountant.

This facility of fast track route will be available to the Indian party only once in a block of three of calendar years including the calendar year in which the investment is made. However, within the overall limit of US $ 4 million and its entitlement of 25% of average annual export/foreign exchange earnings, the Indian party may be permitted to invest equity/provide guarantee, etc. on the fast track route on more than one occasion and in more than one JV/WOS abroad. However, the normal route may be availed of without these restrictions.

Category 'B' - Normal Cases

All applications involving investments beyond US $ 4 million but not exceeding US $ 15 million or those not qualifying for fast track clearance on the basis of the applicable criteria outlined in Category 'A' above and all applications will be processed in the RBI through a Special Committee appointed by the Reserve Bank in consultation with Government and chaired by the Commerce Secretary with the Deputy Governor of the Reserve Bank as the Alternate Chairman. The Committee shall have, as members, representatives of the Ministry of Commerce, Ministry of Finance, Ministry of External Affairs, Department of Company Affairs and the Reserve Bank. The Committee shall co-opt as members other Secretaries/ institutions dealing with the sector to which the case before the Committee relates. A recommendation will be made within 60 days of receipt of the complete application and Reserve Bank will grant or refuse permission on the basis of the recommendations. Such proposals should be accompanied by a Project Report/Feasibility Report submitted by the applicant and by a statement from a Chartered Accountant verifying the ratios, projections made, etc. If the Special Committee is not satisfied with the Project Report submitted by the applicant, the Special Committee may require the applicant to submit the project to an appraisal by IDBI, ICICI, EXIM Bank, SBI Cap. or any other similar agency.

The Committee will, *inter alia*, review the criteria for and progress of all overseas investments under the guidelines and evolve its own procedure for consultations and approvals.

Criteria

In considering an application under category "B", the Committee shall, *inter alia*, have due regard to the following :

i)   The financial position, standing and business track record of the Indian and foreign parties;

ii)   Experience and track record of the Indian party in exports and its external orientation;

iii) Quantum of the proposed investment and the size of the overseas venture in the context of the resources, networth and scale of operations of the Indian party including the EEFC/GDR funds proposed as a component of the overseas direct investment;

iv)   Repatriation (net of that amount of EEFC/GDR funding which would have been eligible for clearance under the EEFC/GDR Fast Track) by way of dividends, fees, royalties, commissions or other entitlements from the foreign concerns for supply of technical knowhow, consultancy, managerial or other services within five years with effect from the date of first remittance of equity to the foreign concern or the date of first shipment of equity exports or the due date for receipt of entitlements which are to be capitalised, whichever is earlier.

v)   Benefits to the country in terms of foreign exchange earnings, two way trade generation, technology transfer, access to raw materials, intermediates or final products not available in India;

vi) Prima facie viability of the proposed investment;

provided that the proposals for overseas direct investment in the financial sector under Category "B" shall also conform to the requirements laid down for this sector.

Indian financial and banking institutions considering to support the venture will examine independently the commercial viability of the proposal.

E) Post Approval Changes

In the case of a joint venture in which the Indian party has a minority equity shareholding, the Indian party shall report to the Ministry of Commerce and the Reserve Bank the details of following decisions taken by the joint venture within 30 days of the approval of those decisions by the shareholders/ promoters/directors of the joint venture in terms of the local laws of the host country :

i)   undertake any activity different from the activity originally approved by the Reserve Bank/Government of India for the direct investment;

ii) participate in the equity capital of another concern;

iii) promote a subsidiary or a wholly owned subsidiary as a second generation foreign concern;

iv) alter its share capital structure, authorised or issued, or its shareholding pattern.

In the case of a joint venture in which the Indian party has a majority equity shareholding or in the case of a wholly owned subsidiary, the Indian party may without prior reference to the Reserve Bank, consent to the following decisions being taken by the foreign concern, subject to the foreign concern having been in operation for not less than two years :

i)   undertake any activity different from the activity originally approved for the direct investment

ii) participation in the equity capital of another concern;

iii) promote a subsidiary or a wholly owned subsidiary as a second generation concern;

iv) alter its share capital structure, authorised or issued, or its shareholding pattern;

provided the following conditions are fulfilled:

a)   the Indian party has repatriated all entitlements due to it from the foreign concern, including dividends, fees and royalties and this is duly certified by a Chartered Accountant;

b)   the Indian party has no overdues older than 180 days from the foreign concern in respect of its exports to the latter;

c)   the Indian party does not seek any fresh cash remittance from India; and

d)   the percentage of equity shareholding of the Indian party in the first generation joint venture or wholly owned subsidiary is not reduced, unless it is pursuant to the laws of the host country.

The Indian party shall report to the Reserve Bank and the Ministry of Commerce the details of the decisions taken by the joint venture or the wholly owned subsidiary within 30 days of the approval of those decisions by the shareholders/ promoters/ directors in terms of the local laws of the host country together with a statement on the fulfilment of the conditions mentioned above.

In the case of subscription by an Indian party to its entitlement of equity shares issued by a joint venture on Rights basis, or in the case of subscription by an Indian party to the issue of additional share capital by a joint venture or a wholly owned subsidiary, prior approval of the Reserve Bank shall be taken for such subscription.

F) Review of the Existing Policy

It was, however, felt necessary to further liberalise the existing policy and simplify the procedure for setting up JV/WOS abroad. The need for reviewing the existing policy was also considered by the High Level Committee on Balance of Payments headed by **Dr. C. Rangarajan**. In its final report submitted in April 1993, the Committee, while expressing satisfaction with the latest liberalisation measures, suggested further review of the existing policy framework keeping in view the following aspects/developments :

i)   While liberalising Foreign Direct Investment (FDI) in India, Indian Joint Ventures abroad should also be encouraged as globalisation would involve close interaction between Indian and foreign companies.

ii)   With the partial convertibility of rupee, the idea that capital flight has to be controlled through regulatory administrative measures will not hold good.

iii)   With increasing opportunities for services sector and skills in India, it should be possible to encourage less capital-intensive and more skill-oriented Indian investments abroad.

iv)   Indian business may need strategic presence abroad because of emerging trade blocks, such as, EEC.

The need for such changed outlook was already reflected in the EXIM Policy for 1992-1997. After considerable deliberations and consultations, thoroughly revised guidelines were issued by the Government of India, Ministry of Commerce (MOC) on the 17th August, 1995.

These guidelines reflect a transparent policy framework in the context of the new developments in national and global set-up and the lessons learnt from our past experience in regard to existing JV/WOS abroad. The basic objectives of this new policy are :

i)   to provide a transparent framework to enable Indian industry and business to gain access to global networks in recognition of the established link between trade and investment flows;

ii)   to ensure that such investment flows, though determined by commercial interest, are consistent with macro-economic and Balance of Payment requirements of the country;

iii) to give liberal access to Indian business for technology-sourcing or resource-seeking or market-seeking as strategic response to the emerging global opportunities in trade in goods and services;

iv) to give a signal that there is a qualitative change in the approach of the Government of India and the Reserve Bank from one of the "regulator and controller" to that of "facilitator and promoter"; and

v) to encourage Indian entrepreneurs in their effort to improve the global image of Indian industry.

G) Salient Features of the New Guidelines

The major changes introduced in the August 1995 policy framework are as under :

i) The work relating to receipt and disposal of applications for overseas direct investment has been entrusted to the Reserve Bank which acts as the Single Window Agency instead of the MOC.

ii) The new guidelines will also apply to investment in financial services, such as, insurance, mutual funds, etc. besides industrial, commercial, trading or service activities.

iii) Overseas investment upto US $ 4 million is eligible for clearance by the Reserve Bank within 21 days of receipt of complete application/full information subject to fulfilment of the prescribed conditions under the Fast Track (Automatic) Route. Earlier, the MOC was clearing proposals involving investments upto US $ 2 million only (with cash remittance not exceeding US $ 0.5 million) under Automatic (Category 'A') route within 30 days of receipt of complete application.

iv) A Special Committee constituted by the Reserve Bank, with the Commerce Secretary as its Chairman, Deputy Governor of Reserve Bank as the Alternate Chairman and representatives of other Ministries/Departments (viz. Finance, Commerce, External Affairs and Company Affairs) and the Reserve Bank as the members has replaced the erstwhile Inter-Ministerial Committee (IMC) to consider the cases coming under the Normal Route (viz. cases not qualifying for clearance under the Fast Track Route by the Reserve Bank).

v) Large Investment proposals, where the investment exceeds US $ 15 million, are being considered, if the additional resources beyond US $ 15 million are raised through the GDR route.

vi) The balances available in the Exchange Earners Foreign Currency (EFFC) account can be utilised by the Indian companies for their contribution by way of equity/loan in overseas JV/WOS approved by the Reserve Bank.

vii) The disinvestment proposals are now being considered by the Reserve Bank for which application accompanied by share valuation and justification for sale price as certified by the Chartered Accountant has to be submitted.

viii) The guidelines also provided for supply of second hand or reconditioned indigenous machinery by the Indian party towards its contribution as direct investment in the foreign concern.

ix) Reserve Bank has notified the procedure for issue of "in principle" approval to the proposals for acquisition of overseas ventures through time-bound bidding/tender procedure.

Even within a period of one and a half years after the guidelines of August 1995 came into effect, further changes, mainly aimed at providing more relaxations to Indian companies, were brought about. These changes include (i) computation of foreign exchange earnings other than exports and the export/foreign exchange earnings of the parent or the subsidiary company for clearance of the proposals under the Fast Track Route, (ii) dispensation of the requirement of technical appraisal by designated agencies and (iii) additional norms for investment in the financial sector. In March 1997 norms relating to rupee investment in Nepal were relaxed; accordingly, it was notified that proposals for rupee investment upto Indian Rupees 25 crores would be considered by the Reserve Bank under its Fast Track Route without any linkage to the past export/foreign exchange earnings of the Indian promoter companies. The requirement of repatriation of entitlements in foreign exchange has also been dispensed with in the case of rupee investments in Nepal. In August 1997 Government of India announced introduction of two new Fast Track Windows for Indian direct investment abroad to be operated without prior reference to the Reserve Bank as under :

i) Investments upto US $ 15 mn., including the amount of investment approved by the Reserve Bank under its Fast Track Route, in a block of three years, would be allowed by authorised dealers from out of the balances held in the EEFC account of the Indian promoter company.

ii) Proposals of investments in JV/WOS abroad upto a maximum of 50% of GDRs to be raised would be cleared by the Government of India, Ministry of Finance under its normal GDR approval process with overseas investments as permitted end-use.

Further, the extant norm of repatriation in foreign exchange of the original investment by way of dividend and other entitlements within a period of five years would not apply to the investment proposals cleared under these Fast Track Windows. However, the requirement of repatriation of dividend and other entitlements due to the Indian promoter companies from their investments in JV/WOS abroad as per the existing Exchange Control regulations will continue to apply.

1.4.3 The full text of the 'Guidelines for Indian Direct Investments in JV and WOS Abroad, issued by the Government of India, Ministry of Commerce, as amended upto date, has been incorporated in Chapter 2. A chart showing the revised approval procedure for overseas investment in JV/WOS abroad under different routes as per the extant guidelines is enclosed as an Annexure to this unit.

H) Recent Relaxations by the Reserve Bank

Consistent with the policy of liberalisation, the Reserve Bank had also made certain relaxations in the Exchange Control regulations relating to overseas investments as under :

i) Earlier Indian companies were allowed to make actual overseas investment by the Reserve Bank only after they obtained the necessary clearance from the Department of Company Affairs (DCA) under the relevant provisions of the Companies Act, 1956, if applicable or produced a certificate from DCA about the non-applicability of such provisions. Approvals for overseas investments issued by the Reserve Bank were no longer linked with production of the clearance certificate from DCA or any other ministry/ agency as may be required under different statutes.

ii) Adequate powers were delegated to the Regional Offices of the Reserve Bank to permit Indian companies to make remittances towards payment of fees, incidental charges, etc. to overseas consultants/merchant bankers/solicitors for conducting preliminary studies, evaluation of the fair price for acquisitions, identification of foreign collaborators, etc. before submitting any formal proposal for making overseas investment subject to certain conditions. Such powers have since been delegated to authorised dealers to allow remittances upto US $ one lakh per project.

iii) Regional Offices of the Reserve Bank were authorised to permit remittance of nominal amounts for acquisition of qualification shares, if required, under the law of the host country by resident Indians who become directors in overseas companies provided the Indian party does not acquire any controlling interest in such concern.

iv) The earlier requirement of obtaining clearance from the Government of India/ the Reserve Bank for acquiring shares offered under bonus issue by the overseas company in which investment has been made by the Indian company with necessary approval was dispensed with. Recipients of such shares are only required to report the details along with the Board Resolution of the overseas company allowing the bonus shares to the Regional Office of the Reserve Bank for issue of holding licence.

I) Performance Reports and Repatriation of Dues

The past experience in regard to reporting of performance of the overseas JV/WOS to the Government of India/the Reserve Bank and repatriation of dues/entitlements from such overseas concerns by the Indian promoter companies has not been satisfactory. Accordingly, the requirement of prompt submission of **Annual Performance Reports** (APRs) has been re-emphasised in the new guidelines. Reserve Bank follows up timely receipt of APRs and other reports/documents, like **Quarterly Progress Reports** (QPRs) on the status of the project implementation, Special Reports for non-repatriation of entitlements, share certificates from the overseas companies, etc. and also repatriation of dividends and other entitlements/dues by the Indian promoter companies. Keeping in view the penal action. which could be initiated by the Reserve Bank against the defaulting Indian promoter companies and in their own business interest, it is imperative that the Indian companies closely monitor the activities of their overseas ventures, prepare reports on their performance for their own use as well as submission to the Reserve Bank and also repatriate all their dues to India in time.

Annexure

Chart showing the existing procedure for obtaining approval for Indian Direct Investment in Joint Venture (JV)/Wholly Owned Subsidiary (WOS) abroad under different routes

(A) FAST TRACK ROUTES (FTR)

I) RBI	II) Authorised Dealers (AD)	III) Ministry of Finance (MOF)
Limit	**Limit**	**Limit**
Investment upto US $ 4 mn. (Rs. 25 crores in Nepal).	Investment upto US $15 mn. out of the balances held in the Exchange Earners Foreign Currency (EEFC) Accounts.	Investments upto 50% of GDRs as approved by MOF [Dept. of Economic Affairs (DEA)].
Application	**Application**	**Application**
Application in Form ODI (4 sets) to RBI, Central Office with documents as under : (a) For setting up a new JV/WOS	Application in Form ODA (3 sets) to the authorised dealer (AD) with whom the EEFC account is maintained with documents as under :	Application to MOF/DEA, as per the usual GDR approval procedure with details of proposed overseas investments (viz. country of location of the proposed JV/WOS, line of activity, amount of investment by way of equity/loans, etc.).
i) Draft JV Agreement/MOU and Articles of Association	i) Project/Feasibility report	
ii) Project/Feasibility Report	ii) CA Certificate on ratios/projections.	
iii) CA Certificate on ratios/projections	iii) Board Resolution for the investment	
iv) Certificate of credit-worthiness from bankers (in sealed cover)	iv) CA Certificate on fair value of share of the foreign concern (in case of partial/full take over)	
v) Bank Certificates in support of export earnings/other forex earnings	v) CA Certificate about networth, profitability, capital adequacy ratio and registration with RBI/SEBI (in case of investment in financial services sector)	
vi) Annual Accounts of the applicant company for the last 3 years		
vii) Board Resolution for the investment		
viii) List of machines/goods to be capitalised (where applicable)		

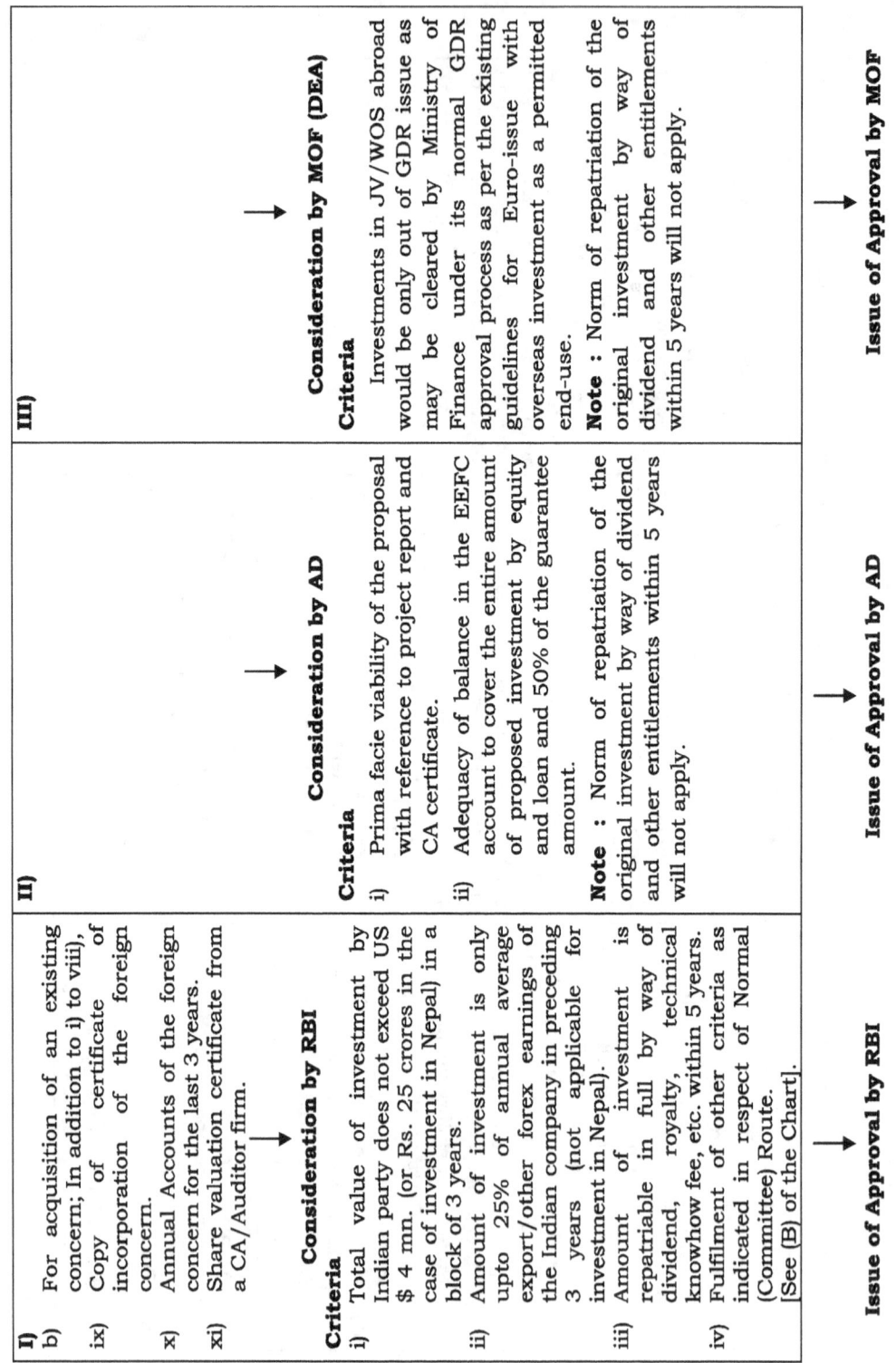

I)

b) For acquisition of an existing concern; In addition to i) to viii),

ix) Copy of certificate of incorporation of the foreign concern.

x) Annual Accounts of the foreign concern for the last 3 years.

xi) Share valuation certificate from a CA/Auditor firm.

Consideration by RBI

Criteria

i) Total value of investment by Indian party does not exceed US $ 4 mn. (or Rs. 25 crores in the case of investment in Nepal) in a block of 3 years.

ii) Amount of investment is only upto 25% of annual average export/other forex earnings of the Indian company in preceding 3 years (not applicable for investment in Nepal).

iii) Amount of investment is repatriable in full by way of dividend, royalty, technical knowhow fee, etc. within 5 years.

iv) Fulfilment of other criteria as indicated in respect of Normal (Committee) Route. [See (B) of the Chart].

Issue of Approval by RBI

II)

Consideration by AD

Criteria

i) Prima facie viability of the proposal with reference to project report and CA certificate.

ii) Adequacy of balance in the EEFC account to cover the entire amount of proposed investment by equity and loan and 50% of the guarantee amount.

Note : Norm of repatriation of the original investment by way of dividend and other entitlements within 5 years will not apply.

Issue of Approval by AD

III)

Consideration by MOF (DEA)

Criteria

Investments in JV/WOS abroad would be only out of GDR issue as may be cleared by Ministry of Finance under its normal GDR approval process as per the existing guidelines for Euro-issue with overseas investment as a permitted end-use.

Note : Norm of repatriation of the original investment by way of dividend and other entitlements within 5 years will not apply.

Issue of Approval by MOF

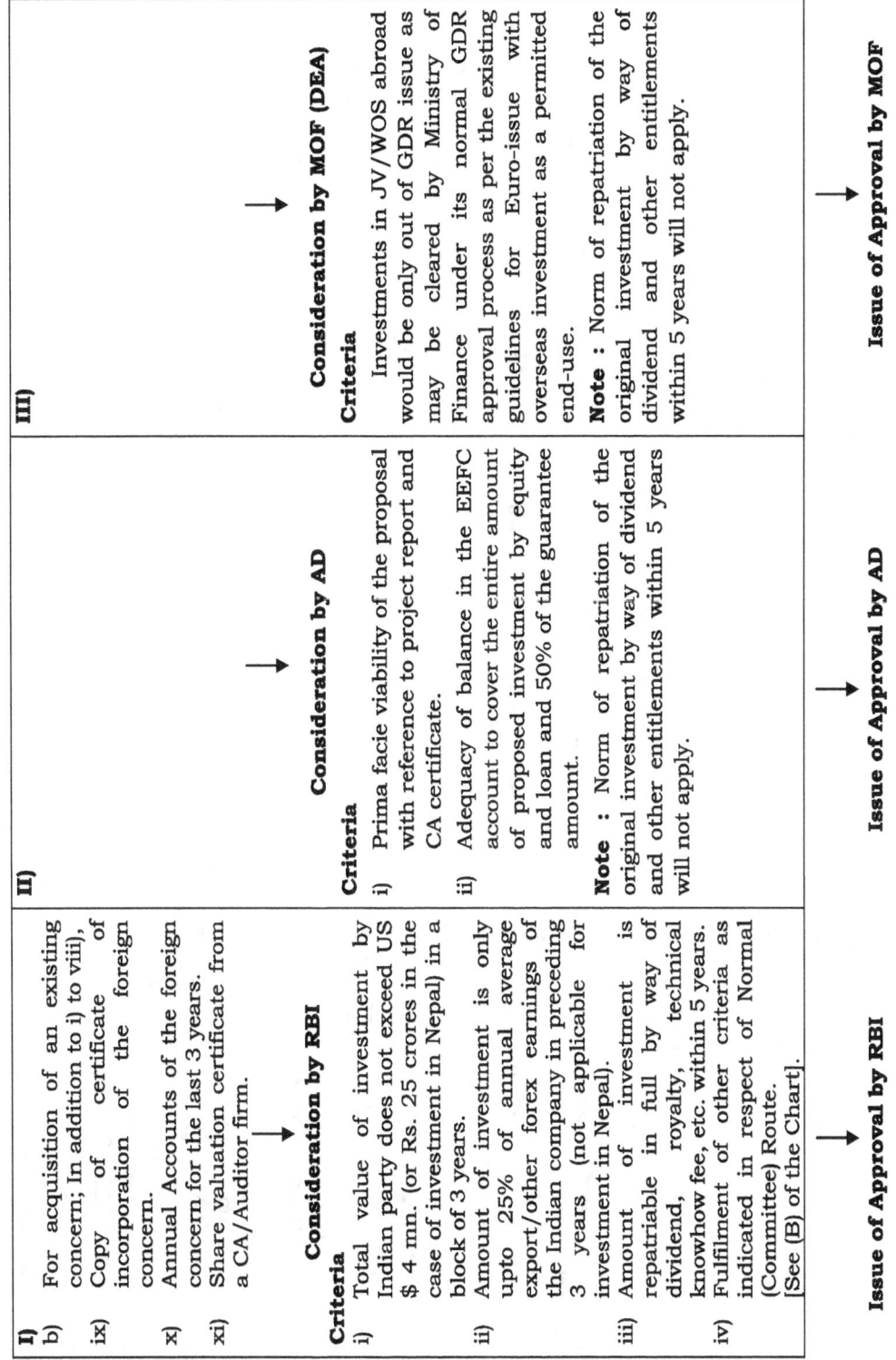

I)

b) For acquisition of an existing concern; In addition to i) to viii),

ix) Copy of certificate of incorporation of the foreign concern.

x) Annual Accounts of the foreign concern for the last 3 years.

xi) Share valuation certificate from a CA/Auditor firm.

Consideration by RBI

Criteria

i) Total value of investment by Indian party does not exceed US $ 4 mn. (or Rs. 25 crores in the case of investment in Nepal) in a block of 3 years.

ii) Amount of investment is only upto 25% of annual average export/other forex earnings of the Indian company in preceding 3 years (not applicable for investment in Nepal).

iii) Amount of investment is repatriable in full by way of dividend, royalty, technical knowhow fee, etc. within 5 years.

iv) Fulfilment of other criteria as indicated in respect of Normal (Committee) Route. [See (B) of the Chart].

Issue of Approval by RBI

II)

Consideration by AD

Criteria

i) Prima facie viability of the proposal with reference to project report and CA certificate.

ii) Adequacy of balance in the EEFC account to cover the entire amount of proposed investment by equity and loan and 50% of the guarantee amount.

Note : Norm of repatriation of the original investment by way of dividend and other entitlements within 5 years will not apply.

Issue of Approval by AD

III)

Consideration by MOF (DEA)

Criteria

Investments in JV/WOS abroad would be only out of GDR issue as may be cleared by Ministry of Finance under its normal GDR approval process as per the existing guidelines for Euro-issue with overseas investment as a permitted end-use.

Note : Norm of repatriation of the original investment by way of dividend and other entitlements within 5 years will not apply.

Issue of Approval by MOF

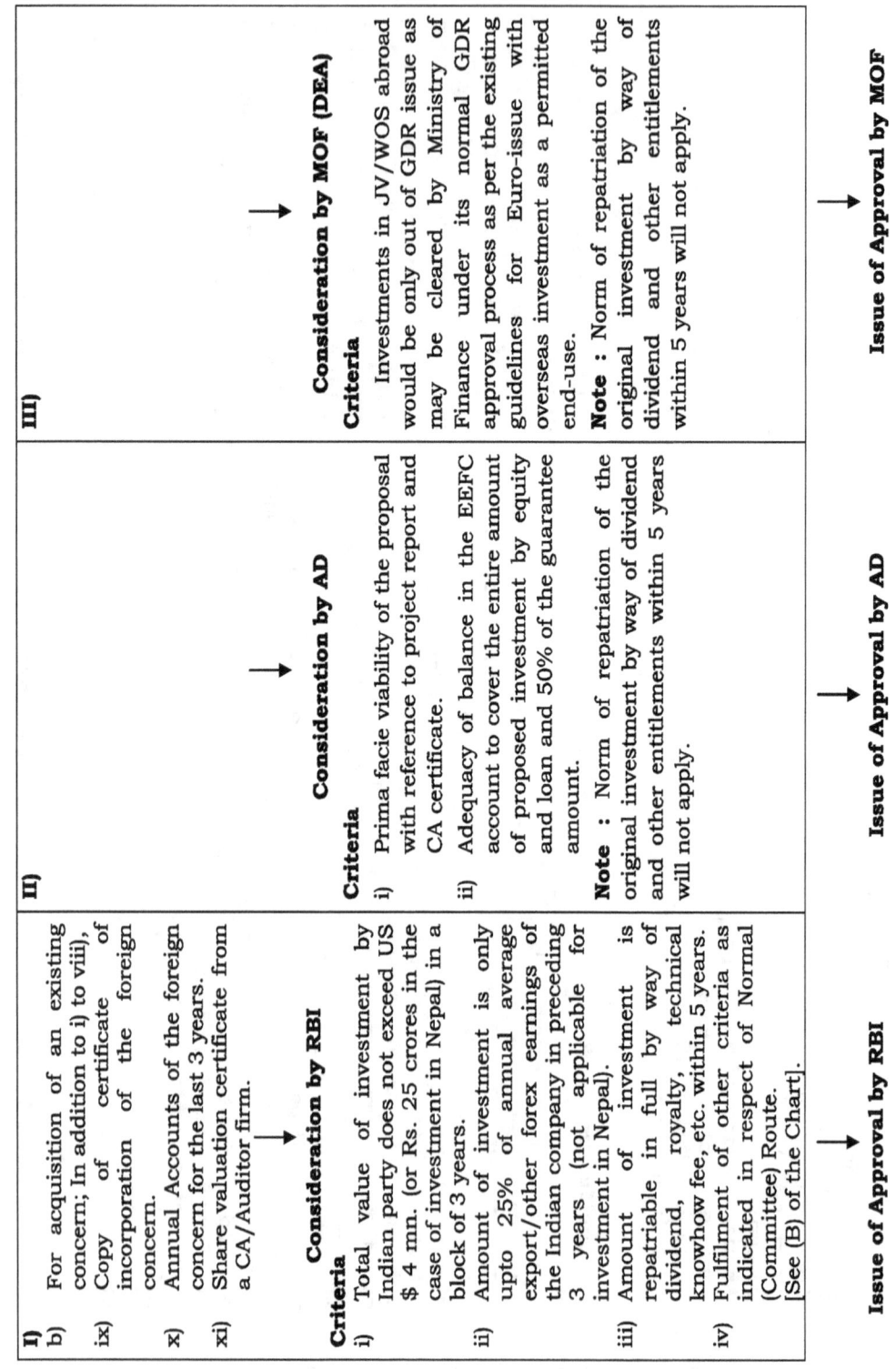

I)

b) For acquisition of an existing concern; In addition to i) to viii),

ix) Copy of certificate of incorporation of the foreign concern.

x) Annual Accounts of the foreign concern for the last 3 years.

xi) Share valuation certificate from a CA/Auditor firm.

Consideration by RBI

Criteria

i) Total value of investment by Indian party does not exceed US $ 4 mn. (or Rs. 25 crores in the case of investment in Nepal) in a block of 3 years.

ii) Amount of investment is only upto 25% of annual average export/other forex earnings of the Indian company in preceding 3 years (not applicable for investment in Nepal).

iii) Amount of investment is repatriable in full by way of dividend, royalty, technical knowhow fee, etc. within 5 years.

iv) Fulfilment of other criteria as indicated in respect of Normal (Committee) Route. [See (B) of the Chart].

Issue of Approval by RBI

II)

Consideration by AD

Criteria

i) Prima facie viability of the proposal with reference to project report and CA certificate.

ii) Adequacy of balance in the EEFC account to cover the entire amount of proposed investment by equity and loan and 50% of the guarantee amount.

Note : Norm of repatriation of the original investment by way of dividend and other entitlements within 5 years will not apply.

Issue of Approval by AD

III)

Consideration by MOF (DEA)

Criteria

Investments in JV/WOS abroad would be only out of GDR issue as may be cleared by Ministry of Finance under its normal GDR approval process as per the existing guidelines for Euro-issue with overseas investment as a permitted end-use.

Note : Norm of repatriation of the original investment by way of dividend and other entitlements within 5 years will not apply.

Issue of Approval by MOF

Global Financial Instruments

The two major categories of equity linked instruments used in international borrowing are IDRs and ECB.

The Global Financial Instruments are shown below in Figure 3.12.

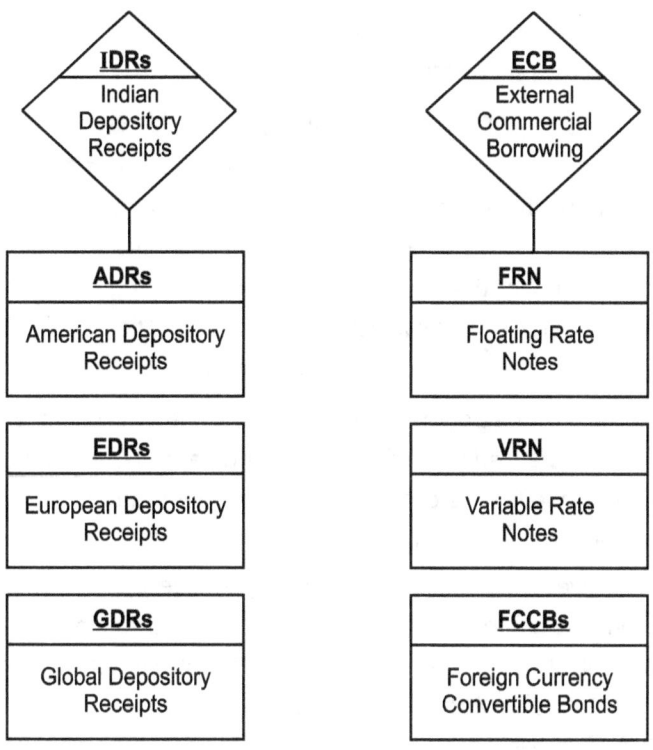

Fig. 3.12 : Global Financial Instruments

The two major categories of equity linked instruments used in international borrowing are Indian Depository Receipts and External Commercial Borrowings.

INDIAN DEPOSITORY RECEIPTS (IDR's)

The various types of IDRs are ADRs, EDRs and GDRs. ADRs are American Depository receipts, created in the U.S.A. wherein a U.S. Depository bank would hold a predetermined number of foreign securities and issue against them tradable ADRs, thus turning them into dollar denominated instruments.

If these are EDRs, there are European Depository Receipts, which are issued to in Europe by an Indian company with an European bank holding the securities of issuing company and Depository Receipts are issued on the basis at the foreign securities held with it and these EDRs are tradable in Europe, where the Clearing system called Euroclear and CEDEL is used.

GDRs are instruments of equity linked nature which can be traded in multiple markets, outside the domestic market of the issuer. A GDR represents one or more equity shares with a right to the holder for conversion into underlying shares. The underlying shares are already listed on domestic stock Exchanges. The holders of GDRs do not carry any voting rights but only dividends and capital appreciation.

The various types of Indian Depository Receipts are as follows :

American Depository Receipts (ADRs)

An American Depository Receipt (CADR) is a physical certificate evidencing ownership in one or several ADSs. The terms ADR and ADS are often used interchangeably.

An American Depository Share (ADS) is it US dollar denominated form of equity ownership in a non-US company. It represents the foreign shares of the company held on deposit by a custodian bank in the company's home country and carries the corporate and economic rights of the foreign shares subject to the terms specified on the ADR certificate.

Concept of ADRs

ADRs are convertible at the option of the holder into the underlying shares. The issue of ADR, requires the SEC clearance in USA for which the details of the issuing company has to be provided to them. The ADRs are optionally convertible into underlying securities but not compulsorily. ADRs are tradable only in the U.S.

ADRs provide US investors with a convenient way to invest in non-US securities without having to worry about the complex details of cross-border transactions, they offer the same economic benefits enjoyed by the domestic shareholders of the non-US company. ADRs are issued by a US bank such as JP Morgan, that functions as a depository on behalf of the non-US company. Each ADR is backed by a specific number or fraction of shares in the non-US company. The relationship between the number of ADRs and the number of foreign shares is typically referred to as the ADR ratio.

ADRs can be listed on any of the US exchanges, such as the New York Stock Exchange (NYSE) and the American Stock Exchange (AMEX) and may be quoted for trading on the National Association of Securities Dealers Automated Quotation System (NASDAQ), the NASD's over-the-counter market or the pink sheets. They can also be privately placed and traded. The concept of ADR has been extended to other geographical markets, resulting in structures known as Global Depository Receipts (GDRs) International Depository Receipts (IDRs) and European Depository Receipts (EDRs), which are generally traded or listed in one or more international markets.

Although ADRs are US dollar denominated securities and pay dividends in US dollars, they do not eliminate the currency risk associated with an investment in a non-US company. The **Types of American Depository Receipts** (ADRs) are shown below in Figure 3.13.

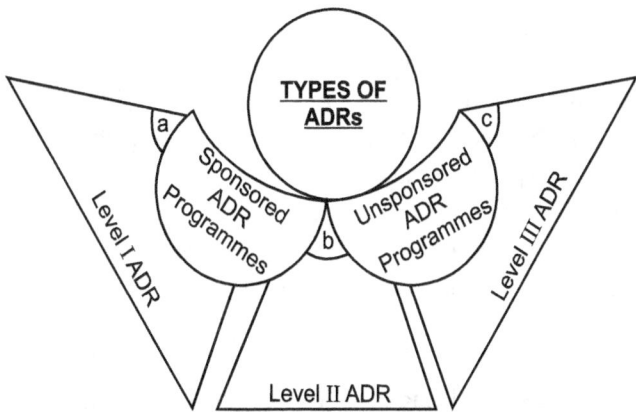

Fig. 3.13 : Types of American Depository Receipts (ADR's)

Sponsored and Unsponsored ADR Programmes

These ADRs are created and offered to the investors with a company's active participation hence the name sponsored ADRs.

Issuers seeking the benefits of ADRs generally pursue what are called sponsored ADR programmes. They initiate the process and working with a depositary bank, actively manage the programme going forward.

The issuer benefits by making a strategic foray into the US market, controlling its image and reputation in the capital markets. In general, only sponsored ADRs can be listed on the major stock exchanges or quoted under the NASDAQ system. While most new ADR programs are sponsored, many unsponsored programmes (in which the ADRs are created and offered to investors without a company's active participation) still exist.

a) Level I American Depository Receipt (ADR)

The most basic form of sponsored ADR programme is a Level I ADR. Level I ADR is used when the issuer is not initially seeking to raise capital in the US markets or does not wish to, or can't, list its ADRs on an exchange or on NASDAQ. Level I ADR programme offers an easy and relatively inexpensive way for an issuer to gauge interest in its securities and begin building a presence in the US securities markets.

Trading

Level 1 ADRs are traded in the Over-the-Counter (OTC) market. With bid and ask prices published daily and distributed by the National Daily Quotation Bureau in the pink sheets. Prices may also be posted on the OTC Bulletin Board (OTCBB). Due to the SEC's recent permanent approval of the OTCBB system, however, effective from 1st April, 1998 all non-US equity securities, including ADRs, must be registered with the SEC pursuant to Section 12 of the 1934 Securities Exchanges Act to remain eligible for quotation in the OTCBB system.

Regulations and Disclosure

Level I ADR programmes currently require minimal Securities Exchange Commission (SEC) registration. The issuer seeks exemption from the SEC's traditional reporting requirements. Under this exemption, the company agrees to send to the SEC summaries or copies of any public reporting documents required in its home market (including documents for regulatory agencies, stock exchanges, or direct shareholder communications). The depository, working with the issuer, also files the Form F-6 registration statement with the SEC in order to establish the programme.

b) Level II : American Depository Receipt (ADR)

In a Level II ADR programme, the ADRs are listed on the US securities exchange or quoted on NASDAQ, thereby offering higher visibility in the US market, more active trading and greater liquidity.

Trading

Level II ADRs can be listed and traded on one of' the US securities exchanges (including NYSE, AMEX, and others). Alternatively, they can be quoted on NASDAQ.

Regulations and Disclosure

Level II ADR programmes must comply with the full registration and reporting requirements of the SEC's Exchange Act, which entails the following :

    i)   Form F-6 registration statement, to register the ADRs to be issued.

    ii)   Form 20-F registration statement, which contains detailed financial disclosure about the issuer, including financial statements and a reconciliation of those statements to US GAAP to register the listing of the ADRs.

    iii)   Annual reports and any interim financial statements submitted on a regular, timely basis to the SEC.

c) Level III American Depository Receipt (ADR)

In the most high-profile form of sponsored AUK programme, Level III, an issuer floats a public offering of ADRs in the United States and lists the ADRs on one of the US exchanges or NASDAQ. The benefits of a Level III programme are substantial. It allows the issuer to raise capital and leads to much greater visibility in the US market.

Trading

Level III ADRs can be listed and traded on one of the U.S. Securities exchanges (including NYSE and AMEX) or on NASDAQ.

Regulations and Disclosure

Level III ADR programmes must comply with various SEC rules, including the full registration and reporting requirements of the SEC's Exchange Act. This entails the following :

    i)   Form F-6 registration statement, to register the ADRs.

    ii)   Form 20-F registration statement, an annual filing that Contains detailed financial disclosure from the issuer, including financial Statements and a full reconciliation of those statements to US GAAP.

    iii)   Form F-1, to register the equity securities underlying the ADRs that are offered publicly in the US for the first time, including a prospectus to inform potential investors about the company and the risks inherent in its businesses, the offering, price for the securities and the plan for distributing the shares.

iv)   Annual reports and any interim financial statements submitted on a regular, timely basis to the SEC and to all registered public shareholders.

Pricing of American Depository Receipts

As per the norms laid down by the finance ministry, companies going in for domestic offering of shares and a simultaneous or follow-on offering in the ADR/GDR would be exempt from the pricing guidelines for overseas offerings, provided the ADR/GDRs are priced at or above the domestic offer price.

To avail oneself of the exemption, follow-on overseas offering has to be within 30 days of the domestic issue.

The Finance Ministry has said that companies going for such simultaneous or immediate follow-on offering will have to take SEBI's approval and that the capital market regulator would specify the percentage to be offered in the domestic and ADR/GDR markets.

In its guidelines for GDRs/FCCBs, the Government had stipulated that the overseas offering should he made at a price not less than the higher of the following two averages i) The average of the weekly high and low of the closing prices of the related shares quoted on the stock exchange during the six months preceding the relevant date; ii) The average of the weekly high and low of the closing prices of the related shares quoted on a stock exchange during the two weeks preceding the relevant date.

The 'relevant date' would be the date 30 days prior to the date on which the meeting of the general body of shareholders is held, in terms of Section 81 (IA) of the Companies Act, 1956, for considering the proposed issue.

The pricing guidelines were part of a major revision of the guidelines on ADRs/GDRs/FCCBs whereby the Finance Ministry has made it mandatory for unlisted companies that have raised funds from such overseas offerings to list on the domestic stock exchanges within a stipulated time frame.

European Depository Receipts (EDRs)

EDRs and GDRs are similar to ADRs that they are primarily aimed at non-US resident investors and are intended to trade mainly in markets outside the US.

EDRs are used by corporations (of whatever country) to enable their shares to be indirectly purchased by individuals in Europe but not in the US market or other markets. EDRs in Europe trade through various Euromarket clearing systems such as Euroclear and Cedel and many are listed on the major European stock exchanges.

By way of contrast, GDRs will trade in two or more markets such as Europe and Asia. Normally, EDRs and GDRs are priced in US dollars thereby enabling non-resident investors to indirectly trade in the issuing company's stock without the risk of holding investments denominated in a possibly weak local currency.

EDRs and GDRs have low commission costs compared with shares bought directly in the overseas markets. EDRs and GDRs also provide the following benefits to issuer companies.

EDRs and GDRs serve to increase the liquidity of the shares of the issuer company globally.

EDRs and GDRs provide a means of accessing international capital markets.

EDRs and GDRs may be purchased through most major brokerage firms and international financial institutions.

A non-residential investor may easily purchase a share ownership interest in overseas companies with the help of EDR and GDR transactions.

Issue of Euro-Convertible Bond (ECB)

Indian companies are allowed to borrow abroad in the Euro-currency markets and foreign capital market since 1992. Thus, short-term paper is issued in the form of Euro currency notes at rates linked to LIBOR. These rates are cheaper than those in India. Besides, Euro-currency bonds of medium to long-term nature are issued as debt instruments. Some of these bonds are convertible into equity shares of Indian companies at a future date. Foreign currency bonds are debt instruments while GDRs are equity instruments of Indian companies, denominated in foreign currencies, quoted and traded in foreign markets. Only companies with high credit rating are allowed to borrow abroad either through FCBs or GDRs. With the globalisation of the market, Indian banks as much as Indian companies have been taking recourse to foreign funds more frequently.

ECB or Euro-convertible bond is a quasi equity instrument, issued outside the domestic market with an option to convert this debt instrument into one or more equity shares at a pre-determined price. Till conversion it carries an interest paid in dollars but this rate is lower than on a fixed coupon bond and the difference reflects the conversion value of the bond. If the company is doing well, stock prices will be rising and the investor in ECB captures the premium. The company as well as the investor benefits from this method. The company can benefit by securing funds when it is not ready to service equity and hopes to earn enough after a period to service larger equity due to conversion of ECB.

Global Depository Receipts (GDRs)

Global Depository Receipts are equity linked instruments, representing the equity shares of a specific number (of 1 to 10 shares) denominated in a foreign currency and traded abroad. Indian government encouraged the companies to go for foreign borrowings and in particular of equity.

A GDR is tradable both in Europe and America, as it raises capital both in Europe and America, through a uniform security. In 1990, Rule 144A was adopted by SEC to facilitate secondary market trading in non-fungible unregistered securities among the qualified institutional buyers. This eliminates the registration requirements of the U.S. Securities Act of 1933, with the SEC. The right of conversion into underlying securities is optional and converted securities do not carry any exchange risk, unless they are sold in the issuing company's country. Issue of GDRs raises foreign funds, enhances the issuing company's image and broadens the market into a global stage.

Many companies seek to raise capital in the US markets privately by issuing restricted securities Under Rule 144A, which do not require SEC review. Rule 144A facilitates the trading of privately placed securities by sophisticated institutional investors (also known as Qualified Institutional Buyers, or QIBs; they must own or manage at least $100 million in securities).

GDRs allow issuers to raise Capital in two or more markets simultaneously, thus broadening their shareholder base. They can be settled outside the US (using a link connecting the two major European clearance and settlement facilities, Euro Clear and Cedel, with the major US clearance and settlement facility, the Depository Trust Company, or DTC) and can be traded in the Rule 144A private market. Under SEC Regulations, securities offered or sold to investors outside the US are not subject to SEC registration requirements.

GDRs being equity, will have no maturity as in the case of ECB. The currency in which it is denominated is generally dollar and its listing is done in Europe and USA, namely, London, Luxemburg, New York, etc. Unlike the ECB it will have no coupon rate, but the price is decided on the basis of the market price ruling in the immediate past. The commission paid on GDR is generally more at say 3-5% as against 2-5% in the case of ECBs.

The issue expenses include management fee (of around 0.5% to 1.0%) underwriting fee (of around 1 to 2%) selling expenses (of around 2 to 3%), leading to a total commission of around 5% in the case of GDRs. The same will be lower at around 3% in the case of ECBs for the simple reason that they are easier to sell due to less risk involved in ECBs.

Role Custodian in GDR Transactions

GDRs do not give any rights of voting unlike equity shares issued domestically. They are something like non-voting shares of Equity. The domestic shares are held with a domestic bank, as a custodian. Besides, there will be depository bank in Europe or America, who issues the GDRs for sale to the lead Managers and underwriters and who are responsible to the investors for the underlying shares, for collection of dividends, rights, bonus and other entitlements to be given to the investors of GDRs on a pro rata basis. The custodian is responsible to the depository bank and has to arrange for sale of underlying shares in the domestic market and remit the foreign exchange proceeds to the depository bank to be paid to the ultimate investor. The custodian has to observe the domestic Exchange Control and Tax laws, as applicable to these transactions.

EXTERNAL COMMERCIAL BORROWINGS (ECB's)

As referred to earlier, Global new issues are in the form of GDRs, ECBs, Straights, FRN, VRN, Warrants and Convertibles. Straights are Euro-bonds in the form of debt instruments with a fixed maturity period and a fixed rate of interest.

ECB Policy of the Government

All corporates and institutions are permitted to raise ECBs upto 20 million U.S. dollars with an average maturity of 3 years, for all corporate objectives except real estate and stock market investments. Corporates with foreign exchange earnings are permitted to raise upto thrice the average amount of annual exports during the previous three years, subject to a ceiling of U.S. $ 100 million without end use restrictions. Holding companies and promoters are permitted to raise ECB upto a ceiling of U.S. $ 50 million to finance equity investment in a subsidiary or J.V. implementing the infrastructure projects. Interest rate spreads are linked to LIBOR and maturity periods. (**London Inter Bank Offer Rate (LIBOR)**).

Corporates can draw on ECBs for 8 years and above but less than 16 years upto an amount of U.S. $ 100 million and above 16 years upto an amount of U.S. $ 200 million. Long-term debt instrument should not include any "Put" or "Call" options which may reduce the stated maturities. All financial intermediaries, including DFIs are required to observe the maturity criteria for on-lending and extend the loans within 12 months of drawing on them. They can also lend for rupee expenditure and ECBs can be used for import of capital goods and services and project related rupee expenditure.

The RBI is the sanctioning Authority for short-term loans upto 3 years and the other cases have to go to the Ministry of Finance. Rollover of an ECB or inter corporate Swapping of ECBs is not permitted. Corporates can, however, undertake liability management for hedging the interest rate and exchange rate risk on their underlying foreign currency exposure without prior approval through interest rate Swaps, Currency Swaps, Coupon Swaps and forward rate agreements.

Changes in ECB Policy of the Agreement

During 2001-03, the Govt. discouraged the external commercial borrowings, due to growing forex reserves. Short-term borrowings in particular are discouraged. External commercial borrowings for infrastructure financing for long-term is the favoured route. In April 2004, there was a revised policy which increased eligibility limits for automatic rate upto U.S. $ 500 million, as against the earlier limit of $ U.S. 50 million.

ECB would be allowed to all corporates, except banks, FIs and NBFCs. FIs are eligible to the extent of their participation in the Restructuring to textile and steel sector. End use restrictions were removed in January 2004, but replaced in April 2004. They are not allowed for working capital or other corporate uses of short-term nature, for repayments of rupee loans or for further lending. The money cannot be used for investment in capital market or the real estate.

Restrictions on the Interest Rate Spreads

There are also restrictions on the interest rate spreads. For maturities of 3 to 5 years, the maximum spread is 200 basis points above six months LIBOR. For ECBs above 5 years of maturity, the maximum spread is 350 basis points above LIBOR. These restrictions are also applicable to FCLBs.

The automatic route upto $ 20 million will be there for ECBs between 3 to 5 years and upto $ 500 million for ECBs above 5 years. Proposals for short-term credit above U.S. $ 20 million are considered by the RBI on merits. Earlier repayments of ECB by corporates are allowed without any limit in more recent years. As the policy is changing from time to time, one has to update the information from financial press or from the RBI publications.

Raising Resources Abroad through FCCB

An Indian company desirous of raising foreign funds by issuing ordinary shares for equity issues through Foreign Currency Convertible Bonds (FCCBs) is required to obtain necessary approval from Government of India, Ministry of Finance, Department of Economic Affairs. A copy of the application made to "in principle" approval already received from the Ministry of Finance for issue of FCCB should be enclosed, alongwith other required documents to the application in form ODI submitted to the RBI for consideration of large overseas investments proposals.

The scheme to permit Indian companies to raise funds from the international market through Euro issues in the form of FCCBs was announced by Government of India, Ministry of Finance vide their Notification No. S-11 (2J) CCI-II/89/NRI dated the 12th November, 1993.

i) **Track Record :**

An issuing company seeking permission for raising foreign funds by Euro-issues having a consistent track record of good performance, financial or otherwise, for a period of three years shall be allowed to issue FCCBs/GDRs.

ii) **Approvals :**

It will need to obtain prior clearance from Foreign Investment Promotion Board (FIPB) before final approval to the Euro-Issue is given by the Ministry of Finance.

iii) **End-use :**

A company shall be required to specify the proposed end-uses of the issue proceeds at the time of making their application and will be required to submit quarterly statement of utilisation of funds for the approved end-use duly certified by their auditors.

iv) **Repatriation of Proceeds :**

Companies may retain the proceeds abroad or may remit funds into India in anticipation of the use of funds for approved end-uses.

v) **Validity :**

Both the "in principle" and final approvals will be void for three months from the date of their respective issue.

The policy and guidelines for Euro-Issues will be subject to review periodically.

FOREIGN INSTITUTIONAL INVESTORS (FIIS)

Foreign Institutional Investors (FIIs) during the last one decade have become an integral part of Indian equity markets. They have been an incredible source of money ever since. The clout of the FIIs is such that their arrival is anticipated with breathless anxiety by the market players. This reputation of the FIIs is a well-earned status. The authority of these institutions is evident from the very fact that by the mere news of their arrival it is sufficient for the market to supplement itself with a double-digit growth.

As per the definition of RBI, a FII is an institution established or incorporated outside India, which proposes to make investments in Indian securities. Such institutions have been permitted to invest in Indian securities markets starting from September 1992 when the then authorities issued suitable guidelines. The FIIs are subject to stringent monitoring. They are required to register with RBI and the SEBI before they commence their operations.

Foreign Financial Institutions (FFIs) have been permitted by SEBI to operate in India since 1993. They got registration from SEBI and from the RBI under FERA. The registration is valid for 5 years.

These are Foreign Institutions such as pension funds, Mutual funds, Investment Trusts, AMCs, Institutional Portfolio Managers, etc., who operate generally in all money and capital market instruments abroad. They are now operating in Indian money and capital markets as well, but through accepted brokers.

The criteria for granting registration to the FFIs are their track record, professional competency, financial soundness and their experience in their own countries.

Activities Allowed to FIIs by the RBI :

The general permission from the Reserve Bank will enable the FIIs to :

i)   Open foreign currency denominated account (s) with a designated bank,

ii)   Open a special non-resident rupee account to which all receipts from the capital inflows, sale proceeds of shares, dividends and interests could be credited accordingly.

iii)   Transfer sums from the foreign currency accounts to the rupee account and vice-versa, at the market rates of exchange permitted by RBI.

iv)   Make investments in securities in India out of the balances in the rupee account.

v)   Transfer repatriable (after tax) proceeds from the rupee account to the foreign currency account (s).

vi)   Repatriate the capital, capital gains, dividends, incomes received by way of interest, etc., and any compensation received towards sale/renouncement of right offerings of shares.

vii)   Buy, sell and realise capital gains on investments made through the initial corpus remitted to India.

viii)   Subscribe/renounce rights offerings of shares and invest on all recognised stock exchanges through a designated bank branch.

ix)   Appoint a domestic custodian for a custody of investments held.

Rational of Foreign Institutional Investment in India :

Because of following reasons FIIs are optimistic about investing in India.

i)   Exchange rate is stable.

ii)   Domestic Private investment is being encouraged.

iii)   Government's attitude is conducive for healthy competition and industrial growth.

iv)   Economic activity is beginning to rely more on price and market mechanisms.

v)   Macro-economic fundamentals are much stronger today.

vi)   Fiscal reforms have succeeded in a large measure in curtailing inflation.

vii)   The forex position is fine.

viii)   Liberalisation of trade has been accompanied by convertibility of the rupee for trade transactions.

ix)   Progressive management with good credentials.

x)   Sound technological base, quite possibly with foreign collaborations.

xi)   International competitiveness and good export potential.

xii) A widely dispersed share-holding, that rules out the possibility of family funds destabilising the management and performance.

xiii) Market capitalisation greater than ₹ 100 crore or so.

xiv) Participation by other financial institutions like IFC, ICICI, etc.

xv)   The FIIs are investing in Indian stock market because of adoption of the liberalisation measures, political stability, the end of industrial recession, growing marketing potential.

xvi) The stock market booming in other developing countries are flattened out. In India, the situation is otherwise and the foreign funds incoming has been surging in.

SEBI Guidelines for FIIs :

As the regulatory authority of the Indian Capital Market, the SEBI has issued a list of guidelines for FIIs. Some of the important guidelines are listed below :

i)   FIIs would be required to obtain an initial registration with Securities and Exchange Board of India (SEBI), nodal regulatory agency for securities markets, before any investment is made by them in the securities of companies listed on the stock exchanges in India, in accordance with these guidelines. Nominee companies, affiliates and subsidiary companies of a FII will be treated as separate FIIs for registration and may seek separate registration with SEBI.

ii)   Since there are foreign exchange controls also in force, for various permissions under exchange control, along with their application for initial registration, FIIs shall also file with SEBI another application addressed to RBI for seeking various permissions under FERA, in a format that would be specified by RBI for this purpose. RBI's general permission would be obtained by SEBI before granting initial registration and RBI's FERA permission together by SEBI, under a single window approach.

iii) For granting registration to the FII, SEBI shall take into account the track record of the FII, its professional competence, financial soundness, experience and such other criteria that may be considered by SEBI to be relevant. Besides, FIIs seeking initial registration with SEBI shall be required to hold a registration from the securities commission, or the regulatory organisation for the stock market in the country of domicile/incorporation of the FII.

iv)   SEBI's initial registration would be valid for five years. RBI's general permission under FERA to the FII will also hold good for five years. Both will be renewable for similar five years period later on.

v)   RBI's general permission under FERA would enable the registered FII to buy, sell and realise capital gains on investment made through initial corpus remitted to India, subscribe/renounce right offering of shares, invest on all recognised stock exchanges through a designated bank branch, and to appoint a domestic custodian for custody of investments held.

vi)   There would be no restriction on the volume of investment-minimum or maximum for the purpose of entry of FIIs, in the primary/secondary market. Also, there would be no lock-in period prescribed for the purposes of such investments made by FIIs. It is expected that the differential in the rates of taxation of the long-term capital gains and short-term capital gains would automatically induce the FIIs to retain their investments as long-term investments.

vii)   Portfolio investments in primary or secondary markets will be subject to a ceiling of 24 percent of issued share capital for the total holding of all registered FIIs, in any one company. The ceiling would apply to all holdings taking into account the conversions out of the fully and partly convertible debentures issued by the company. The holding of a single FII in any company would also be subject to a ceiling of 5 percent of total issued capital. For   this purpose, the holdings of a FII group will be counted as holding of a single FII.

The RBI has now restricted the foreign institutional investors quota in primary issues. This decision has been taken after complaints that companies are reducing the quota for NRI's in public issue while allotting the full 24% to the FIIs.

viii)   The maximum holding of 24 percent for all nonresident portfolio investments, including those of the registered FIIs, will also include NRI corporate and non-corporate investments, but will not include the following :

   a)   Foreign investments under financial collaborations (direct foreign investments), which are permitted upto 51 percent in all priority areas.

   b)   Investments by FIIs through the following alternative routes :

   c)   Offshore single/Regional Funds :
        • Offshore single/Regional funds;
        • Global Depository Receipts; and
        • Euroconvertibles.

ix)   Disinvestment will be allowed only through stock exchange in India, including the OTC Exchange. In exceptional cases, SEBI may permit sales other than through stock exchanges, provided the sale price is not significantly different from the stock market quotations, where available.

x)   All secondary market operations would be only through the recognised intermediaries on the Indian Stock Exchange, including OTC Exchange of India. A registered FII would be expected not to engage in any short selling in securities and to take delivery of purchased and give delivery of sold securities.

xi)   A registered FII can appoint as custodian an agency approved by SEBI to act as a custodian of securities and for confirmation of transactions in securities, settlement of purchase and sale and for information reporting. Such custodian shall establish separate accounts for detailing on a daily basis the investment capital utilisation and securities held by each FII for which it is acting as custodian. The custodian will report to the RBI and SEBI semi-annually as part of its disclosure and reporting guidelines.

xii) The RBI shall make available to the designated bank branches a list of companies where no investment will be allowed on tile basis of the upper prescribed ceiling of 24 percent having been reached under the portfolio investment scheme.

xiii) RBI may at any time request by an order, a registered FII to submit information regarding the records of utilisation of the inward remittances of investment capital and the statement of securities transactions. RBI and SEBI may at any time conduct a direct inspection of the record and accounting books of a registered FII.

xiv) FIIs investing under this scheme, will benefit from a concessional tax regime of a flat rate tax of 20 percent on dividend and interest income and a tax rate of 10 percent on long-term (one year or more) capital gains.

REGULATION OF FOREIGN CAPITAL

Guidelines of RBI

Participation in Joint Ventures (JV) /Wholly Owned Subsidiaries (WOS) abroad will involve remittance of cash, export of plant and machinery/goods from India towards the Indian promoter company's contribution and acquisition of shares in the overseas concern and will, therefore, require the Reserve Bank's approval under the relevant provisions of the Foreign Exchange Regulation Act (FERA), 1973. Approvals are issued by the Reserve Bank, Exchange Control Department, Central Office in accordance with the revised Guidelines for Indian Direct Investment in JV/WOS abroad notified by the Government of India, Ministry of Commerce vide their Notification No. 4/1/93-FP(OI) dated 17th August, 1995 and further amendments/ modifications as may be notified from time to time

These guidelines do not apply to portfolio investment by Indian parties in foreign concerns. These are also not applicable to direct investment in the banking sector which are separately considered by the Department of Banking Operations and Development, Reserve Bank of India /Department of Economic Affairs, Ministry of Finance under a different set of guidelines. All approvals issued so far by the Regional Offices of the Reserve Bank on the basis of approvals given earlier by the Government of India, Ministry of Commerce shall continue to remain in force subject to the terms and conditions stipulated in the relative approval letters issued by the Government of India and the Reserve Bank and such other directions/instructions as may be issued by the Government of India and the Reserve Bank from time to time.

Procedure for Approval of Proposals by the Reserve Bank

Proposals involving Indian investment not exceeding US $ 4 million (to be contributed through cash remittance and/or capitalisation of exports, technical know-how fees, etc.) will be processed and cleared by the Central Office of the Reserve Bank under the 'Fast Track Route' within a period of 21 days from the date of receipt of, complete application provided i) the investment is upto 25% of the annual average export/other foreign exchange earnings of the Indian party (other than equity exports to their JV/WOS abroad) in the preceding three years, ii) amount of investment is repatriated in full by way of dividend, royalty, etc. within a period of 5 years and iii) the other criteria laid down in the extant guidelines are fulfilled. Proposals for rupee investment in Nepal (in Indian currency) upto 25 crores will be considered by the Reserve Bank under this Fast Track Route without any linkage to the past export/foreign exchange earnings of the Indian promoter companies. However, the requirement of repatriation of the amount of investment by way of dividend, royalty, etc. within a period of 5 years as indicated above will continue to apply in such cases. The Indian promoter company can, however, repatriate all its entitlements in Indian rupees instead of foreign exchange.

Proposals, which do not qualify for clearance under the above Fast Track Route of the Reserve Bank or the Exchange Earners' Foreign Currency (EEFC)/Global Deposit Receipts (GDR) Fast Track windows indicated at paragraph 3.5 below would be processed by the Special Committee constituted for this purpose by the Reserve Bank. The Committee, while considering such proposals, will take into account .the quantum of EEFC/GDR funds to be utilised by the Indian promoter companies for their overseas investment, their net worth, scale of operation and other criteria laid down in the extant guidelines. Proposals involving investment in excess of US $ 15 mn. will be referred to the Ministry of Finance for clearance. After the proposals are cleared by the Committee/the Ministry of Finance, the Reserve Bank will issue the necessary letters of approval. Standard terms and conditions which are stipulated by the Reserve Bank for compliance by the Indian promoter company of the JV/WOS abroad are given in **Appendix A**.

Application in form ODI, together with documents as indicated therein, should be submitted in four sets in respect of proposals coming under the Fast Track Route (including rupee investment in Nepal) and in seven sets in respect of other proposals coming under the Normal Route and Large Investment Route with or without GDR/EEFC funds to the Chief General Manager, Exchange Control Department, Reserve Bank of India, Central Office, Overseas Investment Division (OID), Amar Building, Sir P. M. Road, Fort, Mumbai 400 001. Besides, in respect of cases which do not qualify for clearance under the Fast Track Route of the Reserve Bank, a copy of the proposal should be forwarded simultaneously by speed post/courier to the concerned Indian mission in the host country, as indicated in form ODI (please see Appendix C for the addresses of Indian missions). The format of form ODI, and the detailed instructions for filling up the same and the documents to be enclosed thereto are given in Part B of this Hand Book. Applicants should carefully go through the instructions while submitting the application to the Reserve Bank and should specifically note to submit the following documents :

i)   Draft Joint Venture agreement (or Memorandum and Articles of Association in the case of Wholly Owned Subsidiary) specifying the equity structure, management pattern and rights and responsibilities of shareholders and also draft agreement (s) for extension of technical know-how, management support and other services, if applicable.

ii)   Detailed project/feasibility report incorporating, *inter alia*, projected Funds Flow Statements and Balance Sheets for five years, the information on various leverage and profitability ratios like debt-equity ratio, debt service coverage ratio, return on investments, etc. of the proposed foreign concern accompanied by a statement from a Chartered Accountant (CA) verifying the ratios, projections made, etc. in the report.

iii) A certificate of credit worthiness from the bankers of the Indian applicant in sealed/closed cover,

iv) Certificate(s), in form BCX, from the concerned authorised dealers in support of export performance for the last three years (excluding equity exports) and certificate(s), in form BCI, from the concerned authorised dealers/certificate from Chartered Accountant in support of foreign exchange earnings other than exports, if any.

v) Copy of application made to/'in principle' approval letter obtained from the Ministry of Finance for raising GDR resources for overseas investment, if applicable,

vi) Last three years' Annual Accounts, i.e., Balance Sheet and Profit and Loss Account along with Directors' report of the Indian applicant company,

vii) A list of the plant and machinery/goods proposed to be exported from India against equity in the following proforma, where applicable. (This should be accompanied by a Chartered Engineer's Certificate certifying that the plant and machinery are indigenous and that the prices quoted are reasonable) :

Proforma

List of Plant and Machinery / goods to be exported against equity.

(Amount in INR '000)

Sr. No.	Item with broad specifications	Name and address of the supplier/manufacturer	Number of units	FOB value/unit	Total FOB value	Remarks

viii) A copy of the resolution of the Board of Directors of the Indian promoter company approving the proposed investment,

ix) Additional documents, as under, if the application is made for partial/ full takeover of an existing foreign-concern :

    a) A copy of the certificate of incorporation of the foreign concern;

    b) Copies of Annual Accounts, i.e., the Balance Sheet and Profit and Loss Account alongwith Directors' report of the foreign concern for the last three years; and

    c) A valuation certificate from a Chartered Accountant/Auditor firm justifying the price of the shares/assets of the overseas company,

x) In case of proposals coming under the Fast Track Route of the Reserve Bank, when the applicant does not have the requisite exports/foreign exchange earnings and proposes to avail of the benefit of export/foreign exchange earnings of its parent/subsidiary company, a letter of disclaimer from the latter to the effect that it has not availed of and will not avail of investment, etc. facility under the Fast Track Route to the extent of credit afforded to the applicant company, and

xi) In cases where overseas investments have been made under the EEFC Fast Track Window operated by the authorised dealers, a statement showing the details of such investments (viz., date of approval, RBI identification number, amount approved for each JV/WOS, country of their location, etc.) duly certified by the applicant.

Where the Indian companies require approval under the Companies Act, 1956 or any other law for the time being in force for the proposed overseas investment, it shall be their responsibility to obtain such approvals from the appropriate authority. The requirements under the Companies Act have been indicated in Chapter 4.

Approval letter issued by the Reserve tank will contain the terms and conditions to be complied with as also the procedure to be followed for making actual investment in overseas concern. On receipt of necessary approval from the Central Office of the Reserve Bank, the Indian party should approach the concerned Regional Office of the Exchange Control Department of the Reserve Bank for making exports towards equity participation, effecting remittance towards equity or loan, etc.

Any proposal for addition/deletion of the terms and conditions of approval, change in size and pattern of investment, extension of loan/guarantee from India beyond the limit approved, etc. should be submitted to the Exchange Control Department (OID), Central Office of the Reserve Bank, with a copy to the concerned Regional Office, justifying the need for the proposal along with the latest information on progress and achievements of the overseas concern and the revised projections relating to profitability and repatriable entitlements, wherever necessary. In addition, in respect of supplementary proposals envisaging enhancement of equity and extension/ enhancement of loan/guarantee to the overseas JV/WOS or involving major changes in the existing terms and conditions of approval resulting in revision in the projections of profitability of the overseas concern and the promoter company's entitlements therefrom, application in form ODS should be made to the Reserve Bank for prior approval.

Controlling Authority for Regulating Foreign Capital

There are eight controlling authority which are regulating foreign capital which are,

i)   Government of India, Minister of Finance, Department of Economic Affairs.

ii)   Reserve Bank of India.

iii)   SEBI Act, 1992.

iv)   FERRA 1973.

v)   Securities Contract (Regulation) Act, 1956.

vi)   Foreign Exchange Management Act, 1999.

vii)   Foreign Contribution (Regulation) Act, 1976.

viii) Foreign Trade (Development and Regulation) Act, 1992.

Foreign investments provide a great stimulus for growth to the Indian economy. The continuous inflow of foreign direct investment (FDI), which is now allowed across several industries, manifests the faith that foreign investors have in the country's economy. FDI inflows to India increased to 17 percent in 2013 to reach US $ 28 billion, as per a United Nations report.

India received cumulative FDI inflows (including equity inflows, reinvested earning and other capital) of US $ 331923 million during the period April 2000-May 2014, according to the data published by Department of Industrial Policy and Promotion (DIPP) Government of India. Total FDI equity inflows in India (including amount remitted through RBI's - NRI Schemes) during April 2000 - May 2014 stood at US $ 222,890 million.

FDI inflows in India (US $ in million)

2000-01	2463
2001-02	4065
2002-03	2705
2003-04	2188
2004-05	3219
2005-06	5540
2006-07	12492
2007-08	24575
2008-09	31396
2009-10	25834
2010-11	19427
2011-12	28403

Source: onemint.com.

QUESTIONS FOR SELF-STUDY

I. Theory Questions :

1. What is "Financial Services" ? State the classification of financial services.
2. Define the term 'Merchant Banking'. State the functions of Merchant Bankers.
3. Explain the term 'Merchant Banks' Explain the services rendered by Merchant Banks.
4. What is 'Merchant Banking' ? Explain the recent trends in Merchant Banking.
5. What is 'Mutual Funds' ? State the history and growth of Mutual Funds in India.
6. Define the term 'Mutual Funds'. Explain the functions of Mutual Funds.
7. Explain the term 'Open Ended Funds'. Explain the important features and drawbacks of Open Ended Funds.
8. What is 'Close Ended Funds' ? Explain the important features of Close Ended Funds.
9. Define the term 'Growth Funds'. State the important features of Growth Funds.
10. What is 'Mutual Funds' ? State the advantages and disadvantages of investing in mutual funds.
11. What do you understand by 'Portfolio Management'. Explain the important aspects of Portfolio Management.

12. Explain how the risk and return of a two security portfolio can be measured.
13. What is 'Credit Rating' ? Explain the need of Credit Rating.
14. Define the term 'Credit Rating'. Explain the functions of credit rating firms.
15. Explain the term 'Credit Rating'. Explain the Credit Rating Agencies in India.
16. Distinguish between : i) Fund based financial activities and Non-fund based financial activities, ii) Open ended funds and Close ended funds, iii) Income funds and Balanced funds, iv) Systematic risk and Unsystematic risk.
17. What is 'Foreign Investment' ? State the need of Foreign Investment.
18. Define the term 'Foreign Investment'. Explain the importance of Foreign Investment in Indian Capital Market.
19. Explain the following important terms related to Indian Direct Investment Abroad i) Direct Investment, ii) Host Country, iii) Indian Party, iv) Joint Venture and v) Wholly Owned Subsidary.
20. State the importance of Indian Depository Receipts as a equity linked instrument used in international borrowings.
21. What is 'American Depository Receipts' ? State the types of American Depository Receipts (ADRs).
22. What is 'External Commercial Borrowings' (ECB's) ? Explain the ECB policy of the Government.
23. Define the term "Foreign Investment Investors". State the activities allowed to Foreign Institutional Investors by the RBI.
24. Write short notes on :

    i) Classification of financial services, ii) Origin of Merchant Banking, iii) Merchant Banking in India, iv) Merchant Bankers Commission, iv) Pre-issue Management Functions of Merchant Bankers, vi) Post-Issue Management Functions of Merchant Bankers, vii) Organisational Structure of a Mutual Fund, viii) Role of SEBI in Mutual Fund Industry, ix) Features of Income Funds, x) Features of Balanced Funds, xi) Growth Funds, xii) Index Funds, xiii) Off Shore Funds, xiv) Time Value of Money, xv) Portfolio Management Services, xvi) Features of Credit Rating, xvii) Credit Rating Codes, xviii) Methodology of Rating, xix) Credit Rating Information Services Ltd. (CRISIL), xx) Investment Information and Credit Rating Agency of India Ltd. (ICRA), xxi) Credit Analysis and Research Ltd. (CARE), xxii) Future of Credit Rating, xxiii) Foreign Investment, xxiv) Need of Foreign Investment, xxv) Direct Investment, xxvi) Need for RBI Guidelines for Indian Direct Investment Abroad, xxvii) European Depository Receipts (EDR's), xxviii) Euro-convertible Bond, xxix) Global Depository Receipts (GDRs), xxix) Rational of Foreign Institutional Investors in India, xxx) Regulation of Foreign Capital.

4...

Securities
and
Exchange Board of India (SEBI)

The SEBI Act 1992, established SEBI with statutory powers for protecting the interest of investors in securities, promoting the development of the securities market and regulating the securities market. Its regulatory jurisdiction extends over corporates in the issuance of capital and transfer of securities, in addition to all intermediaries and persons associated with securities market. SEBI can conduct enquiries, audits and inspection of all concerned and adjudicate offence under the Act. SEBI has powers to register and regulate all market intermediaries and also to penalise them in case of violations of the provisions of the Act, Rules and Regulations made there under. As per the provisions of Act, SEBI has full autonomy and authority to regulate and develop an orderly security market. The Rules under the securities laws are framed by Government and regulations by SEBI. All these are administered by SEBI.

4.1 BACKGROUND

The capital market comprises two components namely, new issues market where companies issues directly securities to the public and the stock market or the secondary market where existing securities are bought and sold.

Trading in old securities is governed by the Securities Contract (Regulations) Act of 1956 and the Securities Contract (Regulation) Rules of 1957. The Act was provided for recognition to the Stock Exchanges and gave wide ranging powers to the Government to control and regulate the Stock Exchanges.

These legislations contained several provisions relating to the issue of prospectus, disclosure of accounting and financial information, listing of securities etc.

Securities market in India witnessed a phenomenal growth in the 1980s leading to financial disintermediation with corporate sector placing increasing, greater reliance on the market for satisfying their long-term financial needs and emergence of new intermediaries and institutions in the country and thereby developing a new awareness and interest in investment opportunities.

For the first time, the securities market showed a potential not only to mobilise the savings of the household market sector but also to allocate it with some degree of efficiency for industrial development. The corporate sector relied on the security market for meeting its long term requirements of funds. Several companies raised large resources from the market especially through debt instruments. The changes in the capital structure of companies gave birth to new intermediaries and institutions in the security market and thereby created new investment opportunities and awareness among the investors.

However, quality of transaction in the securities market was not adequate and theme was lack of professionalism and healthy competition among the various players in the markets.

With the growth of securities market, the number of malpractices also increased in both the primary and secondary markets. The malpractices were noticed in the case of companies, merchant bankers and brokers who are all operating in the market.

Under these circumstances, the Government felt the need for setting up of an apex body to develop and regulate the stock market in India. Eventually, the Securities and Exchange Board of India (SEBI) was set up on 12th April, 1988. To start with, SEBI was set up as a non-statutory body.

It took almost four years for the government to bring about a separate legislation in the name of Securities and Exchange Board of India Act, 1992 conferring statutory powers. The Act, charged to SEBI with comprehensive powers over practically all aspects of capital market operations.

Dual Objectives of SEBI

Securities Exchange Board of India (SEBI) was established on 12th April 1988 with the dual objective of protecting the rights of small investors and regulating and developing stock markets in India. The Board was subsequently upgraded as a fully autonomous body (a Statutory Board) in the year 1992 by passing a SEBI Act on 30th January, 1992.

In place of Government control, a statutory and autonomous regulatory board with defined responsibilities to cover both development and regulation of the market and independent powers has been set-up.

The **basic objectives** of the Board were identified as follows :

i)   To protect the Interest of investors in securities,

ii)   To promote the development of Securities Market,

iii)   To regulate the securities market,

iv)　To promote fair dealing by the issuers of securities and ensure a market place where they can raise funds at relatively low cost,

v)　To provide a degree of protection to investors and safeguard their rights and interests so that there is steady flow of savings into the market, and

vi)　To regulate and develop a code of conduct and fair practices by intermediaries like brokers, and merchant bankers with a view to make them competitive and professional.

Since inception, SEBI has been working towards targeting of securities and trying to fulfill its objectives with commendable zeal and dexterity.

Administration of SEBI

The Securities and Exchange Board of India Act, 1992 came into force on 30th January, 1992. Under this Act a Board named Securities and Exchange Board of India (SEBI) was constituted under the SEBI Act to administer its provisions.

The board consists of one chairman and five members : One each from the department of Finance and Law of the Central Government, one from the Reserve Bank of India and two other persons and having its head office in Mumbai and regional offices in Delhi, Kolkata and Chennai. The Central Government reserves the right to terminate the services of the Chairman or any member of the Board. The Board decides questions in the meeting by Majority vote with the Chairman having a second or casting vote.

Section 11 of the SEBI Act provides that to protect the interest of investors in securities and to promote the development and regulate the securities market by such measures, is the duty of the Board. It has given power to the Board to –

i)　regulate the businesses in Stock Exchanges

ii)　register and regulate the working of stock brokers, sub-brokers, share transfer agents, bankers to an issue, trustees of trust deeds, registrar to in issue, merchant bankers, underwriters, portfolio managers, investment advisors etc.,

iii)　to register and regulate the working of collective investment schemes including mutual funds,

iv)　to prohibit fraudulent and unfair trade practices and insider trading, to regulate takeover, to conduct enquiries and audits of stock exchanges etc.

All the stock brokers, sub-brokers, share transfer agents, bankers to an issue, merchant bankers, underwriters, portfolios managers, investment advisors and other such intermediary who may be associated with the Securities Markets are to register with the Board under the provisions of the Act under Section 12 of the SEBI Act. The Board has the power to cancel or suspend such registration.

The Board is bound by the direction vested by the Central Government from time to time on questions of policy and the Central Government reserves the right to supersede the Board. The Board is also obliged to submit a report to the Central Government giving true and full account of its activities, policies and programmes.

Organisation

Chapter II of the SEB1 Act deals with establishment, incorporation, administration and management of the Board of Directors etc. The SEBI Act provides for the establishment of a statutory board consisting of six members. The chairman and two members are to be appointed by the Central Government, one member to be appointed by the Reserve Bank and two members having experience of securities market to be appointed by the Central Government. Section II deals with the powers of the Board.

The **Activities of SEBI** are shown below in Figure 4.1.

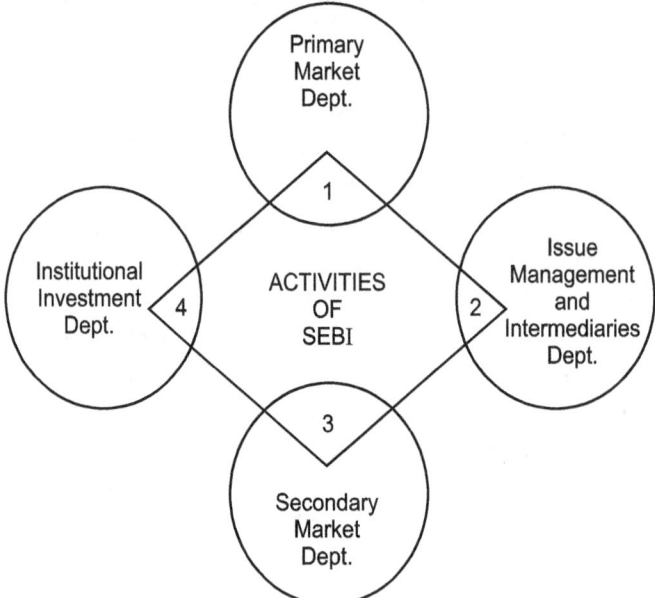

Fig. 4.1 : Activities of SEBI

SEBI has divided its activities into four operational departments namely primary market department, issue management and intermediaries department, secondary market department and institutional department, each headed by an Executive Director. Apart from these, there are two other departments viz., Legal Department and Investigation Department, also headed by officials of the rank of Executive Directors.

1) **Primary Market Department :**

   Primary market department deals with all policy matters and regulatory issues relating to primary market, market intermediaries and matters pertaining to SRO's and redressal of investor grievances.

2) **Issue Management and Intermediaries Department :**

   This department is concerned with vetting of offer documents and other things like registration, regulation and monitoring of issue related to intermediaries.

3) Secondary Market Department :

It looks after all the policy and regulatory issues for the secondary market; administration of the major stock exchanges and other matters related to it.

4) Institutional Investment Department :

This department is concerned with framing policy for foreign institutional investors, mutual funds and other matters like publications, membership in international organisations, etc.

SEBI has two Advisory Committees, one each for primary and secondary markets. The committees are constituted from among the market players, recognised investor associations and eminent persons associated with the capital market. They provide advisory inputs in framing policies and regulations. These committees are non-statutory in nature and SEBI is not bound by the committees.

The Central Government has the power to issue directions to the SEBI Board, to supersede the Board, if necessary and to call for returns and report etc. as and when necessary. The Central Government has also powers to give any guidelines or to make regulations and rules for SEBI and its operations.

The activities of SEBI are financed by grants from the Government in addition to fees, charges etc. collected by SEBI. The fund called the SEBI General Fund, is set up to which all grants, fees, charges etc. are credited. The fund is used to meet the expenses of the Board and to pay salaries of staff and remuneration to officers, members of the Board etc.

4.2 ESTABLISHMENT

Establishment and Incorporation of Board

i)   With effect from such date as the Central Government may, by notification, appoint, there shall be established, for the purposes of this Act, a Board by the name of the Securities and Exchange Board of India.

ii) The Board shall be a body corporate by the name aforesaid, having perpetual succession and a common seal, with power subject to the provisions of this Act, to acquire hold and dispose of property, both movable and immovable, and to contract, and shall, by the said name, sue or be sued.

iii) The head office of the Board shall be at Mumbai.

iv) The Board may establish offices at other places in India.

Management of the Board

i)   Board shall consist of the following members namely :

   a)   Chairman;

   b)   two members from amongst the officials of the [Ministry] of the Central Government dealing with Finance [and administration of the Companies Act, 1956 (1 of 1956)];

c)   one member from amongst the officials of [the Reserve Bank];

d)   five other members of whom at least three shall be whole-time members.

to be appointed by the Central Government.

ii)   The general superintendence, direction and management of the affairs of the Board shall vest in a Board of members, which may exercise all powers and do all acts and things which may be exercised or done by the Board,

iii)   Save as otherwise determined by regulations, the Chairman shall also have powers of general superintendence and direction of the affairs of the Board and may also exercise all powers and do all acts and things which may be exercised or done by that Board.

iv)   The Chairman and members referred to in clauses (a) and (d) of sub-section (1) shall be appointed by the Central Government and the members referred to in clauses (b) and (c) of that sub-section shall be nominated by the Central Government and the [Reserve Bank] respectively.

v)   The Chairman and the other members referred to in clauses (a) and ((d) of sub-section (1) shall be persons of ability, integrity and standing who have shown capacity in dealing with problems relating to Securities market or have special knowledge or experience of law, finance, economics, accountancy, administration or in any other discipline which, in the opinion of the Central Government, shall be useful to the Board.

Term of office and conditions of service of Chairman and members of the Board :

i)   The term of office and other conditions of service of the Chairman and the members referred to in clause (d) of sub-section (1) of section 4 shall be such as may be prescribed.

ii)   Notwithstanding anything contained in sub-section (1), the Central Government shall have the right to terminate the services of the Chairman or a member appointed under clause (d) of sub-section (1) of section 4, at any time before the expiry of the period prescribed under sub-section (1), by giving him notice of not less than three months in writing or three months' salary and allowances in lieu thereof, and the Chairman or a member, as the case may be, shall also have the right to relinquish his office, at any time before the expiry of the period prescribed under sub-section (1), by giving to the Central Government notice of not less than three months in writing.

Removal of member from office :

[1][* * *] The Central Government shall remove a member from office if he –

a)   is, or at any time has been, adjudicated as insolvent;

b)   is of unsound mind and stands so declared by a competent court;

---

1   "(1)" omitted by the Securities Laws (Amendment) Act, 1995, w.e.f. 25-1-1995.

c) has been convicted of an offence which, in the opinion of the Central Government, involves a moral turpitude;

d) 2[* * *]

e) has, in the opinion of the Central Government, so abused his position as to render his continuation in office detrimental to the public interest.

Provided that no member shall be removed under this clause unless he has been given a reasonable opportunity of being heard in the matter.

Meetings :

i) The Board shall meet at such times and places, and shall observe such rules of procedure in regard to the transaction of business at its meetings (including quorum at such meetings) as may be provided by regulations.

ii) The Chairman or, if for any reason, he is unable to attend a meeting of the Board, any other member chosen by the members present from amongst themselves at the meeting shall preside at the meeting.

iii) All questions which come up before any meeting of the Board shall be decided by a majority votes of the members present and voting, and, in the event of an equality of votes, the Chairman, or in his absence, the person presiding, shall have a second or casting vote.

Members not to participate in meetings in certain cases :

Any member, who is a director of a company and who as such director has any direct or indirect pecuniary interest in any matter coming up for consideration at a meeting of the Board, shall, as soon as possible after relevant Circumstances have come to his knowledge, disclose the nature of his interest at such meeting and such disclosure shall be recorded in the proceedings of the Board, and the member shall not take any part in any deliberation or decision of the Board with respect to that matter.

Vacancies, etc., not to invalidate proceedings of Board :

No act or proceeding of the Board shall be invalid merely by reason of –

a) any vacancy in, or any defect in the constitution of the Board; or

b) any defect in the appointment of a person acting as a member of the Board; or

c) any irregularity in the procedure of the Board not affecting the merits of the case.

Officers and Employees of the Board :

i) The Board may appoint such other officers and employees as it considers necessary for the efficient discharge of its functions under this Act.

ii) The term and other conditions of service of officers and employees of the Board appointed under sub-section (1) shall be such as may be determined by regulations.

---

2 Omitted, *ibid.* Prior to omission, clause (d) read as under :
(d)   is appointed as a director of a company';

4.3 FUNCTIONS OF SEBI

So as to ensure that interests of the investors are well protected and the development of the securities market is well promoted, the SEBI has to perform two major functions, viz., **regulatory and developmental** as shown below in Figure 4.2.

Fig. 4.2 : Functioning Role of SEBI

i)   Regulatory Functions :

Under regulatory function, the SEBI has to perform the job of regulating the business in stock exchanges and other securities market, registering and regulating the working of stock brokers, sub-brokers, share transfer agents, bankers to an issue, merchant bankers, underwriters, etc., and regulating the working of collective investment schemes including mutual funds.

Another regulatory function of the SEBI is to prohibit fraudulent and unfair trade practices in the securities market and regulate substantial acquisitioning of shares and takeover of companies.

Further, the SEBI can call for information, undertake inspection, conduct audit of stock exchange and intermediaries, etc. It also levies fees or other charges for carrying out its responsibilities.

Section 11 of the SEBI Act specifies the **Regulatory Functions** of SEBI as follows :

a)   Regulation of stock exchange and self regulatory organisations.

b)   Registration and regulation of stock brokers, sub-brokers, registrar to all issue, merchant bankers, underwriters, portfolio managers and such other intermediaries who are associated with securities market.

c)   Registration and regulation of the working of collective investment schemes including mutual funds.

d)   Prohibition of fraudulent and unfair trade practices relating to securities market.

e)   Prohibit insider trading insecurities.

f)   Regulating substantial acquisitions of shares and take over of companies.

ii)   Developmental Functions :

The SEBI has also to perform as a **development institution** in order to serve as an effective body to develop securities market and safeguard interests of the investors. The SEBI has to educate investors and make them aware about their rights in clear and specific terms and train intermediaries of securities markets. It has also to promote self-regulating organisation.

The SEBI has to help the corporate sector in raising funds through securities from the market without any problem and at low cost.

The SEBI is required to develop a proper infrastructure so that the market automatically facilitates expansion and growth of business to middle men like brokers, jobbers, commercial banks, merchant bankers, mutual funds, etc. This will enable them to render efficient services to investors and corporate sector at a competitive price.

The SEBI is also expected to make more effective the law in the existing status as far as they relate to the industrial securities, mutual funds, investment in units, LIC savings plan, chit-fund companies and securities issued by housing/industrial societies and corporations with the purpose of making investment in housing/industrial projects.

The SEBI has to create the framework for more open, orderly and objective conduct in respect of takeovers and mergers so as to ensure fair and equal treatment to all security holders and to facilitate such takeovers and mergers in the interest of efficiency by prescribing a mechanism for more orderly conduct.

Finally, the SEBI is expected to conduct research and publish information useful to all market players.

In brief, **Developmental Functions of SEBI** can be summarised as under :

a)   Promote investor's education.

b)   Training of intermediaries.

c)   Conducting research and published information useful to all market participants.

d)   Promotion of fair practices. Code of conduct for self regulatory organisations.

e)   Promoting self regulatory organisations.

4.4 POWERS OF SEBI

1)   Subject to the provisions of this Act, it shall be the duty of the Board to protect the interests of investors in securities and to promote the development of, and to regulate the securities market, by such measures as it thinks fit.

2)   Without prejudice to the generality of the foregoing provisions, the measures referred to therein may provide for –

   a)   regulating the business in stock exchanges and any other securities markets;

   b)   registering and regulating the working of stock brokers, sub-brokers, share transfer agents, bankers to an issue, trustees of trust deeds, registrars to an issue, merchant bankers, underwriters, portfolio managers, investment advisers and such other intermediaries who may be associated with securities markets in any manner;

   [ba] registering and regulating the working of the depositories [participants], custodians of securities, foreign institutional investors, credit rating agencies and such other intermediaries as the Board may, by notification, specify in this behalf;]

c) registering and regulating the working of [venture capital funds and collective investment schemes], including mutual funds;

d) promoting and regulating self-regulatory organisations;

e) prohibiting fraudulent and unfair trade practices relating to securities markets;

f) promoting investors' education and training of intermediaries of securities markets;

g) prohibiting insider trading in securities;

h) regulating substantial acquisition of shares and take over of companies;

i) calling for information from, undertaking inspection, conducting inquiries and audits of the [stock exchanges, mutual funds, other persons associated with the securities market], intermediaries and self-regulatory organisations in the securities market;

[ia) *calling for information and record from any bank or any other authority or board or corporation established or constituted by or under any Central, State or Provincial Act in respect of any transaction in securities which is under investigation or inquiry by the Board;]*

j) performing such functions and exercising such powers under the provisions of the Securities Contracts (Regulation) Act, 1956 (42 of 1956), as may be delegated to it by the Central Government;

k) levying fees or other charges for carrying out the purposes of this section;

l) conducting research for the above purposes;

[la) calling from or furnishing to any such agencies, as may be specified by the Board, such information as may be considered necessary by it for the efficient discharge of its functions;]

m) performing such other functions as may be prescribed.

[2A) *Without prejudice to the provisions contained in sub-section (2), the Board may take measures to undertake inspection of any book, or register, or other document or record of any listed public company or a public company (not being intermediaries referred to in section 12) which intends to get its securities listed on any recognised stock exchange where the Board has reasonable grounds to believe that such company has been indulging in insider trading or fraudulent and unfair trade practices relating to securities market].*

[3) Notwithstanding anything contained in any other law for the time being in force while exercising the powers under [clause (i) or clause (ia) of sub-section (2) or sub-section 2A)], the Board shall have the same powers as are vested in a civil court under the Code of Civil Procedure, 1908 (5 of 1908), while trying a suit, in respect of the following matters, namely :

i) the discovery and production of books of account and other documents, at such place and such time as may be specified by the Board;

ii) summoning and enforcing the attendance of persons and examining them on oath;

iii) inspection of any books, registers and other documents of any person referred to in section 12, at any place;]

iv) inspection of any book, or register, or other document or record of the company referred to in sub-section (2A);

v) issuing commissions for the examination of witnesses or documents].

[4] *Without prejudice to the provisions contained in sub-sections (1), (2), (2A) and (3) and section 11B, the Board may, by an order, for reasons to be recorded in writing, in the interests of investors or securities market, take any of the following measures, either pending investigation or inquiry or on completion of such investigation or inquiry namely :*

a) suspend the trading of any security in a recognised stock exchange;

b) restrain persons from accessing the securities market and prohibit any person associated with securities market to buy, sell or deal in securities;

c) suspend any office-bearer of any stock exchange or self-regulatory organisation front holding such position;

d) impound and retain the proceeds or securities in respect of any transaction which is under investigation;

e) attach, after passing of an order on an application made for approval by the Judicial Magistrate of the first class having jurisdiction, for a period not exceeding one month, one or more bank account or accounts of any intermediary or any person associated with the securities market in any manner involved in violation of any of the provisions of this Act, or the rules or the regulations made there under :

Provided that only the bank account or accounts or any transaction entered therein, so far as it relates to the proceeds actually involved in violation of any of the provisions of this Act, or the rules or the regulations made thereunder shall be allowed to be attached;

f) direct any intermediary or any person associated with the securities market in any manner not to dispose off or alienate all asset forming part of any transaction which is under investigation.

Provided *that the Board may, without prejudice to the provisions contained in sub-section (2) or sub-section (2A), take any of the measures specified in clause (d) or clause (e) or clause (f), in respect of any listed public company or a public company (not being intermediaries referred to in section 12) which intends to get its securities listed on any recognised stock exchange where the Board has reasonable grounds to believe that such company has been indulging in insider trading or fraudulent and unfair trade practices relating to securities market.*

Provided further *that the Board shall, either before or after passing such orders, give an opportunity of hearing to such intermediaries or persons concerned.*]

Board to regulate or prohibit issue of prospectus, offer document or advertisement soliciting money for issue of securities.

1) Without prejudice to the provisions of the Companies Act, 1956 (1 of 1956), the Board may, for the protection of investors,

   (a) specify, by regulations –

      i) the matters relating to issue of capital, transfer of securities and other matters incidental thereto; and

      ii) the manner in which such matters shall be disclosed by the companies;

   b) by general or special orders

      i) prohibit any company from issuing prospectus, any offer document, or advertisement soliciting money from the public for the issue of securities;

      ii) specify the conditions subject to which the prospectus, such offer document or advertisement, if not prohibited, may be issued.

2) Without prejudice to the provisions of section 21 of the Securities Contracts (Regulation) Act, 1956 (42 of 1956), the Board may specify the requirements for listing and transfer of securities and other matters incidental thereto.]

Collective Investment Scheme

1) Any scheme or arrangement which satisfies the conditions referred to in sub-section (2) shall be a collective investment scheme.

2) Any scheme or arrangement made or offered by any company under which –

   i) the contributions, or payments made by the investors, by whatever name called, are pooled and utilised for the purposes of the scheme or arrangement;

   ii) the contributions or payments are made to such scheme or arrangement by the investors with a view to receive profits, income, produce or property, whether movable or immovable, from such scheme or arrangement;

In short, SEBI has been vested with the following important powers :

i) Power to call periodical returns from recognised stock exchanges.

ii) Power to call any information or explanation from recognised stock exchanges or their members.

iii) Power to direct enquiries to be made in relation to affairs of stock exchanges or their members.

iv) Power to grant approval to bye-laws of recognised stock exchanges.

v) Power to make or amend bye-laws of recognised stock exchanges.

vi) Power to compel listing of securities by public companies.

vii) Power to control and regulate stock exchanges.

viii) Power to grant registration to market intermediaries.

ix) Power to levy fees or other charges for carrying out the purpose of regulation.

x) Power to declare applicability of Section 17 of the Securities Contract (Regulation) Act is any state or area to grant licences to dealers in securities.

4.5 ACHIEVEMENTS OF SEBI

Achievements of SEBI can be highlighted with the help of the following points :

i) The SEBI has put in place regulations and codes of conduct for intermediaries. It has endeavoured to encourage investors association and self-regulatory organisation of merchant bankers. The SEBI has brought out series of educational advertisements for investor protection guidance. It has persuaded stock exchanges to have broad-based boards and to go for prudential norms of capital adequacy for brokers and norms for brokers-client relationships and has undertaken inspection of stock exchange.

ii) The SEBI has also been constantly seeking to solve the problems of settlement delays and higher transaction costs associated with physical, paper-based trading procedures.

iii) The SEBI has, of late, issued guidelines to modify the entry norms for unlisted and listed companies accessing capital market, relaxed norms with regard lo both entry and pricing for bank shares, provided for uniforms promoters' contribution for public issues at 20%, gave flexibility to issuers to fix maximum marketable lot on the basis of offer price, facilitated raising of funds by infrastructure projects and introduced the 'Modified Carry forward' 'System and Securities Lending Scheme'.

iv) The SEBI is currently engaged in the task of developing a strong cash market for the benefit of investors and trying to encourage transparency and fairness in market transactions.

v) The SEBI took several measures for widening and deepening different segments of the capital market and for promoting investors protection and market development. It tightened eligibility norms for companies intending to access capital makets for equity funds. A three-year dividend paying records (out of the proceeding five years) was made mandatory for companies accessing the capital market. However, new manufacturing companies with their project appraised by public financial institutions could also access the market. Also, the SEBI advised all stock exchanges to set up clearing corporations, or settlement guarantee funds. All exchanges have been directed to introduce weekly settlements. Exchanges have been allowed to expand the on-line screen based trading terminals outside the existing jurisdiction if they meet certain criteria.

vi) One of the remarkable success which the SEBI claims to have made has been in pushing screen-based trading. It is true that India is probably the only country in the world of its size where all the exchanges have screen based trading.

vii) Dematerialisation of shares is another area where the SEBI has made significant headway. Dematerialisation of shares, like screen-based trading, is going to change the way trading is done across the country. Computerised trading has led to reduction in the scope for price-rigging and manipulation, De-materialisation will push the process further.

viii) The SEBI has, together with the exchange, evolved certain mechanisms to improve surveillance. Introduction of price caps, price bands, circuit filters, margins, mark to market margins and stock watch are someway of keeping a strict vigil on the market. In the two years, the volatility in the market has increased manifold due to domestic and international reasons, yet not a single broker has failed.

ix) The SEBI is trying to breathe some life into the primary market. Recently, it carne up with a list of guidelines for infrastrutcture issues. For other companies too, the SEBI board has decided that the primary issue should be compulsory through the depository mode. These guidelines will certainly help the promoters to be flexible in structuring, the capital of the company which will atleast make sure that these projects can be financially closed.

x) Biggest success which the SEBI has scored is in the areas of mutual funds. When some mutual funds planned to renege on their promises to investors by unilaterally amending the terms of assured return scheme, the SEBI put its foot down and compelled them to make good their promises. For instance, when Can Bank Mutual Fund attempted to wriggle out of its Canstar issue commitments by delinking the repurchase price from prices assured at the time of launch, the SEBI intervened and insisted that the move be ratified by unit holders through a postal balloon.

xi) Following the Government invention in 1992 to evolve a comprehensive set of guidelines for the operation of mutual funds, the SEBI was authorised to issue directives to the mutual funds. As per the guidelines, mutual funds are authorised for business by SEBI. Mutual funds can be operated only by separately established Asset Management Companies (AMCs). The AMCs are authorised for business by SEBI on the basis of fulfilment of certain stipulation. In order to oversee the working of these funds, the SEBI was given the right to call for any information regarding the operations of the funds, lay down accounting policies and impose penalties for violating the guidelines, as may be necessary with the concurrence of the RBI and the Government.

xii) Stock invest was designed by the SFBI in consultation with RBI and banks as an additional facility for making applications for new issues. The stock invest facility is available to individuals who can approach the bank with whom they maintain an account for issue of stock invest of required denominations for payment of application money while making an application for shares. The stock invest scheme envisages that the investor's account gets debited only on the allotment of shares. The investor, therefore, has to part with his funds only when he is eligible to get allotment of shares. Till such time, the investor's fund remains in his account and continues to earn interest, whi6r is normally four months.

4.6 REGULATORY ASPECTS OF SEBI

SEBI has introduced from time to time the comprehensive regulatory measures, prescribed registration norms, eligibility criteria, code of obligations and code of conduct for different intermediaries like, bankers to issue, merchant bankers, brokers and sub-brokers, registrars, portfolio managers, credit rating agencies, underwriters and others. It has framed bye-laws, risk identification and risk management systems for clearing houses of stock exchanges, surveillance system etc., which has made dealing in securities both safe and transparent to the end investors.

SEBI has brought out a number of guidelines separately, from time to time, for primary market, secondary market, mutual funds, merchant bankers, foreign institutional investors, investor protection etc. These guidelines are described below :

1) SEBI and Primary Market :

Any company or a listed company making a public issue or a rights issue of value of more than ₹ 50 lakhs is required to file a draft offer document with SEBI for its observations. The company can proceed forward only after getting observations from SEBI. The company has to open its issue within three months from the date of SEBIs observation letter. SEBI has also laid down several entry norms for companies who are to make a public issue.

Major Guidelines for Public Issue :

i)   Abridged prospectus has to be attached with every application.

ii)   A company has to highlight the risk factors in the prospectus.

iii)   Objective of the issue and cost of project should be mentioned in the prospectus.

iv)   Company's management, past history and present business of the firm should be highlighted in the prospectus.

v)   Particulars in regard to company and other listed companies under the same management which made any capital issues during the last three years are to be stated in the prospectus.

vi)   Justification for premium, in the case of premium is to be stated.

vii)   Subscription list for public issues should be kept open for a minimum of three days and a maximum of 10 working days.

viii) The collection centres should be atleast 30 which include all centres with stock exchanges.

ix)   Collection agents are not to collect application money in cash.

x)   The quantum of issue, whether through a right or public issue, shall not exceed the amount specified in the prospectus. No retention of over subscription is permissible under any circumstances.

xi)   A compliance report in the prescribed form should be submitted to SEBI within 45 days from the date of closure of issue.

xii)   Minimum number of shares per application has been fixed at 500 shares of face value of ₹ 100.

xiii) The allotments have to be made in multiples of tradable lot of 100 shares of Rs. 10 each.

xiv) Issues by way of bonus, rights etc. to be made in appropriate lots to minimise odd lots.

xv) If minimum subscription of 90% has not been received, the entire amount is to be refunded to investors within 120 days.

xvi) The capital issue should be fully paid up within 120 days.

xvii) Underwriting has been made mandatory.

xviii) Limit of listing of companies issue in the Stock exchange has been increased from ₹ 3 crores to ₹ 5 crores.

2) SEBI and Secondary Market :

Stock Exchange Regulations :

i) Board of Directors of stock exchange has to he reconstituted so as to include non-members, public representatives government representative to the extent of 50% of total number of members.

ii) Capital adequacy norms have been laid down for members of various stock exchanges depending upon their turnover of trade and other factors.

iii) Working hours for all stock exchanges has been fixed to be from 12 noon to 3.00 p.m. For Bombay Stock Exchange from 9.00 a.m. to 3.30 p.m. w.e.f. 4.1.2010).

iv) All the recognised stock exchanges will have to inform about the transaction within 24 hours.

v) Guidelines have been issued for introducing the system of market making in less liquid scrips in a phased manner in all stock exchanges.

Section 3 of SEBI Act protects the interests of investors in securities and also promotes the development of, and regulates, the security market and related matters.

The following are the financial products/instruments which are controlled by SEBI :

Equity Shares, Rights Issue/Rights Shares, Bonus Shares, Preferred Stock/ Preference Shares, Cumulative Preference Shares, Cumulative Convertible Preference Shares, Participating Preference Shares, Bond, Zero Coupon Bond, Convertible Bond, Debentures, Commercial Paper, Coupons and Treasury Bills.

SEBI has taken the following initiatives in the Secondary Market :

i) Reconstitution of Government Boards of Stock Exchanges to have :

a) 50 : 50 broker and non-broker representation in the board.

b) Arbitration, Disciplinary and Default committees of exchanges to have 60% representation from non-broker members.

c) Change of tenure of Vice President and President such that they are not able to hold office for long periods of time without break.

ii) To ensure impartial and fair governance by public representatives and government nominees on governing Boards of the stock exchanges.

iii) Filing of criminal Cases against unrecognised stock exchanges.

iv)   Compulsory audit of broker books and filing of audit reports with SEBI.

v)   Amendment of SCRA Section 19 (2b) to reduce the minimum percentage of securities to be issued to public from 60% to 25%.

vi)   Reporting of off-market deals by a special committee.

vii) Set-up of 3 tier margin system to curtail build up of speculative volumes on brokers to ensure curtailment of speculative volumes and price rigging.

viii) Guidelines for introduction of market making in less liquid scrip in a phased manner for the first time.

ix)   Continuous monitoring of stock exchanges by inspection.

3) SEBI and Mutual Funds :

SEBI formulates policies to regulate the mutual funds for protecting the interest of investors. Mutual funds either promoted by public or by private sector entities including ones promoted by foreign entities are governed by these Regulations.

SEBI approved Asset Management Company (AMC) manages the funds by making investments in various types of securities, custodian, registered with SEBI, holds the securities of various schemes of the fund in its custody. The general power of superintendence and direction over AMC is vested with the trustees.

According to SEBI guidelines, two tricks of the directors of trustee company or board of trustees must be independent. They should not be associated with the sponsors, 50% of the directors of AMC must be independent. All mutual funds are required to be registered before they launch a scheme.

In April 1992, Scheduled Commercial Banks and public financial institutions were allowed to set up Money Market Mutual Funds (MMMFs). The initial conditions were relaxed between Nov. 1995 and July 1996 to make the system more popular and add depth to the market. Several steps were initiated subsequently viz. allowing them to invest in corporate debentures and bonds with residual maturity less than one year, reducing minimum lock in period of MMMF units from 30 days to 15 days and MMMFs were allowed "cheque writing facility" in tie-up with banks. Effective from 7th March, MMMFs have been bought under the regulatory purview of SEBI.

4) SEBI and takeover norms :

SEBI has also laid down norms for takeover. These are :

i)   Imposing curb on off-market deals,

  a)   Upto a threshold level of 5 percent, off market deals are allowed.

  b)   Between 5 percent and 15 percent all deals should be made only trough stock market.

ii)   SEBI has laid down the reduction of time limit for completion of the open offer from 4 months at present to 3 months.

iii) SEBI has put restrictions on the sale of shares by the acquirer during the open offer period.

iv) SEBI has made it mandatory for the board of directors to give independent comment to the shareholders of the target company regarding its future plans.

v) Merchant Banker must stop dealing in the shares of the target company, following his appointment as manager to the offer and disclose its shareholding in the offer document.

5) SEBI and Brokers :

The work of the SEBI unfortunately started with registration of brokers which has remained unsolved so far. As an attempt at regulating the stock market activity, it initiated its work with registration of brokers. The issue could have ended up on a favourable note but for the condition of fee. The Board issued regulations requiring every stock brokers to make an application for the grant of a certificate of registration. For getting the certificate, the brokers should be eligible to be admitted as a member of a stock exchange, should have necessary infrastructure should have experience in the business of buying and selling of securities and be subjected to disciplinary proceedings under the rules. Further, the broker holding the certificate of registration should abide by the code of conduct envisaged under the rules. The registration is subjected to the payment of specified fees by brokers and sub-brokers Annual turnover is taken as the basis for the fixation of fees by the SEBI.

6) SEBI and Merchant Bankers :

The Government of India using its powers under Securities Contracts Regulation Act issued guidelines for merchant bankers providing that any person or body engaged in the business of merchant banking would need authorisation from SEBI. Exercising the powers conferred by section 30 of the SEBI Act, the Board issued regulations for merchant bankers. These regulations make it obligatory for the merchant bankers to get themselves registered under the Act.

7) SEBI and Insider Trading :

So as to regulate insider trading and ensure its smooth operation, the SEBI issued requisite regulations. These provide for various measures including the Board's right to investigate and inspect the books of account of any insider and render the act a criminal offence punishable with fine or imprisonment up to one year.

While the intentions of SEBI are laudable in curbing insider trading, it is not easy to establish the relation between unpublished information and its price sensitiveness.

Guidelines for preservation of "Price Sensitive Information"

Employees/directors shall maintain the confidentiality of all Price Sensitive Information. Employees/Directors shall [not] pass on such information to any person directly or indirectly by way of making a recommendation for the purchase or sale of securities.

Need to know

Price Sensitive Information is to be handled on a "need to know" basis, i.e., Price Sensitive Information should be disclosed only to those within the company who need the information to discharge their duty.

Limited access to confidential information

Files containing confidential information shall be kept secure. Computer files must have adequate security of login and password etc.

Pre-clearance of Trades

All Directors/officers/designated employees of the company who intend to deal in the securities of the company (above a minimum threshold limit to be decided by the company) should preclear the transaction as per the pre-dealing procedure as described hereunder.

An application may be made in such form as the company may notify in this regard, to the Compliance Officer indicating the estimated number of securities that the designated employee/officer/director intends to deal in, the details as to the depository with which he has a security account, the details as to the securities in such depository Mode and such other details as may be required by any rule made by the company in this behalf.

An undertaking shall be executed in favour of the company by such designated employee/director/officer incorporating, *inter alia*, the following clauses, as may be applicable :

i) That the employee/director/officer does not have any access or has not received "Price Sensitive Information upto the time of signing the undertaking.

ii) That in case the employee/director/officer has access to or receives "Price Sensitive Information" after the signing of the undertaking but before the execution of the transaction he/she shall inform the Compliance Officer of the change in his position and that he/she would completely refrain from dealing in the securities of the company till the time such information becomes public.

iii) That he/she has not contravened the code of conduct for prevention of insider trading as notified by the company from time to time.

iv) That he/she has made a full and true disclosure in the matter.

Other Restrictions

All directors/officers/designated employees shall execute their order in respect of securities of the company within one week after the approval of pre-clearance is given. If the order is not executed within one week after the approval is given, the employee/ director must pre-clear the transaction again.

All directors/officers/designated employees shall hold their investments in securities for a minimum period of 30 days in order to be considered as being held for investment purposes. The holding period shall also apply to subscription in the primary market (IPOs). In the case of IPOs, the holding period would commence when the Securities are actually allotted.

In case the sale of securities is necessitated by personal emergency, the holding period may be waived the compliance officer after recording in writing his/her reasons in this regard.

8) SEBI and Custodian of Securities

i) The custodian of securities shall maintain the highest standard of integrity, fairness and professionalism in the discharge of his duties.

ii)   The custodian of securities shall be prompt in distributing dividends, interest or any such accruals of income received or collected by him on behalf of his clients on the securities held in custody.

iii)   The custodian of securities shall be continuously accountable for the movement of securities in and out of custody account, deposit, and withdrawal of cash from the client's account and shall provide complete audit trail, whenever called for by the client or Securities and Exchange Board of India.

iv)   The custodian of securities shall establish and maintain adequate infrastructural facility to be able to discharge custodial services to the satisfaction of clients and the operating procedures and systems of the custodian of securities shall be well documented and backed by operations manuals.

v)   The custodian of securities shall maintain client confidentiality in respect of the client's affairs.

vi)   Where custodian records are kept electronically, the custodian of securities shall take precautions necessary to ensure that continuity in record keeping is not lost or destroyed and that sufficient back up of records is available.

vii)   The custodian of securities shall create and maintain the records of securities held in custody in such manner that the tracing of securities or obtaining duplicate title documents is facilitated, in the event of loss of original records for any reason.

viii)   The custodian of securities shall extend to other custodial entities, depositories and clearing organisations all such co-operation that is necessary for the conduct of business in the areas of inter custodial settlements, transfer of securities and transfer of funds.

ix)   The custodian of securities shall ensure that an arms length relationship is maintained, both in terms of staff and systems, from his other businesses.

x)   Every custodian of securities shall exercise due diligence in safe-keeping and admi-nistration of the assets of his clients in his custody for which he is acting as custodian of securities.

xi)   a)   A custodian of securities or any of his employees shall not render, directly or in directly any investment advice about any security in the publicly accessible media, whether real-time or non-real-time, unless a disclosure of his interest including long or short position in the said security has been made, while rendering such advice.

        b)   In case an employee of the custodian of securities is rendering such advice, he shall also disclose the interest of his dependent family members and employer including their long or short positions in the said security, while rendering such advice].

9)   SEBI and Foreign Institutional Investors (FII) :

i)   Foreign institutional investors have been allowed to invest in all securities traded in primary and secondary markets.

ii)   There would be no restrictions on the volume of investment for the purpose of entry of FIIs.

iii)   The holding of single FII in a company will not exceed the ceiling of 5% of the equity capital of a company.

iv)   Disinvestment will be allowed only through stock exchanges in India.

v)   FIIs have to pay a concessional tax rate as prescribed by law from time to time.

10) SEBI and Derivatives Trading :

Derivatives trading takes place under the Act 1992, and the framework including suggestive bye law and its clearing corporation/house has been laid down by Dr. L. C. Gupta Committee, constituted by SEBI.

11) SEBI and Investor :

Investor protection is the major responsibility of the SEBI. SEBI has taken various measures to protect the interests of investors.

Regarding New Issue

The issuing company should provide fair and correct information. Allotment process should be transparent and not tainted by any bias.

The draft prospectus of the companies is scrutinised for full and fair disclosure.

No delay in refunds or despatch of share certificates. Underwriting obligations is necessary to inspire confidence of investors.

Risk factors and highlights should be fairly stated without any bias in the prospectus.

Listing should be timely and transferability is ensured.

Both stock exchange and companies are responsible for investor protection in respect of free trading and transferability of shares.

The investor protection is to be ensured by not only the Director/Secretary of the company but by all the parties in the new issue process namely merchant hankers, Registrars, collecting banks, stock exchange and SEBI.

Recently, SEBI has instituted the system of appointing its representatives to supervise the allotment process to ensure that no malpractices take place in the allotment process.

Investor Education

SEBI has issued a few investors guidance, advertisements and published a hook on 'Investor Grievances - Rights and Remedies' SEBI has also registered certain active Investor's Association.

SEBI has issued an Advertisement Code for the issuers to ensure that the advertisements are fair and do not contain statements to mislead the investors or vitiate their informed judgement.

Grievance Cell

An Investor Grievance Cell is set up to handle investor complaints.

Parliament passed the SEBI (Amendment) Bill, 2002 giving more powers to SEBI to punish market offenders. The Bill entrust SEBI wide Powers including seizure of books and accounts, impose fine upto ₹ 25 crore on insider trading, slap a penalty of ₹ 1 lakh a day and upto ₹ 1 crore in cases where small investors were cheated. The SEBI is being given powers to suspend the governors of the stock exchange. It is also being empowered to impound the proceedings of the exchanges.

The SEBI's governing board itself would have Powers to appoint investigating agency.

12) SEBI and Portfolio Managers

Like the merchant bankers and mutual funds, the activities of portfolio managers have also been brought with in the ambit of SEBI. Such portfolio managers are required to register themselves with SEBI. This is intended to ensure fair play towards investors.

Regulatory reform is a dynamic process given the pace of financial evolution world wide. Besides autonomy and independence of SEBI, two other critical elements are in the building up of human resources and expertise in the system. Consultative mechanism should be put in place which can bring in a wide array of information and knowledge from the financial community into the regulatory system. SEBI should avoid becoming a controlling authority substituting CCI. It should function more as a market regulator to see that the market is operated on the basis of well laid down principles and conventions. SEBI has both a regulatory and developmental role. The challenges will be to balance the efficiency and cost and risk reducing benefits of an integrated system.

4.7 RECENT CHANGES AND EMERGING TRENDS

(I) To ease the process of implementing stronger corporate governance norms by listed firms, regulator, SEBI recently relaxed various provisions of the new law, especially for smaller companies and extended the deadline for appointing atleast one women director to April 1, 2015. Changes have been made to the new regulatory regime, which would come into effect from October 2014.

The listed companies would have till 1st April, 2015 (comply with the woman director - related provision).

SEBI has also exempted smaller companies - those having equity share capital of upto ₹ 10 crores and net worth not exceeding ₹ 25 crores, as also listed on SME platforms of the stockexchanges - from the mandatory compliance to the new code for the time being. Since implementation of the New Companies Act, w.e.f. 1st April, 2014, the Ministry of Corporate Affairs has issued various circulars on matters related to corporate governance clarifying certain provisions of the new law.

Recently, the SEBI accepted the recommendations of the Takeover Regulation Advisory Committee (TRAC) in respect of acquisition of shares of listed companies.

Also an amendment to the SEBI (Prohibition of Insider Trading) Regulation has been carried out with respect to shareholding disclosure by the promoter.

SEBI has approved amendment to the SEBI (Prohibition of Insider Trading Regulations, 1992 mandating certain disclosures to be made by promoters and persons who are part of promoter group of a listed company.

(II) Changes regarding "Foreign Investment in India by SEBI registers Long term Investors in Government dated securities"

(As per A.P. (DIR Series) Circular No. 13 dated July 23, 2014.

The present limit for investments by SEBI registered Foreign Institutional Investors (FIIs) SEBI registered Qualified Foreign Investors (QFIs), and long term investors registered with SEBI in Government securities stands at USD 30 billion, out of which a sub-limit of USD 10 billion is available for investment by long term investors in Government dated securities.

On a review, RBI has decided to enhance in investment limit in government securities available to FII (QFIs/FPIs by USD 5 billion by corresponding reducing the amount available to long term investors from USD 10 billion to USD 5 billion within the overall limit of USD 30 billion. The incremental investment limit of USD 5 billion shall be required to be invested in government bonds with a minimum residual maturity of 3 years. Further, all future investment against the limit vacated when the current investment by an FII/QFI/FPI runs off either through sale or redemption shall also be required to be made in government bonds with a minimum residual maturity of 3 years.

RBI has however clarified that there will be no lock-in period and FIIs/QFIs/FPIs shall be free to sell the securities (including that are presently held with less than 3 years of residual maturity) to the domestic investors.

(III) Infrastructure Facilities and Submission of Periodic Reports:

SEBI has issued Circular No. IMD/FIIC/09/2014 dated 28-04-2014 whereby it has been decided in order insure proper functioning of the Foreign Portfolio Investors (FPI) regime, it is imperative that Designated Depository Participants (DDPs) should have adequate infrastructure facilities and appropriate systems and control in place. Accordingly, it has been decided:

(i) Every DDP shall maintain arms length distance from other businesses carried out by it.

(ii) Every DDP shall have necessary infrastructure.

(iii) Every DDP shall have a complete manual, setting out the systems and procedure to be followed for effective and efficient discharge of its functions as DDPs.

(iv) Every DDP shall have adequate mechanisms for the purpose of reviewing, monitoring and evaluating its controls, systems, procedure and safeguards.

(v) Every DDP shall submit periodic reports to SEBI.

The provisions of this circular would be applicable upon commencement of Foreign Portfolio Investor (FPI) regime.

(IV) SEBI raises Threshold Limit for Cash Investment in Mutual Funds to ₹ 50,000/-

SEBI vide its Circular No. IMD/DF/10/2014 dated 22-05-2014 has decided to increase the limit of cash transactions in mutual funds from existing limit of ₹ 20,000/- per investor, per mutual fund, per financial year to ₹ 50,000/- per investor, per mutual fund, per financial year, subject to (i) compliance with Prevention of Money Laundering Act, 2002 and Rules framed thereunder, the SEBI Circular(s) on Anti Money Laundering (AML) and other applicable AML rules, regulations and guidelines and (ii) Sufficient systems and procedures in place.

It has been further decided that in the guidelines for Investment/Trading in Securities of Employees of Assets Management Companies (AMCs) and Trustees of Mutual Funds, alongwith MMMF schemes, liquid-schemes shall be added in the list of securities to which the guidelines do not apply.

QUESTIONS FOR SELF-STUDY

I.   Theory Questions :

1.   What is 'SEBI' ? Explain in detail the background of SEBI.

2.   What is 'SEBI' ? State the basic objectives of SEBI.

3.   State the establishment and management of SEBI.

4.   Explain the power of SEBI.

5.   State the functions of SEBI.

6.   What is 'SEBI' ? Explain in detail the achievements of SEBI.

7.   Explain in brief the recent changes and emerging trends in SEBI.

8.   Write short notes on :

i) Background of SEBI, ii) Basic Objectives of SEBI, iii) Administration of SEBI, iv) Organisation of SEBI, v) Regulatory Functions of SEBI, vi) Developmental functions of SEBI, vii) SEBI and Primary Market, viii) SEBI and Secondary Market, ix) SEBI and Mutual Funds, x) SEBI and Brokers, xi) SEBI and Custodian of Securities, xii) SEBI and Investor, xiii) SEBI and Portfolio Managers, xiv) SEBI and Derivatives Trading.

Glossary

- **Arbitrage :** Arbitrage in idealised market conditions is a trading activity which can result in generation of riskless profit without any investment, by taking advantage of price variations in different markets, in given assets. In practice, due to various factors like transaction costs, taxes, frictions/restrictions of various kinds, etc., it may not be possible always to realise such riskless profits.

- **Auction :** On account of non-delivery of securities by the trading member on the pay-in day, the securities are put up for auction by the Exchange. This ensures that the buying trading member receives the securities. The Exchange purchases the requisite quantity in auction market and gives them to the buying trading member.

- **Bad Delivery :** SEBI has formulated uniform guidelines for good and bad delivery of documents. Bad delivery may pertain to a transfer deed being torn, mutilated, overwritten, defaced, or if there are spelling mistakes in the name of the company or the transfer. Bad delivery exists only when shares are transferred physically. In "Demat" bad delivery does not exist.

- **Basis Point :** $1/100^{th}$ of 1%. In other words, one basis point = 1%/10 = .01/100 = .001.

- **Bear Market :** Sometimes the market goes through a period of months or even years when it keeps going down overall. This has occurred a number of times in the history of the stock market. When the stock market is in a bear phase, it means that the major market indices Sensex and Nifty are declining. People sell their stocks for whatever price they can get. In general, the economy is weak, and corporate earnings are declining. A bear market is depressing. People begin to avoid the stock market and put their money in gold, or bonds. The majority of brokerage houses/firms stops hiring or lay off employees and tries to cut down expenses. Since the stock market often predicts what will happen to the economy, a lengthy bear market may signal that a recession is looming. No one can predict how long a bear market will last, although bear markets in the past have been relatively short.

- **Book-Closure/Record Date :** Book closure and record date help a company determine exactly the shareholders of a company as on a given date. Book closure refers to the closing of register of the names or investors in the records of a company. Companies announce book closure dates from time to time. The benefits of the name appears on the company's records as on a given date, is known as the record date. An investor might purchase a share-cum-dividend, cum rights or cum bonus and may therefore expect to receive these benefits as the new shareholder. In order to receive this, the share has to be transferred in the investor's name, or he would stand deprived of the benefits. The buyer of such a share will be a loser. It is important for a buyer of a share to ensure that shares purchased at cum benefits prices are transferred before book-closure. It must be ensured that the price paid for the shares is ex-benefit and not cum benefit. In case of a record date, the company does not close its register of security holders. Record date is the cut off date for determining the number of registered members who are eligible for the corporate benefits. In case of book closure, shares cannot be sold on an Exchange bearing a date on the transfer deed earlier than the book closure. This does not hold good for the record date.

- **Break Out :** At certain points, the market finds its resistance or support. Thus, the market either has support or resistance, when it gives the break out, it brings in a rush of buyers or sellers. Thus, investors will buy the stock when the price breaks below support. This is called break out point.

- **Bull Market :** Bull markets are very profitable for most traders and investors. During a bull market, there are plenty of jobs, and investors are flush with cash that they eagerly use to buy more stocks. Everyone seems to be in a stock buying mood, and the major indicies have no where to go but up. People are optimistic about the direction of the country. Everyone is talking about how much money they made in the market.

- **Call Option :** It confers on its buyer the right to buy the underlying, whereas the put option grants its buyer the right to sell the underlying.

- **Circuit Breaker :** Circuit breaker is also known as circuit filter or, Price Band which set the upper and lower limit within which a stock can fluctuate on any given day. A price band for the day is a function of previous trading day's closing. Circuits breakers or trading halts can be resorted in case there is any adverse or out of the ordinary happening, like movement in a stock's price which is at large variance from the stock's daily average variation, on the trader volume on a particular day gone beyond the average daily volume. In order to arrest any extraordinary movement in the trading pattern, automatic circuit breaker mechanism is put in place. In case the average daily variation in the price of an instrument is crossed at any point of time during the trading hours, the circuit breaker would come in operation immediately, halting the trading forthwith. It is a time out measure enabling the market to stop, halt the knee-jerk reactions, if any and assess/evaluate and correct imbalances/anomalies, if there. The method and content of the mechanism has to be customised as per the needs of the situation and would differ from market. At present circuit limit which is decided 20/10/5/ and 2%. Circuit breaks or filts is not applicable on A group companies, FNO scrips, Sensex and Nifty scrips. Also on the day of listing of new company there is no circuit breaker (only for one day, that is day of listing).

- **Contract Note :** Contract Note is a confirmation of trades done on a particular day on behalf of the client by a trading member. It imposes a legally enforceable relationship between the client and the trading member with respect to purchase/sale and settlement of trades. It also helps to settle disputes/claims between the investor and the trading member. It is a prerequisite for filing a complaint or arbitration proceeding against the trading member in case of a dispute. A valid contract note should be in the prescribed form, contain the details of trades, stamped with requisite value and duly signed by the authorised signatory. Contract notes are kept in duplicate, the trading member and the client should keep one copy each. After verifying the details contained therein, the client keeps one copy and returns the second copy to the trading member duly acknowledged by him.

Details Mentioned on the Contract Note : A broker has to issue a contract note to clients for all transactions in the form specified by the-stock exchange. The contract note inter-alia should have following : i) Name, address and SEBI Registration number of Member broker, ii) Name of partner/proprietor/ Authorised Signatory, iii) Dealing Office Address/Tel. No./Fax no., Code number of the member given by the Exchange. iv) Contract number, date of issue of contract note, settlement number and time period for settlement, v) Constituent (Client) name/Code Number, vi) Order number and order time corresponding to the trades, vii) Trade number and Trade time, viii) Quantity and kind of Security bought/sold by the client, ix) Brokerage and Purchase/Sale rate, x) Service tax rates, Securities Transaction Tax and any other charges levied by the broker, xi) Appropriate stamps have to be affixed on the contract note or it is mentioned that the consolidated stamp duty is paid, xii) Signature of the Stock broker/Authorised Signatory.

- **Correction and Crash :** Correction is natural reversal of the trend up to an extent of about 10% to 20% of the last movement band of index/price of scrip. E.g. : Index has moved for 2100 points continuously. Then if it falls for about 200 to 1000 points it can be termed as correction to find the level of stability and justification of the new prices. In rising market → Profit Booking. In falling market → Buying as people feel it is now cheap to buy. Crash is basically a panic selling due to external conditions. People in such sentiments have a feeling that "World is going to end." Sell at any cost and salvage whatever you can.

- **Credit Risk :** It is the conventional counterparty risk. In other words, it is the risk that the counterparty may fail to fulfil his obligation as per the terms of the contract, thereby putting the other party to a financial loss.

- **Derivative :** It is a financial contract whose value depends on the value of an underlying, which can practically be anything. As their value is essentially derived out of an underlying, they are financial abstractions whose value is derived mathematically from the changes in the value of the underlying. All derivatives have finite life after which they expire.

- **Diversification :** Diversification is a risk management technique that mixes a wide variety of investments within a portfolio. It is designed to minimise the impact of any one security on overall portfolio performance. Diversification is possibly the best way to reduce the risk in a portfolio.

- **Exchange-Traded Derivatives :** These are those which are traded on the floor of an exchange (physical), generally, on an open outcry basis or on an electronic basis.

- **Ex-Date :** The first day of the no-delivery period is the ex-date. If there is any corporate benefits such as rights, bonus, dividend announced for which book closure/record date is fixed, the buyer of the shares on or after the ex-date will not be eligible for the benefits.

- **Forward Rate Agreement (FRA) :** It is a simple derivative which is essentially an agreement between two parties that determines the interest rate that will apply to a notional future loan/deposit of an agreed amount. It is the simplest example of an OTC interest rate derivative and is used for hedging single period interest rate risk.

- **Forwards :** These are bilateral contracts in which the buyer and the seller agree upon the delivery of a specified quality and quantity of asset at a specified future date at a predetermined price.

- **Futures :** These are financial agreements to deliver (sell) or take-delivery (buy) of a standardised quantity of an underlying commodity/instrument, at a pre-established price on a regulated exchange at a specified future date. Simplistically speaking, futures contract is an agreement to buy or sell an asset at a certain time in the future at a certain price. Futures can be constructed on various types of underlying like commodity futures (on wheat, meat, gold, silver, etc.,); financial futures (on money market paper, T. Bills/notes/bonds, etc.,); currency futures (on U.S. dollar, Pound Sterling, Euro, Yen, etc.,); index futures (on S&P 500, Japanese Nikkei Index, NSE 50, etc.).

- **Hedging :** It is a strategy whereby specific exposure to a particular market, say currency, commodity etc., are sought to be covered with a view to stabilise cash flows. The decisions in hedging operations are driven due to fear of market movements. Hedging represents a defensive strategy in financial matters aimed at neutralising adverse market movements.

- **Large - Cap Stocks :** Most of the blue chip companies are generally known as large cap stocks in the market which include Reliance Industries, State Bank of India, Infosys, TCS. The advantage of these companies is that they have at their disposal large reserves of cash to venture new business avenues. As they are very much established in their business. The advantages to the investor are they pay dividends regularly also during correction or crash if they fall sharply but due to their fundamentals being very sound their recovery is very fast.

- **Legal Risk :** It is the risk associated with unenforceability of contracts due to defective documentation or due to various laws or any other lacunae.

- **Market Risk :** It is the risk arising out of movement in market variables. In financial markets, interest rate is the single most important variable. Hence, interest risk is a prime example of market risk. Other examples of market risk are currency risk, commodity price risk, equity price risk, etc.

- **Market Trends :** There are basically three types of market trends namely, Bull, Bear and sideways Market.

- **Mid - Cap Stocks :** Market capitalisation in the range of 250-4000 crores are generally the mid cap stocks, and are well-known companies, recognised as seasoned players in the market. They offer two advantages of acquiring stocks with good growth potential as well as the stability of a large company. Many baby blue chips companies are included in mid caps and they too show steady growth backed by a good track record. They are like blue-chip stocks but lack in their size. Over a long term these stocks tend to grow very good.

- **No-Delivery Period :** Whenever a company announces a book closure or record date, the Exchange sets up a no-delivery (ND) period for that security. During this period only trading is permitted in the security. However, these trades are settled only after the no-delivery period is over. This is done to ensure that investor's entitlement for the corporate benefit is clearly determined.

- **Non-Availability of Shares in Action :** If shares are not bought in auction i.e. if the shares are not offered for sale, the Exchange squares up the transaction as per SEBI guidelines. The transaction is squared up at highest price from relevant trading period till the auction day or at 20% above the last available Closing price whichever is higher. The pay-in and pay-out of funds for auction square up is held along with the pay-out for the relevant auction.

- **Off Market Settlement :** It is an internal transfer of shares from your DP A/C TO Other PP A/C of your own/family member/friend. However, you cannot use for private sell/buy deal with other person since any sell/buy deal without exchange intermediately is not legally recognised.

- **Operational Risk :** It is the risk arising due to inadequate systems and procedures, internal control, computer failures or frauds by employees.

- **Options :** These are financial contracts which give the holder or buyer of the option the right to buy or sell an underlying at a pre-agreed price in the future, without the concomitant obligation to do so.

- **OTC Derivatives :** These are contracts traded on a private basis and bilaterally negotiated. A typical example of an OTC derivative is the forward contracts.

- **Pay-In and Pay-Out :** Pay-in day is the day when the securities sold are delivered to the exchange by the sellers and funds for the securities purchased are made available to the exchange by the buyers.

  Pay-out day is the day the securities purchased are delivered to the buyers and the funds for the securities sold are given to the sellers by the exchange. At present the pay-in and pay-out happens on the 2nd working day after the trade is executed on the stock exchange.,

- **Portfolio :** A Portfolio is a combination of different investment assets mixed and matched for the purpose of achieving an investor's goal(s). Items that are considered a part of your portfolio can include any asset you own-from shares, debentures, bonds, mutual fund units to items such as gold, art and even real estate etc. However, for most investors a portfolio has come to signify an investment in financial instruments like shares, debentures, fixed deposits, mutual fund units.

- **Risk in Finance :** It is defined as the 'possibility or probability of loss.

- **Rolling Settlement :** Under rolling settlement all open positions at the end of the day mandatory result in payment/delivery 'n' days later. Currently, trades in rolling settlement are settled on T + 2 basis where T is the trade day. For example, a trade executed on Monday is mandatory settled by Wednesday (considering two working days from the trade day). The funds and securities pay-in and pay-out are carried out on T-2 days.

- **Short Delivery :** For pay-out, you have bought 100 shares budget the delivery of only 70 shares so there is short delivery of 30 shares which exchange will buy it in auction and gives you after 4 days. In case there is no availability in auction, close - out is issued.

- **Sideways Market :** One hates a sideways market because it's hard for anyone to make money in such a market. In a sideways market, the market indicies attempt to go up or down but end up just about where they started. People just sit on the sidelines, holding their cash and refusing to participate in the market.

- **Small - Cap Stocks :** The Companies whose price volatility is in the range of upto 250 crore are small cap stocks. If an investor wishes to generate significant gains in the long run, then these stocks are the best option for them, but at the same time they should not think such about dividends. Most of these companies are relatively new, it is difficult to predict how they will perform in the market. They being small enterprise, growth spurts dramatically affect their values and revenues, sending prices soaring, but some time during correction or crash in the market these stocks decline dramatically and take a substantial time to recover. Aggressive mutual funds and FIIs are also enthusiastic about adding small-cap stocks in their portfolios, as they have the advantage of being highly growth oriented.

- **Speculation :** It is a strategy wherein market opportunity are sought to be utilised for raking in profits. The decisions are based on the expectation of market movements and the speculator may or may not have an exposure in the underlying market. Speculation represents an aggressive strategy in financial matters to reap the benefits of market movements.

- **Standard Deviation :** It a measure of dispersion of a set of observations from their arithmetical mean. In finance, standard deviation is used as a measure of risk.

- **Stock Split :** A Split is book entry wherein the face value of the share is altered to create a greater number of shares outstanding without calling for fresh capital. There is no change in the proportional holding of shares. Splitting a stock may lead to increase in the stock's liquidity, since more investors are able to afford the share and the total outstanding shares of the company have also increased in the market.

- **Swaps :** These are the most versatile of derivative products. Swap literally means an 'exchange'. Swaps can be of two types – foreign exchange swaps and financial swaps. A foreign exchange swap is a contract where a currency is simultaneously bought and sold for two value dates – one leg may be spot and the other may be forward or both the legs may relate to two different forward dates. A financial swap in a derivatives market is a contract between two parties known as counterparties, whereby they exchange two streams of cash flows over a defined period of time, usually through an intermediary like any financial institution.

- **Tick Size :** It is the minimum market price movement of a given contract.

- **Treasury Bills/Notes/Bonds :** These are instruments for borrowing money from the general public by the governments. The only difference among them is the tenor for which the amounts are borrowed. While bills are used for raising short term money i.e., generally upto one year: notes are used for raising medium-term money i.e., generally upto 5 years, while bonds are used for raising long-term money i.e., generally beyond 5-7 years.

- **Types of Trading Styles :** There are basically two types of trading styles viz. i) Delivery based buying and day trading. **i) Delivery Based Trade :** Delivery based trade is a trade in which settlement will occur based on normal settlement cycle for the security being traded. Limitations of Delivery Based - Helpless during correction or falling market, Cannot Short sell etc. **ii) Day Trading :** Day Trading involves taking a position in the markets with a view of squaring that position before the and of that day. A day trader typically trades several times a day looking for fractions of a point to a few points per trade, but close out/square off all their positions by day's end. **iii) Derivatives Trading :** Derivative is a product whose value is derived from the value of one or more basic variables, called bases (underlying asset or index), in a contractual manner. The underlying asset can be equity, forex, commodity or any other asset. Derivative contracts have several variants. The most common variants are forwards, futures, and options. The following three broad categories of participant's hedgers, speculators, and arbitrageurs trade in the derivatives market.

- **Underlying :** It is the basis upon which the value of a derivative depends. The underlying can be agricultural commodities, individual stocks or stocks indices, financial instruments, currencies or interest rates.

- **Valuation of Derivative :** It means the evaluation of its financial interest economic value on a given date. This is useful essentially for trading and for balance sheet purposes.

- **Value Date :** It is the date on which actual cash flows in a financial contract are exchanged.

- **Variance like Standard Deviation :** It is a measure of dispersion of a set of observations from their arithmetical mean. Variance is calculated as the square of standard deviation.

- **Volatility Standard Deviation :** It is expressed in annualised percentage terms. It is known as volatility and it can be of three types – historic, implied and expected. Volatility in the value/price of the underlying plays a predominant role in deter-mining the value/price of options.

- **Yield Curve :** It is the graphic representation of the term structure of interest rates. The interest rates may be of deposits/advances in money, capital or forex markets.

- **Yield-to-Maturity or YTM :** It represents the yield earned on the financial asset if it is held till maturity.

- **Zero Rate or Zero-Coupon Rates :** It is the rate of discount applicable for the concerned period.

Abbreviations

AMC	Asset Management Company
AMFI	Association of Mutual Funds in Indian
ATM	At-The-Money
BIFR	Board for Industrial and Financial Reconstruction
BLESS	Borrowing and Lending Securities Scheme
BMC	Base Minimum Capital
BSE	The Stock Exchange, Mumbai
CBDT	Central Board of Direct Taxes
CC	Clearing Corporation
CCIL	Clearing Corporation of India Limited
CDSL	Central Depository Services (India) Limited
CFRS	Carry Forward under Rolling Settlement
CH	Clearing Hose
CM	Clearing Member
CM Segment	Capital Market Segment of NSE
COSI	Committee on Settlement Issues
CP	Custodial Participant
CRAs	Credit Rating Agencies
CRISIL	Credit Rating Information Services of India Limited
CRR	Cash Reserve Ratio
CSE	Calcutta Stock Exchange
DCA	Department of Company Affairs
DDBs	Deep Discount Bonds
DEA	Department of Economic Affairs
DIP	Disclosure and Investor Protection
DNS	Deferred Net Settlement
DPs	Depository Participants
DSCE	Debt Securities Convertible into Equity
EFT	Electronic Fund Transfer
ELSS	Equity Linked Saving Schemes
EPS	Earning Per Share
F & O	Futures and Options
FDI	Foreign Direct Investment
FDs	Fixed Deposits

FIBV	International World Federation of Stock Exchanges
FIIs	Foreign Institutional Investors
FIMMDA	Fixed Income Money Markets and Derivatives Association
Fis	Financial Institutions
FVCIs	Foreign Venture Capital Investors
GDP	Gross Domestic Product
GDRs	Global Deposit Receipts
GDS	Global Domestic Services
GNP	Gross National Product
GOI	Government of India
G-Sec	Government Securities
GTC	Good Till Cancelled
GTD	Good Till Days/Date
IBRD	International Bank for Reconstruction and Development
ISSA	International Securities Services Association
IT	Information Technology
MFs	Mutual Funds
MNCs	Multi National Companies
MOU	Memorandum of Understanding
MTM	Mark-To-Market
NASDAQ	National Association of Securities Dealers Automated Quotation System
NAV	Net Asset Value
NBFCs	Non-Banking Financial Companies
NCDs	Non-convertible Debentures
NCDS	Non-convertible Debt Securities
NEAT	National Stock Exchange Automated Trading
NGOs	Non-Government Organisations
NPAS	Non-Performing Assets
NSCCL	National Securities Clearing Corporation of India Limited
NADL	National Securities Depository Limited
NSE	National Stock Exchange of India Limited
OIS	Overnight Index Swaps
OTC	Over the Counter
OTCEI	Over the Counter Exchange of India Limited
P/E Ratio	Price-of the Money

PAN	Permanent Account Number
PDO	Public Debt Office
PDs	Primary Dealers
PSUs	Public Sector Undertakings
PV	Present Value
RBI	Reserve Bank of India
ROCs	Registrar of Companies
SAT	Securities Appellate Tribunal
SC(R)A	Securities Contracts (Regulation) Act, 1956
SC(R)R	Securities Contracts (Regulation) Rule, 1957
SEBI	Securities and Exchange Board of India
SEC	Securities Exchange Commission
SGF	Settlement Guarantee Fund
SGX-DT	The Singapore Exchange Derivatives Trading Limited
SIPC	Securities Investor Protection Corporation
SLR	Statutory Liquidity Ratio
SPAN	Standard Portfolio Analysis of Risks
SSS	Securities Settlement System
T-Bills	Treasury Bills
TDS	Tax Deducted at Source
TM	Trading Member
TRI	Total Return Index
VCFs	Venture Capital Funds
WAN	Wide Area Network
WDM	Wholesale Debt Market Segment of NSE
YTM	Yield to Maturity
ICSE	Inter-Connected Stock Exchange of India Limited
IFSD	Interest Free Security Deposit
IOSCO	International Organisation of Securities Commission
IPF	Investor Protection Fund
IPO	Initial Public Offer
IRDA	Insurance Regulatory and Development Authority
IRS	Interest Rate Swap
ISIN No.	International Securities Identification

✳✳✳

www.ingramcontent.com/pod-product-compliance
Lightning Source LLC
Chambersburg PA
CBHW081142020726
47504CB00009B/1970